That Potent Alchemy

Tess Bowery

This is a work of fiction. Similarities to real people, places, or events are entirely coincidental.

THAT POTENT ALCHEMY

First Edition, 2018.

ISBN: 978-17753003-3-5

Written by Tess Bowery.

http://tessbowery.com

Dedication

To R, who will always be Isaac to me.

Contents

Chapter One

"You want to go to a fortune-teller." Grace Owens' bemusement fell flat in the noise of the mid-day London street. Between the children underfoot, the horses and carriages in the road and the voices of merchants calling out into the bustle, it was a wonder Lucy could even hear her reply at all.

"Not just *any* fortune-teller." Lucy tossed her head full of red curls in a gesture not nearly as artfully practiced as one might expect from an actress. She gestured with her hands as she spoke, the little bag hanging from her wrist swinging back and forth in wild arcs across the front of her patterned calico dress. "Madame *Raiza*. They say her predictions come true almost every time."

"Do they really?" Black-haired and brown-eyed Meg asked from Grace's other side, her crisp pink gown almost sedate compared to her usual cascades of girlish frills and ribbons. "Do you think she can predict what shows we'll be cast in next? I'd *die* for a princess or a duchess role. Something with lots of jewels and some good speeches."

"I don't think Madame Raiza predicts *casting,* my dear Miss Ceniza," Lucy replied loftily, and it was all Grace could do not to roll her eyes at the pair of them.

"If you think a fortune-teller can predict anything beyond whose pockets have the most coin in them, then you're both fools who deserve to be fleeced." Grace stepped out of the way of a couple of red-coated soldiers who came swaggering down the street in their direction.

The young men didn't bother to hide their leers, looking Meg and Lucy up and down with the sort of naked appreciation of libidinous boys everywhere. Grace, with her cloud of black hair tucked up under a cap, her dark skin and tidy figure hidden beneath loose trousers and a homespun shirt, was ignored. Meg—beautiful, and with a well-established patron who kept her in the best of care—lifted her chin imperiously and ignored them, but for a little amused smile.

Lucy turned to watch them go, walking backward for a few paces to keep them in sight. "I do adore uniforms," she sighed after a moment, then scurried to catch up and match Grace's pace once more.

"I think they adore themselves as well."

"You're terrible," Meg replied fondly, swatting at Grace's arm as she did so. She glanced up at the sky, the sun riding high towards noon, and she frowned. "Though I shall have to fly, or I'll be late for rehearsal. Be well, darlings, and be sure to tell me all about your fortunes when next we take tea!" She blew a kiss from the tips of her gloved fingers and darted across the street toward the Olympic Pavilion as Lucy waved farewell.

A moment later, Meg gone and the pair of them alone again, Lucy huffed out a breath and shook her head, her eyes narrowing and her curls settling down around her shoulders. "Honestly, I know you're fond of the girl, but she gives me the vapors."

Grace arched an eyebrow, biting back the ruder comments which came to mind.

Patience. Lucy is the one you'll be working beside for the rest of the summer.

"You don't find her amusing?" Grace asked instead, ignoring the faint twinge of disloyalty.

"I find her exhausting." Lucy seized Grace's arm, pointing down the street at a small sign, tucked in among the store fronts. "There! Come on, and don't be such a spoilsport. Madame Raiza can sense the energy of the disbeliever." She waggled her fingers at Grace as though to evoke said mystic energies, and Grace let herself be pulled along in Lucy's wake.

It was more of a tent than a building, really. Canvas walls staked down in the hard-packed earth of a little corner garden gave the impression of a desert encampment, or at least the stage-set of one. A hand-lettered sign in front of the dark red draperies read:

Tarot Tea and Fortunes Read
Palms and Heads Mapped and Explained
For the Entertainment of Ladies and Children

"Oh, for heaven's sake," Grace muttered under her breath. Lucy ignored her and made her way inside. The flap fell behind her, narrowly missing Grace. She ducked, shouldered her way past the weighted canvas, and stepped in.

The interior of the tent was far gaudier than the outside. The details of the painted silk hangings and the brightly colored rugs were partly obscured by the haze of sickly-sweet smoke that coiled up from a silver salver set upon the small, round central table. Other bits of furniture took up most of the rest of the cramped space. More silks and threadbare velvets half-covered mismatched sideboards and chairs that looked like they'd been rescued from a rubbish tip. Countless knickknacks and bottles of odd-looking substances covered those surfaces again. In the middle of all the clutter, tinted red from the sunlight beaming through the dyed canvas, stood a woman that Grace recognized, despite all the effort she had gone to in order to change her appearance.

Her hair was tied back and covered by a vibrant scarf, her eyebrows and lashes darkened—unless Grace had missed her mark—with stage paint. She contained her milkmaid's figure in a bodice that looked fair to burst at the seams, and had layered a half-dozen skirts and petticoats on beneath to give herself the impression of an explosion at a textile mill.

"Velcomme," 'Madame Raiza' said with a dreadful pretense at an accent, gesturing to them both with fingers bedecked with a multitude of glittering rings. "Come and sit, ladies, and have your futurrres told."

"She's from *the mysterious East*," Lucy whispered dramatically.

"She's no more from the Orient than you are a Moor," Grace said back, not bothering to pitch her voice any lower than a stage whisper.

"I see vee haf an unbeliever in our midst." Raiza glared hotly at Grace, but put the smile back on her face when Lucy moved toward the chair. "Come, child of faith. Tell Raiza vat you want to know." She took a pinch of yellow powder from a dish on the sideboard and sprinkled it into the tiny flame in the salver. The flame flashed green and the thick smell of spices filled the air. "The flames see all."

Wide-eyed, and clutching a little more firmly at the shawl around her shoulders, Lucy passed a coin over. It vanished into Raiza's voluminous sleeves.

"Ask your question, child."

"Tell me about my employment," Lucy said, blinking nervously. "Will I be famous on the stage?"

The fortune-teller hemmed and hawed, then waved her hands over the table. She passed them through the smoke, dropping in a small handful of fine white crystals. The flame crackled, popped and blazed bright orange, and Raiza stared into it as though she were actually seeing something there. "You vill come to great success, child."

Lucy leaned forward, frowning. "Is that all?"

"Shhht! I am speakink." Raiza flapped her hand at Lucy, not pulling her eyes away from the little fire. "You vill come to great success, as long as you trust the right people. Many vill seek to thwart you, but surround yourself with true friends!" She shot one finger up in the air, narrowly missing Lucy's nose, and Lucy flinched back. "And you will be known throughout the land."

Grace folded her arms in front of her and hung back, the thickness of the air making her head feel full and heavy. The tent itself seemed to draw closer around them, get smaller, though the furniture didn't shift at all. Lucy and Raiza's voices seemed to soften and come from very far away, as though they had gone in to a cave. Grace's head swam.

A moment later (only a moment? It felt longer), Lucy was standing and heading for the tent flap, and Raiza was pinching out the candle wick with long-nailed fingers. The wash of fresh air pushed away the heady smells of spices and dying flowers, and Grace's head returned to her own shoulders and stayed there. She turned to follow Lucy, but a hand grabbed her arm, and tugged her back around.

Madame Raiza frowned, her cork-darkened skin streaky in the brighter light of the sun. She turned over Grace's hand and held it there. She was stronger than she looked, and Grace couldn't pull away without putting real strength into it. Raiza's brow furrowed deeply, her pupils blown wide. And when she spoke to Grace, it still sounded like the words were coming from very far away.

"Great change is coming, and with it, pain. A man will bind you and keep you in chains. An angel falls from dark to dark, and the life you know will end in evening's fire."

A sudden burst of fear shot up through the base of Grace's spine and sank its claws into her lungs. She yanked her hand back, Raiza's head jerked up, she blinked, and the spell—whatever it had been—was broken.

"So you're saying I'm going to hell?" Grace sneered, rubbing her hand. The feeling of Raiza's fingers digging in still lingered. "I assume if I pay you enough money, that can be reversed."

Raiza looked her up and down and snorted, her voice, when she spoke again, missing any traces of her terrible accent. "Suit yourself, I'm sure." And then Grace found herself outside the tent, the flap being noisily tied shut behind her, and Lucy waiting for her in the bustling street.

"What did she say to you?" Lucy asked. Grace was too

busy sucking in deep gulps of fresh air to answer immediately. "Did she see something in your future?"

"Are you addled?" The last of the fog burned from Grace's mind, now that her feet were back on steady, open ground. She swung back in to step beside Lucy, shoving her hands into her trouser pockets. "That fraud? I could tell you more about your future right now, and without charging you a penny." The fear still lingered even through her bluster, burning lines of tension across her shoulders.

"Many people swear by Madame Raiza," Lucy sniffed. The clock in the square chimed, and she began to walk faster.

"Her name isn't Madame Raiza, first off," Grace cut in before she could get another lecture. "Her name is Hortense Pullet, and she's an old whore from Shropshire. She used to live upstairs from me in Charing Cross."

Lucy wasn't nearly annoyed enough, waving off the complaint. "You have no sense of *mystery.*"

"The only mystery is how she convinced you to part with a day's pay for some smoke and mirrors."

Lucy's smile was a little too enigmatic for Grace's tastes. "Oh, but when her predictions come true, a day's pay at my current wages will seem like nothing more than trifles. We must look to the future, Miss Owens, and seize opportunities when they come our way." She trotted up the back stairs to the actors' entrance, and opened the Surrey's door wide. "After you."

"Thank you." It may have been churlish to end so curtly, but Grace's reasonably good mood from the morning had already faded away. Her head ached at the temples from whatever god-awful powders "Madame Raiza" had been burning, and her all-black eyes burned into Grace's memory. There had been something eerie about that woman, in that instant, fake fortune-teller or not.

An angel falls from dark to dark.

Absurd. It was gibberish, or some stolen fragment of an obscure poem. If Miss Hortense *Pullet* thought that Grace was going to let *any* man put her in chains, she was a worse fortune-teller and judge of character than even Grace had been willing to give her credit for.

They walked into the rehearsal hall to the cheery sounds of the cast assembling, men and women alike poring over cheaply-bound scripts or tying themselves into rehearsal costumes. Grace's plain cotton rehearsal dress hung on a nail on the wall behind the simple screen. She was a girl for this part, no matter how she had felt upon waking up this morning. One more layer of the role to be assumed.

She shook off the trials of the walk along with her shirt and trousers, sliding in to the sleeveless petticoat and her character all in one. A man's face had looked back at her in the mirror this morning, yesterday's soft edges hardened and her power in her strength. But the character's skirts weren't *wrong* for him the way wearing a gown would have been. Here in the rehearsal space she could be whomever the play needed her to be, without the itch beneath her skin.

There was a perfect kind of peace and quiet in a theatre before the actors arrived. The stage was a blank slate, slowly filling with the pieces of set and properties that would make the shape of a world for an hour, perhaps two.

From his perch up on the catwalk, Isaac had the whole universe spread out below him. His open toolbox lay directly below, half-unpacked across the stage, evidence of the long list of minor repairs he'd been working on throughout the morning. A stack of backgrounds rested in the time-polished grooves cut into the sides of the stage. Everything from a stormy sea to a king's palace sat in place, just waiting to be rolled out.

He pulled on the rope hanging beside his head—a little tug, just to test. The pulley squeaked at him again. Another swipe from the greasy rag should oil it well enough to survive another few goes—assuming the rope didn't fray to pieces first.

"Oy, Caird!" Colby's voice rang out from the floor two stories below. Isaac glanced over the side and waved his hand once, to show the chief painter that he'd heard. "They're coming in to use the space. Finish whatever it is you're doing and clear the stage."

"I thought they were in the rehearsal hall until tomorrow?" Isaac asked, shoving the rag into the pocket of his waistcoat. He grabbed hold of the railings and slid down the ladder, feet barely skidding along the steps until he reached the bottom and landed with a faint thud.

Colby shrugged, hands in the air and a vibrant rainbow of paint splashes haphazardly strewn across his old, worn shirt. "So did we. God knows what pole Elliston's got up his arse this time, but he's been in a foul mood for a week now. Best to play along and stay out of his way."

"How does he expect us to have the place ready for

opening when he keeps interrupting the work?" It was a pointless complaint. The theatre manager neither particularly knew nor cared *how* or *when* the technical pieces were placed in order, only that they *were* by opening night, and with as little trouble brought to him as possible.

Colby, short, round and already perspiring in the day's heat, swiped the top of his balding pate with a kerchief and shrugged eloquently before vanishing back down the stairs to the paint shop.

And that, as they say, was that.

It took a few minutes to repack his tools in their proper places. His kit wasn't a massive one, only two drawers and a ditty box to hold the smaller blades and files, but every tool had its place set between bits of notched wood, and every drawer had the right order in which to pack it most efficiently. It was petty, perhaps, to fuss over small bits of wood and metal, but if there had been one thing that old Ned had impressed upon Isaac during his years of apprenticeship, was that a man's livelihood—and sometimes his life—rested in the proper care of his tools.

It meant, though, that Isaac was only just throwing the latches on the brass-cornered box when the actors began to wander in to the hall. A few of them, he recognized. Red-haired Lucy Sullivan, who believed more strongly in astrology than most men believed in the Church of England; Frederick Poole with his pompous airs covering the attacks of nerves he suffered before every performance night; young John Bright who collected saucy broadsheets and woodcut prints and saved them all in a scrapbook.

And there among them, someone he hadn't seen before. Isaac set his tool chest down in the wings, where he—and it—would be well out of the way, and watched for a moment more.

She was dark, that was the first thing he noticed. Darker than he was, the creamy color of the petticoat she wore set in contrast against the rose-warm heat of her brown skin. Some of her hair curled down around her face in the careful-set spirals of modern fashion, the rest held back in bands that kept it close to her head.

She wore no rings on her fingers, no wedding band. That didn't necessarily *mean* anything, but his eyes went there nevertheless, lingering only a little too long on the elegant curl of her fingers, the graceful movements of her arm, the poise with which she held her head high and surveyed her world.

Her figure was slim, trim and neat, and if she wore stays beneath her costume they did little to nothing to enhance her small bust.

She held herself like a dancer, and when she moved, she moved like a queen.

Familiar footsteps sounded behind Isaac. When he turned, Colby was there again, the stench of wet paint rising off him. A couple of boys dragged a set piece across the back stage behind him, and a new blue smear had been added to the collection across his sleeve.

"Who is she?" Isaac asked without preamble, tangling his forearm in a rope that hung down the pillar, and casually leaning into it. It held his weight easily, and could have taken far more. His eyes stayed on the group of actors taking their places on the stage. The beauty stood in the wings on stage right, across from them, but her eyes remained on the director and the prompt boy now taking his cross-legged position on top of the table set downstage for his use.

Colby thought for a minute, then nodded. "Miss Owens, that's 'er name. Grace Owens, I think. She was in a show at the Olympic last month, one of those bits of excitement with part of the set going up in flames every night. Terrible messes those are to clean up. Lord willing the *ton* will be going mad for something tidier next."

"Grace Owens," Isaac murmured, impressing the name into his memory. "And it's 'Miss'? You're certain of that?" he asked quickly, Colby's disinterested expression turning rapidly into a smirk.

"Oh, aye. Reasonably so. The missus likes the plays at the Olympic. Always dragging home playbills and programs and such."

"Has she got a patron?" He'd shown too much of his hand now; Colby would never let him live it down.

Colby clapped Isaac on the shoulder, leaving a red spot of paint behind on the sleeve of Isaac's shirt. "Watch yourself, lad. It's never a good idea to piss where you eat." And he tapped the side of his nose sagely before moving off.

Scolding erupted from the crossover behind the stage a moment later, and the boys reappeared, dragging the wooden replica of a bluebonnet cluster back the way they had come.

It wasn't bad advice, as such things went. Normally, Isaac would agree with him. Actresses were beyond the reach of the machinists and crew. They glittered on the stage in their silks and jewels, basking in the attention of the men in the expensive boxes on the other side of the lights. He'd taken enough extravagant bouquets backstage and looked the other way when dressing room doors were locked to know how the land lay.

It wasn't the same for the men and women who toiled behind the scenery. The designers had their moments on the playbills, and there was always one wardrobe master or another who had connections and had his name bandied about Town. But the bulk of them toiled anonymously in the days between other, more gainful employment, putting sweat, tears, and sometimes blood into mounting a production.

And Isaac? His job was to make sure that no one *noticed* him doing his job. When a machinist or a stagehand went right, the show carried on without a hitch. When he went wrong, *that* was when people learned his name.

It wasn't enough.

He had plans for more: an unending brew of experiments and designs bubbling around in his head, on scraps of paper, recipes jotted down in the little dog-eared green ledger he carried with him to workroom and home alike.

Two hundred years ago, Inigo Jones had taken the court of King James by storm. His designs had clothed courtiers and turned palace ballrooms into fantastical worlds of endless possibility.

Isaac Caird was going to be next. Not at the court, perhaps, but by the time he was old, fat and happy, and at the end of his career, the whole city of London—no, all of England!—would know his name.

The play had begun, and on the set, Miss Owens

moved to center stage and spoke her first lines. He didn't hear the words, didn't care particularly what they were. It was her voice that mattered, rich and textured, as warm as the sun and as compelling as the tide.

"Miss Owens," Isaac murmured to himself. "I'll remember your name, too."

He would have been hard pressed to rush back to his work after that. It was more tempting by far to stand there in the wings and watch the rehearsal, keep an eye on the actors as they went through the motions, discussed the blocking and framing of scenes, filled up the space with movement and color. And in the middle of it all, a lithe dark girl in a white petticoat, floating through the swirling chaos, calm and untouched.

So of course, in true dramatic fashion—because theatre people could never do *anything* sedately—the doors to the hall crashed open. Were this two hundred years ago, or a proper staged event, Isaac would have expected official-looking men to enter wearing livery and tabards, perhaps bearing trumpets to announce their presence.

These were less flamboyant times. It was nothing but a man in a plain dark suit, and a boy carrying a folded notice, sealed with red wax. "Elliston!" the man announced, and the theatre manager flinched. Isaac moved forward in the wings, enough to see and hear what was going on.

A few others followed suit, rough-hewn men in working clothes drifting in from the backstage shops to find out the cause of the sudden commotion.

"What's going on?" Tottenham—one of the older stagehands—asked, scrubbing his stubbled jaw with blunt fingers.

"Not a notion." Isaac shook his head and leaned in from his post in the wings. "But I'll guarantee you, it's not going to be good news."

"It'll have to do with the Olympic or the Royal again, mark my words," Colby grumbled from Isaac's other side. He paused with the other two men and watched the exodus glumly. "Elliston hates them houses, and they hate 'im. Too many plays and not enough arses in seats to watch 'em all."

Elliston strode down from the stage and took the letter from the messenger boy. He opened it, and a deep frown settled on his face. He and the other man argued for a moment, Elliston gesturing dramatically in the air, and the visitor only responded with a firm shake of the head. Elliston's shoulders slumped. A buzz went through the cast gathered on the stage, and then they all fell quiet.

Elliston turned, raised his hands, and called out to the cast and crew, "Take half an hour! I must take a brief meeting, and then I will return and disclose all. Go, go." He shooed them off, as though it were his benevolent decision to give them free time, and not a reaction to some kind of brewing catastrophe. "Off with you. Have your tea, return promptly at the half hour mark."

The two men turned and headed for the main doors, the boy following. The moment the doors closed behind them again, the stage erupted into a hubbub of conversation, worry etched bright on all the faces.

"It's not a good sign, whatever it is," Miss Sullivan was saying to Miss Owens as the two of them left the stage. They passed so closely by Isaac that he could have reached out and touched Miss Owens' arm, but neither of them looked his way.

"Great change is coming," Miss Owens said softly, her eyes distant and brow furrowed. Isaac turned to watch them go. The confident woman who had owned the stage was gone. Instead, she looked, for lack of a better word, afraid. But of what?

How very, very odd.

Chapter Two

"Let me be clear—no one is getting sacked."

It wasn't as much of a relief as Elliston likely intended it to be.

Robert Elliston, owner and manager of the new Surrey Theatre, had the kind of round and open face that lent itself to comedy. No one in the crowd currently gathered in the ground-floor saloon was laughing. Grace folded her arms across her chest, leaned back against the rough-hewn wooden post behind her, and waited it out.

Half an hour had only just been enough time to brew a cup of tea, wait for it to cool, and then leave it behind at her dressing table. She *had* taken the chance to change, mind you, out of the rehearsal skirts and back to the trousers and homespun she had started the day wearing. Whatever Elliston was up to, she could face it better feeling like she was in the right skin.

"I've just been to the Office of the Examiner of the Plays, to meet with them and with Kemble from the Theatre Royal," he announced grandly, as though that could be anything but the forerunner of bad news.

A rumble of complaints went up among the gathered

employees and cast, the men of the orchestra muttering darkly amongst themselves from their table in the corner.

"You know what this means," Lucy sighed from behind Grace's ear. "We're all out of a living this season."

"Don't give us up yet," Grace murmured back. "We're only a week into rehearsals. There's time for changes."

Except there wasn't, not truly. The patent theatres could afford delays. The minor stages, those without the support of the crown—they needed whatever money could be drained from the pockets of the wealthy before they all left Town for their country estates. If the Theatre Royal wanted *Skirts of the Camp* for their summer season, the Surrey would have to start all over again.

Across the way, beyond the long tables packed with actors, musicians and stage hands, a tall, dark-skinned, strong-limbed man made the same sort of grimace that Grace herself was probably showing. His tightly curled black hair looked recently shaved close and his skin was the color of red chestnut wood. He wore the same simple shirt and trousers as the other men of the backstage crew, but with a gray wool waistcoat buttoned up to showcase a slim waist and narrow hips. It gave him a dashing, gallant sort of look, and something about him seemed almost familiar.

He had been in the wings earlier that afternoon, watching the start of rehearsal.

He seemed to feel her eyes on him, however brief her examination had been. He glanced over at her, an eyebrow flickering up for a moment before he tipped his head in a nod and smiled.

"Kemble has been given the license to put on *Skirts* at

the Royal," Elliston finally admitted, calling Grace's attention back to the front of the room. The swell of protest that went up all but turned into a roar.

The manager waited a few beats for the noise to begin to die down, and then raised his arms in the air to try and settle the furor himself.

Gray Waistcoat leaned back against the wall, rolled his eyes—dark, but Grace was too far away to see what color of dark—and shook his head.

"Now what do you suppose we'll do?" Lucy groaned from her perch on the beam beside Grace.

"Find some other comedy, I suppose," Grace frowned. "He's got the cast for one, and he needs a simple play if we're still to open on time."

"He's lost his mind if he thinks we can learn a whole new script and blocking in under three weeks." Lucy made a face, her pert nose wrinkling under her scattered freckles.

"Speak for yourself."

"No indeed," Elliston continued bombastically. He took two running steps and bounced up to the tabletop before him. He posed upon it, spreading his arms wide. "We are better than that! There will be no more running after Covent Garden's leftover scripts, nor begging for scraps at the Examiner of the Plays. This season, the Prince Regent himself has commended all the playhouses to put on their best, for his pleasure. This season—" He let the moment swell, holding his words until half the room seemed to be holding their breath. "The Surrey shall perform *Macbeth*."

Actors frantically crossed themselves and spit, musicians looked stunned to silence. Even Gray Waistcoat straightened up away from the wall, wide-eyed surprise crossing his chiseled, strong-jawed face.

"He *is* mad," Lucy decided aloud.

"You can't possibly—"

"We don't have a license for Shakespeare!"

"We'll be shut down!"

"We'll be *jailed.*"

"The *curse.*"

"Angels and ministers of grace defend us," Grace murmured, her only concession to that old superstition.

The overlapping protests brought the noise back up again to something almost unbearable before Elliston commanded them all back down to hushed murmurs.

"License or no license, this summer we do the Scottish Play. Let Covent Garden foam at the mouth! Two ballets will be inserted and music played throughout, making the show a burletta, for which we have *always* had permission."

The reaction this time was much calmer overall, but one word rang too loud in Grace's ears, drowning out any relief she might otherwise have felt.

Ballet. She'd come back to the theatre on the promise of never having to deal with that world again.

That had been the plan: keep the stage and the performance-rush, the bubbles of excitement in her veins, but leave behind the bruises and the blood, drown out the endless litany of failed expectations.

Elliston was staring at her, his jocular, narrow-set eyes gleaming in a highly suspect way. "While Mrs. Elliston will be providing the corps from her excellent academy, we are lucky to have some fine dancers within our current cast. Roles will therefore be reshuffled, to permit them to focus on learning the choreography."

He held out his hand and the prompt-boy handed him a small leather-bound notebook. He flipped it open, cleared his throat theatrically, and began to list off parts. Grace held her breath until her chest felt like bursting, waiting for the only information that mattered.

"Miss Owens will be moved from the speaking cast to principal dancer in the ballet, under the direction of Mrs. Elliston as ballet mistress."

Oh no.

Grace fought to keep her expression bland, though the floor seemed to drop out from under her and the world veered sideways on a cantilever. The rest of the meeting passed in a blur, the list of roles and call times washing over her, unheard.

When Elliston dismissed them at last, she was already moving. She pulled her cap down further to shield her eyes, and pushed her way past a cluster of chattering prop boys.

The door was only a few more feet away. She'd get the gossip from Lucy later on. Right now her mind was too clouded, her heart thumping too wildly to be able to remember anything anyway.

She didn't make it far enough. Gray Waistcoat caught her arm right as she hit the threshold, swinging her around too quickly. "Are you all right?" he asked, his voice warm with concern and thrumming deep as a heartbeat.

Grace looked up. His eyes were brown after all. They were also flushed dark with a bewildering concern that seemed too deep for a stranger to another stranger. His moment of pause gave her time to pull her arm free from his hand and slip out the door before Elliston began hectoring them again.

The door swung closed behind her, cutting off the noise. The silence that fell over her, cotton-wool and heavy, was just as bad. The street outside would offer no respite, no chance to sit and think things through. This tight and claustrophobic back hall ran down along the side of the building, and she had seen stairs at the far end.

Trailing her fingers lightly along the wall, grounding herself in the feel of the plaster under her fingertips, Grace moved quickly down the corridor, turned into the stairwell, and headed up the long flight. She wasn't entirely clear on where these stairs led, but anything open and quiet, right now, was better than here.

The second-floor landing opened out to a familiar hallway, the doors to the dressing rooms closed, while the meeting took place downstairs. The old horse stalls from the circus had been turned into a passable saloon, but the dressing rooms had not been altered in at least twenty years. She would find no space for contemplation in front of those mirrors today.

Up again, then, the winding staircase here shifting beneath her feet, less sturdy than the better-used sections below. The wooden door in front of her stood partly open, the room beyond silent. Sunbeams crossed the rough wooden floor from banks of windows to the east and south, picking up glints of dust rising in the air.

Grace pushed the door open wider, and slipped inside.

The attic space had been storage, once, from the looks

of things—back when the Surrey had been a horse-circus and not a playhouse. An old table littered with properties stood against the south windows, the beakers and apothecary jars catching the light. A pile of discarded scene pieces lay atop a pile of rubble in the far corner, next to a trunk with tarnished brass findings. And there, some old pallets that must have belonged to some long-ago stable boys, years since grown and gone.

The sounds of the street beyond were muffled through the window glass and the three stories she rose above it. She could hear the sounds of life elsewhere in the building, voices raised and the pad of running feet, the distant creaks and groans of the ropes and pulleys in the stage wings. But up here, everything was muted and distant.

She seized the edge of the top pallet, dragging the narrow, straw-tick mattress across the floor. A little dust rose, winking, into the light. There, where the sunbeams met and created a warm patch on the floor; she laid the mat down and herself upon it. The sun warmed her skin, a surface repair for a chill that went much deeper.

I have to dance again.

Her body ached despite the warmth of the sun, and old memories ripped through her mind's eye.

~TANZEREI mit Herr Laselles und Fräulein Owens, bei deren ersten Bühnenauftritt in Wien~

~Avec une scène de ballet ouverte par l'incomparable Mademoiselle Owens~

~A dance starring Miss Owens, a child prodigy of unusual skill, beauty and grace~

Had her father had it all in mind already, before she

was even born? Had he chosen her name with the thought of having it inscribed upon playbills, posters and signs?

And now, once again, a man was trying to take charge of her future. But she had choices in this life, where she hadn't before, and they were too hard-won to abandon now.

Grace closed her eyes and let the sun's heat seep into her skin, muscle, and bone. It felt like a lover's touch, a tender kindness, clearing away the rubble of memory.

Should she stay, or quit? It would be hard to find another theatre position now. They all had their casts and summer plays arranged. Her small savings were only enough to carry her through a few weeks, perhaps a month or two if she was frugal. On the other hand, a girl could do many things with a month's worth of living expenses, if she was clever.

Elliston would have to wait a little longer for his answer. Grace had some serious thinking to do.

The small bag secured in his waistcoat pocket and a hum on his lips, Isaac vaulted the last few stairs up to the loft. The meeting over and the actors dispersed to do whatever it was that actors did, he had the rest of the afternoon to read over the new play and consider.

Witches; there are to be witches. Smoke powder, then, and bits of green glass for the reflectors to make them properly ghastly.

Better not to mention that in front of the actors, mind. That lot hated looking any less than perfect, even when a character was supposed to be hideous.

The door had swung farther open than the way he normally left it, and Isaac paused on the landing to look inside. Something had definitely changed. His workbench was undisturbed, but Miss Owens hadn't been asleep on the floor the last time he'd been upstairs.

She was as lovely in sleep as on stage. She had stretched out upon one of the old pallets, an arm flung over her eyes and one knee bent. Her ochre-dark skin gleamed like polished gemstone in the rays of the afternoon sun, and the linen shirt she wore fell in supple folds around that lithe, slim body. First question answered—she didn't seem to be wearing any sort of stays. The hat she'd worn during the meeting lay beside her on the floor, a few of those curls broken free from captivity and surrounding her face like a saint's halo.

Perhaps she dressed in loose shirt and trousers like a dockhand to hide her figure, but even so her hips called to his hands, firm and delicately curved. Her mouth was a promise and he could easily imagine tasting it, drawing the fullness of her lower lip between his teeth and gently biting—

She stirred and he cut that line of thinking off immediately, before the rising heat in his blood caused visible problems in his breeches. He was a man of almost thirty, for God's sake, not a boy barely out of the schoolroom with the lack of control to match.

Any moment now she would open her eyes, and he'd be caught staring. Isaac took his hand off the door and strode in as though he had every expectation that he was welcome. "You sure you're well?" he asked, carrying on his question from downstairs as though the conversation hadn't been interrupted by her panicked flight.

Miss Owens bolted upright as though she'd never been asleep, her eyes wide. They too were beautiful—dark, large, framed with black lashes that Cleopatra would have envied. He pretended to ignore her movement, heading for his workbench. He pushed aside the bits of scrap wood where he'd sketched out some of the mechanism designs for Jupiter's descending chariot. That project would have to wait a little longer.

"What are you doing up here?" she asked, and even laced with tension her voice matched her lips, warm and full.

"It's a good space to get my work done. Good light, enough room to spread out. Staked my claim to it last summer when I signed on with Elliston. No, don't get up," he offered, looking back over his shoulder just long enough to nod at her. "If you don't mind me, I won't mind you."

He started to empty his pockets onto the cluttered surface, already strewn with various bits and pieces of his more recent experiments. Copper strips, distilled spirits in a vial, and the little bag of nuts that held the possible proof of his latest theory.

She moved behind him, his senses so attuned to the rustling sounds that he could all but pinpoint the moment she stood, brushed the dust from her clothes and stopped to watch him work.

A glance out of the corner of his eye showed that he'd been mostly right. She was frowning at the workbench, not at him.

"Isaac Caird." Isaac introduced himself, rolling up his shirtsleeves to just below his elbow. "You're new this summer, aren't you?"

"That's right," she replied coolly, with more confidence than she'd had before. She bent and scooped up her hat from the floor, holding it in her hand rather than setting it back on her head. She moved like a dancer, all clean movements and long limbs. No wonder Elliston had recast her. "I just came off a play at the Olympic Pavilion. Grace Owens."

It was probably not the smartest thing to tell her that he'd already spied out her name.

"That's a nice stage," Isaac replied, to keep making conversation. The pewter bowl he'd liberated from the tavern sat on the other side of the desk and Isaac circled to grab it, along with his flint and tinder. Elliston had enough troubles without him burning the place down around their ears.

A single pistachio would do to start; into the bowl it went, shell and all. "Not a lot of space in the flies, but the sound's good."

Miss Owens padded forward and came around the other side of his workbench, taking in everything. "And what is it that you do here, Mr. Caird?"

"Here in the theatre, or here in the loft?" He grinned, striking the flint to light the small bundle of kindling in his firebox. It caught after only a couple of sparks, and he shielded the smoldering ember with his hand. "I'm just your everyday machinist. Stagehand, rope-hauler, and set-mover. Jack of all trades, master of none."

A long splinter of wood caught at the end, and he carefully lowered the tiny flame down into the bowl with the single, lonely pistachio.

He waited. She waited, one perfectly curved eyebrow arched with such a look of skepticism that he could almost hear the incredulous question in it.

The nut didn't explode. The shell caught on fire satisfactorily enough, burning with a merry little flame, exactly like any other small, thin piece of wood might. The faint, acrid smell of smoke wafted up from the bowl. And that was all.

"Damn," Isaac muttered under his breath, forgetting himself. "Begging your pardon, Miss Owens."

"I've heard worse, believe me. What *are* you doing?" She stood with her arms crossed in front of her, shifting her shirt and lifting her breasts purely by accident, he was sure. She had the sort of figure that could get away with such brilliantly indecent liberties, her bust high and small, each breast the perfect size to be completely hidden by a man's palm.

"An experiment, of sorts," Isaac replied, clearing his throat and forcing himself to look away. At the bowl, at the aggrieved and irritated look in her large brown eyes, anywhere but at her curves, outlined in coarse linen. "You know Three-Fingered Ned, the propmaster down at the King's Theatre?"

Miss Owens nodded, the tension in her shoulders relaxing somewhat when he started to speak. "Who doesn't? That man can make a story last through two pints of beer, as long as someone else is paying." But she said it with a certain amount of fondness that took the sting out of her commentary.

"That's the one," Isaac agreed, setting a candlesnuffer down over the still-burning shell to put the fire out. "He claims he saw a ship's hold erupt in a tower of flame from a barrel of pistachios that weren't properly packed in brine. There's a power in them, so he says, and I'm wondering how best to make use of it."

"Planning a little arson?"

"Nothing of the kind. If I can figure out their secrets, these little things might serve for some half-decent stage explosions. Safer than black powder, and cheaper to boot. The witches for the Scottish Play will need some kind of magic to make their entrances interesting." He fished a couple of nuts out of the bag and cracked one to eat.

The slow, speculative smile that curled over Miss Owens' lush lips was enough to make a vicar think of sin. "You're just a stagehand?"

"Just a stagehand." He returned the smile, offering the bag to her.

"No," she said, looking him up and down. He caught himself all but holding his breath under the weight of that firm, unwavering regard. "Are you sure there's no touch of the alchemist about you?"

What could he say to that? Isaac shrugged, his hands sliding into his waistcoat pockets and his grin widening into a smile. "Maybe so. Doesn't hold any weight with the manager unless I can make my magic work." He waggled his fingers at her in an imitation of Macbeth's witches over their spells, and was rewarded with a faintly tolerant smile.

Back to the workbench, then, and two pistachios into the bowl, plus some kindling under them. The little fire was still smoldering away in his tinderbox, the coal glowing red. "If you don't mind my asking," he said, his curiosity finally getting the better of him, "why'd you look so upset downstairs? I imagine that being recast is a nuisance, but you looked more like you'd been kicked."

The memory of her face in that instant—the warmth draining out of her brown cheeks until she almost looked pale, the way her eyes had narrowed at Elliston—it sat with him, and he couldn't shake it off. It wasn't the reaction of someone who'd only been a little disappointed; more like a child half-sunk into a nightmare. And then, of course, was the way she'd turned and all but run from the room the moment the meeting was over.

She didn't look half-interested in answering. "I don't like change," was all she said. He looked up from the little pewter saltcellar, a pinch of salt crystals between his fingers. Her expression was carefully blank, a drama-mask as effective as any wall between neighbors. "I wasn't expecting it," she added, almost as a concession.

What could he say to that? Isaac hummed, a non-committal sound, and added the salt to the bowl. Pistachios were normally packed in salty water for safe passage— maybe that made a difference. He dipped the slightly-charred taper into the tinder box long enough to light it up again, and carefully, his touch light and his movements cautious, laid it down in the bowl with the tinder and the split-open pistachios.

Once again, the shells caught, but nothing sparked. The little flame burned orange from the salt, and Miss Owens' gaze snapped to it, watching the new color.

A moment hung there, something expectant in her eyes, and then the fire consumed the salt and the flame returned, sadly, to its normal, un-explosive state.

"I have the growing notion that Ned was putting you on," Miss Owens said, one corner of her mouth quirked up in a smile.

"You wait and see. I'll have this figured out within the week." He dusted his hands off and pushed a few piles aside across the surface of his workbench until he found his ledger. The little green book had never filled its purpose as a list of accounts, being bent, rather, to more arcane purpose. Chewing on the end of his pencil stub, Isaac jotted down a few things in his narrow, clean hand.

Nut alone = n / shell bns. N + sel + tind. = burns again. No boom.

Miss Owens had begun a slow walk around the loft by the time he looked up again, as though she were measuring out the space in her controlled paces. She wound up by the door, and he called out before she could vanish.

"I'm happy enough to share the space. No one but me comes up here." She seemed to hesitate, glancing down toward the stairs. "The sunlight is best between two and five in the afternoon," he added, and at that, she smiled.

"I'll remember that." She slipped soundlessly through the open door, and out of his line of sight.

The loft felt cold, suddenly, and some faint hint of perfume lingered in the air, so faint as to be unidentifiable. "So will I."

The evening was too pleasant and Isaac's day too eventful to make returning home in time for the supper rush an attractive option. The prospect of being called upon to draw pints at the bar or run to tables balancing serving trays sat ill on him when compared to the fire of excitement bubbling fiercely in his veins.

The pistachio experiment may have been an utter failure from beginning to end, but there was still so much to be planned, and so much that could be *done* with a show like the Scottish Play.

If only they had longer than three weeks to build and rehearse.

That thought sparked a moment of guilt that he was leaving the theatre at all. But he had no firm plans for his next designs, nor any kind of clear notes from Elliston as to what the manager wanted to see.

He headed north and across Blackfriar's Bridge without another qualm, the river glinting dark and reflecting the torches perched high above as streaks of yellow stars.

The tavern at Chelsea Place was a beckoning gleam of light in the growing dark, the cheap ale a draw to the tradesmen and theatre-crews, the rooms tidy and lit enough for a man not to have to keep his hand on his purse at all times.

He took the stone steps two at a time, the heavy wooden door pulling open easily on well-oiled hinges. The heat and light from inside welcomed him as pleasantly as a woman's arms, and a handful of familiar faces at the bar made his choice of seating obvious.

"What ho, Caird!" came a cheerful shout, and Isaac slid onto the empty stool next to Philip Thilby. He was dressed as though he'd just come from work, his shirt streaked with something that looked like lamp black, his straight mouse-brown hair flopping limply across his forehead and the powerful tang of sweat and linseed oil scenting the air around him.

"What ho yourself," Isaac grinned easily, and clapped the other machinist's meaty shoulder. Thilby and Isaac were of an age and reasonably matched temperaments and had apprenticed together under old Ned. Though Isaac would always privately maintain that he was the smarter of the two by far.

Thilby had thrown his lot in first with the Olympic Pavilion when Isaac had been hired on at the Surrey, designing and crafting stage illusions and tricks that had received some small measure of praise over the last few seasons. Only this summer he had been taken on by the Theatre Royal, a grand step up into the world of patent theatres and royal patronage.

"Heard you lot have been having trouble with the Examiner of the Plays," Thilby commented, waving the barman over. The air whistled slightly between his teeth on that terminal S. "A pint for my good friend here—he'll be needing to save his pennies." He whistled again.

If I were he, I'd avoid using plurals altogether.

"I'll take the pint but you'll be singing small for it. Elliston's got a plan." The mug arrived at Isaac's elbow and Thilby obligingly coughed up the coin for the barman. Isaac picked up the mug, the pewter cool and solid in his hand, and obligingly toasted his colleague before tipping it to his lips. The drink flowed easily, the taste smooth and exactly what he craved after a day like this one.

Thilby was hard to dissuade, though. "Oh yes, we're all familiar with Elliston's sort of plans. I guarantee you, whatever disaster he can hack after will be nothing to commend. The Royal's troupe will do a better job with *Skirts* than the Surrey ever could." He stabbed in the direction of Isaac's chest with one raised finger, his ale sloshing in his mug.

"Watch yourself, Thilby," one of the men on Thilby's other side laughed. "That's 'is manager and 'is livelihood you're after. A man's got 'is pride."

"The Surrey can take it, I warrant," Isaac called back, taking another long drink. "And your paying audiences as well. No insult from a half-grown strutting cockerel like this one could upset me."

"Ask your sister how half-grown I am," Thilby leered, and the very notion of Thilby ever getting within arm's reach of Isaac's sister, never mind having the chance to despoil her, was so absurd that Isaac laughed along with him.

"She already told me—how d'you think I know?"

"Oooh, he slid between the ribs on that one, boy." Thilby's friend all but hurt himself laughing, though Thilby's smile was fading and the gleam in his hooded brown eyes was growing.

"You're that sure of yourself?" Thilby asked, and his tone had changed to shake off the laughter and the jesting.

"I'm that sure." Isaac tipped his mug toward Thilby to punctuate his statement. "Even if the script is terrible, the dancers clumsy cows, the actors mumble-mouthed, and the orchestra drunk, my effects alone would be enough to fill the Surrey's seats as full as the Royal's."

"Oh ho, from confidence to arrogance in one. I'll lay odds

you can't fulfill that promise," Thilby grinned, his narrow lips stretching wide. "You against me, as it used to be."

A bet? Isaac's ebullient mood flamed higher. If there was anything he was certain of, beyond his family's love, it was his skills at his work. "I'll take that wager," he said before he had fully thought it through.

"Fewest seats empty on opening," Thilby said smugly, before Isaac could come up with a suggestion of his own.

"The Royal's got more seats than the Surrey, so that's no fair measure. Plus it needs to be your work against mine, not the breasts of the ingénues. Best spectacle," Isaac suggested instead. "Something new to each of us, not one we've done before."

Thilby frowned at that, then nodded. "Victory to be determined by the reviews and the second-day audiences."

"Done. Wager?" The discussion alone was enough to send Isaac's mind racing through his options. Thilby was obsessed with fire and lights—they were instant pleasers for any crowd and he'd undoubtedly choose something along those lines. Isaac would have to take a different direction, something magnificent without flame and bombast.

"A pound sterling." Thilby had a challenge in his eye, hardly something any man of any pride would allow to go by without answering.

"Only that?" Isaac scoffed. "You don't think much of your skills. Two pounds."

Thilby bristled, his mobile lips pursing tight. He brushed his stringy hair back off his forehead. "I can win more than that in a single hand of cards. I'll wager you can't match me at five."

"Five?" his friend echoed from behind. "That's a month's wages, you caper-witted chucklehead."

"Then Caird here better make sure he has enough set by to pay up."

Isaac drained the last third of his ale all in one and set the mug down on the bar victoriously. "Take your own advice, Thilby. I'll have the crowds of London remembering *my* name in the morning."

"Ye're lucky if a *girl* remembers your name in the morning." But Thilby spat in his hand and held it out. Isaac took it without hesitation, shaking it firmly.

"Witness," Thilby pointed at his friend, and the gray-haired laborer nodded.

"Five pounds," Isaac repeated, wiping his hand on the front of his trousers. "Payable after opening, for the grandest stage spectacles London has ever seen. And let London be the judge."

"Start running now, Caird," Thilby chuckled. "Your only hope or prayer is to be in France by the time we open. You've not seen the smallest piece of what I can do."

Perhaps. Perhaps Isaac's memories of Thilby's rushed and poorly-measured contraptions were out of date or incorrect. But Isaac had a trump card to play, and until then, he would keep his hand close to his chest. So he saluted, bought the next round, and fell into the easy give and take of jesting. And all the while his mind was working away at a competition that had just become so much bigger than Elliston's plans, or the Price Regent's fickle approval.

His pride was on the line. And he knew just the thing.

Chapter Three

Isaac wasn't due to arrive at work until just before noon, but he woke almost with the sun. Sleep had come uneasily, when it had come, his mind preoccupied with images of long, slender limbs, night-dark skin, and the way sunlight had flickered across a sleeping girl's gentle curves.

He was being foolish, that was true, but there was something about the way Miss Owens had moved, the timbre of her voice... And there he was, mentally reciting lists of her fine features again, when the sun was only now peeking between the slats of his window shutters and the smell of freshly-baked bread was filling the air.

The tavern on the ground floor of the house on the Chelsea Road wouldn't open until much closer to the dinner hour, but his parents would already be up and about their preparations.

And Miss Owens' spectacular personal qualities aside, he had a wager to win.

He washed and dressed rapidly, buttoning his waistcoat across his stomach. A dandy he was not, nor a fashionable fop with lace kerchiefs and fancy gilded watch chains hanging about every which place, but there was no shame in starting the day with the illusion of respectability. Even if his employment did amount to manual labor, punctuated by short periods of experimentation with odd substances and odder chemicals.

Brushing his hands across his pockets, however, one finger slid over a rip of some kind that hadn't been there before. Off the waistcoat came, and he held it up in the light. A small black-singed hole was burned right through the gray wool. He put a finger in the pocket and was able to stick it right through. *Well, damn.* That could have been from the fire in the salver, or possibly the bit of acid he'd bought from the chemist. It hadn't been strong enough to do much of anything to the silver plate he'd been testing it on, but apparently wool wasn't nearly as hardy.

He tossed it over his chair and took another from the trunk, checking for any rips or holes before he put it on, this time. Repairs and apologies to the tailor would have to wait until—or, no. Perhaps they wouldn't. Perhaps he could kill two birds with one stone. Isaac picked up his ruined waistcoat instead, folding it under his arm and taking it with him.

Isaac vaulted down the two flights of stairs, taking them two or three at a time. Father stuck his head out from the dining room as Isaac flew by, calling out a "good morning, and what's the rush?" that Isaac didn't stop to answer. They kept the wine in the cellar, rows of shelves designed to keep the various bottles from souring. The expensive shelves were to the back, and he avoided those, tucking a smaller bottle of middling quality under his arm along with the waistcoat.

Mother stepped out into the hall from the kitchen door

as he came up the stairs, wiping her fine-boned hands on her apron, her golden hair braided and tucked beneath a clean white cap, and a dusting of flour along her peach-pale cheek.

"Up so early?" she asked, eyebrows raised, and he stopped long enough to bend and kiss the top of her head.

"Things to do," he apologized, but didn't turn for the door fast enough. She spotted the bundle under his arm and frowned.

"Tell me that's not your good coat ruined. You're going to end up getting yourself killed if you keep messing about with black powder and all those potions of yours."

He grinned, trying the smile that women occasionally found charming, but got only a tapped foot back at him in reply. "Waistcoat, it's only the pocket, and I'm taking it to be fixed," he explained, and his mother only shook her head and sighed.

"I don't know what I'm going to do with you, Isaac Caird." But she reached up and patted him lovingly on the cheek, so he took it for the compliment it was probably not intended to be. "Except wait patiently for you to get married," his mother added pointedly, "so that your clothing mishaps become another woman's problem."

"It could happen!" he replied with another grin, taking his coat down from the hook and slinging it over his shoulders. "Stranger things have taken place." His hat next, not an elegant gentleman's hat, but a serviceable cap nonetheless.

"Hmmph," was all he got back. "I'll believe *that* when I see it."

He didn't reply, heading out into the bustling city street and letting the door swing closed behind him. Twenty-nine was hardly old to be unmarried, not for a working man. He'd not thought himself particularly deprived, either. His parents had room enough to keep him, in return for rent and some help about the tavern once in a while. He had steady work, friends, and the occasional short-lived love affair to keep himself in good company.

It was hard to deny the appeal of something new, though. He had money saved to consider a house of his own, and he could afford to keep a wife in reasonable comfort— as long as she didn't demand rubies and diamonds, or a carriage and four. But all of that was immaterial, really, until he found someone to share it.

Unless, of course—

But that was getting far too ahead of himself, based solely on the allure of a pair of large dark eyes.

The doors to the theatre were open when he arrived, light flooding through the windows of the main hall. Down the back stairs and a handful of twists and turns through the rabbit's warren of little hallways led him to the tailor's shop, tucked in behind the propmaster's workshop and the painters.

This door, painted red and gold with little scrollwork flourishes on the edges, opened into a different world than the dusty halls stacked with unpainted veneers and stretched canvases. The costume workshop had been designed to be a broad and open workspace, but actual use had not followed suit. Two long tables took up the bulk of the floor, dressmakers' dolls standing along either side, half-covered in pinned fabrics and partially sewn robes. There were male ones and female ones, each a splash of vibrant color and sparkles in the bright light cast by a pier glass with a rack of candles sat before it.

The closer end of the room was entirely taken up by a mock sitting room, cushioned chairs and even a low chaise making three sides of a square, a table covered in sewing supplies and bits of patterns set between them. A little fire burned merrily in an equally little hearth—where the chimney went and how it vented the smoke he could not begin to imagine. A pair of Mr. Byrne's infamous fur-lined slippers had been set to warm on the hearthstone, but the doughty Irishman himself was nowhere to be seen.

A couple of Byrne's apprentices sat cross-legged on the farthest table with laps full of fabric, their needles pausing for a moment at Isaac's entrance. Mrs. Byrne rose to standing from her chair by the fire, the equally stout and gray-haired woman next to her bobbing her head at Isaac in a friendly nod. She didn't otherwise stir from the silk-covered frame standing in front of her and the complicated gilt embroidery spooling out beneath her fingers.

"Any sign of Paddy today, Mrs. Byrne?" Isaac let the door close quietly behind him, and the boys bent back to their labor, ears undoubtedly wide open. Pádraig Byrne's costume shop was like every other Isaac had ever known— the true center of all gossip, rumors gleefully heard, tutted over, and then passed on by the tailor, his boys, embroiderers, and mantua-makers alike.

"Oh, he's already been and out again," Mrs. Byrne exclaimed, bustling over to draw a chair out for him. "There's a ship in with his orders from away, and you know how he likes to be doing everything himself. Doesn't trust a single man jack o'them to check the shipments over proper-like before signing." Her eagle eyes spotted the bundle beneath Isaac's arm before she finished speaking. "Have you something there for him?"

He perched on the edge of the chair carefully. One false move and he'd sink into the wonderfully soft cushions, not to be heard from again for weeks. "Only a small repair to my waistcoat, and it can wait." He did hand her the wine bottle, though. "A gift, to say thank you in advance."

"Oooh, lovely!" Mrs. Byrne beamed at him, as though the tithe-for-labor was a surprise and not universally understood part of the routine. "Is it your mam's?" She patted her friend on the arm until the other lady looked up; spectacles for close-work made her eyes seem alarmingly huge. "Isaac's mam is one of the finest brewers in London, my dear Mrs. Westby. She puts up such beer as you've never seen the like."

"It's not, I'm afraid," Isaac apologized before she could get too carried away on her torrent of praise, "but she does have a batch coming up to be bottled soon. I'll set some aside for you."

"You're a good lad," she replied promptly, nudged a kettle back onto the center of the iron rack in the fire, and settled into her chair. She picked up her sewing once more, a moss-green silk gown with a perfect line of her tiny stitches marching like cross-hatched soldiers along the hem. "So what's new in your world, my lad?" And she looked at him with a shrewd and knowing expression.

"Not too much," he began, but at her chuckle, he grinned. "There's no putting one past you, is there?"

"Not on your life," Mrs. Byrne answered cheerfully.

"Who've you got your eye on, my dear?"

He leaned forward, elbows on his knees. There was a protocol to all of this, as easy in the back-and-forth as any script. He grinned, she echoed it back, and he drew a line in the air with his finger, back and forth. "Now this is just between you and me."

Mrs. Byrne pressed her hand solemnly to her ample chest, and nodded. "On my saintly mother's grave, my lips are sealed." Mrs. Westby beside her pretended not to be listening, and when Isaac stole a quick look, one of the apprentice boys quickly dropped his head back to his work.

Not that he minded particularly if word got about that he was interested. If nothing else, it might keep other fellows from pressing their luck. "Do you know an actress here this season? Miss Owens? Tall, slim—similar coloring to mine," he added, just to be clear. There were more than enough dark-skinned actors and actresses around, but she was the only one at the Surrey this season.

"Grace Owens?" Mrs. Byrne nodded with satisfaction. "Oh yes. She was down here only just last week for fittings. Of course that's all changed now and we'll have to have her down again. Poor Mr. Byrne was up in the closets all last night, pulling out bits and bobs from the last time we did any kind of serious show. Can't have comedy colors and Harlequinos wandering around in ancient Scotland."

She took a few more tiny stitches, peering closely at her work, before continuing. "She's a nice enough girl. A right funny duck, what with the breeches and all, but you can always see the wheels turning. She's got a clever mind."

"The cleverest people are the ones who say the least that's foolish," Mrs. Westby added sagely, giving Mrs. Byrne rather a pointed look over the thick rims of her spectacles.

"You do say the oddest things, Mrs. Westby," Mrs. Byrne trilled. "In any matter, we were speaking of Miss Owens. Is there anything in particular you wanted to know? She's not a trusting soul—keeps her lips buttoned tight on 'owt to do with her personal business."

What did he want to know? Everything. *Does she have a family already? A lover? What does she like in her men? What kinds of kisses make her blood run hot?*

He shrugged instead. "I suppose the only important question is whether she's married or not, but I've heard that it's 'not.' Unless she has an understanding with someone…?" He left the question open-ended. An "understanding" could mean anything from an engagement to being the mistress of a wealthy patron, and an entanglement on that scale would put him firmly out of the running.

"Nothing that I've ever heard tell of," Mrs. Byrne said thoughtfully, and Isaac could feel the relieved grin spreading across his face. Grace was shy, then, perhaps reticent, rather than unable to answer his attentions. That, he could work with. But then Mrs. Byrne kept talking, shaking her head. "Oh, lad, I'd turn your eye elsewhere for your bit of fun."

"And why's that?"

"Because it's a fool's errand." She tutted sadly. "That girl's not interested in lovers. She's a spinster and content to stay so. Said it herself when I was fitting her for her gown only a week ago. Alls I said was that she'd be lovely enough in that dress to snare any man she wanted, despite her advanced years, and what do you think she said?"

He was drawn in despite himself, sitting back down on

the edge of his chair. "What's that?"

"That there was no man alive worth putting in the effort." Mrs. Byrne sighed and shook her head, while Mrs. Westby snorted softly. "Fancy that."

Was that all? No vows of chastity or Sapphic sins to keep her set apart, then, but a general distaste for worthless males? All he would have to do to win her, then, would be to prove himself different than the men she had known before. Given the sort of self-obsessed gentlemen who haunted the stage doors and fancied themselves lovers, that was a challenge that he could readily accept.

"I hope you don't think so," he flirted, winking. Mrs. Byrne blushed and swatted at his arm in an "oh, *you*" sort of gesture that was by now easy and familiar.

"Off with you now." She shooed him away. "And leave that waistcoat here. I'll have Mr. Byrne take a look once he's back."

He left, bowing his thank-yous and retreated, his mind already humming. The first step to getting Miss Owens to lower her defenses was to show her that he could be kind, and thoughtful. He would send her something, then. A small, unobtrusive, but obvious sign that he both remembered and enjoyed the short conversation they had shared, and then see what came of it.

"Quit? You're not going to quit." Lucy sounded very sure of herself, and her reflection frowned at Grace from the mirror set at her spot in the women's dressing room. "What on earth for?"

It was the question Grace should have anticipated, and the one it was most difficult to answer. At least not without delving into aspects of her tiresome life story that she would much rather remain untold. She tipped her head back against the wall for support, only to have a few strands of her hair catch in the splintered wood. Running her hand behind her head pulled them loose easily enough, but it was the *principle* of the thing.

"I signed a contract to act, not dance." A change in contract could be good enough reason for anyone.

Lucy didn't seem to be so convinced. "Your pay's the same, isn't it?"

"But the work isn't. I haven't danced in four years, not on a stage. It will take time and long hours of training to even get back half of what I used to have. And that's time I *won't* be paid for."

"But if you're learning again from Mrs. Elliston, it'll be for free," Lucy pointed out, stabbing her paintbrush in Grace's general direction before returning to scrutinizing her face in the mirror. "So think of it as being paid in kind, lessons for training hours. Besides, you won't have to learn any lines that way, or dodge Bixby's fingers when he gets all pinchy in rehearsal."

"I might enjoy learning lines, you know." Grace replied, but there was so little point to the argument that she may as well not have bothered. Lucy had said her piece. She was probably right, which was the worst of it. Finding a new contract now, with every company in Town already open or in rehearsals, would be next to impossible. No matter which way she twisted and turned the problem in her mind, it made better sense to stay.

Sooner or later Elliston and his wife would see that she was nowhere near the star they expected her to be. And then they would either fire her or move her back to the acting cast, where she would be relegated to whatever background part was still open. It was hardly the way she'd prefer to spend the summer, especially since she had expenses.

And then there was Mr. Caird. He was a puzzle, no matter how wide his smiles or how easy his patter. He dressed like a gentleman down on his luck, spoke like a boy from Oxford despite his thoroughly Scottish name, and worked as a stagehand for pennies a week.

She had barely been able to pull her eyes from the bunch and flow of the muscles of his forearm, his sleeves rolled up to his elbows. He had broad hands, but handled his tools with the delicacy of a jeweler.

It had been a very long time since Grace had—

No. That was a pursuit that would only end in disappointment. Only a few months ago she had been lecturing Meg on men's dishonesty and avarice. Nothing had changed between then and now.

Except that Grace was notoriously poor at taking her own advice.

If she left the Surrey now, she was unlikely to secure a contract with Elliston again. That meant leaving the mysterious Mr. Caird to *stay* a mystery.

"Perhaps it would be worth at least meeting with the ballet mistress and see what she has planned," Grace mused aloud, halfway to hating herself for the concession.

"That's the ticket," Lucy replied with a commiserating smile. "You'll see. It won't be as bad as all that. Consider this—the stars have seized upon the chance to teach you something and guide you to a new path."

"Is that another fortune for me, oh Lady Dee?" Grace teased. She hardly felt like it, but spilling out her miseries to Lucy in any detail was not in her plans for the day.

"It could at that," Lucy agreed, appearing to take no offense. "If you allow it to be."

The dance school was less impressive than the extravagant baroque academies Grace had once known well in Vienna. This one was a wide low building that might once have housed a boxing ring or fencing school, the broad double-doors badly in need of fresh paint. They swung open easily at her touch, though, the well-oiled hinges silent and smooth.

Appearances can be deceiving? Is that my first lesson?

Hardly. Things in life happened because people made them so, not because of stars or fate, nor even black cats and spilled salt.

The entryway opened to a wide hall, cozy and less grand than others Grace had seen. The tall arched windows let in a great deal of light, the sunbeams splashing golden across the smooth wooden floor. A bowl of flowers sat on the mantle above an unused fireplace, a summer screen painted with delicate running vines blocking the hearth off from view. A pair of overstuffed chairs in discordant shades of blue and green looked as though they had been pinched from some henpecked husband's study, fancy embroidered work draped over arms that would no doubt be slightly threadbare beneath the exquisitely stitched linen.

And in the distance, the sounds of a pianoforte, the rise and fall of voices, and the heady, familiar scent of rosin tinged with the acrid tang of sweat.

Home, declared a hateful, treacherous voice inside.

Hell, Grace insisted, and turned her attention toward the maid approaching her through the open side door.

The slim girl in her starched white apron led Grace through the hall, past closed doors that hid who-knew-what behind their mysterious blank surfaces. Grace's steps slowed despite her determination, her booted footfalls echoing loudly in the otherwise empty corridor.

"Just through here, Miss," the maid chirped pleasantly, opening the door at the far end of the hall. The plunking sound of the pianoforte doubled in volume, and a woman's voice chanted out the steps of an exercise to the steady rhythm.

"Thank you," Grace muttered out of sheer habit. Her internal war was hardly the girl's fault, and she didn't deserve rudeness simply because Grace was fighting the urge to run. She stepped through the door and entered the studio.

The memories struck her in a flash, a flood that tumbled down over her and all but knocked her off her feet.

She was a child of six, standing in a white dress, Monsieur Dauberval circling her as though she were a prize horse at auction. *She has a good length to her limbs; if she is clever as well, she will do.* Her father paid him with a small bag of coins, a small investment to be repaid in full in Grace's sweat and blood.

Grace was a girl of twelve, rising up *en pointe* in pink silk slippers, the rough darning in the end of the shoe scraping painfully against her toes. But she stayed up a little longer every time she tried. She glanced in the rippled and distorted looking glass on the wall, enthralled by her growing strength, her shape a slim white line with dark ends. Her ankles wobbled, a cramp shot up her leg and she collapsed back down to flat feet. Mme. Lavalle's stick across the back of her thighs hurt less each day.

At eighteen she was an adult, and dancing had become her escape. She floated across the stage on the balls and toes of her feet, curled her arms just *so* to beckon her lovers, a falling dove folding to the stage in clouds of delicate silk chiffon. Or she was a prince fierce and proud, in breeches and cravats, arms outstretched to take his bows. For an hour each night, she was weightless in her skin, she was music, she was *free.*

By twenty-two, any romance in the dance had long since faded and died. Every week was another stage, another grand plan to get her closer to the courts and the extravagant ballrooms, every coin and note, every jewel from an admirer vanishing forever into her father's gold-embroidered pockets.

Grace had been twenty-three when she had sworn that she would never dance again.

Now, at twenty-seven, nothing and everything had changed, except a knee that stiffened in the winter rains. The row of young men and women in their snug breeches and knee-length skirts stared at her, then murmured and tittered to one another behind elegant, long-fingered hands.

A solid, round man with graying sideburns plunked his

thick fingers down on the keys of the pianoforte one last time, then stopped. Mrs. Elliston, her high-waisted brown dress falling neatly to her ankles and her hair up in rolls and a ribbon, smiled, and approached. She moved quietly across the polished wooden floor, slippered feet barely seeming to take her weight, an ebony stick tucked neatly beneath her arm. "Miss Owens."

"Mrs. Elliston." Grace nodded, fighting back the urge to sweep into a curtsey. Old training died hard, in some cases. "I am told you have some choreography for me. I should warn you, it has been a very long time since I danced."

"It will come back to you in no time." Mrs. Elliston said with confidence, a mirror opposite of Grace's own last thought. "I have no concerns, child. You have had good training from the start, from what I have heard, and the muscles will remember. Now, come here and let me look at you."

Mrs. Elliston's good cheer seemed almost catching, with her easy laugh and the wrinkles that appeared around the corners of her eyes when she smiled. Even still, she carried an aura of authority that Grace was loath to contradict. She set down her bag, smoothed the front of her dress, and moved to the center of the room.

Another rush and murmur of sound rose from the young dancers behind her. She held her head high, her arms at her sides, and ignored them all. There was only one small mirror here upon the wall, no sheet of silvered glass in which she could see every distorted imperfection.

Mrs. Elliston regarded her solemnly, raising her stick to prompt Grace's arm to lift. Grace rose with it, holding her arm out, her fingers just so, the *porte a bras* as natural a stance even now as *en garde* became to a lifelong fencer. "Lovely," Mrs. Elliston murmured, and Grace's face must have registered her shock, for Mrs. Elliston stepped back and lowered her stick, allowing Grace to drop her arms to her sides once more.

"I can see why you were a serious dancer," she said then, and her words were not at all what Grace had expected to hear. "You have that dignity that lends itself so well to the sublime, the slow movement of the high dance forms."

She's lost her mind. Grace had been trained for the serious forms instead of comic, yes, but that had been years ago, and the slow, ponderous movements of the formal dances had been falling out of fashion for years.

"Mr. Elliston is adamant that we move to the semi-character forms for this production," Mrs. Elliston went on to explain, faint irritation in her voice. "And so we must make sure that you relearn your jumps and gambols. Audiences these days expect fine legs, high leaps, and women whose strength is as great as any man's."

Grace shook her head. "I think you overestimate my skills, Madame. I've never been a caperer or a jumper—"

"Women of your age have developed better strength, especially in the legs and hips," Mrs. Elliston replied briskly, and the buoyant feeling of relief that had begun to percolate up through Grace's innate suspicion burst, faded, and died. One look answered her suspicions.

The rest of the class were young, some of the boys looking barely old enough to grow a proper beard. Grace was the only one older than twenty, if she had to guess, certainly the only one with the chance of a gray hair or two creeping into her curls. *Of my age, indeed. Perhaps* that's *why they wanted me.*

"And the serious style of dancing required greater strength than our new styles of gambols and turns. We will make a new Camargo of you, my dear, if you put your trust in me."

Grace had seen images of *La Camargo* before, but only those. The dancer who had invented almost everything beautiful about the new forms of ballet had died a decade or more before Grace was born, and had aged out of dancing thirty years before that. "La Camargo was a legend, Madame. I'm only—"

"You are only our new star," Mrs. Elliston interrupted. "And we have a great deal of work to do before we may open. So go and change out of that frock, my dear child, and into rehearsal dress. We will begin with the class, in stretches and *aplombs*, and we will see what your body remembers."

Grace's body remembered much less than she'd hoped.

Not that she had made a complete sammy of herself, at least not in front of the *corps de ballet*. But she had forgotten how much a human body could sweat. Or perhaps she was farther gone than she had realized, for her rehearsal dress was wet from sleeves to waist when she peeled the knee-length white costume from her body and tossed it in the general direction of her bag.

Sitting down on the wooden bench in the school's dressing room, Grace took her inventory. Knees and hips less flexible; her breath coming faster and sooner than it had when she was young.

She had once been able to keep on one raised foot for an *aplomb* for at least a twenty-count, and now her legs began to tremble at five. It was best not to think on jumping at all, especially with the young sylphs beating their toes on their calves and soaring as though they hung on wires.

Grace peeled her slippers from her feet, the toes almost worn through. She hadn't taken the time to darn the soles, the new satin already wearing down to the canvas from the scraping of her feet against the floor. The rising blisters were her own fault, her own pig-headedness to blame.

She hurt everywhere, in places she hadn't remembered existed on a body.

And yet, at the same time—Grace stretched, linked her fingers and pressed her arms up toward the ceiling. She folded forward, slowly, so as to feel the ache of her back and shoulders, the delicious pull through her hips, the solid certainty of being inside her skin that came after rough work, hard work.

Ballet masters, directors, parents, lovers—they could tell her which way to move, put dialog in her mouth, pretend that she was what they wanted her to be. Let them dream. Even days when her sense of self shifted, skin and muscle seeming to stretch and change overnight, that ache was what kept the knowing in place—that she was real. Man's eyes in the mirror or woman's, that thing that was *Grace* remained the same. The proof that in all its myriad forms, this body was hers.

Today even that was irritating. It was foolish, but she didn't *want* to feel good. It felt as though she was betraying something that had become essential.

Grace changed briskly, washed, and packed her bag once more, heading out into the bright afternoon. The sun was too hot, the walk from the school to the theatre too long, and the salve she'd rubbed on the raw skin on her feet was doing nothing useful.

Why had she agreed to this? Because she didn't feel like looking for new employment, and worse yet, because she had been briefly swayed by the thought that she might find a man attractive. Honestly, what had become of her?

She was supposed to be calm, steady Grace. Supportive, strong, independent Grace. That was what everyone expected of her. Not whatever sort of…acquiescent, submissive *girl* she was turning back into.

Of course there were times when she longed for someone to take her under their wing, the way she had done for so many others. For it to be *her* turn to have someone draw a hot bath, rub liniment on her sore muscles, brew a cup of tea for her and set a hot Chelsea bun on the plate beside. Just because. But that didn't make her *weak,* or childish, or easy to push around.

Elliston and his wife had no business trying to force her into a role she was uneager to play. If they wanted La Camargo back, let them go to Belgium and dig her up in the churchyard.

And fie on Mr. Caird for that matter, who couldn't have simply left her alone. If he hadn't started those conversations, she'd never have been curious about him. If she'd never been intrigued, then she would have had nothing to keep her at the Surrey. And if she'd quit like she *should* have, well! Her feet wouldn't be hurting now, would they?

So it was all, essentially, his fault.

Grace had worked herself into a properly indignant strop by the time she arrived back at the Surrey to find the building mostly empty. Rehearsals had ended for the day, the theatre deserted but for a few boys having a war with their brooms on the stage. Lucy had already gone. \The dressing room above stairs was empty as well, except for the usual debris—shoes kicked under the bench, a sweaty shift badly in need of laundering draped over the arm of a chair, and three washcloths piled in a damp heap on the stand beside the water jug.

And at Grace's usual mirror, her boy's cap set on the corner of her dressing table, something new. A white gauze sweet bag, tied with a delicate satin ribbon. Grace set her own satchel down and approached her dressing table slowly. There was no card or note, no suggestion of the giver or the intended recipient. Perhaps it was meant for Lucy, or one of the other girls?

She picked up the bag and tugged on the ribbon; that was when she knew. The little sweet bag fell open, the sides bulging from the contents. It held a good handful or two of candied nuts, the warm sugar smell of the confection cloying and too sickly-sweet.

Mr. Caird.

Who else would have left her *nuts*? She had turned him down upstairs, refused his offer of sweetmeats there. Was this his reaction? To press gifts upon her again, in the hopes that she wouldn't know whom to refuse?

Honestly, he'd caused enough trouble for her already.

Her stomach growled and she ignored the urge. He

would know, somehow, even if she only ate one. And that would mean he was winning.

Winning what, *precisely?* She had no answer for that, but still the feeling lingered.

Grace took the bag and headed around the corner, up the stairs again, until she reached the little door that led into the loft. It was closed, which meant she could just slip in, give back the bag, and slip out again.

She turned the handle, then held very still. Were those footsteps beyond? Was he in there? Running in to Mr. Caird again had *not* been part of her plan.

She waited, holding her breath, her heart thumping treacherously in her chest. The shuffling sound didn't come again.

With more desire than ever to get the entire thing over with, she pushed open the loft door, and strode inside. The setting sun meant no warm golden pools of light on the floor this time. That was for the best. Her eyes played tricks on her when a shadow seemed to shift at the far end, but when she looked right at it, the room was still.

Exhaustion, that was what it was. Already overworked, and it was only her first day.

Grace strode purposefully across the room, and set the sweet bag firmly down on the middle of Mr. Caird's workbench, where he would be sure to see it. And then for good measure, she searched the messy tabletop until she found a little bit of pencil, the wooden end splintered and chewed, and the little green book he'd used to make all his notes. No, she wouldn't rip a page from a book—she wasn't that far gone.

A different scrap of paper, then, without too many scratched-out annotations on it, and a blank side on which to write. Grace licked the end of the pencil and wrote her note. *I don't accept gifts from strangers.* She left it propped up beside the bag. Let that be an end to all of this nonsense.

Chapter Four

The short and pithy note on his workbench was not the way Isaac had hoped to begin his day. The more he looked at it, though, the more things suggested all was not, in fact, lost. It was written on one of his own scraps, so the note had been left impulsively. And she hadn't told him to sod off— at least not in so many words. That left some room for him to become no longer a stranger at all.

He flipped the note back over, his half-baked sketches on the other side a reminder of other projects he'd yet to start. The pistachio experiments had been an utter failure, and not because of his methods. He needed something far larger and more impressive to beat Thilby this time around.

The trunk down in the storage room called to him.

Isaac had stumbled on the dusty, nondescript coach trunk at the end of the previous season, climbing over a pile of broken-down chairs looking for shelves on which to store the parasols and hatboxes left from the summer's shows. His arms full of paper and card gewgaws, he'd barked his knee on the low wooden box with its steel corners, hinges and locks.

A locked trunk wasn't the sort of thing one came across

backstage, generally speaking. Oh, they had boxes, ranging in size from little jewel cases to massive wardrobes meant for secret lovers to hide in. And they had false locks of every conceivable size and shape, to be stuck on prison gates and doors of wayward daughters' bedchambers with paste and finishing nails.

This one was different.

Isaac had set his armful of properties down on the floor, not caring about the dust and footprints accumulated over years of hard-soled boots tromping in and out of the storage room. He had knelt down in front of the mysterious trunk, and run his fingers over the sides, the hasp, and the bottom. Just to see what could be found.

And wonder of wonders, the key had been there, in a small leather bag tucked beneath the trunk, all but flattened under its weight. It had taken him a few minutes to work the bag free, pick out the old and tangled knot in the drawstring, and shake the small brass key into his waiting hand.

The lock had opened as though it had just been oiled, or was somehow waiting for him to try. And inside, the treasures of an age.

Set designs, painted in watercolor and ink wash. Sketches for mechanisms, half-scribbled out, with notes in a variety of hands. The paper was old, the pencil and ink faded from time, or crumpled from use.

A wine splash across the center of one page smeared the ink as though someone had tried to mop it up, the drips along one side the last attempt to hang the drawing of a wind-making machine out to dry.

Below that there had been old cast lists, drafts of

playbills, tailor's warrants—all the bits and pieces of paper that some manager years ago had collected, used, then stashed away for later. And then somewhere in between then and now, the box had been locked, brought to the Surrey, packed away, and forgotten.

Until Isaac.

And now, today, those water-damaged and faded diagrams called to him again. Something in there could be of use. Even if all the working parts weren't noted or labeled or even included on the drawings, as was so often the case (*thanks for nothing, whoever you were*), he could still get enough of an idea.

With enough time and work, he could resurrect some of the old spectacles, the kinds of dramatic machines that had so delighted old King James, and might appeal to the aristocrats now. Perhaps even the Prince Regent himself.

Then his fortune would be made, Elliston's and the Surrey's along with it, and he could rub Thilby's greasy face in the dirt.

Down the long stairs, then, and he only paused on the second-floor landing long enough to look down the hallway and see that the dressing room doors were closed fast. If Miss Owens was around, she was not receiving callers.

Colby bumped into him on the first floor landing, already shaking his head and grumbling. "Have you seen it?"

"Seen what?" Isaac paused, hand still on the railing.

"Elliston." Colby snorted derisively. "He's brought in a bloody guillotine. For the Scottish play. 'E says it's 'topical.'"

Only one word in that really gave Isaac pause. "Wait. *Bloody?*"

"Cursin', not describin'."

"Ah."

"We're all going to be in trouble if the *ton's* in the wrong mood on opening, I tell you what." And with that final proclamation of doom Colby headed up the stairs, grumbling audibly all the way.

There was little point in going to find out more; either the piece would break, it would be cut at dress rehearsal, or Elliston would think better of turning Lady Macbeth into some kind of metaphor for the Terror and make it disappear. And if none of those happened, Isaac would be much better off knowing as little about it as possible.

The coaching trunk sat in its usual place in the smaller property room, now pushed back against the wall with a table pulled alongside, the key clipped on to the ring in Isaac's pocket. He could sit here undisturbed for a while, leafing through the weathered pages, the paper smooth under his fingers and the mapped-out lines telling stories of wonders not seen in decades. He reached for his notebook but it wasn't in his pocket. He must have left it upstairs, damn it all, but he wasn't about to go back to find it now.

Rock that opens to release horse and rider—no. Chariot designed as a cloud that descends from the flies with a winged cherub riding...no. Hardly appropriate for a tragedy.

He normally passed right over the costume sketches, as prettily colored as some of them were. That was hardly his department. But he turned the page in the folder on his knees, gently smoothing the crinkled edges, and one image stopped him cold.

The watercolor was of a ballet dancer standing on her toes, her other leg swept out behind her. The dancer wore a delicate white dress in an old style, the full, knee-length skirt trimmed with flowers and delicate trailing vines. Her skin was fair, her hair curled around her ears and intertwined with rosebuds.

He couldn't help but think of the dancer he knew. The cream and white of the dancing dress would highlight her beauty all the more, the little rosebuds in her curls an invitation to touch, to trace his fingertips down the sweet line of her cheek.

The dancer in the picture stood easily on the very point of her toes, little silken wings on her back to make her into a fairy, perhaps. *Midsummer Night's Dream?*

The caption said *Flore et Zéphire*, no name given to the designer, but it was the next line that caught Isaac's eye and held it there. *Desine pour flying apparati,* the handwritten scrawl seemed to read, as best as he could make out, in a funny combination of languages. *Linnes to pulleys, deux pour une danceuse, three for Didelot as N Wind.* Rigging to send a dancer flying like a bird, or a sprite.

There was more at the bottom of the page, but the edge of the paper had been eaten away by bugs or mice. All Isaac could make out was a signature, the angular hand reading *Liparotti 1794.*

Miss Owens had been pulled from a lead role into a supporting place as a dancer. What if he could give her back that honor? Recreating such an effect would turn the ballet from a pro forma piece, inserted only to obey the laws for non-patent theatres, into a spectacle the like of which had not been seen for, if the date was to be believed, almost twenty years.

What better way to woo a performer, than to give her the ultimate platform for her performance?

What better way to amaze a crowd than to achieve the impossible, and make a dancer fly?

Isaac flipped through the folder one more time, on the off chance that another page might be lurking—something with actual details, perhaps, or the name of the theatre where the original spectacle had been performed. No such luck. He rolled up the precious page and tied it with a piece of string from his pocket.

All right, then. With no further guidance to be had in the archives, he would have to figure it out by himself.

In the meantime, to show that he had not abandoned her, Isaac chose a sweet white rose from a flower seller with a very fancy hothouse, and had a boy deliver it to Miss Owens in the ladies' dressing room.

We are not strangers, but colleagues, said the note.

The rose returned immediately by the same boy, with Isaac's note stuck firmly on one of its thorns.

Sunday was a day of rest, of sitting in the loft after church and dreaming up plans, his sketches and half-formed ideas for the improved flying mechanism unspooling across salvaged scraps of card and paper. He never had found the dratted notebook. It must have been buried somewhere among his papers. It would turn up eventually.

On Monday, Mrs. Elliston happened to mention to Mrs. Westby who told Mr. Byrne that Miss Owens had torn a ribbon from her slipper during rehearsal that day.

Ribbons were a little out of Isaac's area of expertise, but Mrs. Byrne showed him which ones to buy.

The ribbons came back to him still coiled in the little paper packet, but not until the next day.

Grace knew better than to open the letter sitting on her dressing table. She had made it a point to stay late at the school the last few days, stopping only at the theatre to retrieve any notes or changes for the following day. It should have been easy to avoid Mr. Caird and his capering attempts to win her attention.

The little watercolor painting inside the card was small but exquisitely detailed, a rendering of the Theatre Royal at sunset, the golden light shimmering on the building's marble columns and staircases. The signature was not Mr. Caird's, but that of a man who sold his artwork along one of the lanes in Chelsea.

The note inside read, *I saw this and thought of you.—IC.*

Grace ran her fingertips gently over the ragged edge of the card stock, the splashes of muted color exquisite in their subtlety. It was exactly the sort of image that might have caught her eye as she passed the artist's stall.

Whatever else he might be, Mr. Caird's taste was not vulgar. And whatever it was that he wanted from her, he was going to great lengths to conceal it.

No matter how considerate the gift, she couldn't keep it.

Grace sent it back again, with a note. *It is highly improper for a single lady to accept any kind of gift from a gentleman.*

If he tried again, it would be as good as admitting either that he was no gentleman, or that he did not consider her a lady. Let him chew on *that*.

The next morning, along with her call times for the next three days, Grace found a book sitting in her message box at the theatre. The little novel boasted a paper cover, not leather, and some of the pages were crumpled along the edges, as though it had been read before. *The Castle of Vivaldi,* proclaimed the lurid print upon the cover. *Or, the Mysterious Injunction.*

A note stuck out of the top on a separate sheet of paper, as she should have expected. With a heart that started both to sink and to race treacherously fast all at once, she tugged the slip of paper free.

Consider this a loan, not a gift, and you can return the book to me when next we meet. I think you will find the story diverting, and should like to hear your opinion of the hero and his heroine. IC.

The white-hot spot of indignation that burned tight in Grace's chest could be attributed both to Mr. Caird's infernal persistence, and to the realization that he had bested her at her own game.

"Ugh!" Grace dropped the book on the desk and

stormed from the theatre lobby. If he wanted his precious book back, he could come find it. *She* wasn't going to be dancing at his beck and call!

She left the Surrey and made it halfway to Westminster Bridge before curiosity got the better of her. She stopped, turned around and went back. The book still lay where she had dropped it.

If Grace stayed up through the night and burned an entire candle stub down to finish reading it, well. She would package it up and send it back to him the next day. There was no reason Mr. Caird would ever have to know.

"Women like jewels," Colby said to Isaac over supper, as the paint dried on one of the false walls for Inverness Castle. "But if you've got money for jewels, what are you doing working here?" He guffawed loudly.

"Don't ask me," Thomas Hunter drawled, stretched out and lounging on the stage. His fencing gear lay beside him, along with the pages of fight choreography that he would have to beat into Macbeth and MacDuff the next day. He smiled with inner amusement, flicking his dark hair out of his eyes. "I've never courted a woman in my life."

"Chelsea buns," Lucy Sullivan told him, and she cocked her head and studied him with a measuring gaze. "Grace has a fondness for Chelsea buns. But don't let on

73

that I told you, or I'll have to listen to her go on again for hours."

The Chelsea bun, purchased hot and delivered still warm from the oven, did not come back. But a rather frazzled-looking Lucy Sullivan did meet Isaac on the stairs to the theatre loft, and pressed a coin into his hand. "She asked me to tell you," Miss Sullivan sighed dramatically, "that this should recompense you for the bun and for your troubles, and that this should be an end to it."

Isaac took the shilling and turned it over in his fingers. A grin caught the corner of his mouth as he flipped the coin over his knuckles and back again. "How did she sound when she said it?"

Miss Sullivan's smile quirked up in mirror of his. "Reluctant."

"Truly?"

Miss Sullivan folded her arms and shook her head at him. "Truly. There was nothing on her table this morning and I would swear she looked disappointed. At least until the boy showed up with the bun." She looked him up and down, taking his measure with her eyes. "I don't see why you're wasting your time and energy on a girl who won't give you the time of day, mind. There are others about who would appreciate that sort of attention."

"I imagine there are," he replied. He was flirting. Miss Sullivan's smile back showed that she knew it too, but his attention was not on the wordplay. No, he had other things to consider.

Grace shouldn't have eaten the bun. She knew it, *he* would know it, but it had been sitting right *there* in the packet, and it had smelled so very good, and she had been nervous enough before rehearsal yesterday that she hadn't eaten anything at all to break her fast.

How had he known that she would be starving, and that the unexpected arrival of one of her favorite treats would be enough to tip her over the edge into accepting a gift she'd never intended to accept at all?

The last thing she needed was to encourage the man. He'd already shown himself to be persistent beyond all reason, and irritatingly…well, no. He hadn't been irritating, because he hadn't approached her himself, only sent notes which could be thrown away, ribbons for her shoes after her old ones had frayed away, and a sweet pastry when she was hungry.

But *why* was he doing it, that was the question. What did he want? When would he decide that he had given her enough, and now she owed him something in return?

The thoughts plagued her at night, when she dragged her weary body home. She couldn't escape them even after she'd bathed, rubbed liniment into her sore and abused muscles, and wrapped her hair in its silk scarf for the night.

Thoughts of the situation, mind. Not thoughts of the two times she had spoken with Mr. Caird, his voice rich, deep and warm. Nor of the afternoon in the loft when she'd opened her eyes to see him standing there, his long, lean body casting a shadow across the loft floor.

Nor even of yesterday, when she had seen him standing on the stage and she'd stopped in the wings to watch. He'd been pacing something out across the empty stage, looking up into the flies and muttering to himself. He'd chewed on his thumbnail in thought and his mouth had given her wicked ideas before she'd shut the notion down and hurried herself away.

None of it was worth the risk. Once a man thought he had power over you, that was when he drained you dry. Everything you had would be his: money, if you had any; time and energy spent taking care of him that could have been used for other things; love—until he lost interest and moved on. Better not to start.

So since she wasn't ever going to give him the response he was hoping for, it made sense that he would give up. That she would come to the theatre the next day and find her table empty, no note, no gift, and no sign of him whatsoever.

What didn't make sense was the disappointment that rose up inside, sour and sad.

Even worse, that feeling grew stronger as the evening progressed, even once she was home, with no knock at the window or messenger boy slipping a note beneath her door. Not that she'd expected anything. He didn't even know where she lived.

I don't want his stupid gifts anyway. Why should I care that he's stopped sending them?

Besides. If he were really interested, he wouldn't have given up so easily.

The feelings were contradictory and laughable, but the one thing they had in common was a very comfortable sort of irritation leveled at infuriating, annoying, *disappointing* Mr. Caird.

Grace had just become settled in her mind with the knowledge that Mr. Caird had given up his intrusive attempts to get her attention when that dratted boy appeared again, right in front of her, as she was leaving the dance school late the following afternoon.

"What is it now?" she snapped, then immediately felt terrible for snapping. The boy, one of the young ones who cleaned and did small errands backstage, didn't seem to mind.

"Gift for you, Miss Owens." He held out another packet, this one flat and small, not shaped at all like ribbons, roses, or a Chelsea bun. "And begging your pardon, Miss, but Mr. Caird says that if you want to pay him back for it, you'll have to do it in person this time." He tugged on the brim of his cap and vanished back into the throng on the busy city street.

Oh she *would*, would she? Why, of all the overbearing, intrusive, infantile demands!

Not bothering to open the packet, she shoved it down into her satchel and headed for the Surrey, her long, purposeful strides enough to send passers-by hastily out of her way. Wearing breeches today had been a good choice—it meant she could stomp up the back stairs without worrying about tripping on her hem.

She wouldn't have minded her stays, though. They were armor against the world, a protective layer that, some days, made her feel strong. But today had been a breeches and boys-clothes sort of day, and Mr. *Caird* was just going to have to deal with that.

The door to the loft sat open, the oncoming evening dimming the natural light. A low lamp glowed in the wide space, casting a warm glow over the sparse furnishings. Mr.

Caird seemed to be expecting her, turning at the sound of her footsteps in the door. It looked as though she had interrupted him at work, though, his waistcoat off and his shirtsleeves rolled up to his elbows, his pants too long and loose to be breeches, but cupping his hips and rear end as perfectly as though they had been.

No—she was not here to be distracted by arses, arms, or thighs. Grace swept into the room, ignoring the coaching trunk sitting by the workbench, and the scads of diagrams mapped out in chalk across the table's newly uncluttered surface.

"Miss Owens," Mr. Caird greeted her, his mouth pulling up in a smug and hateful grin, and she slammed the new gift down on the table in front of him, sending a puff of chalk dust up into the air. The motes glinted in the lamplight as they settled back down around her hand.

"I always send these back. Why do you keep bothering?" She burned to say more, but bit her words off there. Less for him to turn back around onto her.

Mr. Caird seemed nonplussed, moving around to her side of the table with easy grace. The soft light loved his skin, caressing the ripples of muscle on his lean, strong forearms with shadows, then with a warm brandy-glow.

"Because one day," he answered, his eyes not leaving her face, "I'll stumble on the thing that you'll want to keep. And then I can send more of the same." He stopped moving once he was beside her, standing barely a hand span away. He was taller than she remembered, and she had to tilt her head up to keep matching him look for look. His shirt fell open at the neck exposing a vee of smooth skin, the barest hint of dark hair a shadow at the bottom.

He would taste like golden rum, feel hard as cordwood under her lips.

Stop that.

She had to keep her head, and not focus on the warmth spreading low throughout her body. The point of this visit was to make him leave her in peace. "But *why?*" she insisted. An answer for that would tell her what she needed to hear, and then she could put an end to all this nonsense.

He didn't seem to understand the script. "It brought you up here and talking to me again, did it not?" Mr. Caird had dropped his voice low. It surrounded and encompassed her, as though he were creating a circle of heat around them.

Grace swallowed, her breath unaccountably difficult to find. Her heartbeat raced. Surely he had to hear it, hear it and mark it and *know* that he was winning. "I don't understand," she said, and that was the moment.

She had lost.

Mr. Caird touched her face, stroking his thumb down along her temple with the faintest of pressures. He studied her intently, his eyes never leaving her, and brushed his fingertips lightly across her lips.

I should bite him. He's close enough.

But the small, angry voice in the back of Grace's head could not stand against the rush of heat that knocked her breath from her lungs, gooseflesh prickling along her arms and her nipples—oh!—pulling up tight. He was going to kiss her, and she would have to kick him, or…or *something* to make sure that he didn't press further.

"I want to show you something," he said, and that was far more forward than even she had expected!

"You want to what?" she exclaimed, recoiling. Grace's eyes flew open—she'd closed them somewhere in the moment, and he was laughing at her! Or possibly not *at* her, but his eyes were sparkling nevertheless.

"Now who's making assumptions?" His words were teasing but his smile never wavered, still so all-encompassing and intent upon her that he seemed to eclipse everything else in the room.

She should have bitten him while she'd had the chance.

"Come with me," Mr. Caird coaxed her, back to that low, rumbling voice that seemed to resonate right through her nethers. "Only just to my table, and I promise you I won't press any gifts upon you. But you must see this, and I knew you weren't likely to come to me only on my say-so."

He stepped away, opening up space for her to breathe, to consider her next move. The pool of light shining down on the table illuminated the design he'd been sketching out, and now she could see the streaks of chalk dust on the thighs of his trousers, the light of creation in his eyes that had burned there when they had first met.

When he'd been lighting nuts on fire.

Curiosity drew her back into his orbit—curiosity, and not a single thing more.

"As you like, then." She refused to give him more satisfaction than that, folding her arms across her chest as she approached. His eyes dropped to her bosom—more fool he, for there was little enough there to see!—and then he turned away and gestured at a confusing mass of lines inscribed upon the tabletop. "What is it that I'm supposed to make of this?"

"I have an idea," Mr. Caird began, leaning his palms on the edge of the table, chalk sticking to the heels of his hands, "to make this production of the Scottish Play one of the best that London has ever seen. The most exciting, the most thrilling—let the Royal have *Skirts of the Camp.* We'll outshine them with this. Look, here."

He drew his finger along a series of lines that resolved themselves into a box, a jutting stage, the walks high above—she was looking at a diagram of the Surrey, stripped down to the ropes and bars that made up its scaffolding, and hanging from them, something strange and new.

"This sits up in the flies." Isaac traced his fingers around a box filled with circled pulleys, and lines for ropes that passed between them. "And works on the same principles we already use to raise and lower the scene drops. The dancer wears a harness beneath her costume, and the controller may raise and lower her at will. The traveler is free to move across the uppermost bar, and so the dancer may traverse the width and depth of the stage at her leisure, and at any height."

She'd seen something like it once, but not to the extent he described. It had been in Italy, perhaps, a dancer hauled up to stand on the very pointes of her toes and move across the stage without making a sound. This seemed higher, and a great deal more treacherous.

Grace frowned, her brow pulling tighter. "Is it safe?"

Isaac nodded. "As safe as any ship's rigging in a calm harbor."

"A great many things may happen to ships, even in harbor," she riposted, and raised an eyebrow when he didn't seem dissuaded in the slightest.

81

"Which is why you should only trust the best sailmaster in the business." He grinned at her skepticism, his enthusiasm infectious.

"You talk a great game, Mr. Caird, but I've yet to see a reason for my involvement."

He cocked his head and straightened up. "Can't you?"

Grace frowned. "No. I'm no machinist, to help you construct such madness."

"No, but you are a dancer, and as rumor would have it, one of the greatest in town," he replied too smoothly and easily, and he didn't seem to be making fun of her any more. No, he leaned in, all earnestness and confidence. "Who else could I possibly ask to be my spirit? Think of it—you would be a star, the centerpiece of the moment. The triumph of spectacle would be yours."

"As well as yours," she interrupted him, finishing his sentence. "You want me to perform in your magical flying machine in order to set off *your* work to its best advantage." Somehow, she should have known.

"No, you have me wrong," he argued, taking a step closer to her. He cupped one of his hands below her elbow. His grasp was firm but not confining. She could break away from him if she chose, but in the meantime his heat seeped into her, fighting the chills that were threatening to take over. "I want to use *my* skills to make *you* shine. You were a lead and now Elliston has you as a dancer in the ballet interval— I know you were hurt by the change, I saw it in your eyes. But if you fly with me, no one will be able to deny your talents."

He was mostly wrong, of course, at least about the

reason for her unhappiness, but he wasn't *entirely* wrong. "You spin tales like a fishwife," Grace told him off, and he only chuckled. "I'd wager you don't believe half the things you say."

"I speak only truth to beauty," he fired back, pressing his hand flat over his heart in a gesture imitating sincerity. Then he seemed to get serious, one final time, and reached out for her hand. She didn't give it, and he let his hand fall back against the table again. She felt a small pang at that, guilt, perhaps, but said nothing. "Come with me to speak to Elliston," Mr. Caird urged. "I need his approval and funds to build the rig, and your support could make the difference."

"I haven't agreed to take part in this madness yet," Grace reminded him, but she could feel her confidence waning. And so, it seemed, could he. "Let me think about it."

"Don't take too long," he urged, and she folded her arms beneath her breasts again.

"I said I would think about it," Grace answered, turning to leave.

"Be here tomorrow, first thing, before your class."

She answered without thinking, her mind still caught up in the notion of being hauled up and flown around the stage. "Tomorrow."

He pounced on it immediately. "Then you will come!"

Grace paused by the door, and even as the words left her lips she knew she was going to follow through. Out of professional courtesy, and curiosity. Nothing more. "I'll think about it." And with that, she left the room, and Mr. Caird, behind her.

Chapter Five

"You live to make things difficult for yourself, Mr. Caird." Elliston circled his desk to look at the plans from the other side, as though upside-down would change Isaac's proposal to something different. "And you propose to build this infernal contraption?"

"Hardly infernal, and safe as anything we ever do." Isaac protested, looking across the book-lined office to Mrs. Elliston, sitting in her husband's leather armchair, her expression pensive. Miss Owens stood silent by the window, her arms folded with her shawl draped over them, the neckline of her simple yellow dress curving sinuously around the top of her bosom, covering almost all but the sweet divot in the center of her collarbone. She frowned, watching the diagrams rather than meeting his eyes.

"That is all well and good—safety is of course important. But lifting dancers an inch or two into the air has been done before." Elliston reached into his pocket for his cigar. He drew it halfway, out, stopped, looked at the ladies, and tucked it back in. "You said you had something impressive to show me."

"A few suggestions, more than anything."

Elliston raised a single eyebrow. "I'm listening."

Isaac launched into the description of his first idea, spreading his hands wide in the air. "Imagine, then, the stage. A wall of mist as the bottom of a great waterfall. The dancers emerge from the mist as nymphs, and—"

"How do you suppose they will then *dance* on a stage covered in water?" Mrs. Elliston interrupted.

Something he hadn't completely considered. "A secondary set of risers?"

Elliston drummed his fingers on the edge of his desk. "Next idea."

It wasn't "get out of my office," a minor blessing.

"Fly the dancers across the stage, using harnesses and pulleys. I can suspend them above the stage completely, never touching the ground."

"Flying isn't dancing," Miss Owen said, as though she'd been thinking over the proposal during the night. She was less enthused than he had hoped for, but at least she had turned up.

Elliston nodded. "And flying isn't a ballet, which is what we need to get the event past the Office of the Examiners. Try again." His brow was lowering which meant one last chance for Isaac to make his case. Five pounds sterling rested on Elliston's decision. And more important, the chance to impress himself further upon Miss Owens, to work beside her, bend his talents toward making hers shine.

At the moment she was looking at him with thoughtful consideration rather than admiration or awe, and that had to change.

"Picture this," Isaac began, leaning forward, hands splayed on the papers laid out on Elliston's desk. "The curtain falls on the second act. Duncan is killed, the conspirators fled, and the servants whisper of strange and unearthly happenings in the night. Then! Four torches which have stood on the corners of the stage all along, unlit—they burst into flame, seemingly untouched by human hand!"

Miss Owens had drifted closer to the table as he spoke, and she tugged her shawl about her shoulders. "How?"

Isaac nodded solemnly at the good question. "Witch meal will flare when passed through a fire of wine spirits. The rest is a trade secret." And he winked, boldly and broadly. Mrs. Elliston made a soft exasperated noise, and a small smile flickered briefly across Miss Owens' full and tender lips. "Now—if I may continue?"

He carried on without waiting for Elliston's permission. "The torches blaze up, the low music begins. Dum-dum-dummm—the backdrop changes to a pale and solid thing, forms in the mist. The stage lights turn to rainbows, and then through these rainbows of color, light most prodigious and magical, the fairies descend on their wires—"

Elliston cut him off with a slash of his hand. "We are not doing *Midsummer*," he complained.

"Angels, then." Isaac changed direction, and his eyes lingered on Miss Owens as he spoke. "Let the stage be the dark and unruly portents of doom, the torches lighting Duncan's fallen form. Angels descend, in flawless white, the reflections from the prisms bathing them in God's light." Miss Owens lifted her eyes to his, interest and wonder and some sad and distant thing resting in the glory of her eyes.

"The pillars of fire stand before them," Isaac spoke softly, drawing the three listeners into his vision. "The rainbows behind them. The dancers lift Duncan and carry him away from the licking fires of hell and to the redeeming grace of heaven."

Mrs. Elliston was nodding along—he had her thinking of the possibilities, at least! Elliston pulled out his cigar and stuck one end in his mouth, unlit, to chew on it pensively.

Miss Owens, whose opinion was most important of all, approached the desk. She put her fingers over his, only long enough to lift his hand and move it off the diagram. She stepped in beside him and took a long and measuring look at his design.

"The fire will not burn us?" She flicked her gaze up toward him, her question soft and considering.

"It will be cool to the touch," he promised her and her alone. The doubt he saw in her eyes stirred up that same rough need from before, to sweep her into his arms and make reckless promises—that he would do nothing to harm her, that whatever hardships she had overcome in the past, he would willingly be the one to keep her safe. "I will not let you burn."

Elliston chomped on the end of his cigar, then, slowly, nodded. "If you can do what you claim, this will be a spectacle indeed. Miss Owens?"

She kept her eyes on Isaac, searching for something in whatever expression she saw on his face. She frowned, but below it, something new was unfurling. Miss Owens broke the look first, and behind her, Mrs. Elliston was hiding a small smile. "I will try," Miss Owens replied. "Only in so far as the contraption does not hinder my ability to move."

"Good, then that's settled," Elliston proclaimed, seemingly oblivious to the tension that made the air in the office so heady and thick. "Good lad—this could be the making of the Surrey's season, and more. The Regent has a fondness for a good spectacle, and patents to give away. The Royal may have stolen our comedy, but if we can give him a thrill! Ah, with royal patronage we could have our pick of the plays and the run of the season."

His satisfaction emanated off of him, and Isaac resisted the combating urges both to cheer in victory and wince at the over-confidence.

"Have a prototype ready for testing by next week. Miss Owens and Mrs. Elliston will need time to rehearse with it, and time runs short."

"Aye, captain," Isaac replied jauntily.

"And don't drop anybody," Elliston continued, in a jovial mood now. Miss Owens froze, as though the thought had not occurred to her. "We have no replacements for the ballet corps."

"With God as my witness," Isaac said, keeping his tone light as could be to prevent the fear from settling in.

It wasn't until he began to roll up his diagrams that the enormity of his proposal really began to hit home. *Can I do this? I must. More than pride is on the line now. And more than five pounds.*

Miss Owens had begun to come around. He would not disappoint her now.

"He's a good-looking fellow, then?" Meg smiled oh-so-innocently up at Grace. Her artfully tumbled black curls were tied up under her bonnet in such a way that it looked like one tug on her ribbon would send the whole business spilling down around her shoulders, and her startling décolletage was the sort that would tempt men to try. "Then I hardly see the problem." She tucked her arm more firmly in Grace's as they crossed the street, picking her way daintily between the potholes and wagon ruts.

"It's not so simple as all that," Grace objected, though it was bound to fall on deaf ears. She lifted the hem of her own dress slightly to keep it free from the mud, her sore toes seeking out every pebble and divot in the ground through the thin soles of her shoes. A free afternoon was not a luxury to be ignored, especially one with fine weather that meant she could spend some daylight hours outside of the dance school.

Company other than the young girls in the corps helped a great deal, even if Meg's priorities were, as always, somewhat different from her own.

"I don't see why not." Meg smiled prettily at a stout gray-haired gentleman who passed them, inclining her head in greeting. He didn't stop to chat, only nodded his head at both women before moving on. "Mr. Bertram," Meg confided. "His wife died of childbed fever last year, and he's been *such* a fixture at the patent theatres ever since. I do believe he's got one of the new girls at the Royal put up in an apartment in Chelsea. It's not Mayfair, of course, but heaven knows there are few enough men who can afford that sort of thing."

Grace didn't reply to Meg's prattle and received a sharp look from the girl in return for her silence. "Now there's a thought," Meg said thoughtfully.

"I beg your pardon?" The shop windows along the side of the street reflected Meg and Grace as they passed, two women, one young and one less so, in clean and simple dress, bonnets, and gloves, out for a promenade in the sun. A life filled with only moments like that would be so much simpler, in many ways. Dull, but simpler.

"A patron," Meg announced, and Grace's attention snapped back. "Why not allow him to keep you? If you like him and you trust him, and he *certainly* seems to like you..."

"I'm not in the market for a patron. And in case you've forgotten, Mr. Caird is a stagehand, hardly the sort of profession with which one could support a mistress. Assuming I wished to be one, which I don't. And as far as I know, he has no inheritance to supplement his income like your Mr. Glover."

"Oh pish," Meg replied airily, waving off Grace's objections. "Marry him, then. Unless he already has a wife."

"As far as I know, he's not yet married." Meg tugged Grace's arm to steer her down another street. Grace let herself be pulled, but not distracted. "But you have entirely too glib a view of the world, Meglet."

"And you are a curmudgeon. If he can make you smile, then as far as I'm concerned, he's done everyone a magnificent favor. Come on! There's practically no line at all at Gunter's and I want something sweet."

"It's just past luncheon!"

"That explains the lack of a line. Besides, ginger candies are the only thing that settles my Sarah's stomach these days." Meg was relentless, and Grace allowed herself to be bullied into the front door of the confectioner's shop with limited resistance.

A little while later, a muslin bag of almond comfits in Meg's hand, Sarah's ginger sweets in her reticule, and a sugarplum tucked resolutely in Grace's cheek, they were off again to sit on a bench in the square and watch the stately carriages roll by.

"Are you excited?" Grace settled in on the bench, eyeing Meg's reticule with some suspicion.

A small frown creased Meg's brow. "I suppose. It will change things for a while, certainly, having to share her with a baby as well as a husband. But Sarah is pleased, and James is pleased, and I love them both, so I shall be pleased for them." She nodded defiantly, her black curls bouncing with the movement and her dark eyes shining with amusement. "Besides, I have the privileged place of the mistress. I can play with the child as often as I please, and then hand it back when it's messy or in a strop. It's ideal, really."

"Until the moment when it isn't." Grace tried to imagine Meg with a baby in her arms, and had little trouble doing it. It was much more difficult to picture her rising in the wee hours of the morning to tend to a sick or hungry one, mind you. Could Grace? Would Grace? She poked at that place in her heart where she supposed maternal instinct was supposed to lie, and found any sentiment there directed more at Meg and their friends than at some supposed future child.

No, Grace would not be nearly so saturnine at the prospect, which made it all for the best that Meg was the one of the pair of them to have a lover *in the family way*.

The breeze toyed gently with the ends of Grace's bonnet ribbons, playing with the rippled edge of her lightweight cotton dress. The softly dotted yellow nankeen clung and draped well, carefully shaped today by her long stays. She had felt girlish today when she dressed, tugging the laces down the front of her stays for a satisfying, snug fit.

"I know your trouble." Meg slipped off one of her delicate gloves to dig in the bag for a candy, her skirts settled down around her on the bench so that she looked like a dark-haired cherub in a soft green cloud. "You are bound and determined to stay miserable. You don't know what to do with yourself when you're happy."

The words struck Grace in the pit of her stomach, so pointed that she couldn't reply for a moment. "That is harsh, Meglet, and entirely unfair."

"Not in the least." Meg turned, curling one leg beneath her so that she faced Grace head-on. Her dark eyes were liquid and filled with concern, an expression all too serious for laughing, flippant little Meg. "And I don't only mean the sour face you just made at the thought of families and babies. Take only this past week. You used to love dancing. I could see it in your eyes when you told your stories. And then you stopped, which is fine, but now you have the chance to do it again, something that once made you happy, and all you can think of is your distaste."

"Meg—"

"Hush and let me finish. This is a perfectly good

speech, and I shan't have you ruining it."

"Someone ought to have turned you over her knee a great many years ago."

"Is that an offer?" Meg batted her eyelashes outrageously, and Grace couldn't fight the small smile that surfaced. "But listen. You have been alone for as long as I've known you, always giving, always ready to tell me when I'm being a fool, or to help me out of a jam. And now you have a kind, handsome, amiable fellow pursuing you, and you're contemplating ways to shake him off. Do you know what I think?"

"Am I going to have the opportunity to guess?"

"No. I think that you're afraid to be happy, because you don't know who you are when you're not being a grump." Meg gestured at Grace with her almond. "Suck your sugarplum. And try to remember to enjoy it."

Grace wanted to give Meg a talking-to about respect, or scream out her frustration, or...or *kick* something hard enough to get the tangled roar out of her brain. It wasn't fair—Meg was a silly girl, and she certainly wasn't right!

Or was she?

There were more than enough irritations in Grace's life to keep her well-set for complaints. And life turned out to be disappointing more often than not. Loved ones turned their backs, honest employment came and went capriciously, and avaricious men used women and then discarded them once they had served their purpose.

But what of this moment in time?

The playful breeze was back, tugging at her ribbon-ends. The sun filtered down through the canopy of trees in the shaded square, laying dappled light on the ground, the bench, the two girls sitting there in silence. Dogs barked in the distance, lively chatter flowed from open shop windows and promenading families, and the confection Meg had insisted upon buying for her was sweet and rough-edged on her tongue.

Her toes hurt. Her legs and core ached from new and renewed use. She had ribbons to mend and a dance to learn from the first steps, and now Elliston was muttering about needing a second one to make sure the proportions of dance to play were within the law.

Sugar melted slowly in her mouth, the sweet nectar trailing down her throat. She lived in the greatest of all English cities, it was summertime, and yesterday a man with eyes like shadowed pools and hands as deft as a musician's had looked at her like he would be willing to press her lips with sweet and potent kisses.

Men were all selfish.

"I want to use my skills to make you shine."

No. She knew at least one who wasn't. At least not completely.

Grace settled back against the bench and folded her arms across her chest. She pursed her lips and squinted at the sun. Then, fighting her better instincts, she let go the tension in her shoulders, one aching muscle at a time. A butterfly flitted past, bright splashes of color flickering against the green of the grass.

Meg raised an eyebrow. Grace conceded defeat, her head quieter now than before. She smiled.

It felt good.

Meg smiled back, and while she said nothing, her *I told you so* was somehow audible throughout the park.

Grace did not find herself annoyed.

The cast had the day off and that meant an open stage for work, so Isaac found himself awake early in the morning. He headed down the stairs toward the kitchen with a spring in his step.

Isaac's father stood at the chopping block, his knife working its way through a shallot with such speed as to make the blade itself seem to blur, and surely put his fingers in grave danger. Capons sat ready for the pot in a trough itself half-submerged in cool water, and the rich scent of simmering broth suggested that he and Mrs. Sedgewick had been at work for some time already.

"And where were you last night? Not out and about with your brother, or you'd have been in before cock-crow." His father looked up from his work long enough to fix Isaac with a look that stopped him for a moment in his tracks. "You don't look like you've a bad head, so I'm guessing it wasn't carousing."

"I'm a grown man, father of mine, I shall carouse when and if I feel the urge." Isaac kissed his father on the top of his curly, graying hair, and snagged a carrot from the basket of vegetables waiting for his father's skillful knife. "But no. I stayed late to work, and am on my way back there now."

"Elliston's going to work you into your grave, and for what? Pennies a week?" Andrew shook his head at his son. "You're better than that, lad."

His brogue had thinned in the four decades since Andrew Caird had come down from Edinburgh. There had been little for him in Scotland, where their family had lived as far back as anyone could trace.

In those days black skin marked a man as a slave, freedman, or son of a freedman, no matter how many generations of his family had been farming the same plot of land. Owning a tavern in London had been a much brighter option by far, and now he was a solid fixture in the neighborhood.

Isaac bit the end of the carrot off defiantly. "I agree wholeheartedly, but raises come to those who earn them. Just wait until you see what we have in mind for this show, Da. You'll be calling me Merlin the Magician." A day-old loaf, a hunk of cheese, two trimmed stalks of rhubarb, and a handful of dried apple rings vanished into Isaac's pouch, and he slung the bag over his shoulder.

"I'll be calling you no son of mine if you don't get your thieving posterior out of my kitchen haste-post-haste." Andrew shook his knife blade in Isaac's general direction, his eyes twinkling even as he visibly fought to keep from smiling. "If you see Colin, tell your brother to get himself back here before mid-day. And keep your fingers out of the puddings. Those are for *paying* customers."

"I love you too, Da," and Isaac left, ducking through the door while he still had the last word.

The sun shone down on the Chelsea Road, the breeze just enough to add an edge to the air. Isaac's pouch thumped gently against his thigh as he walked along the side of the street. Quinton's mail coach came along after a few minutes, his timing excellent.

Isaac ran along beside it for a few paces then seized a handhold, swinging himself up to stand on the board until the coach passed Westminster Bridge. He dropped off again with a wave and a salute, Quentin flashing a rude gesture at him from his seat above.

On such a day as this, nothing could ruin his mood.

"If you ass-backwards boot-licking sons of goats and bitches don't get yourselves ship-shape and Bristol-fashion by the time I come back, I'll fire every last useless one of you!"

The shouting was the first thing Isaac noticed when he came through the back door of the Surrey. Elliston's voice was as recognizable at a bellow as it was when he whispered, and right now some poor sods were being tongue-flayed at top volume.

The smell was the second thing that hit him as he climbed the short flight of stairs to get into the stage wings. The whole backstage area reeked of lamp oil and the stage shone slick despite Colby and Tottenham's combined efforts with rags and broom. Isaac moved slowly around the corner—Elliston had the stage boys in a cluster in the crossover, waving his arms and shouting at them as though they'd personally and individually set his mother on fire and pissed into the flames.

Setting down his bag and rolling up his sleeves, Isaac headed out onto the stage to lend his hand to…whatever was going on. "What's the trouble, gents?"

Colby groaned, leaning on the stick of his broom.

"Willem was out to fill the argand lamps. Clod-pated lout tripped and dropped the jug, sent oil everywhere. Here." He handed the broom to Isaac. "Now that you're 'ere, I can get back to work."

Colby took two steps toward the stairs and then his feet went out from under him. His arms pinwheeled and he scrabbled for purchase, tilting forward, then canting back, and finally falling hard on his ample posterior before sliding the rest of the way into the wings.

There was a moment of reverent silence as Colby vanished behind the flies, followed by a series of thumps that sounded like the stairs, and an explosion of creative language.

"All right?" Isaac called, biting the inside of his cheek to stop himself from laughing and further bruising the man's dignity.

"Bloody *hell*," came the answer back. Colby did not reappear.

Isaac turned back to his work, pushing the puddle of oil toward a bank of rags laid down across stage right.

"It's the curse, you know," Tottenham grumbled, and he didn't seem at all amused.

"The curse?"

"Don't be daft. Everyone knows the Scottish Play carries a witch's curse. 'E's not only courted 'is own misfortune, but all of ours along with 'im." Tottenham gestured around him at the stage, the orchestra pit below, and the empty banks of red-covered seats out in the gloom beyond the row of lights.

"And look what's happened. It'll only get worse from here," he predicted, an air of gloom settling down around his shoulders.

"There's no such thing as curses," Isaac insisted. "Only apprentices with their minds not on their jobs."

"You'll see," Tottenham muttered under his breath as he started back to scrubbing. "Just wait."

By the evening Isaac was almost ready to admit defeat. It wasn't the oil on the stage that had done it, or even the fraying rope that had almost sent an entire painted backdrop crashing down on Tottenham's head, or, miraculously, the escaped box of extremely excited puppies that one of the boys had smuggled in to the men's dressing room and had been feeding on the sly.

(They were somewhat less of a secret now that Willem and Bert had chased them into the orchestra pit and bribed the puppies back into their box with bits of sausage and cheese.)

No, it was definitely the moment when Isaac stood there at the side entrance to the theatre, flinging the heavy door back and forth to clear at least some of the billowing clouds of putrid smoke that hung thick in the air everywhere on the ground floor. The smoke bucket sat in the alleyway, still smoldering defiantly even after being doused with water as well as sand.

Boot steps came out of the cloud, stomping forcefully toward Isaac until he could make out a form. Elliston tried to loom over him, proving difficult as Isaac was a little taller, which only angered the manager further.

"What is the *point,* I ask you, of casting witches at *all* if all the audience is going to see is *smoke?*" he snarled. "I asked for a little mist, Mr. Caird, not a thrice-damned forest fire!"

Isaac hung against the door for a moment, then started swinging it again to keep the foul air moving outside. "I've no idea why that happened. It shouldn't have, to be perfectly frank. It's the same mixture I've used every time. Maybe the air from the oil on the stage—"

"Maybe the air from the oil—" Elliston repeated, waggling his head back and forth. He was in a righteous fury, and there was nothing to be said or done except wait for the storm to pass. "Do I pay you to work, Mr. Caird, or to think? Get this cleaned and get out. I want everyone out."

He stormed off back toward the still fogged-over stage, vanishing into the cloud again. "Out, out, everyone out! Leave my theatre! Don't come back until tomorrow! And then don't come back at all—send your cleverer siblings in your places!"

A shadow loomed toward Isaac out of the fog again, the shape only a little more recognizable as the smoke slowly cleared.

"Cursed," Tottenham said solemnly. "Witches'll do that."

He left and Isaac watched him go, sloping down the alleyway with curls of smoke blowing after him and vanishing into the air.

Chapter Six

"We could hear his raging all the way through the floor, we could." Mrs. Byrne puttered about the wardrobe room, bringing Mr. Byrne his tools as he called for them. Grace fidgeted with the hem of her shirt and got her hand tapped for her troubles. "That man will give himself a palsy one day, mark my words. Hold yourself still, dear. Only a few more measurements to go."

"Is this really necessary?" Grace sighed, holding herself still as Mr. Byrne unspooled his measuring tape along the length of one of her arms. He jotted something cryptic down in his notebook.

Mr. Caird, drat him, was grinning from his seat on one of the Byrnes' comfortable old armchairs, the fire burning low and casting a glow on the hearth. "Unless you want a set of stays cut too wide, I'd reckon so. We wouldn't want you sliding out of them from six feet up."

"If I do, you'll wind up six feet under," Grace threatened, and Mrs. Byrne tutted at her with a merry wink.

"Caird, do come here and make yourself useful," Byrne grumbled at him, and Mr. Caird took a moment to unfold himself from the deep cushions. Even that was distracting, the way his hips moved, the power of his arms as he pushed himself upright, and Grace firmly looked away. Any minute now Byrne would send him on some errand and get him out of the room, and she could relax again.

"Hold this end here, there's a lad." Mr. Byrne set the end of the measuring tape against the hollow of Grace's throat and—good God in heaven—had Caird take over while Byrne himself spooled the tape down the full length of her body.

Caird placed two of his fingers where Byrne's had been. His fingertips were warm, the metal end of the tape cool in contrast. His skin barely brushed against the edge of her collarbone, a whisper of feather-light touch that sent a lightning bolt shivering through her. She couldn't look at him or he would know. He would see that she was having trouble breathing, his heady musk a far stronger pull on her senses than the smoke of the fire or the metal tang of the hot iron.

He stood so close beside her that she could lean over and press against him, but the only place he touched her was the point at her throat where her pulse beat against her bones.

"Now show me where exactly you need the attachment points, and be specific. I can't guess at your trade any more than you could cut a coat."

"Here—" Caird let go of the tape and traced his fingers along the curve of her collarbone, lightly, softly, out along to the point where her shoulder joined her throat. "And on the other side the same, a finger-breadth wide. Along the back—" He circled her, not moving any farther away, trailing his fingertips along her shoulder and to the nape of her neck.

Every inch of skin that he touched burned at the

102

contact, his skin so hot—or was it that hers was cold? The linen of her shirt might as well have been transparent silk, for all the good it did. She could feel every ridge and callus on his fingertips as though he touched her naked body.

"Two points here, and here, and then again on the hips, here and here."

He didn't touch there, nor drop his hand, which was for the best. Either she would have turned around and slugged him, or kissed him, and neither would be acceptable behavior in the middle of a wardrobe fitting.

Grace lifted her chin, turned her head to look, to tell him to go away, to tell him that she would hold the tape for the rest, or Mrs. Byrne, anything but the feeling of his two fingers sitting snug against the nape of her neck. Except that when she looked into his eyes, his pupils were blown wide, wider than before, and if she could see her own expression she would wager that it was a mirror of the one she saw on him.

Whatever this surge and burn was, lust or something else, he was feeling it too.

"All right, there we are, all done now." Byrne stood up and collected his tape, Caird let go and stepped back, his eyes not leaving Grace's. Not until she forced her chin own and turned her own head away, focused on shaking out her arms, sore from being held out and still.

"Are you sure you've done everything?" she grumbled, trying to shake off the sensation of Caird's knowing hands, his gentle fingers, the coarseness of his hot skin. "Or do you need me to stand still some more while you spin the thread and weave the fabric?"

"Patience, young one," Mrs. Byrne clucked from her

seat by the fire, her feet up on the hearth and her lap full of muslin. "Measure twice, cut once, as they say."

"Indeed they do, missus," Mr. Byrne agreed amiably. "And a right good philosophy it is, too."

Caird waited by the door, looking pensive, until his eyes fell on Grace once more. "That sounds as though it's time to take our leave," he said aloud. "That is, if you have everything you need from me?"

"If I need anything more, young man, I know where to find you," Byrne replied, waving them off. "Back to your attic and leave me to my labors."

"To your tea and biscuits, you mean," Caird teased, and dodged a swat from Byrne's wife in return. Something odd ached inside Grace at the side of the easy back and forth, the camaraderie of people who were comfortable in each other's worlds.

She was the outsider here, and she felt it all at once. Grace stayed silent as she and Caird left the room, but he brushed his hand against her elbow as she passed him, and she drew up short.

"Come upstairs for a moment?" He was looking at her with those eyes again, speculative and wanting. A thrill raced through her. It seemed to start both in her elbow where his fingers now lay, and in her collarbone where they had pressed only minutes before. "You left your gift there yesterday, and still unopened. Come up and retrieve it."

She wavered on the razor's edge, but tamped down the swelling something deep within with reminders. *Men are not to be trusted. No matter how kind they may seem. They are all takers at heart.*

"I don't know why you bother," she replied sharply, glancing about to be sure they were still entirely alone in the narrow hall. "I've yet to accept any of your bribes, for that's what they are. I simply have yet to determine what it is you hope to gain by them."

"Perhaps I simply want to know you better." His breath was sweet like cinnamon, heady and warm on her skin, his fingers trailing gently, so gently, along the curve of her jaw.

This was the moment, then. Grace closed her eyes, the pull toward him too heady, too strong. He was the undertow and she a hapless swimmer—she could drown in him without another word. And then she would be gone.

She took a quick few steps sideways and out of his reach, his hand falling away and the thick haze around her head vanishing with the distance. Grace sucked in air, a deep breath that tasted of lamp oil and the dry miasma of dust.

"And what if I don't want to know you?" she asked, though the lie in it had to be obvious to both. Especially after the energy that had just charged between them. She wore no stays, only a working man's rough linen shirt. Her nipples rose hard and high against the rub of the fabric, and the treacherous glow of the lamp's light cast shadows across her body as deep as those playing over Mr. Caird.

"Is that what you truly feel?" he asked, staying where he was, and the path clear between her and the stairs. "Because if you tell me so, flat out, no more games or wordplay, then this will be an end to it. I'll not force myself where I'm not wanted."

She could say no, could leave, any moment now she would do exactly that—

She didn't.

His touch alone had been enough to set her mind at odds with her body. She was empty, aching, burning with a reignited need that she hadn't felt in—since—since longer than she could really remember.

"No. That is…" Grace hesitated, cursing herself internally at the loss of words. "I don't know what it is that I want." There, that was true enough, and if it was more of herself than she usually liked to show, so be it. Not like anyone would believe him if he started declaring that strange, mannish Grace had all of a sudden become a frail and dithering girl.

His brow furrowed and he made as though to take a step towards her, but then he stopped. His head tilted as he regarded her, but there was nothing dangerous or upsetting in his stare. "Are you a maid?" he asked gently, and Grace burst into laughter. Not at the question, or at his kindness in the way he asked, but at the sheer absurdity of the moment and the tension building hot and thick inside the core of her body.

"No," she assured him through the laugh and he relaxed, though he still looked at her as if she were a particularly interesting puzzle he meant to figure out.

The tension of the moment gone, her hands twitchy at her sides for lack of something to do with them, Grace took a few steps and leaned back against the wall.

"Do you take lovers?" Caird asked, leaning against the wall opposite in a mirror of her pose. The muscles in his arms made a show of themselves against the light. His legs, long and lean, spread out in front of him, the thickness of his muscular thighs pulling the fabric of his trousers snug.

And oh, there was a solid roundness there as well, imprisoned behind the layers of linen and cotton.

But then, that was the beginning and end of problems with men. That organ, capable of delivering so much pleasure when properly wielded, was more often than not solely a tool solely for their own delights.

"Why should I?" Grace snorted, her equilibrium resettling and her heart rate starting to slow. She was affecting him as she had expected, and she knew how to deal with such things. There was no mystery here, only a lusty man who believed everything he heard about actresses. "There's nothing a man can do for me that I can't do for myself, and better."

She had shocked him with that, his eyebrows going up, and that thrill of perverse pleasure ran through her at his discomfort. *I'll not be your weak and willing prey as long as you fancy yourself a hunter.*

Except that he didn't seem to take the hint. He pushed himself off from the wall, his brown eyes gleaming. "I would almost say that sounds like a challenge."

Those few words, spoken in the return of that low, round rumble of a voice, sent fire blazing through Grace's body, enough to make her blood feel fizzy in her veins. But that would be too easy—she was making this too easy for him.

"Sounds like you need your ears cleaned." She moistened her lips, his eyes dropping right to her mouth. "If you're that desperate for *le petit mort*, go find yourself a girl elsewhere. There are plenty in the neighborhood who could use your coin."

He should have taken some kind of insult at that, but his answer wasn't the kind of rebuttal she had expected. Instead of protesting about affection, or like minds, or even twaddle about the risk of the pox—he simply said, "I'm not thinking of mine."

"Men only think of theirs," she shot back fiercely.

"Who's hurt you so badly?" He crossed the space between them as he replied.

"Why must I have been hurt? Is everything in a woman's life product of a man's actions? Perhaps I am simply an excellent observer of human behavior."

"Fair enough." He shrugged, one-shouldered. "I still say you've misjudged me."

Grace sighed, the war between her body and her mind swinging wildly in all directions. "Let me guess. You are not like other men."

"How can I prove it?" His slow, disarming smile should not have been enough to make her body clench, dampness pooling hot at the join of her thighs.

"You can't."

"And yet you're still here talking to me. There must be something you find redeemable."

"Enjoying conversation doesn't mean I want to fondle your prick."

Liar. But what she actually wanted to do was, as always, beside the point. There were a great many things she enjoyed, or thought she might enjoy, but never if they were *expected*. Let lovemaking be a rush and an improvised, all-consuming flame, not a menu of items to perform for a man's whore-accustomed delight.

"You're trying to shock me but I know better," Caird said, infuriating man. "Come upstairs, sit with me, tell me about yourself, your life, your world. I long to know it all."

"No," she said, and the look of disappointment that flashed in his eyes was enough to make her reconsider. "Not tonight."

"Not tonight, but another?" he tried again, irrepressible and unflagging in his pursuit, and damn her, she was tempted. "Dine with me."

Grace took a deep breath and settled her twisting insides, all her attention still focused on the spot where he touched her arm, where their bodies met. "Yes," she found herself saying. "But not at a tavern. I would rather not be the stuff of gossip."

Something akin to disappointment seemed to flash across his face, but she had to have imagined it. "Here, then," he suggested. "In the loft. I am a reasonable cook, if you can bring yourself to believe that. Tomorrow night, after rehearsals have closed."

"Tomorrow," she heard herself agree, and couldn't find the energy to be angry at herself for it. She still had time, after all, to change her mind.

Chapter Seven

"I'm beginning to regret agreeing to this." Grace picked up her skirt so she wouldn't trip on the hem as she climbed the theatre's back stairs. "How did you manage to cook a meal in the theatre? Not over your tinderbox, I hope."

"Not at all," Mr. Caird replied, that grin on his face that she was starting to suspect meant trouble brewing, "but you shall have to wait and find out for yourself. I was starting to imagine that you liked having me surprise you."

She faltered on the step and he stopped close behind her, near enough that her body flushed with his warmth, his breath playing lightly across the sensitive skin on the back of her neck so it tingled, alive with awareness. His hands brushed her elbows, offering support if she chose to take it. She steadied herself with one hand on the railing and started to climb again.

"Unless you've changed your mind," he continued behind her.

He was offering her an opportunity for escape that she would be wise to take. But she had come to the Surrey of her own will, and to back out now would be an admission of regret. "You promised me a dinner, Mr. Caird. I shall stay and eat."

Meg's voice rang loud in Grace's ear as she opened the door to the attic space. *You are determined to be unhappy.* Perversely, the urge to prove Meg wrong burned stronger than the twisting in her gut that wanted her to turn and run.

Going home now would keep everything as it was, safe and tidy in neat little boxes marked "work" and "friendship" and "A Vaguely Regrettable Incident."

Living in the moment, trusting in what was to come—it would be messy and bewildering, frustration a predetermined end.

She lifted the hem of her dress again and stepped over the threshold into the dark attic space.

Caird's hand settled at the small of her back, a gentle pressure that returned her mind to the here-and-now. His hands were large—they all but spanned half her waist, laid out like that across her back. She could lean into his touch, put her hands on his forearms and feel the ripple of muscle there when he moved.

"You think too much," he said softly, low and close behind her ear.

The familiar, delicious tightening in her lower belly was a warning sign. "You would prefer a lover who did not think at all, I suppose," she fired off, and turned her head just in time to see the faintly wounded look cross his expressive face.

"Hardly that. But I can see from here that something troubles you." He moved away from her—even in the almost total darkness she could feel the instant when he was

111

no longer by her side. The dark pressed in around her, empty and cold, and even wrapping her arms around herself did not stop the momentary shiver.

A shuffle, a clink of metal sounded, and a tiny shower of sparks flew, then died. Another, and a light flared up above the workbench. Caird cupped his hand around the small taper, reflecting the glow of the match back to highlight the strong angles of his cheeks and jaw, the fullness of his lips.

It was a poor idea to linger on the fantasy of that mouth on her body, the pleasure he might be able to draw from her. But linger she did, and remembered other fantasies she had indulged in the night before, on the feel of his hands running rough over her breasts and thighs, the way his breath might shudder as their bodies came together, the heat of touch on her body once more after years of self-imposed solitude.

He set the match to a wick and the lamp caught, light guttering and then taking hold as he adjusted the shade above. Grace closed her eyes for a moment, and when she opened them again, Caird had closed his tinderbox and set it aside.

The room was set with a small table, places for two upon the immaculate white cloth. The stoneware settings and plain crystal glasses made for a simple and elegant arrangement, a bouquet of brilliantly colored early summer flowers collected in a low crystal bowl. Caird set his taper to the lamp and caught the end again, heading for the table and lighting the two tall candles there with a deft and certain touch.

"New candles, crystal, silver—one would think you were entertaining a fine lady, Mr. Caird."

She meant it as a joke, of sorts, commentary on the grandiosity of his efforts. But the way he looked at her in the cozy, flickering candlelight, his dark eyes black and fixed intently upon her, his hand sliding into hers—he was taking her seriously.

"But I am," he said, and his voice rolled over her like distant thunder. "A very fine lady indeed." He straightened, his coat pulling snug against his fine, strong shoulders, and he brought her hand to his lips. The pressure of his mouth against her fingertips was muted by the cotton of her gloves. Unexpected as it was, even so, it still froze her in place, her mouth suddenly dry and her mind empty of thought.

Almost empty, other than the rush of desire to step in, press her body against his like an unrestrained wanton, drag his coat down off those toned and powerful shoulders and expose his shirtsleeves to her touch.

Her breath caught tight in her throat and he smiled, a slow growing curve of those lips that was far too knowing. He stepped in a little closer, not enough to touch but enough that the gentle falling folds of her dress brushed against his thighs. "You are a fine lady, Miss Owens. And deserve to be treated to all that is pleasant and pleasurable in the world."

You, I want to treat myself to you—

Wanton wench! Honestly. Show some decorum.

Grace tried to ignore her battling inner voices, and forced her shoulders to relax down and away from her ears. "You've quite a way with words, Mr. Caird. It must come from spending all your time around actors." That seemed to deter the ardor in his eyes.

"Maybe it does. But that doesn't mean I'm untruthful."

He squeezed her fingertips and led her to her chair. He drew it out from the table for her and waited to push it in until she was seated, then reached beneath the table to draw out a basket and a handsome blown-glass decanter.

The candlelight reflected off the dark red wine inside, a deep and vibrant shade that shone like the deepest garnets in the orange glow.

A bottle ticket hung about the neck of the decanter, the silver gilt shining and the handwritten label difficult to see from her angle. In the dim lighting it seemed to have a crest pressed in to the metal—a tavern sign of some sort. It hardly mattered, because he lifted the decanter and poured the wine into her glass, flicking the decanter expertly as he raised it up again to prevent any drips from staining the cloth.

"You've done this before," she observed dryly. "Do you often bring women to private dinners in secluded places, Mr. Caird?"

"I would have brought you home, or taken a basket to the park, but as I recall, you insisted on the location, Miss Owens." He filled his own glass and set the decanter aside, then proceeded to unpack the basket, laying one dish after another on the table with a flourish and a smile.

He set out a cold collation of meats, but more delicately cut and plentiful than most such meals she could remember. There were rolls of ham sliced so fine she could read a script right through them, two or three types of cheese, fresh grapes and brilliantly red apples, surmounted by deep yellow plums. And beside that, with a flourish and a wave, he uncovered a plate of sweetmeats and nuts, including—and what could she do but laugh?—a handful of candied pistachios.

"Those are to be your signature from now on, I take it?" she asked, and he chuckled.

"Perhaps, as long as the memory makes you smile."

And with that the tension was gone, the doubts and fears that gnawed at the back of her mind vanishing into the dark shadows that ringed the room. But in their little globe of candlelight, across a table set for two, she could find no earthly reason to be upset.

It was a disconcerting sensation.

Mr. Caird tucked bread onto her plate and set about serving her the choicest pieces from each tray until her plate was so laden that the stoneware designs had entirely vanished. "How much do you imagine I can eat?"

"Given how many hours you spend in ballet rehearsals, I imagine you must be constantly starving. Mrs. Elliston will work you into exhaustion or injury before we open, if she's not careful." He served himself about the same and sat down across from her, setting his napkin across his lap.

The guilt—oh, the guilt, when he was being so solicitous! "About that." Grace pressed her lips together and glanced up at him through her lashes.

"You've not been required to work all those late hours," he guessed, leaning in on one elbow.

"It is easier to stretch and practice drills there than to do so at home," Grace objected weakly, but he was laughing at her silently, and she shrugged. "The longer the hours I stay there, the less likely I am to encounter you when I come back here. I attempted to have my notes and call sheets redirected to the school, but Mr. Elliston would have none of it."

"All that effort, just to avoid me?" Mr. Caird still

seemed more amused than angry, toying absently with the stem of his glass.

The wine made for a momentary escape, a burst of dark flavor on Grace's tongue. "You don't make it easy."

He steepled his fingers and chuckled darkly, arching an eyebrow just like Bixby when he was playing an arch-villain. "And now my master plan has come to light."

"And what does that entail? Ravishing me across the supper table?" She meant it to come out dryly, a sarcastic comment to cut short his foolish posturing. Her fickle mind supplied images to accompany the suggestion even as the words left her mouth, though, and much of the edge was lost as her cheeks tinged warm.

His answering smile and long, lingering look at her mouth only sent that rush of heat burning higher, as though she could already feel his hands on her, those skillful fingers working at the buttons and lacings of her dress and stays, or his lips, his tongue, trailing hot along her skin.

"I had thought perhaps somewhere more comfortable, but when beauty commands, man must answer."

"Keep your horses hitched, sir," Grace objected, laughing—the very idea that she might be considered beautiful! Her age, manners and the abiding comfort she took in dressing like a boy half the time destroyed *that* notion irrevocably. He was as ridiculous as he was overbearing, and she was encouraging him just by staying here. But then— "You are distracting me on purpose."

"And I promise I shall not attempt to scare you off any further." He drew a cross across his chest. "At least, not until after you have been fully sated."

Grace refused to give him the benefit of showing that she had understood, but the corner of her mouth quirked up in a small smile nevertheless.

"You're speaking of Three-Fingered Ned." Grace turned the wineglass in the light, the candle flames burned down low enough now that the orange and yellow fire reflected in a dozen scattered flashes off the irregular crystal. The cold collation had been put to bed along with the remnants of the fruits and nuts some time ago, and now there was only an inch, perhaps two, of the good red wine left in the base of the heavy decanter.

"Did you never wonder about how he lost the other two?" Caird asked, lifting the decanter and draining the last of the wine first into her glass, and then his. The sight of the dregs settling back to the bottom of the crystal beaker struck a sudden and inexplicable pang of disappointment somewhere deep in Grace's chest.

"I suppose—yes, fine, I have. But I've never had the audacity to ask him about it!"

"That's where being a nosy young apprentice will get you farther than respect." And he tapped the side of his delicious nose, a knowing smile playing over his full lips. The attic room had stayed warm even against the cool night air that occasionally rattled the shutters, the shadows playing in the corners old friends by now.

How long had they been talking, as the wine level fell and candles sank down in their sticks? It hardly mattered— this little world of theirs was a cozy place, a comfortable one, where she wore lace-trimmed gowns and he a blue waistcoat, double-breasted, with his top button open over his broad, strong chest.

"Are you going to tease me or tell me?" she dared him, and that smile of his turned wicked, the very tip of his tongue moistening the center of his lower lip.

The lightning sprang between them, fire in his eyes. Then he continued talking and the moment passed by unclaimed.

"Ned was a gunner on one of His Majesty's mighty warships—"

"Him?" Grace could hardly help sounding astonished—the elderly propmaster at the King's Theatre was far more widely known for his love of ale and horse races than for any patriotic devotion. "When you said he'd seen a ship on fire, I thought you meant in harbor."

Caird nodded nevertheless. "Press gang got him coming out of a brothel. Totally innocently, you understand," he added, a grin wide on his face.

"Mmm-hmm." She hardly needed to reply at all.

Caird pressed his fingertips against his chest, and affected an air of innocence. "He was there to mission to the ladies, to pray for their eternal souls."

"I'm sure you've both spent a lot of time there upon your knees." She was trying to shock him now, because that face was simply asking for it.

He laughed long and low, shaking his finger at her as though she were a naughty child. "So Ned was pressed into the navy and became a gunner, learned everything black-powder related. He got his damn fool fingers blown off in a skirmish against the American rebels, and retired to become a propmaster and professional irritant."

Grace chuckled. "And then you apprenticed to him?"

Caird nodded. "And he taught me everything *he* knew about explosives and chemical reactions, which brings me to the illustrious position I hold today."

"Making stage smoke for witches and tempests."

He leaned forward, as though he meant to whisper something in her ear. Grace found herself drawing in to him, pulled closer, but he didn't tilt his head, nor murmur something soft and sweet.

Instead he took a pinch of salt from the tiny saltcellar set between them, and sprinkled it above the candle flame. A bright orange fire leapt from the candle and consumed the grains even as they fell, sparking into brilliant flares of light that extinguished before they hit the linen. "I make magic," he intoned solemnly, and snapped his fingers. Another spark lit, floated, and died.

An angel falls from dark to dark—

Grace's heart lurched sideways in her chest, the flame colors all too close and too bright, triggering the memory of hazy words and sickly-sweet smoke all in a rush.

He wants to make me into an angel.

A man will bind you, and keep you in chains...

She blinked and shook it off, but not before his brow furrowed. He had seen her reaction. "More like alchemy," Grace said lightly. "Nothing I know anything about."

He shook his head. "It's all just proportions, knowing what elements can come together to make something greater than the sum of its parts." He rose to his feet, then.

"What salts and earths in what quantities to hold a spark."

He stepped around the table that had stood as a bulwark between them, and extended his hand. His eyes glimmered in the darkness above the warm, soft sphere of candlelight. For a moment, Caird standing tall and strong above her, she felt small, delicate, her breath catching low in her throat.

She put her fingers in his hand. He closed his around her and drew her gently to her feet, but did not stop her. He tugged her in, moving at the same time, so that they stopped with barely a fingerwidth between them. His chest rose and fell faster than before, and Grace's heart set a double-time that had to be visible in the pulses at her wrist, at her throat.

When he spoke again it was in a low murmur, his head bent down and his lips moving against her ear. "How much heat on a mixture will ignite a flame."

How much, indeed. Desire burned through her, her knees trembling to hold her up. She ached at her core, empty and hollow, all the awareness in her body collecting at the one point where they touched, where his hand fit so completely around hers.

His cheek brushed against hers, his jawline betraying the faintest of rough prickles. His breath was sugar-sweet, and when her lips parted and he kissed her, he tasted of marzipan dainties and pistachio nuts. His hand came up to splay across her lower back, the other cupping her jaw, his fingers pressing hot and firm against the side of her neck. Caird's lips moved over hers gently, exploring, brushing his mouth against hers once, twice, before she melted against him entirely.

Then he changed, his hand on the small of her back drawing her tight against his body, the long, firm length of his thigh sitting against her legs, his hip riding up ever so slightly against the desperate, growing ache at her core. His tongue slipped between her lips for a moment only, his kiss a questing thing growing in strength and in passion.

She held on, her arms coming around his neck, and she opened her mouth to him, parted her legs and let his thigh press between. Forget control; he was consuming her as though she were a wanton, and for the moment she wanted it that way, needed it, craved the moment she could let go and let him take it all.

Then his mouth was gone from hers, pressing soft kisses down her throat, and when she opened her eyes he was moving to stand behind her, his hand never leaving the small of her waist, slipping from her back to her hip, flattening against her stomach.

"Please," he murmured.

He would feel little but her stays through that, the snug-laced protection that closed her off from the world. But she could feel him, his chest against her shoulder blades, his mouth trailing along the back of her neck, the bare skin displayed by her high-dressed hair.

Tingles and shocks exploded from the points of contact and she shivered, opening her eyes long enough to look down, see the broad expanse of his hand spanning her front, holding her close and drawing her hips back, slowly and inexorably.

She felt him then, the hard, fierce length of his cock pushing against her backside, layers of fabric between them. Grace tilted her hips back, pressed harder against him, memorized the shape and size of it, the firm pressure against her body. He let out a low groan, her fingers clenching in

121

the lavender folds of her dress. He grazed the back of her neck with his teeth and a shuddering gasp tore from her lips.

"Yes."

The sound seemed to unleash him, because his hand moved up her body to cup her breast, his thumb brushing firm against her nipple, hard against the top edge of her stays. He gathered up her skirt and shift with the other hand, running his fingers up her thigh, her hip, across the sensitive skin of her belly. It tickled and she laughed, breathless against the mix of sensations coursing through her.

He nipped at the back of her neck, traced the tip of his tongue across the back of her earlobe, closed his mouth over the gold wire of her earring and sucked at the spot where it penetrated her skin.

"Grace," he whispered, harsh and raw, his hips riding up against her buttocks and his hard prick pushing insistently against her. He made no move to touch himself, stroking her breast, cupping and molding his palm around it. And with the other—with the other he drifted lower, his fingers teasing along her skin, diving into the thatch of curls between her thighs.

There, there, oh there—his fingers, clever fingers, they found the place she needed, two stroking across the hard nub of her pleasure. She trembled, arched at the shock of sensation and he held her there, his body strong and firm behind her, unwavering and solid.

He rocked against her as his hands moved, teasing and drawing out ripples and spikes of need and pleasure all tangled into one. She ached, empty, and as though she'd said it out loud his fingers slipped lower still, teasing around her entrance, pressing gently inward then retreating, just enough to feel that she would part for him, she would give in to him, let him in.

He took his fingers back instead. Her eyes flew open just in time to see him bring them to his lips, swirl his tongue around the tips. He pressed them to her mouth and she opened for him, tasting herself on his skin, salt-sour-sweet all blending together and over it all the hazy musk of desire that set her trembling.

"Please," she said, only *please*, and he buried his face in the back of her hair, his gasps in time with the rocking of his hips and the splay of his hand across her lower belly. And there, he would not disappoint, the press of his hand over her mound, and those fingers back between her nether lips, rubbing tight circles over the hard nub of her clitoris.

She needed, she needed and he gave, holding her against his body, his arms wrapped around her and holding her safe, the sins in his hands drawing her closer to the precipice with every flick and rough brush of friction.

There—the world fell away beneath her and she fell with it, shaking apart in his arms, clenching tight around emptiness. He stroked her through the tremors, sliding fingers deep along her cleft, circling her entrance and then back again, down and back, until her shaking stopped.

Grace sagged back against him, limp in the moment of her utmost vulnerability, and he did not let her go. He held her close, let her dress fall back down to cover her legs as she began to shiver, pressed kisses along the back of her neck, the few inches of her shoulders that her dress left bare.

And through it all he kept himself still, his hands on her. Grace drew in breath, a deep trembling pull of air that stopped the last of her trembling. Turning in his arms, she

123

rose up on her tiptoes impulsively to press kisses to the corners of his mouth. He sighed and caught her chin in his hand, covering her mouth with his in a kiss that turned fierce, hot and suddenly entirely too—too something.

Too much, too far, some feeling that sank deep down into her core and set barbed hooks there.

She broke away and the air around them changed. A frown flickered across his face, his eyes black with desire and his trousers pressed out in the front. Caird held still, not touching himself, nor reaching for her, waiting to see what she would do.

He had pleasured her without asking for anything in return, made no move to grab her, or toss her down and take what he needed.

That—that was a restraint that she could admire. It deserved some form of reward. She reached out, running the tips of her fingers lightly down the outside of his fall-front trousers, tracing the outline of his rigid cock.

Mr. Caird's hands balled tight at his sides and he gasped, his eyes fixed on her and a faint sheen of sweat glowing on his forehead. "Grace," he said, so solemn and soft that it sounded like a prayer.

It was his turn now to be vulnerable, but the open need in his eyes seemed anything but. She cupped him, running her hand firmly down the length of his bulge. Though her body still floated on a lazy haze of satiation, the flare of curiosity took over. Her mouth dry, his eyes on her every move, she popped open the buttons on his trousers and let the front flap fall.

A shroud of fine white linen covered his dark skin and

she pushed it aside, impatient. She drew out his prick and it rose, towering in her hand, his dark skin darker still along his length from the rush of blood. He shuddered at her touch, a shiver running through him, and he closed his hand about her hip.

His prick gleamed with wetness at the top, his foreskin sliding easily in her hand, riding up along the hard length. He cried out, a wordless sound, and he thrust up into her hand. She closed her hand and stroked him, hard, and he grabbed her by both hips, resting his forehead against hers. They traded breaths and desperate kisses, his teeth grazing her bottom lip and his prick hot, so hot in her hands.

Mr. Caird groaned when he climaxed, a low, desperate sound that set off resonance in her gut, her core aching.

He would split her in two if she rode him now the way her body wanted her to. It would spear her and drive away everything else, no room left for doubts or troubling thoughts.

Not now, though. Now he came over her hands, hot and white, his passion spilling from him until, spent, he covered her hands with one of his.

He didn't speak nor did she, breathing into each other, standing at the edge of the circle of light.

Seconds, minutes, or hours later, Mr. Caird's prick softening and returning to its normal state, he lifted his hand from hers and she let him go. She didn't look him in the eye as he rearranged his clothes and bought out a handkerchief with which to clean them both. Not until she made a move to start packing away the leftover food did he reach out again, catching her by the elbow.

"Will you come to me again?" he asked softly. "Or let

me come to you?"

"You're a strange and foolish man," she said, equally softly, letting the moment of uncertainty linger. "I'm not the woman you need."

"Perhaps. But you may be the grace that I am looking for."

... He did not.

He kept his face utterly serious when she jerked her head up and glared at him, nothing moving or twitching to suggest that he had been making fun.

She held her gaze steady. He arched an eyebrow.

She set her mouth in a firm line. The corner of his lip twitched, just once.

"Ah-hah!" she crowed, stabbing her finger at him.

"I can hide nothing from you, Miss Owens," he replied cheerfully, and gave her a roguish wink that set alarming things fluttering in the pit of her stomach.

She snorted, and began to wrap the cutlery in the napkins for safe transport. "That's because you're a babbling fool."

"You wound me." He set the glasses inside his basket and moved up behind her, a swagger in his step that had not been there before. Grace held still and he ran his hands up her arms, toying with the little bit of lace that finished the ends of her short sleeves. "And you never answered my question. Will you come to me again?"

Shivers chased each other down her back, delicious and trembling. But her mind was back in control, and the last thing she needed was to let him think that he had somehow won her over, or that she would be a doxy to come at his call.

"And what incentive could you have to offer me?" she temporized, buying herself a moment to think of better replies.

He nuzzled in, his breath warm and his lips brushing against the shell of her ear. Everything that had been slowly going dormant flared back to life, her body aching.

"I want to be inside you," he murmured, the over-confident creature!

Grace stepped out of his arms. "You first," she purred. And frankly, it didn't sound like a bad idea at all.

He stopped abruptly. "Sorry, what?"

So she elaborated. "If you want to be inside me, I get to be inside you first. It only seems fair."

He dropped his gaze to the general region of her groin, then slowly tracked back up toward her face, a worried furrow etching deep into the space between his brows. "...how's that going to work, then? Do you have a prick I don't know about?"

Grace smiled, and took up her bonnet and shawl. "I keep it in a box," she replied, stepping toward the door. "For special occasions."

She paused on the edge of the circle of light and looked back over her shoulder. He stood where she had left him, and there might as well have been a large question mark painted on a sign above his head. He reached up to rub the back of his neck, looking stymied. She smiled.

Grace left the loft, her body humming. She swung her shawl around her shoulders and set her bonnet on her head. *Let's see if you have the fortitude to deal with me after this, Mr. Caird. Somehow, I doubt you'll be man enough to try.*

127

Chapter Eight

Distraction. That woman was a horrible, wonderful distraction that had done as much damage to Isaac's view of the world in the last two days than a keg of black powder could ever have managed.

What in the name of all that was holy could she possibly have meant by "I keep it in a box"?

And was it incredibly wrong to be so very curious about her suggestion?

He would be far better off concentrating on the tangle of ropes and pulleys before him on the stage. He needed hammered iron for a track, to mount above the catwalk, and—

"I get to be inside you first."

Men were hardly built for such things. Though sodomites had presumably discovered some techniques that made it possible. And, one presumed, pleasurable.

That couldn't possibly be what she had meant.

Could it?

It was an affront to the natural way of things—men *had* pricks, and women took them.

What would *that feel like? To have a prick up in your arse?*

Ow.

There were more than enough mollies around that there had to be some sort of appeal. He could hardly go and ask Thomas, even though his proclivities were a loosely held secret. The fighting master would laugh in his face. Then, more than likely, run Isaac through with one of the fencing blades Thomas kept close to hand, for the audacity of even asking such a question.

Which suggested that such pursuits did not necessarily sap a man's strength, nor his potency.

"You first."

When she put it like that, it almost sounded fair.

She keeps it in a box?

"And what are you so pensive about, my good sir?" The flirty voice was not Grace's, but it was familiar, and Isaac nearly jumped out of his skin at the intrusion. *Did she hear what I was thinking? Does she* know? But Miss Sullivan showed no sign at all that she had read Isaac's mind, or picked up any of his aberrant mental wanderings.

"Miss Sullivan," he replied, sitting back on his heels to give himself time to reconcile his mind to the current setting. The actors had been released for their break and he was supposed to have had the stage to himself, more time to figure out the mechanisms behind the flying equipage before he had to present his prototype to the Ellistons. But none of that close timing was Lucy's fault.

"What can I do for you?" he asked, with the hope that his inner debates were not showing themselves on his face.

"Is there aught amiss?"

"No, but I am a miss who ought," she replied smartly, and her green eyes twinkled. He laughed, and waited for her to continue.

Miss Sullivan set her hands behind her back, her pretty blue dress a bright spot of freshness in the dusty theatre, and she strolled leisurely around his half-completed project. "What is this you're working on?" she asked, bending down to look at the way he'd laid out the pulleys to test their bearing strength.

"An experiment," he hedged, "nothing more."

"Surely you can tell me *something*," she cooed, turning to follow the lines of ropes with her fingertips. "You always have such interesting contraptions for us." And the eyes she made at him then, wide and deep sea green, some kind of tint making her fair lashes dark, and a coy little peek over her shoulder, *well*.

He did grin back her, because any man would be flattered. Miss Sullivan had the kind of round-bosomed, cheerful beauty that promised entertainment. But Isaac stood instead of taking her well-dangled bait. "And they're much more interesting as a surprise."

She pouted prettily. "You aren't any fun, Mr. Caird."

"I suppose not." He didn't stop her when she moved across the stage to look over his sketches, though. Whatever she could glean from the scribbled notes on those was information fairly won. The loss of his notebook still nagged at him, mind you. There were ideas and calculations in there that would have been useful, if he could remember what he last done with the thing.

"How go rehearsals today?"

"Well enough." She waved off the question. "There are a great many more lines for the leads to commit to memory, of course. But I'm only a witch now, so what would I know of that?" and the little laugh she gave at the end was bitter.

"Come now," he coaxed, beginning to coil the rope up around his arm to pack it away. "There will be other roles, other seasons. And you shall have had the honor of appearing in a Shakespeare at the *Surrey*, despite the laws."

"I suppose." Miss Sullivan straightened again, and settled her disappointment away, replacing the look with a smile. "And there's no changing anything about now, unless something untoward happens again."

"Don't mention that around Tottenham—he's got his head in a twist about the 'curse' as it is. He'll have you watching your back for weeks."

She only smiled at his wry chuckle, toying with the chain of her reticule. "Watch your own back, Mr. Caird. I am a witch, after all." She waggled her fingers at him as she left, descending the stairs in the wings and disappearing into the darkness of the backstage.

Leaping out of bed early in the morning had never been Grace's forte, nor her pleasure. It was even more difficult now when her nights had been taken over by the urge to relive delicious memory. She could close her eyes and be back in the loft, feel Mr. Caird's hands on her body, delicious sensations that her own hands could almost—but not quite—replicate to her satisfaction.

It was one thing to know oneself, and another entirely to have the new and foreign touch of a lover, the weight and heat of a body against yours, the taste and smell of a man's skin and sweat on your tongue.

And so even though she had not gone to him in a few days, her distraction had made sleep elusive. Nevertheless, it was easier, as always, to arrive at the school before the younger dancers, where she could stretch her aching limbs in private.

There had been a time when she could arrive before the dancing master, poised and ready in her simple rehearsal gown and slippers, stretch to her toes and rise in the postures without pain or hesitation, no stiffness in her bones at the end of the day.

Only a few years, and she had already lost so much.

The young ones were close to surpassing her in technique, their jumps and turns pushed farther, higher, more passionately than anything she had ever been taught. The old style had been languid, slow, drawing the viewer's eye through sweeping gestures and perfectly placed limbs. The new fashion for speed and precision had left her firmly behind.

All the more reason to come early and leave late, to warm her muscles and practice her steps before the rehearsal room filled with bucks and misses in their prime of youth.

Except this morning, someone had beaten her to it.

Miss Mayes, a pretty, bright little thing, was carefully treading out her measures in the center of the otherwise empty room. Grace paused for a moment, half in the doorway, and watched. Miss Mayes had all the sparkle and liveliness that were in demand, her dusky skin lighter even than Caird's golden brown—just enough of a hint of some other blood that she would be considered "exotic" against the usual pale and golden-haired English beauties.

Grace must have moved, her boots scuffing heavily against the floor, for Miss Mayes stopped, came to an easy rest with her arms floating down to her sides, and turned to look. She blinked in surprise, a quick motion that suggested she was taken aback by the shapeless shadow in the door.

"My apologies," Grace said, before the girl could say anything. She tugged off her cap to reveal her hair, expose more of her face to the light, and Miss Mayes visibly relaxed. "I didn't realize anyone would be here this early."

"It's only you, Miss Owens, there's no need to apologize." Miss Mayes said, entirely at ease now, running lightly across the floor to take up the towel left hanging over the back of a chair. "I thought for a minute it was one of the trade apprentices again, come to spy."

She was smiling, but a flicker of outrage ignited in Grace's chest at the casual suggestion. Miss Mayes barely came up to Grace's shoulder, tiny as she was, and Grace herself was not tall. She felt the sudden and powerful urge to place herself between Miss Mayes and the theoretical disrespectful onlookers, and keep her safe.

"Do they do that often?" Grace stepped in to the room and into the light. The mirror on the wall showed her a distorted reflection of herself, a young man in loose trousers and a laborer's rough coat, her figure artlessly concealed beneath the fabric.

"Only when a few of the girls are about, and even then

they mostly keep their distance. You'd think they'd never seen legs before." Miss Mayes said cheerfully, the hem of her white rehearsal dress floating lightly about her knees as she folded easily to the ground and began to adjust one of her slipper ribbons.

"Given the company they could keep in this town, I'm sure none of them are as innocent as they may claim." Grace's reply came out dry, and Miss Mayes' returned look was startled. "Of course, some of them may just enjoy the dancing."

She laughed knowingly, and something inside Grace thawed a little more. "I'm sure—that's why we never see them when the lads are rehearsing alone." Miss Mayes tipped her head and regarded Grace solemnly for a moment, her dark eyes inscrutable. "Isn't that why you dress the way you do?" she asked candidly. "To put off their attention?"

The question caught Grace off-guard, asked as frankly and openly as that. She paused, balancing on one foot and still tugging off her boot, to find the explanation that would reveal just enough of her mind. "Not precisely? Though it is a side benefit." She set her foot down, laces untied and loose across the wooden floor. "Some days the world is only right if I move through it as a man."

And some days it seemed just as wrong. Those were days when frills and silks were called for, setting her curls with pale ribbons and taking long walks with Meg.

How did one make sense of it all, talking to someone who seemed as though she had always been perfectly comfortable in the role she was born to play?

Miss Mayes, though, just nodded sagely, as though Grace had explained enough. "It would certainly make things safer in the evenings," she mused aloud. "Though I don't know that I could manage it as well as you. I'm so little, I would be picked up as a lost child and put into the foundling hospital."

The image of some well-meaning Bow Street Runner tucking Miss Mayes up under his arm and carting her off to the children's home was enough to start Grace laughing. That set Miss Mayes off as well, with a high giggle that turned into a snort. Her eyes flashed wide and she slapped her hands over her mouth and nose, her embarrassed squeak triggering Grace's laugh again.

A door slammed somewhere in the distance and voices echoed down the hall. Grace picked up her bag and smiled. "I should go and make myself ready for rehearsal." It felt like an apology, though for what, she couldn't quite be sure.

"We've an hour or so yet."

"I've interrupted your time."

"It's no bother, I promise you." Miss Mayes rose easily to her feet, brushing down her layers of gauzy white skirts so they hung neatly again. "If you're willing, Miss Owens, I would be pleased if you would consider working here. There's space enough in the studio for two to be quite free to move, and—"

"And?" Grace paused, waiting.

"And I would be grateful for your advice on turns," Miss Mayes said frankly. "You have a way about yours that makes the motion effortless, and so perfectly centered. I'm afraid I always give the impression of a child's top about to fall over."

Caught off-guard, and not for the first time that week,

Grace shook her head slowly. "You don't want my advice. I'm old and my joints creak. You're better off learning from someone who knows what they're about."

"Old?" Miss Mayes seemed about to burst out laughing again. "Mrs. Elliston has ten years on you, I'd wager. And you could still dance circles around the best of the rest of us. If you wanted to." She waved off whatever Grace might have been about to reply. "But if you disagree, then who am I to say contrary?"

"Thank you." Contemplating the available options, Grace headed for the dressing room to change. She could just as easily go to another room in the school—there was always some empty space where she could test the day's limits for her joints and her wayward, uncooperative feet.

Or she could take Miss Mayes up on her offer, and possibly emerge on the other side of this whole business with a new friend.

She shed her skin in the dressing room, put herself into another. It felt less familiar today, a second layer of costume upon costume—man to woman, then woman to dancer. White dress swishing about her knees and her boots replaced with delicate satin slippers, the toes and heels newly darned with tiny, even stitches, Grace went back to the hall.

Miss Mayes dipped her head in a nod when Grace entered, saying nothing other than "thank you," and "how would you like to begin?"

Despite herself, Grace found herself smiling when she answered. "I will show you my tricks for turns, Miss Mayes, but in return you must agree to teach me. I'm of an older school, and feel very much at sea. I—" The words caught in her throat. "I am ill prepared for the work I still have to master."

Tension burned across Grace's shoulders, braced in the habit of anticipation. Nothing happened.

No hand, no crack of a stick across the backs of her legs for daring to admit her failure. No sign at all that the universe had heard or marked her confession in any way.

She was a silly fool.

"Then I shall endeavor to row you back in to shore." Miss Mayes clasped Grace's hand.

There was something kind and vaguely Meg-like about her. With fear still a yammering little goblin down inside her heart, Grace followed her lead.

"Phosphorus costs *how* much?"

Addison turned the book around to face Isaac, pointing at one entry in the ledger with a crooked, skinny finger. The chemist's shop was set up in one of the narrow buildings that had sprung up around the Royal Institution over the past decade, one of any number of supply shops catering to the Institute's resident population of wealthy, well-educated gentlemen…and a handful of machinists with an excess of time on their hands.

"Phosphorus is a dear chemical," Addison confirmed, his high, reedy voice amplified by the grand resonating chamber of his nose. "It requires vast quantities of bone ash to manufacture and men of the highest skill level of extract. I cannot simply sell it for pennies to the pound!"

"I don't need a *pound*, my dear Mr. Addison," Isaac

wheedled, resting his arms on the high counter and leaning in. "Only a few grams, and it will be going to a most excellent cause."

"More of your tawdry stage spectacles, no doubt," Addison sniffed. "There is nothing *edifying* about theatre, Mr. Caird. There is no *advancement* of man's knowledge of the world. This is a shop for men of *science*, not for providing trifles to entertain the unwashed masses."

"Entertainment is what keeps the unwashed masses away from the Institution lectures and off your doorstep," Isaac felt compelled to point out. "Without our shows, how many more trifling men would be wandering about in the evenings looking for some new diversion?"

Addison peered at him peevishly over the rims of his spectacles. Isaac gave him his most winning smile.

"Half a guinea for a paper's worth." The words dragged out of Addison reluctantly, as though he were doing Isaac the greatest favor in the world by *permitting* him to make a purchase.

"Done." Isaac flipped the page in his new notebook, the old ledger seemingly gone to the winds, and skimmed down the list. "And as I'm here, I'd also like packets of chlorate of potash, sulfur, and a two-penny bottle of sulfuric acid."

Addison rolled his eyes and shook his head at the sky, as though blaming the Almighty Father for their current conversation. "When you have finally succeeded in burning the Surrey to the ground, Mr. Caird, I will take no responsibility. None! I have not seen you, and you were never here." He flung his hands up in the air and stalked off to the back room with all the dignity of an affronted scarecrow.

It would take more than a few minutes for the druggist to repackage and dispense out his purchases. Isaac turned and rested his elbows back on the counter, idly marking the shapes of the passers-by outside the dusty shop window. Pretty girl, harried mother with basket and string of children, young gentleman with hat and cane—and one rather more portly figure who stopped, looked in the window, then turned and sauntered cheerfully in.

"What ho, Caird!" Thilby greeted him just as cheerfully as if they were bellied up to the bar together in Chelsea Place, and not official rivals now with five pounds on the line. "And what are you doing here on such a fine day as this? Not out courting the ladies in the park?" He waggled his eyebrows and grinned lasciviously.

"I'm for the life of the mind today," Isaac replied loftily, but he couldn't resist the urge to return the jab. "But I think you must have lost *your* way. The boys for hire are all down at St. James. That's a good quarter of an hour walk from here."

Thilby growled at him, his jocular mood vanishing for a moment at what Isaac was implying, but he recovered his temper before he could make anything more like a threat.

Make a note—sister jokes are fair game, but catamite jests are less so.

"You're far from home," Thilby said, his eyes narrowing with interest. "Bit far north just to come for some headache powders."

"I could say the same for you," Isaac replied. "Unless the packet under your arm there is a dress for the missus."

Thilby chuckled. "Ah, ah—that's for me to know and

you to guess at. At least until opening." And he shifted the paper-wrapped parcel under his arm reflexively. It squished, suggesting fabric, but Isaac couldn't tell anything more. "On an errand for your mother, I suppose? How is your project coming?" Thilby asked, his words whistling between his teeth.

"Well enough to beat you, I warrant." And with any luck, Addison would not be out with his purchases until long after Thilby had vacated the premises. He was a damp sock of a man, but he was not stupid. No brewer or vintner needed phosphorus—or sulfuric acid! "Ready to concede now and save yourself the trouble?"

"Hah! I'd sooner throw a hand of cards to an apprentice. You wait and see, Caird—you're out-matched."

"Spend your time bragging about your win and you'll find you've run out of hours to accomplish it," Isaac fired back another pseudo-friendly riposte, but his attention was fixed on the door behind the counter.

Come on, get your boasting out and then leave. Go. Off with you.

Addison appeared in the doorway and Isaac's heart sank. Then the druggist checked the packets in his hand, and vanished into the storeroom again. A momentary reprieve.

"Not like you, hanging about druggists and hiding beneath your mother's apron."

"Get out of here before I have to beat you black and bloody," Isaac made the banter sound more jovial than he felt. "Not my fault my parents keep a lavish table and love me enough to invite me to it."

"Ahh, your mother sucks eggs." Thilby whistled,

conceding in his tone if not his words. "But tell her I said hello."

Addison came out of the back room, his arms laden, at the same time as Thilby turned and headed for the door. "I'll see you on the field of battle, Caird," Thilby called back over his shoulder, then the door swung closed behind him.

"Engaging in a duel, are we?" Addison remarked dryly. He set the packets, vials, and bottles out on the countertop and began to write up Isaac's bill.

"Something of the sort."

"Well, keep my name out of it. And for the love of all things holy, don't open that phosphorus while you're anywhere *near* my shop."

In all fairness, the scullery at home was nowhere close to Addison's shop. And Isaac had the sulfuric acid open, and not the phosphorus. So it didn't go nearly as badly as it might have.

All his tools were spread out before him on the solid wooden table in the center of the room, the windows open to let in the fresh air and prevent him from feeling the close-chest tightness that strong chemicals sometimes afflicted. It would have been better if he had this kind of light and air at the loft, but beggars, after all, could not be choosers.

First things first. Isaac dug his gloves out of his pocket and slid them on, the once-fine kid leather now pocked with small scorch marks and stained dark in patches across his fingertips and knuckles. He lost some dexterity, but it was better that than suffering the itch and blisters of healing burns.

Next came the fuel, a half-spoon of fine charcoal tipped into the heavy stone mortar. He tapped the side with the spoon to get rid of the last few specks of the clingy black dust, and then carefully tipped in a matching amount of the chlorate.

"Prrrrp?" Gyb, his father's fat old tom-tabby cat, lifted his head from his paws and looked around. Seeing no mice or anything at all of interest, he stretched out in the sunbeam on the windowsill and returned to his nap.

Careful now, careful—it was not volatile on its own, but any slip would cause him no end of problems later.

Especially if one of his parents caught him using the scullery for a laboratory again.

He stirred the powders together until they blended into a salty-pepper gray, and then a heaping spoonful of *that* went into the borrowed stoneware pie plate.

And now for the fun.

The bottle of sulfuric acid held enough of the potent brew to potentially cause damage to both furnishings and flesh. He uncorked the small brown glass vial with the utmost care, setting it down on the table a decent space away from the volatile powders and dusty pestle.

A few drops were all he needed, decanted into the glass beaker. Isaac raised it to the light to check its quality, the liquid clear enough for his purposes, then tipped it into the pie plate atop the combined powders.

The fizz sound lasted less than half a second before the jet of fire erupted from the plate. "Ha-*hah!*" Isaac jumped back to avoid the explosive column of flame, beaker still in hand.

Gyb startled awake on his windowsill and yowled in alarm. He leapt to his feet, back arched and tail puffed wide. The flame burnt itself out almost instantly, the charcoal giving it just enough life to register. Gyb sailed across the gap, ricocheted off the tabletop and bolted for the door. Bottles and beakers clinked together as the table shook, and the vial of sulfuric acid tipped over.

Why had he not capped it? *Stupid, stupid!* Isaac let go of the beaker and dropper in his hands and scrambled for the shelves on the wall.

The fizzling sound from the table grew louder, and he swatted aside containers and tins that were not what he was looking for. Some fell to the floor with thumps and crashes that would surely rouse the house.

There! The tin of soda ash for soap-making. It was only half-full, and he scooped the opened tin through the cistern beside the hearth, filling it the rest of the way with cold water.

The acid sizzled, hissed and popped as it laid dark brown scorch marks on the pale oak table, eating down through the upper layer.

Isaac clamped his hand down over the top of the tin, no time to look for where the lid had fallen. Shaking the mixture combined it somewhat; hopefully it would be enough.

"Isaac? Is that you?" Colin appeared in the scullery door, his eyes wide, just in time to see Isaac dump out the contents of the tin on top of the growing acid pool.

Some of it splashed into the scorched-bottom pie plate and the reaction screamed like wind through standing stones, or a child learning bagpipes. The rest went all over the table, a mess of water, white powder and a thick gluey paste.

A moment passed when the acid-burning sounds had ceased, and there was silence in the room other than a faint pop-sizzzzzz from the table.

"What the bloody *hell* are you—" Isaac's younger brother managed to say.

The world erupted in warm white foam.

It covered the table, the countertop, the cistern and Isaac, the crackling sound of the fizzy bubbles popping sounding like a hundred teeny-tiny Thilbys all laughing at him at once.

Colin surveyed the room from behind the door, his smartly cut coat and trousers seemingly unscathed.

"Mother is going to *murder* you," he said with something approaching awe.

"Not if she never finds out. Quick!" Isaac scrubbed his face clear of the watery foam with the back of his shirtsleeve and pulled a stack of tea towels down from the uppermost shelf. "Help me!" He started swiping at the table, the foam dissolving into water and a gritty white powder that stuck to the cloths and to his gloves.

"Isaac?" Their mother's voice sounded from somewhere distant—upstairs, perhaps, or out in the front hall?

"Faster," Isaac insisted through clenched teeth. "Come on, Colin."

He'd rather take his chances with Elliston in a rage than his mother in a full-on strop.

"Don't call me that," his brother replied, but he grabbed

up a towel and set to work on the floor, mopping up the splashes of water there as well. "I'm not a child anymore."

"Nic-kin, then?" Isaac teased as a distraction, using their grandmother's old terms of endearment. It had sounded better in her thick brogue, but so be it.

"Keep that up and I'll let you clean this mess on your own," Colin—sorry, *Nicolas*—replied. He kept going, though, tossing the first sodden towel toward the sink and taking up another.

"You'd never."

"I would."

"Have you no loyalty to your older brother?" It was easier to banter than to fret about the approaching footsteps, as Isaac frantically capped his vials and folded up his packets of chemicals, tucking them securely back into his travel case.

Col—*Nicolas* (and that was going to take a while)—snorted aloud, standing and scrubbing hard at the black scorched marks on the table. "None whatsoever. That's why I'm here helping you instead of laughing at your misfortune."

The marks neither budged nor lightened, etched as they were into the table's surface.

"Isaac?" Their mother called from the hall outside the kitchen. "Are you in there?"

"Damn," Isaac cursed under his breath. The scullery was still a mess despite the nearly-cleaned-off table: the containers he'd knocked over in his haste scattered on the floor, and a lump of sodden towels hanging over the edge of the sink basin.

"Go!" Nicolas pointed at the door to the yard, his brown eyes laughing. "Go, go go go! I'll say I haven't seen you."

"A blessing on your head and on your house," Isaac pledged, and bolted for the door.

"You owe me!"

He almost made it, too, pushing open the door and his foot landing on the first of the three steps outside. Then, oh then, he heard her come into the room behind him. He closed his eyes. He was a dead man.

Her voice rose in pitch and volume with every word.

"Sweet merciful Mother of God. Isaac Caird, what have you done to my *kitchen!"*

Chapter Nine

Sometimes discretion was the better part of valor. It wasn't that Isaac was *hiding* from his mother per se. What did he, a man of almost thirty, have to fear from a woman twenty years older, a foot shorter, and half his width?

It was just that he could get more work done at the Surrey.

That early evening, his coat mostly dry and his gloves tossed aside on his work table, he was sorting through some of the papers down near the bottom of the trunk. Not for more information on the pulleys—he had that worked out about as well as it would go—but in case there was anything interesting that he had missed on his first cursory examinations.

Something exciting to do with prisms, perhaps, or torches.

Nothing caught his eye, though. It was all the same sorts of things he'd seen a dozen times before—parts of scripts, stage directions, playbills.

And a familiar name that caught his eye. Isaac tugged the old playbill out of the stack and held it up so he could get a better look in the waning light. The lighter text had faded, some of the rest blotted out by a water stain, but the rest was as readable as he could have hoped.

~**A dance starring Miss Owens, a child prodigy of unusual skill, beauty and grace**~

The production had taken place at Astley's, the year was 1796.

1796. Fifteen years ago, Grace would have been a child indeed. How old was she? She barely looked older than a girl of twenty-two or three, add a little time because beauty like that didn't necessarily age as quickly—she couldn't be older than twenty-five now. So at ten years old, she had been a performer valued enough to be on the playbill, in large print?

Isaac sat back on his heels and frowned at the page that gave him more questions than it answered.

Grace had been dancing since she was a young child, and while he had never seen her himself, she was obviously very good. Why would she have left it all behind? Why go from *that* to acting in small comedies at the Surrey?

An injury? That was what had sidelined Mrs. Elliston after her marriage. Grace had never mentioned one, but then, she hadn't told him much of anything that he hadn't found out on his own.

Somehow, it was all connected. Grace's performing past, her reluctance to dance on stage...her mistrust of strangers, and of men?

And that led to an entirely too plausible situation that he never, ever wanted to consider.

The very idea of someone hurting *her*, his Grace, drove the air out of his lungs and replaced it with white-hot rage. It flashed bright then sank to a simmer, smoldering anger that had no target.

He had the key to her now, here in his hand. The trick now was to find out which lock it opened.

Isaac folded up the playbill and tucked it in his waistcoat pocket. Grace would be home by now, the lamps starting to be lit in the street below. He would go by her lodgings, then, perhaps bring a sweet treat or a bottle of wine. And if she invited him in, he would have a chance to ask.

No one would be allowed to hurt her. Not while he drew breath.

Grace had all but settled in for an early night. The kettle sat to boil on the hob, the fire licking lazily at the newly-added wood. It crackled and spit, the warm smoke-smell popping with the sudden bursts of air and sparks.

It might be summer on the calendar, but tonight was cool and damp, the chill finding a way into her bones. A quiet evening at home, that was what she needed. Peace and calm, with a novel and a cup of tea, and no thinking about ballet, or plays, or *men*.

She had already tied up her hair and was in the middle of pouring the last of her hot water into the foot basin when a knock resounded at her door.

It wasn't so late in the day that it had to be some kind of emergency, but still. Who on earth could be knocking? Meg, most likely, come to find out all the news about Grace's 'handsome gentleman.' Well, Meg could take herself right back home, and—

Grace opened the door, but it was not Meg on the other side. Caird stood there instead, a bottle of wine in one hand and a small paper packet in the other. "Good evening, Miss Owens."

"Good evening," she said reflexively, her hand on the door. She was well within her rights to tell him to go away. Who came by a woman's lodgings in the evening unless he had some sort of ulterior motive? "As you can see, I'm in no fit state to receive visitors." She drew her wrapper more firmly around herself, covering the simple morning gown she'd yet to remove.

"Nonsense," he said, eyes warm and friendly and teasing lilt in his voice. "I've seen you in worse."

"I told you to go away then, as well," she replied tartly, but stepped aside and allowed him in. "What can I do for you, Mr. Caird?"

"I came by to give you this." He offered her the packet first, not the wine. "Mrs. Elliston tells me chamomile leaves are just the thing to soak tired and aching feet. I assume that, as a dancer herself, her advice is sound."

"She's very kind." It *was* a sweet gesture, but Grace was off-guard, too unsteady in her footing with him, even—*especially*—following their last torrid and impulsive encounter.

No, *she* had been impulsive. He had planned it from the beginning. So what did he have in mind now? Heat flushed through her at the vaguest of thoughts, pooling low in her belly and suffusing her limbs. "And the wine?" she asked, keeping her head up. Please, don't let him guess the direction her thoughts had wandered. If only he weren't so doggedly persistent!

If only he weren't so generous and quick to smile, or so finely built, his waistcoat sitting flat against his lean stomach, wool caressing the supple curves of the muscles in his arms and legs.

"A bottle from my own cellar. The family cellar," he corrected when she cast him a skeptical look. "We've all been going at a punishing pace, cast and crew alike. It occurred to me that you might not be taking the time required to relax."

Grace stepped back, putting some distance between them. She needed to be farther away from the spicy scent he wore, the one that made her want to bury her face in his neck and breathe deeply for hours. "And you thought you might help with that?"

"If you would care for some company."

Once again, he was leaving it up to her whether he stayed or left. He stood there in his coat and hat, not an anxious boy but a calm and self-assured suitor. His height and the breadth of his shoulders should have been a warning, putting her nerves on edge as she watched for the moment when he would abuse his power over her.

So far, he'd done nothing of the kind.

One tiny part of her registered a flicker of disappointment at that—the part that had been in control when Mr. Caird had pulled her against his body and held her firm, stroked down between her thighs and brought her to climax with his hand alone.

She would not squirm in front of him, or show her discomfort.

"You can stay if you wish, though this is the wrong

place to come for scintillating conversation. I was all but ready for bed and have nothing of importance to say." She moved across her small apartment to fetch glasses.

He doffed his hat and took a seat on the end of her settee, paper crinkling in his pocket when he settled.

"I object to that. Your conversation is always important, even when it's frivolous. Though to be fair, I can hardly remember you ever wasting words on frivolity." He accepted the glasses with a nod of thanks, opening the bottle with a deft flick of his wrist.

Grace sat at the other end, curling her bare feet beneath her. The basin steamed away on the hob in the kitchen. She would have to have her soak later. "To be fair," she echoed wryly, "*all* of what we do is frivolous, compared to things such as the war, or debates over laws in Parliament."

"The Quakers say that the job of all godly men and women is to speak the truth to those in power," he countered, pouring both their glasses full of red wine that glowed garnet-dark in the firelight. "What better way than through a play?"

"Where we strut and fret our hours upon the stage?" Grace probably misquoted, but she hardly felt like getting up to go search her bookshelf for the precious Shakespeare volume nestled there.

"There wouldn't be any fretting if it didn't mean something." He had her there and he knew it, handing her the glass of wine as though it were something precious. His fingertips brushed the backs of her knuckles as he drew his hand away, a gentle caress that left trails of fire burning in its wake.

Be calm. Don't let him see. Don't let him know that he's gotten beneath your skin.

"I came upon something today," Mr. Caird said, turning to better face her and drawing one of his feet up beneath him. "I thought you might want to see it." The piece of paper he tugged out from his coat pocket was folded small, yellowed with age and stained dark around the edges.

"If this is a rude woodcut, it's going out the door and you with it," she threatened, and he chuckled.

"No, nothing so vulgar. But it raised some questions in me that I thought you could answer."

"Vulgar" was certainly not the word she'd use for it. Grace unfolded the paper, and she had only made it halfway before she started to see the outlines of letters taking shape through the layers. Opening it in full brought her right back to that moment.

She had stared up at the wall in awe—that was *her* name up there, *her* moment to be the star that father had told her she would become.

Maybe now it would be enough, maybe now he would say. "Grace, I'm so proud of you."

He never did. But she wasn't that child any more, keeping parts of herself secret, craving the approval and affection that she would never earn.

Even so, it took a moment for her to find her voice again. "Where did you get this? It's from so long ago." Turning the page over gave her no answers.

"In among a collection of other old documents, tucked away in storage. How old were you there, ten? Nine? So young to be so talented." He looked at her face, not at the page, and she kept her head down, studying the curve and curl of the text, her name there in black and white.

"Twelve, actually." He reacted with surprise, and she smiled wryly, one corner of her mouth tugging up. "But thank you. I had been dancing on the stage since I was nine, but this was the first time my name was on a bill."

"You should keep this, then, unless your copy is in better quality."

"I never kept one."

His brow furrowed, as though that were something he'd never considered. "Your parents, then. They must celebrate your accomplishments."

"Not as such." Grace sipped from her glass, the wine full-bodied and deep, the heat spreading out through her body a moment later. "I'd rather not discuss it."

"As you like." He drank and didn't pursue the issue further. That startled her—she'd been sure he would press until he had the gossip he wanted, the better to reel her in. Instead the silence lingered, warm and approving, a blanket of safety falling around them. Until he set the glass down and took her foot in his hand.

She cringed and tried to pull back, but he held on, smoothing his thumb gently across the arch of her bruised and swollen foot, her skin spotted red with broken blisters and patches where her heel and toes had been rubbed raw. His touch sent a tingle rushing up her inner thigh, not the tickle he had perhaps been hoping for. "Don't. My feet are unpleasant outside of dance slippers."

"No, they're not. They're working feet, as I have working hands." He held up one hand, calluses and small scars turning his fingers rough. He held with his other hand, infuriating man, even as she tried halfheartedly to pull away. She'd end up kicking him in the jaw if she struggled for real. "And they look desperately sore."

He set to kneading one of her feet with both hands, his strokes firm and sure up one side and down the other, avoiding the spots of broken skin, circling her ankle with his hand, working his knuckles deep into the aches and pains. He seemed to know exactly where she ached, his hands moving expertly from one knot or twist to the next, stroking, massaging, tracing tiny circles just behind her anklebone, trailing up the inside of her shin.

"So much damage in the name of creating so much beauty."

"It would not be so bad if I hadn't quit years ago," Grace grumbled. She gave up the battle against her baser instincts, sliding her other foot out into his lap. Caird folded his large hand around it, heating up her tired muscles underneath. "I'm out of my prime, attempting to gain it all back at once, and that makes everything worse."

"Why did you stop?" It was an innocent question, but there was no way he could miss the way her whole body tensed when it passed his lips. "A…condition?"

"A *what?*" Grace took a moment to parse what he meant, then shook her head. "No, nothing quite so dramatic, I assure you. And I have no children left behind, in a foundling home or otherwise."

The idea of it twisted something deep. There would be no escape from the wrongness with a child inside; no way to see anything but a swollen belly and breasts that didn't belong to her. She couldn't help the small shudder. With any luck he'd imagine it was for different reasons.

"It would be a common enough thing, and for girls young enough that they had little choice in the matter," Caird said apologetically. "I meant nothing by it." He curled his knuckles into the high arch of her foot, a splendid mix of pain-pressure-heat curling up from her instep.

Grace gasped instead of replying with words, Caird's fingers teasing along her skin and raising gooseflesh on the inside of her ankle. "I left because I couldn't bear it anymore," she confessed, before she had fully decided on what she was going to say.

"My father..." and there she broke off. "No, never mind. It is neither your business nor your problem, and I shouldn't be placing my burdens on you."

She drank more of her wine instead.

"I'd like to hear it," he said, and whether or not he was lying, he sounded as though he meant it. "Sometimes even the telling is enough."

Whether it was the wine and the crackling of the fire, the tug and press of Caird's strong hands on her feet, or just the simple fact of his presence, somehow, tonight, it felt safe to speak.

"My father was fascinated with the life of Herr Mozart," Grace began, for that was the simplest way to describe it. "And he fixated on the notion that by beginning a child in an art early, and enforcing strong discipline, any man could produce a prodigy. I was four when he first engaged a dancing master, and nine when I took to the stage. My days were spent in class, my evenings in performance."

Mr. Caird's hands stilled. "When did you ever have

time to simply be a child?" The note of horror in his voice was a surprise. Hers was hardly a unique story. Good parents sought the best for their children, and that sometimes meant driving them too hard, too fast.

"I think I was born old," she said, deflecting the question with a short, sharp laugh. "In any matter, my father was happy enough to book my time and pocket my earnings in return for my room and board. I eventually became tired of it all. I left Vienna against his wishes, and returned home to England."

That was a weak way of phrasing the fights and tantrums that had ensued, but none of that was anything she wished to relive.

"And until last month, that was the last time I danced."

"Not even for pleasure?" He began to move again, drawing firm circles with two fingers, over her instep and under it, around her anklebone and up, first one leg, then the other.

"There was no pleasure to be found in it."

"It must have held some for you once."

He was digging up things better left buried. Grace's head swam with a mixture of the wine and the heady, distracting pressure of his hands sliding up her calves, the muscles there just as tight and sore as her feet. "Once, of course. I could bring an audience to tears with the curve of my hand, become a dove, a fish, a fairy in the blink of an eye—tell a thousand stories with no words at all. The stage was the space where the world ended and I began."

Mr. Caird stroked down her calves, pressing the palm of his hand against the knotted muscle. She quivered inside, her mind flooded with the memory of those same talented hands in very different places. "That's phrased very prettily."

"I have friends who write," Grace snorted, shaking off the fit of melancholy. "Between them and the endless scripts for romances, some flowery poetry must have rubbed off."

"A hazard of the job?"

"Perhaps."

Something tugged at her wrapper, still lain across her shoulders, and Grace opened her eyes. She had closed them somewhere in the moments between words, only aware of the pressure of Caird's hands and the sound of his voice.

He had worked his way up her calves to the bulk of the muscle there, and he gently brushed the hem of her robe up toward her knees. She didn't stop him—more than that, she pointed her toe and let it brush against the inseam of his trousers. He twitched and made a sound like a sudden quick intake of breath.

"What about you?" she asked, cocking her head and watching him now, her toe resting ever-so-lightly on the seam in the fabric right at the top of his thigh.

"My job has plenty of hazards," he joked. "The top of which is beautiful actresses who revel in teasing."

"Uch," Grace scolded. "I mean your family. Or are you another wandering vagabond like the rest of us, with only the key to your wine cellar secreted about your person?"

He trailed his fingers up higher, around the back of her knee. She flinched at the tickle and he pressed the pad of his thumb to the same spot, more intense and not as irritating. "Alas, no such dramatics. My father came down from

Scotland as a young man, seeking his fortune. He married an English girl from a family of brewers, and she brought her recipe collection with her for a dowry. Now they run a tavern in Chelsea, where they regularly feed and water the worst nuisances among the art and music set."

He pursed his lips and glanced at the ceiling for a minute, as though choosing what to reveal next. "I have a sister, married to a solicitor and blissful in motherhood, and a brother still at home, and we all tumble along together in a happy sort of chaos."

It made a wonderful picture, full tables surrounded by friendly faces, the air filled with warmth and easy conversation. Her heart ached and she couldn't name the reason why.

"And what do they think of their laboring son?"

"It's better than the dockyards and safer than the Navy," he chuckled. "My mother is far more insistent on ending my unmarried state than forcing a change in career."

"True; you must be an old man by now," Grace teased, trying in her mind to calculate. He was about her age, surely, with the confidence that experience brought.

"Twenty-nine, not so young that I'll commit foolishly to the first pair of beautiful brown eyes," he said, looking into hers with an intensity that made her flush warm. "But old enough. I mark you at twenty-seven years, if my arithmetic is correct."

"It is," she said curtly. If he was looking for marriage and children, that alone surely put her far out of the running. Assuming she even wanted that, which she didn't. Family was more trouble than benefit, at least for a woman.

"Tell me. In all that those twenty-seven years, have you ever known love?" His voice went deep and dark, all laughter replaced by a new intensity that shot like a lead ball straight through her gut. Embers flared inside her, desire awakened by this new side of him.

She sat up, drawing her leg out of his hands. The heat left her, cold rushing in to fill the void where his touch had been. "I've had lovers, yes. We established that before." She probably sounded more nettled than she felt, but what had that got to do with anything?

"That's not what I asked," he said cryptically. He unfolded himself from his comfortable lounge in the corner of her couch, rising to his feet.

"Mr. Caird." It was a warning and a plea for answers together.

"At this point could we not be Isaac and Grace?" He held out his hand.

Why not?

Because it's dangerous, that's why.

He hasn't hurt me yet.

Why give him the chance?

She'd had this same argument with herself at the school, or a very similar one, about Miss Mayes and friendship. She'd dipped her toe in the water there and not been scalded. She could try this, too. "Isaac and Grace? Are we sweethearts, then, to be using Christian names?"

Grace put her hand in his and let him draw her to her feet.

"You're thinking too much again," he teased. "Friends, to be sure. Lovers, if you'll have me." He stepped in so that there was barely a handspan between them, her eyes at the level of his shoulders. There was his scent again, something cinnamon and sweet.

Her heart pounded hard, trying to escape from her chest.

She had barely touched him, before, only to give him some pleasure and learn how he felt in her hands. Now he was here in her domain, they were alone together. There was no reason in the world not to reach out, flatten her hands against his chest, and feel the heat of his body beneath the wool and linen that clung to him like a second skin.

It was like touching a stone wall, one that drew in a ragged breath when she put her hands on him, his blood pulsing near the surface of his skin. Firm, strong, unyielding—everything she tried to be inside.

Grace rose up on the balls of her feet, the stretch along her arches a gentle pull and not the tight agony it had been before Caird—before *Isaac's*—ministrations. His mouth yielded to hers when she brushed her lips against his.

This was still more of an experiment than anything else. She pressed her hands against his chest, her mouth against his, close-lipped and tender.

His hands came around her and supported her, one splayed wide across the small of her back. "Isaac, then," she said as she withdrew, falling back to flat feet. The embers of desire in her belly sparked back to life, a rushing flame that left her breathless. What would he do?

"Grace," he murmured with delight, as though she had given him a precious gift. "Gracious graceful Grace-"

"Watch yourself, or I'll change my mind," she said

sharply, and he pressed his lips tightly together, his eyes dancing with delight.

"I'd rather watch you," he offered, and his voice was sinking again, into that register that went with his eyes growing darker and the movements of his body more deliberate.

He set his hands on her shoulders, the broad palms almost covering them. She shivered when he slid his hands down her arms, a caress that ended with his hands on her hips.

And then he kissed her properly, tipping his head to seize her mouth with his. This kiss was nothing like the test of a moment ago—he was stone beneath the sensual fullness of his lips, his fingers splayed out and drawing her hips close in to his body. "So beautiful," he murmured against her lips. "Let me see all of you."

She could never remember what she said to him in that moment other than a hushed "yes," but it must have been reasonable and less foolish than that sounded. Because his hands tightened on her and he kissed the side of her neck, up to her ear and back down again to her shoulder, little presses of his mouth that were echoed in the fluttering low in her belly.

He let go of her only long enough to slip the bow that tied her wrapper closed, pushing the light fabric from her shoulders and letting it fall to puddle on the floor.

For a moment Grace regretted the simple white morning dress she'd flung on when she returned home, but the way Isaac looked at her, at the line of contrast where the cotton met her dark skin, the hunger in his eyes—*never mind. I regret nothing.*

It took a moment for him to discover her lacings, tucked down the back, and draw them open.

She slipped her hands beneath the lapels of his coat, ran them over the swells and lines of his muscles, his shoulders, down his arms. She skimmed her hands over the linen that held the heat of his skin, drawing his coat off his arms and tossing it over the back of the couch.

Waistcoat next, the buttons easy, as he pulled the last of her lacings free. The rest of her clothes followed suit, stays and chemise joining her dress and wrapper on the floor.

Grace skimmed her hand over Isaac's bulge, purely to see the look in his eye when she touched him, fire and need and an exhale escaping. She left his trousers on.

Naked now, she shivered, less from the cold than from the openness of it all. He cupped her breasts in his hands, bent his head and pressed reverent kisses against each one, then ran his tongue around the dark brown circles of her nipples. They pulled up tight and he chased them with his mouth, each contact another spark of pleasure that drove the evening chill away.

He picked her up, hoisting her into his arms. Her legs hiked around his waist in pure reflex, her body jolting with the surge of desire and need for the hard body riding against her core.

He locked his forearms beneath her bottom to hold her in place, but instead of kissing her or touching her as he had before, he took the handful of steps across the small room to the screened-off area that concealed her bed.

She propped herself up on her elbows and frowned. "You're up to something."

"That I am," he answered cheerfully, then leaned over her and tugged her scarf-knot free. The soft green silk slipped from her forehead, puddling on the pillow on either side of the dent where her head had been.

A handful of her loose curls fell across her eyes and she blew a puff of air up at them to move them out of her way. He extended a careful finger and brushed them aside, not disrupting the curl.

The silk, though; he wrapped that around his hands, let the scarf slip between his fingers. It had been one of Mrs. Byrne's scraps, a piece from a hem Grace had laid claim to years ago. Against his golden skin it took on a different sort of look—daring, exciting, full of unnamed promises. She shivered, unaccountably.

Isaac set his knee on the bed and gently, softly, pushed her back until she lay supine again. He covered her mouth with his, a careful, probing kiss that sent wings fluttering in her stomach. His tongue tasted her lips and she opened to him, drowning in the heat.

He smiled against her skin. "Do you trust me?"

Chapter Ten

"Do you trust me?" he asked, his eyes still closed and his lips hovering so close to hers that she could feel the shape of the words as well as hear them.

"Yes?" she replied, her hesitation partly from the surge of fear curling up her spine, and partly out of habit.

He drew his thumb down her lower lip to her chin, pausing with the pad right on the point of her jaw. Their eyes locked and his were earnest, the softness from before replaced with a look of naked and vulnerable desire.

"Like before, I'll give you everything. Whatever you want to do in return, I'll accept, even as I burn." That last was said on an agonized breath, as if he hadn't intended to let it slip out. One look proved it though, his fall-fronts already bulging with his desire—his desire for *her*. "A single word from you and I stop."

And what could she say to that kind of plea? It was so far beyond her experience that Grace couldn't find the right words—or any at all.

"You haven't started yet," she pointed out instead, shying away from the feelings lodged inside her breast.

He laughed, low and long, tightening the silk scarf in

his hands. "Impatience will get you nowhere." Kneeling over her, he claimed a searing kiss that curled her toes. Her hips rose despite herself, the sweet spot between her thighs begging for contact, touch, anything like what he had done to her—for her—before.

Isaac's hands pressed gently on her arms, guiding them up above her head. The scarf came next, his touch so deft and light that she barely felt him tie it around her wrists.

Tugging against the fabric made her bed frame rattle, the scarf looped around a single bedpost. The end of the scarf lay within easy reach of her fingers, the knot tied so she could unlock it with a single pull.

"One word," he promised again. He trailed his fingertips across her lips; she let them part and tasted his finger. Wine and salt. She curled her tongue around it and drew him deeper. Isaac groaned, slowly sliding his fingers from her mouth. "Assuming *I* survive the night."

"If you're good, I might allow you to." She teased him on impulse, a way to fight the aching emptiness of vulnerability, the tight compression of excitement and fear combined. She saw the change in his face the moment the words left her lips.

His eyes went wide, his lips parted, and he let out a breath that shuddered down to his toes.

The surge of power that hit her with his look of wonder and awe was almost as delicious as the way he trailed his spit-slick fingers down her body, a heated trail that turned to cool shivers when he followed with his breath.

She twisted her hands, a test, but the silk held.

"Worried about my knotting skills?" he laughed

against her stomach, a warm vibration that moved southward with his questing mouth.

"Even you must be bad at *something*. I'll find it one day."

He kissed her hip, bit, raising goose bumps and shivers. His breath played warm over her nethers—surely any minute now he would begin to kiss her there, and she would know the feel of his mouth.

Isaac shifted on the bed below her, skipping the join of her thighs entirely to move back up the other side of her body, the hand not holding him up cupping her breast. *What now?*

What now turned out to be an assault unlike any she had known before, Isaac's mouth and hands playing a delicate symphony upon her body. He teased and tormented, now his mouth on her breasts, sucking at her nipples and rolling them upon his tongue; now his hands stroking up her thighs, circling closer and closer and never, *ever* touching the places where she burned.

Agony, the anticipation of pleasure that built and built without release, every inch of her skin tingling as he passed over it. She strained against the silk bonds, snug around her wrists. The pull grounded her, kept her safe, returning her to the moment.

He teased, flicking the tip of his tongue across the nub that throbbed in time with her heart. She forced herself to hold still, hide the way he slowly took her apart.

If he knew how much she needed this, he would stop.

The darting, satin heat of his mouth was gone, and he ran his hands up along her sides. "You've had to be strong for so long," he murmured into her skin. "Let me take some of your burden away."

Grace should have said something witty, something cutting, so he knew she was still in control—but when she opened her mouth to speak all that came out was a strangled sort of sob. He cupped her buttocks and lifted her to meet his mouth. She pulled on the silk, arched her back to press against him, get more, and always he moved just out of reach, flickering touches not enough, never enough.

"*Please*," Grace begged. She clutched at the silk wrapping her wrists, tangled her fingers in the taut line.

He slipped his fingers inside, one, no, two, an invasion that pressed her open. His thumb and his mouth stroked hard against her pleasure. She was undone, unmade.

"Please!" she cried out again, then she was lost. Her orgasm rolled over her in waves, each crest building on the last, ripping through her body like a storm-whipped tide. Each time she imagined it was done he kept going, his fingers crooked and pressing against something deep inside, his mouth unrelenting through every tremor and spasm.

Finally, she collapsed. He set her hips down on the bed again, his hands so gentle where a moment ago they had been instruments of the wickedest sort of torture.

Her head ached, throbbing with the release of tension that had been building for what must have been her whole life. Never had she felt such peace inside her buzzing mind, never felt her limbs so languid and heavy. He moved, and a moment later the silk fell loose around her hands. She left her hands up, her fingers tangled loosely in the soft fabric as her heart gradually returned to its normal pace.

The bed dipped beside her, Isaac sitting there. He still bulged, thick and heavy behind his fall-fronts, but he didn't reach for himself. He took one of her hands in his and drew it to him.

Here we go. My penalty. The rush of disappointment was brimming, then—then, the strange and confusing man, he started to rub his thumbs in circles over her wrists.

He smoothed her skin, as though checking for injury or pressure marks. He finished his thorough caress and moved to her other hand, his bottom lip caught in his teeth and his shoulders and back still gleaming with a faint sheen of sweat.

I don't understand him.

But I do like him.

That thought, plus the flutter of desire that stirred to life at the sight of his naked torso, spurred her on to action. She sat up and he let her have her hand back before leaning in to press kisses across her mouth. "You have no idea how beautiful you look, just like that."

"Bound for you?" she asked, because she couldn't avoid it.

"No, for *you*," he replied, and brought his hand up to cup the side of her face. He kissed her with a fierce desperation that had to be eating him inside, his body yearning for hers even as he held himself in check.

The tension in his shoulders and the faint tremble in his arms betrayed him, his kiss insistent. Grace returned it, the warm simmer in her belly sparking softly, his skin smooth under her fingers. "Lie back," she ordered, pushing him lightly in those powerful shoulders.

"You don't need to—"

"I want to." And that much was very true. He was a sculpture carved from wood and honey, nipples dark against his skin. "You were a good boy," she purred, the memory of his reaction from earlier firing ideas that would have made her blush only yesterday.

Isaac groaned and fell back against the bedclothes, reaching for her. "What do you plan to do with me?"

"Only what you've earned." She avoided his touch, slipping off the bed. He rolled up onto his elbow and watched her as she moved to take a wooden box down from the shelf. She didn't have cause to use it often enough to keep it in easy reach, but the vial of oil inside the box was still there.

Opening the box gave her that thrill down her back that came with fear. Only the oil came out for now, slick and sweet-smelling when she tipped a few drops out on her hands.

Placing her hands on his chest woke the banked fire inside. She traced the lines of his muscles, the oil smoothing out her passage down his body. He folded his hands behind his head and watched her, heavy-lidded, his lip caught between his teeth once more.

She lowered her mouth to his stomach and tasted his skin, the salt of his sweat, the sweet tang of the oil, the musk of sex and lust that wreathed him. An accidental brush of her elbow made him groan and jerk his hips up, his eyes wide.

Oil might have been a mistake at this stage, his buttons slippery between her fingers, but the slow reveal made it better for her, anticipation tingling. Worse for him, his thighs trembling with the effort of holding still. But soon enough she had him unwrapped, a present that she would never admit she'd been waiting for.

His cock arched toward his stomach, proud, thick, and dark. She put her hand to it and he groaned, wrapped her fist around it and he cried out, thrusting into her oil-slick palm. His foreskin rode along the fat length of him, and he pushed faster until she let go and he cried out in frustration.

"Patience," she told him, the surge of power coming back again, different than orgasm but almost as good. "I'll tell you when you're allowed."

"Bloody *hell*," he swore, starry-eyed.

She straddled him, her hands roaming free across his body. *Beautiful*, she kept thinking; *so beautiful.*

Flattening herself against him to reach his mouth with hers might have been a mistake, at least as far as her self-control was concerned. His cock pushed against her belly and the fire rose within her again, driven by the slick-slap sound of their bodies moving together as he rocked his hips with urgent need. She pulled back, as he'd done, and the curses spilling from his lips were her reward. "Please," he asked, but without nearly enough urgency.

"Not yet."

They fit together better when she pushed herself upright again, moved forward and settled so that the base of his prick and his balls were caught between their bodies. There, there—she wrapped her hand around him again, her palm sliding slick across his heated skin.

Isaac groaned, grabbing for her thighs and holding

171

tight. She stroked him and he thrust up into her hand, finding a shared rhythm as easily as breathing.

It was hard to see where his body ended and hers began, his cock rising from the space between them. It could be hers, this way, a missing limb slotted back where it should have been. She could feel the motion of her own hand this way, when he thrust into the circle of her fingers— his hips rocking hard against hers and the base of his cock giving friction.

It was hers in this moment, so essential and *right*, every movement and twitch dragging sensation out of her as well. She moved against him, stroked him, used every trick she knew to heighten the desperately tightening pressure coiling deep inside.

His brow furrowed, lines drawn between his brows; he looked more in pain than ecstatic and that didn't make sense at all. Until she remembered—he was trying to do her bidding.

"Now." She tried to infuse the phrase with the sound of command. "Now you may."

He cried out, arched, his fingers digging into her thighs so fiercely that it might bruise, his body shaking itself apart. He came, his emissions white against the dark skin of his stomach, pearling in the black hair on his belly, hot and wet between her fingers.

Grace followed him over the edge, cock in hand, taking her pleasure from him as he held her tight against the world.

Isaac's prick was softening slowly by the time she let him go and rose from the bed. He made a soft noise and reached out as though to stop her, but the jug of water and her washbasin were close at hand.

She didn't need to go far, the cool water refreshing when she splashed it against her face. Droplets fell, glistening and chill, on the slopes of her breasts, her hands wet and cold even after toweling off.

Now what? When they had done this before, she had been in his space and had been able to take her leave whenever she pleased. Now he was in her home, and she had nowhere else to go.

Grace snuck a peek over her shoulder.

Isaac lay sprawled on her bed, a golden Adonis in repose. He watched her, black eyes glittering in the firelight, shadows lying deep along the sinuous lines of his muscles. His cock lay soft and spent against his thigh, a subtle gleam on his skin from the oil she'd used to ease his way and his trousers pushed down to just above his knees.

As awkward as this was bound to become, she found she had no urge to make him leave. Instead she crossed back to the bed with the damp towel, intending to pass it over his prick and his chest, clean away the evidence of their tryst.

He yelped when the towel touched him, flinching away. "That's cold!" he laughed, encircling her wrist with one of his broad hands. "First you order me about, then you try to freeze me. I've uncovered your wicked plan." He claimed the towel from her, then drew his trousers back up about his hips.

"You didn't seem to think it so wicked a moment ago," she replied, and this time let the smile come. Grace took the chance. She stretched out beside him on the bedcovers, her head propped up upon one hand. "You were the one who began the game, as I recall."

"I should know better than to dish out what I might not be able to take in return." He kissed her and she could taste her own heady musk on his lips.

"Remember that," she said incautiously, her body relaxed and at peace for once, no terrors or anxieties nibbling at the edges of her mind. "For a later date."

"Ah yes." He seemed unconvinced. "The prick you keep in a box?"

Grace laughed, and then considered the image they would make together. Him prone before her, she on her knees behind, the ribbon of her toy snug about her hips, his back a serpentine curve of brown muscle and strength. "Sauce for the gander, my dear Mr. Caird."

He traced the curve of her cheek with one finger, his touch as gentle and as sure as ever. "I thought we were beyond Mister and Miss."

"When it suits the moment."

He arched an eyebrow, trailing his fingers along her neck, her shoulder, down to her ribs and along the curve of her waist and hip. "This is a moment for Grace and Isaac," he declared and, reaching out, tugged her down and against his chest. His steady, strong arms came about her, folding her into his body and his protection.

She should object, roll away and dress, tell him to remove himself from the premises so that she could retie her scarf around her hair and go to sleep.

Lying there, the fire's golden glow sliding warm across their bodies, dark and darker, walnut and ebony, she couldn't even summon up the energy to move.

Secure or powerful; fragile, cherished or triumphant, the feelings muddled up together until the edges all bled together. Nothing was settled between them, nothing named, except this—right now, in this instant, all was well.

Drifting on the soft rhythmic sound of his breathing, the faint lump-thump of his heart beneath her ear, the sweet smell of him and the warmth that surrounded her, it was no wonder that Grace lost sense of passing time. Tucked there, beneath Isaac's chin, skin-to-skin and cocooned in his arms, the world itself seemed to pause and give them space simply to *be*.

Eventually the fire burned low in the grate, the room slipping into darkness, and Isaac moved.

"I should be off," he said softly, pressing tender lips to her forehead, "and let you back to your solitude. I've imposed on your hospitality."

She had been floating in the space between dreams and waking, and the low rumble of his voice brought her out of that peaceful place. "Only insomuch as I allowed it." The admission of her complicity was an open weak point, one he ignored.

"Nevertheless." He rose, his hand in contact with her as long as possible before he moved away, searching for his discarded clothes. "Unless you'd rather I stay the night. Though I have no extra clothes. Perhaps you might lend me a shirt?" He was teasing, the wretch, though for a moment she might have imagined him serious.

"My clothes wouldn't fit you, you strapping brute."

She sat and drew her knees up to shield her nudity from the room.

"Sometimes I wonder why they fit you," he said, then seemed to catch himself.

The moment of reckoning. She should have known it would come. Everyone demanded it sometime, an answer to a question she didn't always know how to word, even to herself. Peace overflowed into melancholy, and Grace settled her chin onto her knees. "Do you ever look at yourself and see someone else? No, not *else*—still yourself—but different than what the world believes you to be?"

Isaac didn't recoil, nor look at her with confusion. Instead a half-smile grew, rueful and somehow kind. "Sometimes. Though I'd wager not in the way you mean it."

"Probably not, no."

A moment later he had crossed back to her with her wrapper, and set it gently about her shoulders. *Why?* she wanted to ask. *Why are you kind and gentle, why do you joke when my choices flout the laws of God and man? What do you gain by all of this?*

Instead she caught herself leaning into his touch, the gentle caress of a single finger down her cheek. "I don't understand you." She settled for that declaration.

"And you are the most confounding miss I've ever set eyes upon," he answered cheerfully, sliding his shirt over his head. "So in that we are equally yoked."

"If you can't be serious, we should talk about something else."

"As you wish." He cast about looking for something,

and she kicked his boot towards him. "Ah, there it is. We should be ready to test the flying wire in rehearsal in a day or two," he offered.

That was a safer subject by far. "So soon?" There was a thrill of fear, of course, at the prospect. But then, she had trusted him this far.

"I need to do some testing first, to be sure it will hold up under strain of movement, but other than that I believe it's ready."

She rose from the warmth of the bed, tightening her wrap around herself, and moved to stoke up the fire to something more useful in the dark of night. "How do you plan to do that? Wear it yourself and dance across the stage?"

Isaac's laugh was a rush of joy, wrapping around her like a quilt warm from airing in the summer sun. "Thankfully for my audience, no—I must be at the other end to hold the ropes securely. I was considering strapping Tottenham in it, or Colby. If it holds either of those two lummoxes safely, it'll bear your pretty weight with no strain at all." He straightened up, boots on and waistcoat neatly buttoned once more.

"Now there's a terrifying notion. You should sell tickets at the door."

"We'd make a fortune and the Surrey's coffers would overflow," he replied cheerfully, before setting his arms around her waist and swinging her into an embrace, and then a kiss. "Until tomorrow, Mistress Grace, and a good night's rest for us both."

"Until tomorrow," she said, and surprising herself,

slipped her arms about his neck to return the hug.

He left, whistling, obviously terribly pleased with himself. She sat for a while by the fire, a cooling cup of tea in her hand, until it was reduced once more to embers.

Then, and only then, she took herself to bed.

Isaac caught himself humming on his way home, his feet lighter than air. The tavern off the Chelsea Road beckoned cheerfully to him, the lights twinkling in the windows as Isaac leapt neatly from the back step of the mail coach and headed for the narrow stone stairs. Grace, *his* Grace—she had all but said it, with her body if not with her words. That angel he had seen from across the stage, she who had led him in such a merry chase, had let him make love to her and she to him.

There were a great many other things he was in mind to try with her. One day he would know what it was like to slide into the sheath of her body, to move with her in that most ancient of dances, to make her a part of his soul. But he had plenty of time yet to earn her trust.

Laughter and the buzz of conversation spilled out from the open doors to the front room, but Isaac slipped around the side instead. He'd cleaned up as best he could at Grace's home, but a clean shirt would make all the difference to his appearance. His reputation could take a few stings—hers shouldn't have to.

The back hall was clear. He took a moment to work off his boots, damp and muddy on the bottom from his homeward trek, and hang his hat.

Mistake.

When he straightened up again, his mother stood between him and the stairs, her apron on and her arms folded.

"Mmhm," she said, looking him up and down.

Isaac nodded nonchalantly to try and throw her off the scent. "Mother. Good evening to you."

She wasn't buying it, her irritated frown not budging. "Who is she?"

"Who?" Isaac asked, all innocence. He edged slowly toward the stairs.

"Don't give me that." His mother scoffed, her pale blue eyes staring daggers at him. "Who birthed you and raised you, may I ask? You're a terrible liar, child of mine, and no better at keeping secrets."

"What, me?" he tried again, but the stubborn set of her jaw was all too familiar. He saw a darker version of it in the mirror on occasion. "Fine. As you will drag an answer from me—she is a friend. A dear friend, nothing more." *Yet.*

"She must be a very *dear* friend indeed, to send you home looking like you've just been fished out of a rubbish tip," his mother shot back, and…had she just made an innuendo? *His* mother?

"I'm a laboring man, dearest mam. You can't expect me to return home smelling of rosewater and cognac." Two more steps toward the stairs. Almost past her now—

She put her hand on the newel post at the bottom of the banister, effectively blocking his escape. "Are you keeping a mistress?"

And he had no pithy answer for that one. Technically,

one could call Grace his mistress, in that they were unmarried. But he was hardly *keeping* her. And they weren't precisely *courting*. That is to say, he had an inclination toward it, but mentioning such a thing now would be more likely to scare her into the wind forever.

"No," he settled on after a moment too long had passed. "She keeps herself quite neatly, thank you very much." Mother was going to launch into a lecture at any moment now—he knew that look in her eye from long experience. He moved in to embrace her, setting his hands beneath her elbows. Petite as she was, he lifted her up and out of his way, kissed the top of her head as she sputtered, and mounted the stairs two at a time.

"Isaac!"

He paused, halfway up, and looked down. "Yes?"

"I want to meet her. You'll bring her by."

He couldn't begin to imagine the carnage that would be the result of giving Grace an order like that. "I don't think that would be wise," he demurred. "Not at present." Not until he'd managed to convince her that she was better off with him, than without.

"Why ever not? I want to meet the women in my sons' lives. Unless you're *ashamed* for us to meet her." There was that set to her jaw again, and the glint in her eye.

Father often called Catherine Caird a force of nature, Colin named her as stubborn as a bull. But Isaac was her son in temperament as well as blood. He returned her gaze measure for measure. "Not in the slightest. Perhaps I'm worried more about her meeting *you.*"

Her eyes lit up. What leeway had he accidentally

given? "Since I'm determined to approve of her, that won't be a problem. We'll see you both for tea on Saturday."

"But—"

"Are you actually saying that you're ashamed of your own mother? Isaac Caird, how could you!"

Her eyes were wide with horror that didn't entirely seem feigned, and he caught himself trying to take it back before he hurt her feelings for real. "Mother, no. That's not what I meant!"

Like the sun coming out from behind a passing cloud, she beamed at him brightly. "In that case, Saturday, at half past one, and don't you dare be late."

Damn it.

"Now go and change your clothes before you give Mrs. Sedgewick a fright."

Freed, Isaac headed for his room, already stripping off his too-warm coat. Closing his door behind him gave him privacy once more. He could wash and change, then… then he had to decide how to tell Grace that she was expected at his parents' home for tea.

Exactly what his mother had been angling for.

Blast and feather her, she did it again!

With two such stubborn, irascible, *hard-headed* women in his life, how was a man supposed to stay on an even keel?

On the other hand, putting the two of them in the same room could be highly entertaining. Assuming I'm out of the line of fire.

Or perhaps it would be better to hie himself down to

the docks and book passage for two to India. Or Spain. Or Lower *Canada*. Anywhere would do, as long as he was out of arm's reach by Saturday afternoon.

The mist-moon night was chilly for early summer, dampness lingering in the air. It made for an uncomfortable walk, but an excellent excuse for Lucy to pull her cloak hood forward and hide her face from anyone who might pass her in the street. The roll of papers she clutched to her chest made for an odd shape, but no one so far had come close enough to notice.

She would not be spotted—and if she were, she had excellent excuses prepared. This was destiny playing out its hand, her cards falling on the table as they had been read.

Number seven, Osiris Triumphant. Rebirth after disappointment, triumph over enemies.

The moon hung gibbous overhead, Venus already set and the rest of the stars in good alignment. It was an auspicious night for risk.

A dog barked as a group of raucous young men tumbled by, cheering and laughing, an older woman crossing the street to put distance between herself and them. The thrill of the night lifted Lucy's feet, the excitement of plans coming together giving her wings. The lit windows of the public house were a clarion call, and she hurried toward the old wooden door.

He was there, waiting at the table farthest from the window, a dark coat covering his clothes and a water-stained wide-brimmed hat tossed carelessly on the chair.

It went against her better instincts to enter the room quietly and without drawing all the eyes she could, but this was a clandestine meeting. The less she was recognized, the better.

"Watch yerself, luv," the greasy-haired serving wench scolded, and Lucy hurried to the back of the room. She stood by the chair and waited. He stared up at her, drumming his fingers on the table impatiently.

"Well?" he said after a minute, his voice thick from the smoke curling out of the pipe by his elbow.

She gave a pointed look at the hat sitting on the seat of the empty chair, and after a moment more of the face-off, he removed the hat with a sweeping and sarcastic flourish.

"Thank you," Lucy said, though gratitude was hardly the purpose, and settled herself into her proper place.

"Do you have it?" he asked, leaning forward, his elbows rude upon the table.

"Here." She drew the tube out from under her arm, unrolling the pages across the table. The fine lines of Mr. Caird's designs were only half-visible in the dim light, but her companion seemed fascinated, rising out of his chair and spreading ink- and oil-stained hands across the papers as he traced out the patterns she couldn't understand.

"They're all here?"

"Everything I could find. That, and this." The green notebook joined the papers on the table. "It should be enough to serve your purpose."

He nodded, the first sign of approval he'd made. "You've done well." It was good to hear some recognition, considering what she'd had to go through so far! Struck from her place in the comedy, relegated to an unnamed witch in the chorus, her natural talents dismissed, her concerns ignored. But here was someone who *appreciated* her ambition.

He rolled the pages back up again and tucked the long scroll inside his coat. A small bag of coin came out from some hidden pocket in that same coat, and he pressed it into her hand. "For the notebook, and the diagrams. I'll contact you the usual way once I've set my plans." Air whistled between his teeth to punctuate his sentence as he rose to his feet.

"As you like," Lucy replied, rising as well. "My only care is that you deliver on your end of the bargain."

He took his pipe and stuck it into the corner of his mouth, puffing away. "Have no fear, dear girl. You will be well cared for, as long as you do your part."

"Then we are in agreement," Lucy nodded serenely, ignoring the smoke wreath he sent out to circle her face. "Good night to you."

"And to you."

The tingle ran through her again, excitement making prickles on her fingertips. Elliston controlled her destiny no longer.

Chapter Eleven

Grace should have been sore the morning after her tryst, considering. Instead her legs felt loose, the muscles in her calves relaxed and her feet only tender in the raw spots, and not deep down into her bones.

Lucy joined her on her walk to the theatre, running lightly down the stairs from her lodgings, green bonnet ribbons flying. She tucked her arm securely into Grace's, the soft shush-shushing sounds of their skirts brushing together the metronome of their walk. "You're looking rather well this morning," Lucy greeted her, green eyes sparkling.

"I slept well," Grace replied simply. There was no reason not to trust Lucy. Her reluctance was because she wanted to hold it close and quiet a little while longer. At least until she knew what words to use for the feelings taking up lodgings inside her ribs. That answer seemed to satisfy Lucy, since she kept up a stream of innocuous chatter all the way along the row to the dance school.

The sky arched blue above them, trees in the small garden on the corner rustling in their brilliant greenery. Birds sang somewhere nearby, a faintly pastoral edge to a morning in the center of the city.

"And that's when Elliston said that if Bixby and Frederick didn't—and I quote directly—get their 'god-be-damned act together, there will be throats slit and blood spilled tonight!' He had a rather large knife in his hand when he said it, so do you know, I think he meant it!" Lucy laughed, a nervous edge to her mirth.

"At least in the moment," Grace agreed, her foot upon the bottom step of the school's stairs. Lucy didn't seem at all relieved. "Here's where I must say farewell. Are you rehearsing late today?"

"Until five, I believe, but then…" Lucy's attention was caught by something over Grace's shoulder, and her thoughtful expression turned first to wide-eyed surprise, then to a smile. "I do believe you have a visitor."

She did indeed, walking toward them as though he hadn't a care at all, his coat snug across his shoulders. She knew what he looked like beneath it now: the acres of firm muscle that responded to her touch, his smooth, warm skin and the way he shivered under her fingertips, and the rest of him hidden away behind the tucks and folds of his waistcoat and trousers.

Isaac had a swagger in his step now that she either had not noticed before or that he was putting on for her benefit, a Bond Street Roll that proclaimed him a veritable cock of the walk.

"He's looking smug today," Lucy murmured, her dimple showing. "I wonder why *that* might be, hmm?"

"I have no idea what you mean," Grace murmured back, her cheeks flushing warm.

"Morning, ladies." Isaac nodded respectfully, his smile

merry and his warm brown eyes laughing. "Miss Owens, may I ask for the honor of a moment of your time?"

"You may," she replied, but kept her hand covering Lucy's where it rested on her arm, so that the other girl couldn't run and leave her alone with him.

Why am I nervous now, when I wasn't so tangled up yesterday?

Maybe it was because of the thoughts that had seeped into her mind when she'd woken in the middle of the night, that hour of restlessness between sleep and sleep when she'd stared at the ceiling and pondered the path her life was now taking.

She hadn't come up with any answers then, and she didn't have any better ones now.

Isaac didn't seem to notice her rapid-fire thoughts, joining them in their conversational space. "I was wondering, Miss Owens, if you would care to join me for tea tomorrow." The light in his eyes suggested that he found this whole thing more amusing than complicated, and she wished it were that easy. "My parents have invited me to bring you by."

"Call on your *parents*?" Grace blurted out, aghast. The notion struck through her, lightning-bright and terrifying.

Lucy, undaunted, flicked her handkerchief at Isaac and swatted him on the wrist. "You need to give a lady more advance warning than that, sirrah!"

"Why?" Isaac asked, and he had that look in his eye like he was about to tease her again. "There's no preparation she needs to make. Indeed, Miss Owens could not possibly become more beautiful than she is right now."

Grace sputtered, but Lucy's warm grip on her arm gave her something to hold on to and get her thoughts in order. "You're a flatterer and a flirt, and you should be ashamed of yourself." But she couldn't bring herself to frown.

"A flatterer, maybe, but never a cad," Isaac replied. "May I take that as a yes? I'll call on you at one, say, to escort you."

His *parents*? Never in their conversations had he suggested that he was so serious about their...whatever they might be...to include calling formally on his family, or even to engage in introductions. She was bubbling over with questions, even beyond "*why?*"—what to wear, what should she expect, who else would be there, how much had he told them about her? But with Lucy there, she could hardly ask them aloud. Not without spurring on further questions she had no interest in answering.

"Yes," Grace responded tentatively, and the look on his face was less "overjoyed" and more "realizing what he'd done". "But on one condition."

"Name it."

"You must tell me about them on the way over, so that I am not marching ignorant into the lion's den."

"Agreed," he said, too quickly, and once again Grace was left to wonder—what was she even agreeing *to?* "Until tomorrow afternoon, then. Miss Sullivan." He touched the brim of his hat and off he went, hands in his pockets and whistling something jaunty.

"Well now!" Lucy broke the silence, her bonnet brim hiding her eyes as she watched him go. "You've made yourself a conquest."

How well Lucy had phrased that, however unwittingly. Was Isaac the conquest Grace had made, or had Grace failed, *weakened* and made a conquered woman of herself?

She snorted instead, shaking her head and untangling her arm from Lucy's. "Don't be ridiculous. It will be something far more sensible than that. He needs to assure them that he isn't a molly, or perhaps there's an occasion for which he needs a friendly escort. He has a brother unmarried yet—perhaps this is some sort of event for him, an engagement, or—"

"Or perhaps he's told his parents that he's eloped as part of a plot to get his hands on an entailed inheritance, and now he needs to produce said bride," Lucy broke in, her dimple showing again as she teased Grace merrily.

"If that's the issue, he'll need to give me more than the length of the walk over to learn my lines." Grace smiled wryly. "In the meantime, I shall have to focus on the rehearsal I'm sure of. We will speak later."

"Oh yes," Lucy replied, turning to head off in the direction of the Surrey. "We most certainly will."

"It's not something I intended to talk about before we'd settled things," Isaac was saying, apologizing really, but Grace's heart wasn't in it.

"Before we'd settled what, precisely?" She sounded more peevish than she'd intended, even to her own ears, but she wasn't about to stand down. She toyed with the ribbon on the reticule she'd had to borrow from Meg—*Meg!*—in order to look more like a finer lady than she actually was. If only…

If only what? If only she had stayed a dancer and allowed her father to keep pocketing her earnings? She'd have no more pin money than she did now. Less, likely. And there would never have been the money for extra fripperies or fine gowns that would make her feel more at ease in the current disaster.

She could have said no, or closed the door in his face when he appeared on her stoop. And yet. Here she was, her natural curls set into artificial spirals that bounced around annoyingly in her peripheral vision. But Meg had produced the pretty golden confection of a silk dress from Grace's trunk and shaken it out, proclaiming it 'the very thing!'

At least she *believes that I can pretend to be respectable long enough to fool strangers.*

Would tavern-owners be the sort to believe that all actresses were prostitutes? Perhaps not, since Isaac himself worked in the theatre. There was no way to prove that she *wasn't*, excepting her own word. Even so, she *was* bedding their son without even the mention of an understanding.

And now she was showing up at their doorstep for tea.

For the moment, though, walking beside Isaac through the street on a sunny afternoon—she could almost forget that outside of their own little sphere, their professions were quite disdained. Her curls bounced beneath her bonnet, her kid gloves sat neatly on her hands, and the gentle fall of dainty silk clung and flowed around her body.

Her walking companion was in an excited state of nerves somewhere between happy and, if she had to guess, just as uncertain as she. When she had opened the door to him, Isaac had frozen in place and stared, as though he were at a loss for words, before bowing and kissing her hand. He was dressed neatly too, no shirtsleeves or burn-pocked waistcoat today.

No, Grace had the terrible suspicion that they made a rather smart pair at the moment, moving through Chelsea's busy streets as though they were its lord and lady.

Now Isaac pressed his lips together, offering his arm to her, though they had been walking next to each other perfectly amiably so far. "Before we'd settled whether or not we had the sort of acquaintanceship that requires introductions to parents or not."

"You seem to have decided that for me, considering."

"She caught me in a weak moment. I had full intentions of keeping your confidences—"

"Until caught in a moment of weakness?" Grace arched an eyebrow in his general direction.

He sighed. "You'll understand once you meet her."

That hardly inspired confidence. She took his arm, nevertheless, as they turned the corner and approached the tavern together.

She had half-expected the neat little house from Isaac's descriptions, the sign out the front fresh-painted, bright and cheerful. Window boxes filled with tidy rows of flowers made the Brewer's Arms look less like a tavern or public house, and more like some country bakery misplaced among the row houses and art studios of Chelsea.

The surprise came *inside*, once Isaac had swept open the door for her and led her down a sunlit hall. The woman who stood to greet her in the daintily furnished parlor was not the sort of person Grace had pictured at all.

"Mother, may I present Miss Grace Owens. Miss

Owens, my mother, Mrs. Caird."

What *had* she imagined? Someone strong and no-nonsense, with arms suited to rolling out pastry and kneading loaves, fingers thickened with dish-scrubbing and table-setting, the kind of laboring woman who populated the taverns and shops in Charing Cross. And dark—Grace had expected her to be dark. At least Isaac's shade, if not deeper-toned.

Mrs. Caird appeared to be none of those things.

Strong, possibly; she would have to be to have raised a son like Isaac. But her golden hair was the same as could be seen on half the girls of the *ton*, her skin fair and with only a few wrinkles at the corners of her eyes to suggest that she smiled. She wore a simple day dress in an indefinable shade of beige that only served to emphasize wrists as slim as Grace's and a frame still slender even after bearing children.

Oh.

Grace couldn't help it—her eyes flickered to Isaac's face, the comforting and familiar breadth of his nose, the warm and sultry gold of his skin. There *was* something of his mother there, she supposed, in the crinkles at the corners of his eyes, the shape of his mouth, the line of his chin.

"Thank you for the kind invitation, Mrs. Caird," Grace said as sweetly as she might. Falling back on Proper Manners soothed her nerves some. They were a script like any other, and acting was something she knew.

"The pleasure is mine, Miss Owens." Mrs. Caird's voice carried strength beneath it, a bread-and-butter warmth that was more in line with what Grace had expected. "My boys will forever chide me for interfering, but I do so like to know the important people in their lives. Please, do take a seat."

"Mother." Isaac kissed Mrs. Caird on the cheek and waited for the pair of women to sit before he claimed a place on the other end of the green-upholstered sofa from Grace. He was eyeing his mother warily, as though waiting for something unpleasant.

Mrs. Caird poured the tea from the tray set beside her, her hands swift and confident. There were calluses on her fingers when she handed Grace the cup, and a small red mark that looked like a healing burn. She had working hands after all. Was it odd that such a small thing could be comforting?

The tea poured and delivered, Mrs. Caird settled on the edge of her chair and balanced her cup carefully on her knee. "So, Miss Owens. I understand that you are an actress?"

Grace weighed her options. Protest that she was "not what you think" and reveal that the notion had even crossed her mind? Accept the term without considering the underlying meanings and implications? Or acknowledge that she was not, technically, that at all. Not at the moment.

Isaac raised an eyebrow at her, and she could almost hear his voice in her ear.

You're overthinking again.

"Yes, madam. At the Surrey this season, the Olympic Pavilion in previous years. Though I was originally trained as a dancer."

Does that make this better, or worse?

She wanted to be sprawled out in the Surrey's rehearsal

hall with colleagues about her, laughing and joking at the things that only resonated with others of their calling. Or at the school with Miss Mayes, gossiping about the dancers in the corps. Or home. Anywhere but here, under the steely-eyed interrogation of a little blonde slip of a woman who was supposedly—what had Isaac said?—an award-winning brewer?

Perhaps Grace was guilty of assumptions too.

"A dancer! Now I am even more cross with you for telling me so little, Isaac. He really has been tight-lipped, my dear, so you see I am working from almost nothing."

Isaac sighed in exasperation. "If you would not persist in pushing us about, you would learn all there was to know, once there *was* something to know, in due time."

"I waited two weeks past your time for you to make your appearance, my lad—don't think I intend to spend the rest of my life waiting for you to do anything else in a timely manner!" Mrs. Caird's expression of amused irritation was so similar to the one on Isaac's face that Grace had to bite the inside of her cheek to keep from laughing.

He is certainly his mother's son.

And that thought brought with it a wave of melancholy, but she beat it back. This was neither the time nor the place.

Isaac, meanwhile, had turned to her with a twinkle in his eye. "Now you see what I have been forced to endure."

"I am certain it has been a terrible trauma—for your mother." Grace replied, the dry rejoinder flying off her tongue before she could catch herself. Mrs. Caird didn't seem scandalized, though, when Grace snuck a look. Rather she was smiling and sipping at her tea, as though she regularly entertained guests who insulted her eldest son.

Isaac took it in stride, heaving a sigh. "I knew this would not end well."

"I think it's turning out quite nicely indeed," Mrs. Caird replied.

The door to the parlor opened and conversation halted—that is, Grace found herself momentarily anxious again, just as she had begun to relax. Isaac and his mother, however, greeted the man who entered with easy familiarity.

"Andrew, come in," Mrs. Caird partly rose from her chair, at least until the tall, broad-shouldered presence in the doorway waved at her to sit back down. "This is Miss Owens." And she fixed him with the kind of intense look that meant he was supposed to know Grace's name.

Grace rose automatically, as Isaac did beside her, and he gestured between the two of them as he made introductions. "My father, Mr. Andrew Caird. Father, Miss Grace Owens." And it was so simple, just like that, but somehow Grace felt as though she'd stepped into a play again; some comedy of manners where everyone was wealthy and polite, and tavern owners came to tea in pretty parlors, wearing nicely-tailored suits.

Andrew was the missing puzzle piece, a dark-skinned man of height enough to compensate for Mrs. Caird's petite size. His eyes were Isaac's as well, warm and brown, and he had white scattered in the kinks of hair at his temples and his tidily-groomed sideburns. "Well now," he said, a trace of the highlands still lingering in the roll of his words. "This is a pleasure." And he nodded to her in welcome.

She'd half-expected his voice to boom out from that

barrel-shaped chest, but there was a mellow rumble to his words that suggested a more even temper than all that. His eyes weren't as smiling, though, and that same uncertainty crackled sharp in the air.

"I thought you would be busy in the kitchen," Isaac said, then turned to Grace as he sat again. "I assumed he would be busy," he repeated, "or I would have said something."

"I'm never so busy that I'll pass up a chance for your mother's caraway cake." Mr. Caird—and it was odd to think of another man by that name—slipped a piece off the tray before them and for lack of a plate, balanced it on his hand.

Mrs. Caird sighed heavily and theatrically, took up a saucer, stood, and in short order lifted the cake, placed the saucer in his hand, deposited the cake on it again, and sat herself down, with nary a hair out of place. "Andrew, honestly. We have *company*."

"Ah, Cate. You can take the boy out of Scotland, but you can't take the Scot out of the boy." He chuckled quietly, not angry at the show of correction to his manners, and Grace felt something tight along her spine unwind.

Isaac leaned in, his fingertip brushing against her arm. "There's nothing to be afraid of," he murmured softly, as though he'd seen her reactions, as though he'd understood. How could he, when she couldn't begin to understand it herself?

Mr. Caird settled himself in the armchair, balancing his plate and cake upon his knee. "Now that we're settled, tell me something of yourself, Miss Owens. 'Owens' is a Welsh name, is it not?"

That was an unexpected turn, but something of a welcome one. Grace nodded, and the last of her anxieties slipped away. "It is, though my family is not." Mrs. Caird smiled and nodded, and there was something so calm and welcoming in her, in this sweetly decorated room, that Grace kept talking.

"My father's parents were freedmen, and my grandfather worked with a group of Quakers in the American colonies. The Society of Friends secured him employment with their compatriots in Wales before the war began, and he was able to bring my grandmother—his wife. My mother used to tell stories about distant family still in Barbados, but of course that cannot be proved."

She ran out of air, then. Isaac was regarding her with an odd expression, something more than the admiration and appreciation she had begun to enjoy.

"Yes, of course it cannot—but what an adventure that would be some day, once more nations have caught up with England and such categories as 'freedmen' or 'slave' are unimaginable distinctions." Mrs. Caird reached over and refilled Grace's cup without asking. "My aunt Darby married a Quaker—now *that* caused quite the scandal! You remember Aunt Darby, don't you?" She directed that question at her husband and he nodded, a grimace flashing across his face for a moment.

"Your father's eldest sister? The one who was always talking about horses," Mr. Caird said, with an air of faint exasperation.

"That's her, precisely. Father would have absolutely none of her 'thee'ing and 'thou'ing all over the place. Terrible shame that the Quakers don't drink, mind you—she used to make an exquisite cordial. Though I always did better fancy her scones."

Mrs. Caird narrowed her eyes at Grace for a moment. "Are you Quaker yourself?"

Grace shook her head. "No, madam. I was baptized Church of England. My father never had much use for plain dress."

Isaac's mother nodded, apparently satisfied. "It would be awkward if you were, what with the tavern being the family business and all."

He should have known better than to relax. Family history had seemed like a safe topic when his parents had broached it, and offered him the opportunity to sit back and enjoy the scene spread out in front of him. Grace, her yellow gown turning her into a shaft of golden sunlight, sat demurely among all the trappings of Isaac's youth.

She may have been poised and cool on the outside, but Isaac knew how hot he could make her blood run. The contrast was enough to make his heart beat a little faster, imagining her moving through his world, settling in to his daily routines and he into hers as naturally as she seemed right now.

Until his mother had to steer the conversation around to *hinting* again.

"I hardly think that's something worth discussing at this juncture," he said pointedly. "Since both Miss Owens and I are gainfully employed in the theatre. Not to mention—" and there he trailed off, with an apologetic look at Grace. *Forgive me for this.* "It is not a point of contention."

His father's eyebrows went up and the look he gave Isaac meant that Isaac was going to be hearing about this moment, possibly at length and high volume. He'd told Grace that there was nothing to be afraid of in this house, and he would stand by that until the end of his days. But his father's lack of temper didn't mean that he lacked strong opinions as well.

Grace filled the sudden and awkward silence that followed. "I have tasted some of your wine, Mrs. Caird. Mr. Caird—Isaac, that is—was kind enough to share a bottle. I am no connoisseur, but I found it to be of excellent make."

Isaac's mother's smile at Grace was a little thinner than before, most of her energy going into a glare aimed at her son. "I should have you back later in the evening, when we might better enjoy a glass. We do tend to take our evening meals rather late, mind you, owing to the hours we keep for the tavern."

"My own tend toward the fashionable as well, through necessity rather than preference," Grace replied, her hands still around the cooling cup, and her ankles crossed beneath her. Did her stillness mean anger, or acceptance? Isaac might never know. "Perhaps one night after a show?"

His mother nodded slowly, her expression thoughtful. "Yes, that might work nicely."

The mention of the show gave Isaac the opening he needed to reenter the conversation and the rest of the call whiled away on theatre stories and easy talk of scripts and audiences.

The clock finally chimed the hour, not nearly quickly enough for Isaac's tastes, and his parents would be called back to the kitchen any moment to begin preparations for the evening. He was mildly surprised that Colin hadn't managed an excuse to stick his head in and take a look, but he had to be grateful for the small mercies. His parents weren't about to show him any larger ones.

"Tell me, Miss Owens, do you play at cards?"

His case made in a single point. Isaac paused, his hand held out for Grace to take so he might help her out of her chair. "Mother?"

"I do, on occasion," Grace replied. She set her hand in his though didn't lean on him at all, rising easily out of her seat.

"Excellent. What is your game?"

"I'd make your exit now," his father warned, laughter in his eyes as he stood, but Grace didn't seem inclined to listen.

"Whist, now and again," Grace replied instead, gathering up her bonnet and reticule—frilly things he could not remember seeing her carry before. "Primarily crib, when someone has a board to hand."

"Don't do it," Isaac murmured, shaking his head.

"I've tried my hand at that once or twice," his mother mused aloud. "We should have a set one day, and you can teach me the rules I have forgotten."

"She lies."

His mother tutted at him. "Are you dishonoring your elders?"

"I will leave you two to settle your disagreements

between you," Grace actually laughed softly. "Mrs. Caird, Mr. Caird, thank you once more for your invitation. I should enjoy that game if a time becomes convenient."

"Come, I'll escort you," Isaac's father offered, and with one last inscrutable look at Isaac, Grace followed his father out the door.

Which, as though his parents had planned it, left Isaac alone with his mother for a crucial, terrible moment. Her eyes lost that laughter they had held only a moment before, and she laid a hand firmly on his forearm before he could turn to leave. "She is a quick-witted girl," she said at first, "and very pretty. Her attractions are plain to see."

"But?" he wagered. There was more coming.

"All I want in life is to see you settled and happy," she said, her hand not moving from his arm.

He grimaced. "As would I. But life is not so simple as deciding 'I should like to marry now' and having everything else fall into place. Cues are for the stage."

"Grandbabies, Isaac Caird!" And she squeezed his arm fiercely.

"Slow yourself down!" He all but laughed in shock at the notion. Not that the idea in and of itself was terrible, but he had barely managed to convince Grace to let him court her, however unorthodox his methods. The notion of marriage—even before imagining her nursing his child— was too far away to fix his heart upon. "Children are not in my current plans, I can assure you. You have Nan to look to for that."

All laughter had left his mother's eyes, and the grim set of her mouth told him that whatever she was about to say next, she was as serious as death itself. "It's not a matter of wanting them or not—children *happen*. So if you intend to pursue this for much longer, you'd best get that girl to a church before you do her a damage that even the good Lord Himself can't undo."

Grace was standing in the hallway with Colin when Isaac emerged from the parlor, his mother's words ringing in his ears. He certainly hadn't been about to divulge details to her—nor to anyone!—but the warning was enough to make him nervous. They were playing dangerous games, he and Grace, and the trouble with games was that someone usually ended up the loser.

He'd all but lost his mind earlier today, seeing her in her ribbons and lace. There was something so delicate in her eyes today, unsure and a little bit wary. Isaac had fought the urge to gather her up into his arms—bonnet, frills and all—and pledge to protect her from all the indignities of life.

The side of Grace that preferred to traipse about in breeches and boys' caps would probably kick him in the shin if he tried.

Except the way she looked up at him now, the tilt of her head and the gleam in her eyes reminded him of nothing so much as the way she had challenged him first in the loft—the night he had called her bluff. The night she'd laid her claim on him completely, even if she couldn't see that yet.

Breeches and braces or skirts and stays, she was the same person whatever form she took. *He* was the one who was learning, just beginning to see the shapes of her petals as the flower slowly unfolded in the sun.

At the moment, that exquisite yellow rose was chatting away with his younger brother, a grin on Colin's face that spoke of trouble.

"I found someone wandering the halls," Colin greeted him cheerfully as Isaac moved to intercept. "Father left her in my care. If I'd known you had company calling, I would have made a nuisance of myself much earlier."

"If Isaac had known earlier than yesterday that he had company calling, you would have seen nothing but his wake as he stowed away upon a ship to America," Grace replied, mirroring Colin's sly grin.

"I see you're not doing anything useful with yourself today," Isaac replied dryly. Colin was far too young to be interested in flirting with Grace—especially since he'd shown little interest in anyone until now. He was unlikely to try his first romantic pursuit with Isaac's…whatever Grace wished herself to be.

"On the contrary. I am a font of wisdom, watering untended ground." Colin waggled his eyebrows in a broad gesture probably intended to be lascivious, but it came across only as sarcasm. "Why, Miss Owens has never even heard the story about you, the vial of mercury and Father's good silver."

"I think we've finished our business here," Isaac informed Grace. She was smirking at him, Colin was laughing, and while part of him rejoiced at the comfortable level the two seemed to have so quickly…the rest was rapidly devolving into the kind of "annoyed" that only a pesky younger sibling could generate.

Colin handed Grace her bonnet—and how had he become so comfortable with her so immediately, when there had been nothing but tension between Grace and *Isaac* for weeks? She set it on her head and tied the ribbons neatly and efficiently. "It is a pleasure to make your acquaintance, Mr. Caird," she said to Colin, and he bowed over her hand.

"The pleasure is all mine."

"The boot in the rear is about to be all yours if you don't make yourself vanish," Isaac threatened gruffly, and as usual, Colin didn't take him seriously at all.

"If you ever tire of digging my brother out from beneath his experiments, Miss Owens, I would be honored to be in your reserves."

"Nicolas Caird!"

"Going now."

Grace *laughed*, an honest-to-heaven laugh, as Isaac settled her hand on his arm and led her back out into the warm afternoon sunshine. "I like him," she declared, taking her hand off his arm only to tuck it more securely into the crook of his elbow. "If Meg weren't happily settled, I should think of making an introduction."

"I wouldn't waste too much time contemplating that. I've yet to meet the woman who could turn his head."

"Hmm," Grace murmured, but said nothing more for a minute or two. Then, "It's lovely how you laugh together."

Caught by surprise, Isaac's laugh was more of a bark. "After that? Don't be fooled. He's a pleasant enough fellow, and good, honest company, but he's like every other younger brother the world over. He exists solely to drive me mad."

"I think you're luckier than you realize."

And that—yes, that inspired a different sort of question in his mind. "I feel foolish for not asking long before," Isaac admitted. "But I'm curious to know all about you, neither-a-Quaker-nor-Welsh Miss Owens. Have you many siblings?"

She glanced away from him at the question, looking at the flowers in the window boxes of the shops, the people strolling by on the opposite side of the street, anywhere but at him. "If I do, they haven't revealed themselves." She seemed to regret the smart answer, for she spoke again a moment later. "My mother was older when my parents married. I don't know if that was the reason for it, but I was her only child."

Only child, a troubled relationship with her father, none at all with her mother from what he had seen so far. "You're no longer close with her?" He had to open his mouth, hadn't he? Now she would close up on him again and he would lose all the ground he had gained.

"We never were." Grace's fingers curled around his arm a little more snugly, and he set his other hand over hers—a gentle gesture to support, not to confine. Finally she looked back at him. The carefully studied blankness masked any feelings she did not care to share, but for a downturn in the corners of her eyes.

That didn't sit well with him at all. "A mother and daughter—and more than that, her only daughter? If my own mother and sister are any indication, you should have been more entangled in affections and shared delights than maypole ribbons in a thunderstorm."

Grace shook her head, and the look that flashed across

her face in that instant when her guard was down was one of such despair and bitter loneliness that it almost made *him* feel the urge to weep. "I never lacked for anything," she insisted, her jaw set in some kind of misguided loyalty. "Nothing material, at any rate. Father arranged things as he wished. Mother allowed it. Whether from fear, apathy, weakness—I don't know. More than likely it was simply a lack of regard. She had her friends and her parties—and some affection for but little interest in me. She cared even less about dancing, or the stage."

There it was again, that surge of anger, the impotent rage building inside at the parents who could bring a life into the world and—what? Which was worse? Seeing her only as a tool to garner praise and glory, or not seeing her at all? Either way, Grace had been horribly misused.

"Then she was a fool," he said firmly, brooking no argument. He stopped dead in the middle of the street, seizing her free hand and pulling her about to face him. "She was a fool for not seeing the incredible woman you were going to become. If even I can see it after only a few weeks—your talent, devotion, passion, loyalty—the girl you were back then was someone that any parent with sense would have been proud of."

"How can you say that?" Grace argued, the blank look of determination replaced with steel. *Better. Not perfect.* "You know nothing about the child I was."

"I don't need to. She must have been magnificent, because she became you."

And for the first time, it looked as though he might actually have startled her into silence. Grace stared at him, wide-eyed, tears shimmering and pooling across her long, dark lashes. "You're mad," she said, her voice catching in her throat. "You've gone utterly mad. It's the chemicals you're always playing with."

"I'm not mad." He looked into her eyes, held her hands close between their chests, and willed with every ounce of his strength that she would see the truth reflected in his face. His mother's admonition rang in the back of his mind still— *church, children, do her a damage you can't undo.* Her concern hadn't been for him, but for the woman who had taken over so much of his attention.

"You are a wondrous creature, Grace Owens, and I knew that from the first moment I saw you. But beyond your beauty, or your—dare I say it—dancer's graces, you are so much more. You've been hurt, by those who should have been the ones to love and protect you the most fiercely. I swear to you if it's within my power, I'll make sure you are never hurt again."

Grace turned away, dashing something away from her cheek with a flick of her gloved finger. A streak of dampness marred the surface for only a moment before she dropped her hand and it was gone. "Now I know you need to be shut up in Bedlam." Her words were harsh, but her tone was ragged, broken, and small.

"No indeed," he murmured low, not caring about the business of the street in mid-afternoon, or the shops about them, or the children running noisily past and raising up the dust. "What *we* need is some time to ourselves, so that I can show you exactly how precious you are. Do you have other plans for the evening?"

Grace didn't answer right away, seeming to fight some sort of internal struggle. Then her shoulders relaxed and she shook her head. "No, I do not."

"Now you do."

He let go her hands, and she took a little while to step away, the air between them heated. Only the presence of everyone else around them prevented him from taking her face in his hands, cupping her chin, and lowering his mouth to hers to claim her, forever.

"We're only a short walk from the Bun House. First we stop there so that I might buy us some Chelsea buns." He stopped speaking and looked at her for her reaction. The surprised smile she gave him made the impulsive suggestion well worth it. "Then I will take you home. Your home, I would suggest. I will warm you a bath, massage your feet..."

"Do my washing-up and beat out the rug as well?" she asked tartly, and that was definitely a sign that she was on the road to recovering from the melancholy he had inadvertently caused.

"Is that what the ladies are calling it nowadays?" he teased, and the dark walnut of her cheeks flushed rose-red.

"Perhaps." She held her head high, but the corners of her generous mouth twitched up as though she were attempting to conceal a broad smile. "If you acquit yourself well enough, it might be."

Chapter Twelve

Bringing Isaac home to her little apartments after seeing the house he had been raised in, Grace couldn't help but feel the lack of space and fine furnishings. It was only for a moment—she was a single spinster, after all, and her lodgings were more than enough for her needs—but the self-consciousness remained. After Mrs. Caird's pretty parlor, her own rooms seemed dingy and dull, her stoneware heavy in the hand and her windows too small.

This is what wanting does. It makes you unhappy with the things you earned for yourself.

Isaac, on the other hand, was moving through her space with ease, as though he belonged here, as though from the one time—one!—that he'd come in to her lodgings, he had carved himself a space. He fit into it too neatly. As Grace set aside her bonnet and Meg's reticule, he was already poking up the fire and setting the kettle on to boil. She should be irritated, and found herself pensive instead.

"Your father is kind, and your mother is hardly the ogre I'd been led to expect," Grace said into the silence. She unpinned her hair and let her spiral curls fall free, bouncing about her neck like clockwork springs.

Isaac snorted from where he puttered about with cups and saucers in her tiny kitchen. "That's what she'd like you to believe. But wait until she considers you family, and you'll sing a very different tune."

There would never be a better time to bring up that question—*what are we doing, what do you* want *from me*—and yet Grace couldn't bring herself to do it quite so directly. "There isn't anybody in the world who considers me family," she said instead. She felt a layer peel back inside her heart, the odd and unwelcome sensation of a wound being opened so Doubting Thomas could peer within.

The clinking of china stopped, and she stood at the window, looking out. His hands stroked up her arms, his presence behind her thrilling and terrifying all at once. "That's not true," Isaac objected.

Please don't say "me", please don't—

For a little while she had thought herself in control of their encounters, able to take or leave him as she pleased. How could she have been so wrong?

"You've spoken of your friend Meg often enough, as though she were a sister."

"Meg is…" Grace stopped, thought about it, then shrugged, Isaac's broad, strong hands still resting lightly on her upper arms.

The firm, strong bulk of him stood behind her, and she could feel, even without looking, the ripple of tension in his shoulders, the way he would be tilting his head as he watched her, the line between his brows as he waited for her to finish her reply. "I will grant you Meg," she said finally, and with the kind of deep and abiding fondness that only her closest friend could induce.

"There, you see? And where there is one, there is room for more." He moved around her then, to stand between her and the window. He settled to rest on the window frame and sat there, his head at her own level.

There was the brow furrow, and she reached out impulsively to smooth it away. He tilted his face up and into her caress, the iron bands of fear clamped tight around her chest melting away. "You're very lucky to have the family that you do," Grace tried to explain to him again. "For years I'd dreamed of finding something like that. Somewhere where I could be understood, the way your mother understands you."

"You did dream," he replied, the rumble in the bottom notes of his voice warm and rich with concern. "And now?"

The air trembled, Isaac's hand resting on Grace's hip.

She shook her head. "When I was a child, I spake as a child, I understood as a child, I thought as a child: but when I was grown, I put away childish things." Corinthians had never been her favorite text, but it spoke to her in a way so many other pieces of the Holy Writ did not.

"There is nothing childish about wanting to belong to someone." He didn't rise, but stayed on her level, tugging gently at her hip until she followed where he led. Grace stepped in closer, the breeze from the window faded to nothing, even the pigeons that roosted on the roof silent now.

Time hung in its stillness.

Isaac slid his hand along her jaw, cupped the back of her neck.

The shiver ran down her spine starting from the place where his fingers settled, bursting into heat somewhere deep between her hipbones.

"Don't say anything more," she begged, the fear—of what, precisely? She couldn't name it—rising up and threatening to choke her.

He didn't. He kissed her instead, his mouth moving gently over hers. Tender, sweet at first, she parted her lips and let it deepen. He pulled her in close, hands on her hip and on the side of her face, and she splayed her hands across his chest to keep her balance. His muscles were hard beneath her hands, the shapes of them easy to make out beneath the wool of his waistcoat and the soft linen of his shirt. She trailed her fingers down his ribs to his lean, flat stomach.

His kiss deepened, his tongue teasing along her bottom lip, tantalizing and elusive. She chased it with her mouth, leaning in until he caught her around the waist with both arms and pressed her close against his body.

He stood and pulled the shutters closed, cutting the afternoon light that had been flooding into her room. Grace's heart raced, her fingertips tingled, and the beating throb of her pulse echoed in the core of her sex. This was simpler than talking, easier than picking a way through her confusion.

She rose up on her toes, not waiting for him to make the next move. Her hands curled around the lapels of his waistcoat, the fine wool soft and twined with her fingers.

Isaac caught her about the waist again, his hands spanning across her back, strong and sure. She kissed him and licked into his mouth. She closed her eyes, nothing but the rush of pure sensation allowed in.

His hands fell lower, caressing her bottom, squeezing and lifting, his hips tight, tight against hers. She could feel him stirring, the rise of his desire against her side.

The sound he made when she cupped her hand over his growing bulge was addictive, somewhere between a gasp and a groan.

She stroked him with her thumb, up and over and down the other side, and he sucked in air like a drowning man. "Grace," he pleaded, a hundred things she wouldn't let him say packed into that one word, then let go of her hips to bring one hand to her breast.

He kissed down her throat, sharp nips and bites that stung brightly before fading. There, there—he brushed across her nipple and it tightened painfully quickly. He bent his head to her chest, tugged her bodice down a little and teased the edge of her shift with his tongue and teeth, swiping hot and wet across her nipple.

She worked his buttons until they opened, started to push his waistcoat off his shoulders. He gleamed beneath the white of his shirt, his nipples dark circles beneath the semi-sheer linen. Isaac let go of her only long enough to shrug the waistcoat off and haul his shirt over his head.

When he took hold of her again she went with his grip, rising up on one foot and looping her knee up and over his hip. His hard cock sat right where she needed it now, between her legs and solid against the center of her sex.

He seemed to understand her and set his hand beneath her thigh, holding her steady.

Arms about his neck, his hands stroking and caressing

her, his prick hot and thick against her pleasure, Grace keened softly. She rocked into him with the hunger she had come to associate with Isaac's particular scent, his fierce strength, the singular heat and pressure of his mouth.

When he set her down it was without warning, the loss of his lips and his arms leaving her momentarily cold. Not for long, though, as he took her by the hands and drew her toward her bed. With each step he stopped and pressed a kiss to her lips, her eyes, her nose, smiling into the curve of her mouth as she tried to catch him.

Isaac's hands tangled in her laces and he fought them for a moment before flexing his arms and pulling. The knot broke with a snap and Grace pushed him lightly in retaliation. "You owe me a new staylace!"

"And you owe me a button for my breeches. I never did find the one that went missing here last time. Shall we call it a fair trade?"

"There's little fair about this," Grace laughed, breathless, as Isaac yanked the last of her lacings loose. Her stays fell to the floor and she stepped out of them, pulling at the buttons on his waistband—one newly replaced, apparently—to free him from his clothes.

Bending to kiss her, he took the hem of her shift in his hands and brought it back up with him, stroking her thighs. They were gloriously nude by the time they tumbled to the bed, all but for her stockings, still tied above her knees with pale pink ribbons.

She moved to tug at the bow but he grabbed her hand, stopping her. "Leave them," he asked, propping himself up above her, his long, lean body half-resting between her open thighs. "I like the contrast," he elaborated, his gaze running hungrily down her body—her bare breasts, the slim curve of her waist, down to the line of linen and lace against her thigh.

She'd seen him mostly in the altogether before, but this was a new angle, his cock rising hard into the heated air between them, his muscled arms and shoulders tense as he held himself steady, knees dug into the bed between her thighs.

Isaac ran his hand across the top of her stocking, first over her skin, then with the material between, toying with it. The stocking dragged lightly against her skin, waking up sensation as he circled his fingers around her thigh, brushed the back of his knuckles tantalizingly delicately against the folds between her legs, then trailed his hand up, up to cup her breast and cover it with his mouth.

Grace cried out, her back arching and pushing her breast against his lips and tongue, the pleasure rippling through her as everything tightened in delight and anticipation.

She slipped her hand down between them and seized his cock, wrapping her fingers around the thick shaft. Her first stroke was hesitant but he groaned her name aloud, the sound vibrating down through her skin.

Hollow, she was hollow and empty, and everything she needed to fill that ache was right there in her hand. All she had to do was give in.

Or play with fire, and skirt that edge of yes and no. She pushed up and rolled him over, Isaac going willingly and laughing. He set his hands around her buttocks and rolled his hips up, grinding the hard thickness of his erection against her. She straddled and opened to him, letting his cock slide between her folds. Not inside, not yet, but there—there—she dug her nails into his shoulders, the wave of pleasure so desperate, so intense.

Rolling together like this, his hands tight around her buttocks, his fingers stroking and caressing the sweet slick skin between them, it was too good to be borne. He was so much thicker than fingers, hotter than her toy prick, and he groaned and moved with her as she used him for her pleasure.

"Grace," he begged, his hips moving ever faster, his eyes fixed on her breasts as she moved above him. "Please, I need you, more of you, all of you."

She could do it. All it would take would be a shift of her weight, take him in her hand and guide him inside. He would stretch her, fill her, and stoke the fire that smoldered inside her until she became lightning herself.

Still, there was the fear, the thing that stayed her hand and pushed her hips down against him just as she had been, taking without giving him everything. "Like this," she begged, breathless, and the horizon beckoning, rushing closer with every second. "Like this for now, please, don't stop."

Leaning down to kiss him changed her angle, all of him now sliding against her, balls to head, all riding hard against her clitoris and teasing at the entrance to her core. Now, here, his hand gone from her buttock and slid between them, fingers teasing at the spot where her pleasure coiled tight. Faster, faster again, and there, his fingers and his prick and just the tip of him sliding inside by accident of their motion—

She came, she came and her body shook, convulsed,

around his fingers and the very tip of his cock and the solid power of his shaft between her folds. Everything burned together, a fire that annihilated fear. She ground down, just once, taking the whole length of him inside her.

Just to feel him, just to know, to double her pleasure as his cockhead rubbed hard against the coal of need still aching inside. She arched and came *again*, this time from the inside out, desire shaking her to pieces while he dug his fingers tight into her hips and laughed with delight.

"Love, love, oh love," he gasped out, his voice harsh, low and ragged. His words meant nothing in this context. She would have to force herself to forget them when this was over.

Grace rose up, slid off him, and kissed away his disappointed cry when the cool air hit his prick. Her hand slid easily over him, pumping along his shaft, bringing his hips up, his lips open.

Too soon.

She slowed her hand and Isaac groaned, pushing up into the circle of her fingers with increasing need.

Grace stopped, resting her palm across his erection, teasing her fingertips lightly over the place where his foreskin stopped and the head began.

"Pricktease!" he gasped, tried to rub up against her, and she pulled her hand away completely. "You're going to be the death of me. Do you plan to torment me forever in revenge?" The way his tongue darted out to moisten his lips suggested he might have little problem with that notion.

"I made you a proposition once," she began, the shiver of anticipation mixed with nerves tying her belly into knots.

What if—but he had seemed intrigued, not horrified. "It only seems fair, after all. If you want to take me—"

Isaac stopped moving beneath her and propped himself up on his elbows, Grace still straddling his lap. He cocked his head and his eyes went wide with surprise. "Then you take me the same way first?" he guessed, and there was cautious hesitation in his voice. "You mean you really do have..."

"A prick in a box?" Grace said sweetly, and couldn't help the laughter that bubbled up at his look of surprise. "I told you not to doubt me, Mr. Caird."

"Never again," he swore. "But what *precisely* does that entail? I think I'm entitled to ask that much before agreeing." He was grinning, though, with that look in his eye like when he was about to cause an explosion.

"Stay there, and don't move." Grace eased off of him, found her footing, her knees still wobbling and head spinning. The small wooden box sat on the floor beside the bed where she had left it, the jar of oil on the nightstand.

Isaac rolled on to his side, watching her intently. "I'm fascinated now—you couldn't pay me to leave."

It was not the scenario Isaac had envisioned when walking Grace back to her lodgings, but he couldn't deny that her description had been... "tantalizing" was not quite the correct word, but then neither was "terrifying," as it possibly should have been.

He was curious. Curious in a way that sent shivers of anticipation down his spine at the same time as it made his arse clench. So Isaac focused on hers instead, on the sleek lines of her body as she moved, bent to the floor, rose again; the controlled flow of her muscles and the exquisite beauty of her skin; the way her nipples rose, large and dark, and pebbled at his breath. *Those* thoughts were just about enough to stop the fluttering of nerves in his belly and bring blood back to his member.

"You shouldn't feel too intimidated," Grace told him archly, then brought the wooden box back up to the bed and joined him there. "It's no match for you." Indeed, the leather instrument she brought out was only a few inches in length, something firm covered in dark leather. A ribbon came off either side of the flat base, and those she tied about her hips.

When it came down to it, though, when he kissed her fiercely and she sank into it, when she molded her body against his as though surprised that he was willing to try— for her, he would—when he took her prick in his hand, it didn't seem nearly as odd as he'd expected.

"Must I submit to your punishment now, oh mistress?" he teased, but her expression was solemn.

"You've got it all wrong," she insisted, and hissed between her teeth when he covered her breast with his hand. "A cock shouldn't be a weapon. And I am no one's mistress."

Her breasts were small, firm and magnificent, her hips round and full, and she kissed him as though she were drowning and he her only lifeline. His skin sparked with recognition of her touch, the silk of the ribbons soft under his fingers, pressing lines down into her firm flesh. He wrapped his hand around the toy.

Smooth and firm, some kind of padding lending give,

small enough that he could imagine it passing into him without injury, rising from the nest of black curls between her thighs—

My lady has a prick. And I am surprisingly not upset by this.

When she rolled him over to his knees, he went, and when she coated her hand with oil and stroked his cock to firmness again, he groaned and thrust into that sweet, slick heat. She covered him, her front against his back, her breasts pressed against him, and her fist wrapped around his own erection.

Those fingers went exploring, circling the skin around his arse, teasing the sweet spot behind his bollocks, his prick aching and tension coiling deep inside. The way he kneeled he could feel the sweet-hot bite of her teeth along his spine, and when she slipped her fingers inside, first one, then two, oiled and gentle, he felt a stretch that made him shiver, but no pain.

Was this how it was for women? The feeling of being filled by someone else, of having all your secret, hollow places opened?

It was odd, so strange. He shook with it, fighting the urge to run, or to roll her over and sink into her body himself, reclaim his place in their love play.

You first.

She stroked his cock again, and the pleasure of her hand chased away the last of his fear.

He rocked with it, pushing forward to slide his erection through Grace's tight-closed fist, shocks of desire and heat burning back through his body to where her other hand teased and toyed at his arse, two fingers sliding out of him, and—God in heaven, there it was—her prick pressing gently in.

Too much too much—would she tear him in two? The slow pressure was more than anything he had prepared for. Until she began to move, until a fire within began to stoke higher, and—

"What in God's name is *that?*" he gasped out, when the prick buried in him nudged against something deep inside. Pleasure burst behind his eyes, desire and need for *more* consuming everything he was or would ever be.

His body relaxed, the oil easing her passage, Grace pushed into him again, her hands tight on his hips.

"Please!" he begged, pushing back hard to drive her fully home and find that place inside him, whatever it was that burned for her, for the pressure and the friction, assault by a greater force—no. Not a besieged target, but a hearth-fire stoked by loving hands.

Again she found the rhythm that sent sparks through his vision, his body trembling. Forward into her hand, back onto her prick, and everywhere around him was *her*. Her arms, her mouth, her hands and heat, giving and giving to him until his body shook apart.

Hands clenched in the bedclothes, quilt rough beneath his knees, Grace's teeth scraping along the ridge of his spine, Isaac came. He came with Grace's prick buried deep inside him, with her hand tight and frantic on his cock, her breasts pushed against his back. Shaking and cursing, he spurted over her hand, once, twice and again, his emissions driven out of his body by the force of her thrusts and the place where his body was split open.

The world went white.

When spots swam before his eyes and shapes took hold once more, Isaac had toppled to his side, still in bed.

The splashing of water on the other side of the screen meant Grace washing up. She came back to bed fully nude—no stockings or extra paraphernalia—with a damp cloth in her hand, stroking it gently across his tired body.

He gathered her in his arms and wrapped a leg over hers, folding her completely into his embrace.

"Thank you," he murmured, because the thrum and burn of passion still flared in his muscles, the hazy peace of satiation thick as fog in his brain. "I've never in my life experienced anything like that. It was—you are—"

"Have I done the impossible?" Grace teased him, tracing his lips with the tips of her fingers. "Have I rendered you speechless?"

"I have lost all of my wits," Isaac swore fervently. "I shall have to come back and find them in your bed again."

She kissed him on the nose, a giddy girl in place of the careful woman. "If you think I'd let a witless man in bed with me, you don't know me at all."

Isaac nuzzled against her throat, tasted the faint salt-sweat of her skin. This was home, then, this heavy-thick feeling of comfort, of satiation, of utter relaxation and trust. "Then I'll just have to stay here until they return."

Grace laughed softly, and in that instant he vowed to cheer her so that he could hear that sound every day for the rest of his life. "I shall lay in provisions for the wait."

Had there ever been a man more perfectly content in all of England? Somehow, he could not imagine it at all.

Another clandestine meeting under the cover of darkness, and this time Lucy's nerves were all in a muddle. A mail coach rattled by in the street outside the alleyway where she had stationed herself, the wheels loud over the cobblestones. She jumped, squeaked, then clapped her hands over her mouth to stop herself from making any more noises which might attract attention.

Across the road, shadowy figures moved around the door to the Surrey, the one she had left unlocked. A flicker of movement again and they were gone, the closing door the only sign as to their passage through.

She had to wait here until they finished, then lock the doors again. The key she'd lifted from Elliston's office hung heavy around her neck, the weight of it a hot coal between her breasts.

Whatever was happening inside was not her concern. Her part of the bargain was only this. There was no reason in the world to be nervous or to fear. Who had ever caused a problem by opening a door?

No, her task was simple. The reward would be worth it. All she had to do now was wait.

Chapter Thirteen

Isaac had been caught off-guard and by surprise one too many times over the past few weeks. He'd contented himself the night before with the knowledge that whatever he and Grace got themselves up to in their private hours, it was for them alone. No one ever had to hear details, nor suspect that their relations were anything other than what was generally expected.

He should probably have thought of that before sitting down in the house seats at the Surrey the next day. The ache in his nether regions was a new and not altogether pleasant sensation.

Did women feel the same sort of ache after lovemaking? The distant soreness was a reminder that he carried with him throughout the morning, a constant thrum that proved he was desired, possessed, adored. Perhaps it was the sort of thing a virgin experienced at her deflowering, though *that* comparison made him snicker uncomfortably inside.

All in all it was worth it, considering the mind-rending pleasure that had inspired it. But the chairs off to the side of the stage were uncushioned, and he still wasn't able to hold back the wince when he sat.

"And what have *you* been up to, Caird?"

It had to be Thomas Hunter who spotted him. Because apparently Isaac's luck had turned sour.

The Surrey's fight master draped himself over the back of the chair next to Isaac's and grinned at him with an all-too-knowing smile. "You haven't gone and hurt yourself, I warrant?"

"Me? Never better." Isaac set his jaw and watched the stage, Elliston pacing restlessly across it.

"Could've fooled me, old man. Or is that something other than the rheumatis' setting into your hips?"

"I don't know what you're—" Isaac got halfway through the denial before Hunter kicked the bottom of his chair, sending vibrations up through the wooden seat. He jumped, more from the anticipation of soreness than any actual pain.

Hunter snickered, his eyes alight. "And here I thought I knew all the news there was to know." He rose, clapped Isaac companionably on the shoulder, then leaned in close to murmur in his ear. "Next time, old boy, tell your man to use more oil. Spit and persistence will only carry you so far."

"You're a nuisance and a scoundrel," Isaac informed him, fighting to prevent the flush from rising hot into his cheeks. He had nothing to be ashamed of, though Hunter's assumptions might cause problems at some juncture…assuming anyone believed him. "And you have never been more wrong about anything in your life."

"You keep on thinking that." Hunter stretched and stood, arching as though to put his lithe, buckskin-clad form on display.

Oh, for the love of—

When Isaac didn't blink or take notice other than to roll his eyes, Hunter shrugged and gave him a roguish grin. "Whatever you say, Caird. Your secret is safe with me."

"My brother's keeping secrets?" Colin had come in without Isaac noticing. He tugged up his trousers at the thigh and dropped down into the seat on Isaac's other side. "Other than Miss Owens, that is?"

Hunter cocked his head in puzzlement, his ribbon-tied queue flopping over his shoulder, and he stared at Isaac as though trying to divine the secrets of his soul.

"Nicolas," Isaac sighed, "Mr. Thomas Hunter. He keeps the actors from stabbing each other accidentally. Hunter, my younger brother, Mr. Nicolas Caird. Now, if both of you would stop inventing baseless rumors, I would be much obliged."

"Now where's the fun in that?" Colin teased, and Hunter chuckled.

"I'm surrounded by imbeciles," Isaac muttered darkly, and the other two ignored him. "What are you doing here?" he asked Colin after a moment. "Don't you have better things to do than hang about my workplace?"

"You said you were going to test the flying wire today," Colin pointed out. "After listening to you grumble about the ruddy contraption for weeks now, did you think I was going to miss the grand debut?"

Obviously his younger brother was not going to be still any time soon. "I shall take that as my cue," Isaac said, rising from his seat. "Try not to engage in too much salacious gossip at my expense, gentlemen."

As he pushed his way past his brother and out into the aisle, he heard Hunter joking, "Are you a gentleman?"

"Not I—perhaps he meant you?"

"Highly improbable."

Now there is an unholy alliance in the making if ever I did see one.

He put the thoughts of his brother and his colleague out of his mind once he arrived at the bottom of the stairs which led to the wings. Grace waited for him backstage, and he was going to turn her into a star.

Isaac climbed the stairs two at a time, the half-flight a meaningless obstacle. The harness hung where he had strung it the morning before, thin wires ascending into the darkness of the flies. And up there, the pulleys and ropes at the heart of his design. He tugged on the harness as he passed it, a swift bounce of his hand to reassure himself that all was secure. Nothing moved or creaked that shouldn't have, and he nodded to himself with satisfaction.

"Pleased by your infernal creation?" Grace had come up behind him while he'd been checking the lines, moving so silently in her satin slippers that he actually jumped in surprise at her voice.

"Not yet." He smiled and turned, checking first one way and then the other to be sure they were alone before he drew her into his arms.

This was another side of the girl that he was falling for so desperately—clad in a dancing dress made up of layers of blue muslin, her dark brown skin warm against the delicate fabric tiers. The skirt was cut high, almost to her knee, and the bodice designed as flower petals, curving up and stiffened with rope to capture and raise the glorious bounty of her breasts.

He settled his hands around her waist, tugging her close against his body, every inch of him responding to her perfume, the soft heat of her body, the sting and tug of her teeth against his lower lip when he kissed her deep.

"Is this the costume you'll wear?" he asked when he parted from her to draw breath. "I'd suspect Mr. Byrne of some dark designs on you, if I didn't know that Mrs. Byrne would murder him for it."

"It is." Grace kept her own voice pitched as low as his, and ran her fingers up and down the lapels of his fine golden-orange waistcoat. "Designed by Mr. Byrne, stitched by Mr. Glover—at least the bodice, with all its bones and cords—and embroidered by some nameless apprentices who may someday have shops of their own. We are piecemeal rag bags, all of us, performing on command."

"You are a goddess, and we all live to serve your grand design," he corrected her, capturing her hands in his and bringing them to his lips.

Had it been only yesterday that this glistening, ephemeral fairy had pressed him down to the bed and lain her weight across his back, only last night that she had played the man and plundered his body so thoroughly that he had been made to unlearn everything he thought he knew about the possibilities of passion?

It hardly seemed likely that both worlds could be so perfectly encapsulated in one creature, and yet here she was. And she was his.

"You're impossible," Grace said fondly, and she

cupped his cheek with one warm hand before rising up on her toes to kiss him again. Someone shouted from the house and Grace made a plaintive sound in her throat when Isaac broke the kiss.

"We had best get on with this while we still have an audience," he suggested, forced to take deep, settling breaths to calm his body down after Grace's touch. She glanced down at his distress and laughed softly, a sparkling noise that he would have to do his best to eke out of her again later. Right now, they simply didn't have the time.

"As we must," she sighed. "But we'll continue this conversation later." She looked at the harness with something between disdain and hesitation. He unclipped it from its moorings and held it out to her, in time to see Mrs. Byrne and Miss Sullivan come around the corner and into the wings.

Lucy Sullivan looked askance at the harness as Isaac buckled Grace into it, her lips pressed tight. "Are you sure you're going to go through with this?" she asked Grace, not acknowledging Isaac's presence at all.

"Of course I'm sure," Grace replied, with bravado that Isaac was sure she didn't really feel. "We've all done odder things in the name of our art, after all."

Miss Sullivan didn't seem encouraged. Mrs. Byrne bustled around them, untucked Grace's skirts from where the harness had rucked them up, and patted Grace's spiraling curls back into place. "There we go, my duck. As perfect as God made you."

"Off with you," Grace shooed them away. "Let the man work."

Miss Sullivan hesitated again, seemed about to object, but she bit her lip and hastened away with Mrs. Byrne. To take up their seats in the house, one presumed. Isaac forgot them as soon as they were gone, his whole attention focused on checking the buckles and straps that would support Grace's weight while she was in the air.

"Is everything all right?" she asked, and now that they were alone again, there was uncertainty back in her voice.

"It will be fine," he soothed her. "I had Tottenham's great bulk bouncing about the stage yesterday, with no harm done to him, nor the rig. You're half his weight if you're an ounce."

She nodded, watching the space on the stage. Her lips moved silently and she seemed to be counting out steps, her feet moving in place as she ran through the routine in her mind. After a moment she paused, stretched out her arms, and nodded. "I'm ready."

He took the chance and kissed her one last time, a brush of the lips meant as a promise. "I'll be right here manning the ropes at all times."

She nodded and began to climb the ladder to the flies, ascending into the darkness that swallowed detail and light. He drew up the slack in the ropes as she went, playing the lines.

Grace vanished into the darkness, and he watched until all he could see was the faintest glimmer of pale blue in the shadows. Something cold passed over his spine, footsteps on his grave, and he shuddered. It was nerves; nerves and nothing else. He'd been over and over the setup a dozen times in the past two days. There was nothing that could possibly go wrong.

The ladder up the side of the stage seemed to go on forever, and the odd constriction of the harness around her waist, shoulders, and thighs didn't help to dispel Grace's unease. The leather straps chafed, the edges biting in to her skin.

I'm going to make him put lotion on for me. It's the least he can do.

The delicious fantasy of Isaac's hands smoothing oil over her skin carried Grace up the rest of the way, Tottenham helping her up on to the perch constructed below the catwalk. Isaac reeled in the lines until they were taut above her, and Grace looked down for the first time.

The stage was only about ten feet below but it felt as though she stood on a cliff higher than the white precipices of Dover, looking out over an endless fall.

A flash of red hair in the opposite wings meant Lucy— she'd stayed to watch, her fingers up and pressed against her mouth.

"Any day now," Elliston barked from beyond the stage, and Grace quelled her nerves. This was no more dangerous than lighting parts of the set on fire, and the Olympic Pavilion did that sort of thing on the regular.

Isaac waited below for her signal, her life quite completely resting in his hands.

She tugged once on the rope leading down to the ground below. An answering tug meant he'd received her, loud and clear.

Tottenham whistled the cue, a piercing sound that cut through the busy murmuring of the backstage crew. It was answered with another whistle from below, and Grace's harness tugged taut.

She stepped off the platform.

For an instant she was in free-fall, scrambling to right herself and keep her arms and legs in position. The wires caught, as they should, and the pulleys slid along the bar above, the harness pulling snug against her thighs in an almost sexual embrace.

Grace pointed her toes, relaxed into the safety of the rig, let Isaac glide her down, down toward the stage. For a moment everything was clear; she soared, free and bright, weightless as a feather on the breeze—

The rest seemed to happen in slow motion, each event isolated and complete.

A cracking sound echoed from above, followed by the *sprang* and *poing* of splitting fibres. Someone shrieked.

Grace rocked, unsteady, a wire giving way, and then another—

Nothing held her at all. She fell, the stage rushing up to meet her, and a scream ripped from Grace's throat.

Another crack.

Then there was nothing but silence.

Chapter Fourteen

It didn't seem possible that time could move so quickly around him. It all seemed to take place in an instant, too fast for Isaac to react. Grace soared through the air just like he'd envisioned, and as he'd lowered her toward the stage, her foot extended to touch the planks.

That was when time stopped.

A crack, a scream, the horrible, sickening noise of a body hitting wood.

He ran from the wings, skidded across the stage and dropped to knees to cradle Grace in his arms before his mind had even caught up with the terrible reality.

No blood; thank the Lord almighty, there was no blood, not on her head nor on the stage.

"Ow!" Air hissed out between her lips. She glared at him and struggled to sit up on her own, striking his hands away. "Bastard! Leave me be!"

"Grace!" Lucy darted across the stage then, followed hotly by Elliston and his wife. Tottenham landed at the base of the ladder, rubbing his hands together to clear the sting from sliding down the rungs, and Isaac found himself pushed aside.

Mrs. Elliston helped Grace to sit up, Lucy helping to pull the harness from her and toss it aside. One of Grace's legs curled beneath her but the other stretched out before, and she sucked in a harsh breath when Mrs. Elliston ran her fingers experimentally along her ankle. Her blue dress spread out around her, the delicate layers wrinkled and pushed away.

"Mrs. Byrne!" Mrs. Elliston called out from where she knelt at Grace's side. "Go find Dr. Marshall and have him attend immediately."

"Oh, Grace!" Lucy cried out again, and then her eyes went wide. "It's like Madame Raiza said—an angel falls from the dark!"

"What nonsense are you spouting now, girl? Give them room, give them room." Elliston got between Lucy and the women on the floor and shooed her away. "Miss Owens, can you stand?"

"She shouldn't put weight on it," Tottenham supplied helpfully from behind Isaac. "Could be broken."

"It's not broken," Grace snapped.

Enough of this.

Isaac pushed back past Tottenham to get to Grace, the image of her falling replaying itself over and over again in his mind. She was all right, she was conscious and well, but he still had to touch her to be sure.

"Let me help you up," he said firmly, and set his arm about her waist before she could scold him like before. He didn't bother trying to get her onto her other foot, but slid his other arm behind her knees and lifted her in his arms as though he were carrying her across the threshold. "Arms around my neck."

She did it, but the tension all through her body turned her supple form into sharp ridges and angry edges. Her eyes burned into his, accusing, furious.

Isaac set her down into the prompter's chair on the side of the stage and she let go of him immediately and with such force that he stumbled. "'Trust me,' you said. I did," she spat out, her eyes narrowed and fierce. "And now look! You've ruined me!"

His work, his ideas, his fault—no! His brain rejected the idea as violently as Grace's fall had been. He couldn't accept it, not when it would mean that his own hands had caused the destruction of everything he held dear.

"There was nothing wrong with the rig, you must believe me! I had men twice your size testing it as recently as yesterday."

"And yet it did! Are you so caught up in your own pride that you can't admit that you failed, when the evidence is sitting right in front of you?" Her cheeks flushed red and her hands shook, whether from anger or the shock of the fall, he couldn't begin to guess.

He set his hands on the arms of the chair on either side of her and held her there, to try and impress upon her the truth of his speech. "Whatever happened here was not due to any mistake of mine." Of that, he was absolutely certain!

"You're in pain. You're not thinking clearly or you'd know that I would never put you in harm's way, even by accident. Let me help you. Once your ankle's been seen to, we'll uncover the truth."

"I can guarantee that uncovering anything with me is the *last* thing you will be doing in this lifetime." She leaned back in the chair and stared up at him, jaw set and fire in her eyes.

"Grace, listen to me!" He wanted to grab her up and kiss her, check every inch of her for other injuries or bruising, wrap her in quilts and tuck her into bed where she would be safe, bar the door against anyone who had dared to...

Dared to interfere with the rig? He'd spent the rest of the afternoon at tea with his parents, and the night in bed with Grace—what could have happened in between then and now?

Could anyone at the Surrey have been capable of such total disregard for Grace's life?

"Get away from me," she hissed, her hands coming up to push against his chest. "I don't want anything to do with you, not now, not ever again!" Her face contorted in pain, lashing out at the rescuer as well as the trap.

"Grace!" He hurt along with her, his whole body caving in around his hollowed heart.

A hand seized his arm and Isaac whirled around. Colin held tight and Isaac stared into his brother's eyes, his blood up and thundering in his ears. "Isaac, calm yourself," Colin said firmly.

"I won't leave her," Isaac said.

Colin shook his head. "The doctor is here. And you're doing more harm than good."

"Don't you tell me what to do!" All he could see was her, falling—all he could hear was the horrible noise of her body meeting the floor. Fear blended into anger and all of it sat heavy and hot in his stomach, blotting out his better judgment.

What were his choices? He could fight his brother. Colin deserved a kick in the arse!

Or he could allow himself to be taken aside, to fold his arms and scowl while old Dr. Marshall turned Grace's ankle this way and that, poking and prodding about until she yelped with pain.

Isaac bolted forward, running on instinct and fear, but Grace's dark glare, Colin's death grip on his arm and Marshall's irritated wave of dismissal froze him in place.

Finally, *finally*, Marshall gestured to his boy for his bag, produced a length of linen and a pot of pungent-smelling salve, and bound Grace's ankle. She winced and dug her fingertips into the chair arms as he worked, and Isaac's hands itched to push the doctor away from her, stop him before he did more damage.

"Nothing is broken," Marshall pronounced as he stood, wiping his hands off on a kerchief that he tucked back into his waistcoat pocket. "There is a pull to her Achilles tendon, and a little swelling that will bruise, but that is all. It is nothing serious, my dear,"—he patted Grace's shoulder with a faintly condescending air—"and will not hamper your career. But you must stay off that foot for a few days if you wish to be in good form for the opening. And I do mean completely—should you walk on it at all for the next three or four days, you will set back your healing with your impatience."

"There must be some other way," Grace protested. "I live alone. I cannot stay in bed for the better part of a week."

"I'll come," Lucy blurted out, seizing Grace's hand. "I'll stay and care for you."

"No," Grace objected, taking her hand back. "I cannot ask you to become my nurse, Lucy. You have your own business to attend to, not to mention rehearsals."

"Yes, let us not mention rehearsing at all," Elliston grumbled darkly. Mrs. Elliston shot him a fierce look and he subsided.

Colin stepped forward. "If I may," he began. Isaac started after him, but Colin laid his hand on Isaac's arm again in that same warning. His entire soul chafed against obeying, but he managed—barely— to hold his tongue.

"Miss Owens, if you'll permit the liberty of the invitation, you should come and stay with us. My parents own an inn," Colin explained quickly, as the others reacted with varying degrees of surprise. "We always have an empty room, and our mother would no doubt welcome the company."

"That's kind of you," Grace began, wrapping her arms around herself as though she were cold.

Jealousy and anger flared up hot inside Isaac, the whole mess leaving him muddled and unable to think. Colin and Grace? How could she smile at *him*? Colin was interfering where he didn't belong. Then the guilt crowded in hot on the heels of his anger and fear—for cajoling Grace into participating, for losing his temper and his sense all at once, for doubting his brother even for an instant.

His head swam with the devastating brew, his fists clenching impotently.

Isaac couldn't take anything more. He turned on his heel and strode off backstage. Let the others fuss over Grace if she would not take kindness from him. *He* would find out what had happened, and if the accident had been deliberately caused—well then. Isaac would have a serious reckoning to deliver.

He had promised to protect her, and he'd failed. He'd tried to comfort her and been sent away. The next best thing he could give her would be *justice*.

She'd been wrong to snap at him, probably, but the sight of Isaac's back as he fled the stage like the coward he was meant that she wouldn't give him the satisfaction of hearing an apology. Not ever! He was the one who should be crawling on his hands and knees to beg forgiveness, not turn all high-and-mighty and cling to his pride!

Not that it would make a difference even if he did. Her ankle still throbbed, bruises were already starting to ache on her elbows, and she had wrenched something in her neck that made her wince when she tried to stretch it.

She had trusted him, and look what that had given her.

An angel falls from dark to dark—a man will bind you and keep you in chains.

Nonsense! She hadn't believed it from Hortense the first time, and she wasn't going to let Lucy's silliness about predictions and fortunes send her into a tizzy.

They were all fussing around her like a swarm of chattering starlings, and there was still a question she needed to answer. "Mr. Caird," she said to Colin. "I appreciate your offer, of course. But I don't want to be a burden. I can take care of myself."

"Nonsense. Mother lives for this sort of thing. And before you think of refusing, I can guarantee that if we did not bring you home ourselves, once she hears about your injury, she'll send us packing off to your lodgings to bring you back anyway. So you may as well agree now and save everyone the trouble." He smiled hopefully, as charming as his older brother but without the weight of expectation, and the stone around Grace began to crack a little.

"That's settled, then," Mrs. Elliston said briskly. "Do you have a carriage to bring around, or should I send a boy out to find a hack?"

"Mrs. Elliston!" Grace objected, but it didn't seem to matter. "I can manage. It will be fine by tomorrow. This is all an overreaction."

"And make sure she doesn't stir herself out of bed except for the absolute necessities for the next three days at least—or should we make that four?" Mrs. Elliston faced off against Grace, hands on her hips.

"Three will be enough." Grace wilted under that glare, the rush of angry energy abating, and leaving her as wrung out as sheets in the laundry. He had done it, the bastard, managed to make her weak and then destroyed her. Just like she'd tried to convince herself he wouldn't. The world tilted and reshaped itself, and she was alone. Her pride nagged at her, demanding she be strong.

The truth of it was, she didn't have the energy to fight any more.

Today, just for today, she would let someone else take charge. At least for the moment, she was released—from having to plan, to worry, or even to think.

She just sat. She noticed Lucy scramble off to find Grace's bag and her changes of clothes, watched Tottenham disassemble the pieces of Isaac's machine and haul them off to some godforsaken workshop in the bowels of the theatre, waited for Isaac to come back and tell her it was all fixed now, and he would take care of her until she was quite well again. No matter how many times she had sent him away before, he had always come back.

He didn't reappear. But Colin came for her not long after. He set himself under her arm and acting as her cane so she could slowly, carefully, hobble her way down the hallway and out into the afternoon sun.

The light came as a shock to her senses and the exhaustion rolled over her, worse than before.

"Easy now," Colin murmured, sounding so like his brother that for a moment she almost believed—but no. Isaac had run off and left her to face her pain alone. "No need to race. We're almost there."

He lifted her easily, tucked her into the carriage, and took up a guard post on the opposite seat, settling her foot on the cushion beside him.

"You'll have to forgive my brother." Colin said as the horses began to move. Grace shook her head. "All right, maybe not right away. But you know he's meticulous about his work. And *I* know that if he thought there was any chance at all you might be hurt, he would never have taken the risk."

"Risks are easy to take when they're with someone else's body," Grace said, and the parallels struck her hard in the gut, drove the breath from her lungs.

Another man who thinks I only exist to demonstrate his genius.

"I think that's a little unfair," Colin objected, but Grace

stared out the window at the city streets passing swiftly by and didn't answer.

He seemed to be able to take the hint, thankfully enough, and didn't press her for further conversation. They bumped along the streets in silence, every jolt and jostle sending darts of pain shooting up the back of her leg. The overall ache had begun to subside, but that only meant the soreness clustered around the injury itself, a throb around the tendon that meant swelling, bruising, and sleepless nights to come.

Colin swung himself out of the hack as soon as it drew up in front of the inn, and within moments of his going-in there was an exodus of people from inside, like ants from a tumbled-over anthill. Mrs. Caird, Mr. Caird, a stocky woman in an apron who had to be a housekeeper, Colin himself—they moved as a well-trained team.

Within moments Grace found Mr. Caird gently hoisting her out of the cab, his nice suit replaced today by a coat dusted over with flour, and wreathed in the scent of baking bread.

He took her upstairs, talking over her head with instructions for the others, and set down in a bed so soft that it might as well have been made from the downy feathers of angel wings rather than straw and ticking.

"Now you rest there a moment." Mrs. Caird fussed over her, vanishing out the door for a moment before returning with a pink bolster, cunningly fashioned with ruffles at each end. She cooed over Grace's bandaged ankle, lifting it gently before sliding the bolster beneath.

"This always helped my boys when they did a damage to themselves. Keep it set up high, and the swelling will go down. I'll have Mrs. Sedgewick put up a poultice that will do the rest."

Grace pushed herself up on her elbows. "You're too kind, but truly, I don't need—"

Mrs. Caird snorted, reached behind Grace, and rearranged the pile of pillows there. She pushed lightly on Grace's shoulders until she let go and lay back, half-sitting in the fancy guest bed.

"Honestly, now. Don't go being difficult with me, my dear girl. I've nursed three stubborn Caird men through bumps and bruising of all sorts, and I know a bad turn when I see one. Colin tells me that the doctor's instructions are to stay off that foot, and so that's what you'll be doing."

She bustled across the room, more force of personality than Grace had imagined possible rolling off of this tiny little pixie of a woman. She had Grace's bag unpacked within moments, hanging her dress up to air out. She did pause at the breeches, but folded them and set them neatly in the growing pile.

"You'll not want to be fussing about with stays and bodices such as that while you're recovering," she said, nodding at the gauzy blue costume that Grace was still laced into, under the shawl Lucy had tucked about her shoulders for modesty. "I'll send Isaac around to your lodgings to collect some clothes for you. A dressing gown or two, a nightrail, a morning gown, perhaps? Or you're welcome to borrow some of mine." And she looked at Grace expectantly, as though waiting for an admission of guilt.

Oh yes, that would be ideal. Confess to Isaac's mother that the man had intimate knowledge of where Grace kept her personals, and turn him loose in her apartments. No. She would not be dependent on that man any more than she had been already.

"If Mr. Caird—Nicolas, that is—could speak to my friend Miss Sullivan, at the theatre," Grace said quietly, trying frantically to choose the least-worst of all her possible options. "She has been to my home before. She could pack up what I might need for the short stay. And I promise I'll not be a burden on your kindness, Mrs. Caird."

"I'll tell you the first thing I need you to stop doing," Mrs. Caird replied smartly, and Grace's heart sank.

I've made a nuisance of myself already. I knew I should never have come. She's going to tell me to stay away from her sons.

"Stop apologizing," Mrs. Caird finished, and Grace blinked in confusion. "You'll be a much more convivial patient if you think of yourself as a guest, my dear, and not a burden. I certainly have no intention of running the gauntlet of over-courtesies and overblown social graces every time I bring you a dish of soup. Honestly, who has time for that?"

Grace laughed in surprise, a short burst of mirth that won a smile from Mrs. Caird. "Yes ma'am. That is, I thank you, and—"

"That's precisely what I mean. Enough with all that. And since you're a guest in my home, please do me the courtesy of calling me Catherine."

Would this woman ever stop surprising her? And yet, she inadvertently explained quite a bit about what made Isaac himself.

"I will, Mrs—*Catherine*," Grace replied, a smile

touching her lips. "And please, call me Grace."

The room arranged to her satisfaction, and a simple banyan laid out on the bed for Grace to change into when she had the energy, Mrs. Caird looked around and nodded firmly. "Now, you relax yourself, think of nothing but getting better, and I'll be back up presently with something to eat, and a nice cup of tea. Do you enjoy novels, my dear? Some reading would make an excellent diversion from your troubles. Or would you care for a newssheet to pass the time?"

"Nothing, thank you." Grace shook her head. "I've put you out quite enough already."

"Novels it is, then. Get yourself comfortable, my dear Grace. I'll be back shortly." And Catherine left, closing the door behind her.

Grace looked around her, at the sweet rose-painted room with its vases of summer flowers in the windows, the gauzy curtains rippling in the breeze, and the double bed on which she lay, with its matching mountain of pillows. It was bright and cheerful, a long way from the dark wood and rich brocades of the room in which she had made her own home.

What did Isaac's room look like? Was it another delicately feminine room, his mother's handiwork evident in every doily and curtain sash? Or was it like his workroom in the loft, scattered with half-finished projects and experiments in all stages of completion?

She shouldn't consider it, because it didn't matter. Grace folded her arms and curled her toes on her injured foot, noting with mounting displeasure every twinge and painful pull the movement triggered.

No, charming or not, she could not allow Isaac's family to make her forget. Their lovemaking was something that had happened in a dream world, one where she'd let go of everything about the outside world. This was her penalty. Reality had asserted itself, however harshly, and she had to leave that half-real haze of *feeling* behind.

If he cared he would be here, smoothing her brow and distracting her with easy conversation.

Instead, as always, she was left to deal with things alone.

Isaac climbed the rungs of the backstage ladder, his tool-bag slung over his shoulder and his mind fixed firmly on the task before him.

If he allowed himself to slip, to begin thinking about Grace, he would go right back there in his mind. The fear would bubble up again, along with everything else that had torn through him at the moment of impact—the panic, fury, and the utter certainty that his life was over before it had begun.

That instant had been easily the worst of his life, and also his moment of brightest clarity. What a fool he'd been only minutes before, picturing Grace sprawled in his bed, remembering her sitting and eating at his table, the way she had sat demurely in the sunlight in his mother's parlor. He'd imagined every possible future they could have together, now that he was on his way to winning her heart.

Every future but this.

He reached the platform and the beams that spanned

the width of the stage, swung himself up to straddle one of the broad oaken posts. He was woolgathering again, thinking about the things he promised himself he would deal with later.

Once the work was done.

Then he could go to Grace with all the information he currently lacked, lay the truth of the incident out before her—whatever it might be—and swear before everything holy that he would see justice done.

Damn the theatre, damn opening night, damn Thilby and his blasted five pounds! None of it was worth one split hair on Grace's head.

The beam ran from one wing to the next up here in the flies, worn smooth from years of able hands doing just what Isaac was doing now. He pulled himself forward, keeping his knees tight about the beam as though he posted on a horse, one hand on the rope that crossed the same span. He'd made this crossing a thousand times before, never once giving thought to the vast emptiness that yawned beneath his feet.

Not until today, anyway. Now everything seemed dark and ominous, every creak of a rope or echo of a voice sending chills speeding along his spine.

It did not improve once he reached the dangling remnants of his mechanism, the system of pulleys and gears that controlled and directed the flying wire. Isaac hauled himself to standing, finding his footing on the six inches of smooth-sanded wood.

Here was the pulley through which the main rope fed, connecting to the clamp below, the belaying line that attached to the all but invisible wires. It was in one piece, showed no signs of wear.

The secondary pulleys, though—one had snapped clean in half, the two ends hanging, ragged-ended and splintering, broken clean through along the groove. The rope hung down into the abyss, the harness unclipped and already taken away.

The other pulley held and the rope was still solid. Thank God and all the saints in the heavens for that blessing. If it had broken then both ropes would have given way at once, and Grace would have plummeted to her death.

Isaac leaned over the empty space to grab the broken pulley, tugged it toward him as he regained his balance. The pieces slid obligingly off the loose rope and he fit them together, turning them this way and that to try to find the weakness.

Had he not been careful enough? Maybe he'd slipped with the chisel during the tooling, and made a notch that had turned into a crack.

Or maybe he'd missed a knot in the wood, or a hint of rot.

If so, then he would have to spend the rest of his days trying to earn Grace's forgiveness.

The two segments fit together snugly, only a handful of splintered bits missing. There was nothing obvious to his eye, not in the dim half-light of the flies.

He took everything down, coiling the ropes and packing all the pieces of his pride away in his bag. To his workshop then, and put himself to task. Isaac slid down the ladder and headed for the stairs. He had light and a pallet to sleep upon in the loft, food and drink to last him a few days while he worked.

Grace was being cared for; there was nothing more he could do for her that someone else couldn't do just as easily.

The things he wanted to do—hold her, gather her up in his arms, and press careful kisses over every inch of her body, smooth curatives over her skin and bind her ankle again, fluff her pillows and soothe her fears—he had no illusions that she wanted him anywhere nearby to even try.

She had sent him away, after all.

She believed he'd betrayed her—she had every right to despise him.

And the next time he went to her, he would go armed with the truth.

Chapter Fifteen

Catherine had done as she'd threatened and set a small stack of well-thumbed-through novels on the table at Grace's bedside. Her cheerful breeze in and out again had snapped Grace out of a turn of self-pitying thoughts, but it had also left her unsettled.

She tried to read, but the first book she'd opened had begun with a young woman tripping on the stairs. Grace hadn't meant to think about her own fall—one had nothing to do with the other—but the room spun and wheeled around her, and the floor rushed up to meet her.

She shut the book and pushed it back on the table, ignoring the others.

The sounds of life filtered in through the open window, voices from the tavern downstairs, the clink of stoneware and cooking pots, the rattle of coaches on the cobblestones of the street. The sun would be setting soon; it was already sitting low behind the buildings, casting longer shadows across the bedroom.

What she needed was someone to talk to and distract her from the dark thoughts jostling for attention in the back of her mind. Where was Meg right now? She'd be home, most likely, preparing for the evening's show.

If only Isaac were here, to tell her stories and make her laugh, forget all about the throbbing pain in her ankle and the bleakness that hovered around her heart.

But he *wasn't* here. He'd run off somewhere and not even checked on her once to make sure she was all right. When it was his fault she was injured in the first place!

The anger flared up hot inside and she clung to it, the first real emotion that had broken through the shock and numbness. At least that was something she could *feel.*

Grace pushed herself up to sitting, pointing the toes on her injured foot and rotating her ankle first this way, then that. It didn't hurt nearly as badly as she'd feared it would. A twinge of warning ran up along the back of her calf, but the wrapped bandage held the joint stable.

She didn't need to stay after all—the doctor must have been wrong. She could take this burst of energy and walk right out of there, leaving Isaac's family and his house behind. The thought of owing him anything, even by proxy, was enough to set her teeth on edge.

And to think she had trusted him! Not only with her body, though she was more relieved than ever that she'd never allowed him to fully consummate their love-play, but with her deeper secrets and her inner thoughts as well. He had seen her vulnerable.

(She had seen him that way as well, mind you, his back curved so deliciously underneath her and his cries echoing in her ears. His body had been so hot and tight; he had opened for her so well, her fingers sliding inside as though he had been made to take them. Isaac had groaned and gasped beneath her, riding up greedily as she curled her fingers down, pressed rough into that core-deep spot that made men quiver and sigh. And then the sounds he had made when she opened him up with her prick, his arms trembling and the taut muscles of his back golden and slick with sweat.

She had pushed inside and ruined him, pressed her hands along his spine and held his hips firm, stroked his hard cock with an oil-damp hand. Her body had thrummed with it, the friction of the ribbons tied about her hips, the solid weight of her prick putting pressure and friction on her mound, the sensation setting her own desire ablaze once more. She could have stayed there forever, buried inside him, moving with him, his pleasure entirely and completely in her hands. And then he'd shaken apart beneath her, claimed, possessed, *taken*—)

Enough!

His mother's house was hardly the place for that kind of memory, not now, with her foot bound and all future employment in question, her body aching with pulled muscles and new bruising, her soul bearing a void in the shape of *him*.

That was the price she was to pay, then, for letting him in.

Now there was one more person that she was going to miss.

Grace swung her feet over the edge of the bed, her wrapper falling down to cover her legs. The bindings felt odd beneath the arch of her foot but her ankle seemed stable enough. Her breeches sat on top of the neatly folded pile of her clothes. She could take the handful of steps across the room, dress, and be on her way home within minutes.

Her ankle had other ideas. Grace stood, one hand on the bedpost, and the pain blazed hot up the strained tendon as though she'd banged against an open stove. She sucked in breath, heard the air whistle between her teeth. The flare subsided and she gritted her teeth. She could do this.

One step, then another—she'd have to let go of the bedpost to make the last two steps over to the trunk where her clothes lay, but that was no problem.

It was a problem.

The moment she let go of the bedpost and put real weight down, her ankle screamed at the insult. The sharp stab of pain ran up and down the back again, and it wouldn't carry her. Grace toppled, grabbed for the back of the chair, and managed to slow her fall, landing hard on her knees on the woven rug beside the bed.

I will not cry.

Her eyes didn't listen, filling up with water anyway.

What's the point of crying? It won't fix anything.

The humiliation swamped her, there on the floor of the bedroom. She wrapped her arms around herself, choking back the anger and the dark grief that seemed to come up out of nowhere. The creak of the door opening was the absolute last sound she wanted to hear.

Grace tried to push herself up from where she knelt, but her foot refused to bear her weight. She dashed the treacherous tears from her eyes with the back of her hand, but they spilled out faster and faster no matter how hard she tried to blink them back.

"Shh, dear girl." Catherine knelt beside her and

gathered Grace into her arms. Grace stiffened, tried to resist, but Catherine stroked her shoulders and her back. "It's alright, poppet. I'm here."

So unfamiliar and so strange, to be held like this, like a mother rocking a hurt and tender child—Grace choked on a sob that forced its way out, and Catherine only held her closer, solid and maternal.

The world could shatter in that instant and somehow, Grace knew, Catherine would not be moved.

In the face of such tenderness from a woman who was almost a stranger, Grace lost the last tenuous hold she had on her pride.

The grief and struggle ripped her lungs apart, coming out in gasping sobs that burned her throat.

"How could everything go so wrong so quickly?" she managed to get out, burying her face in Catherine's shawl. The tears flowed freely then, pulled out of her by Catherine's gentle hands and the warmth of her embrace.

Catherine either didn't notice or didn't care that Grace's tears were soaking her clothes right through. "Everyone is tested sometime. It will all come out right in the end, poppet; you'll see." She spoke with such conviction that Grace almost believed her.

Once the tears began it was impossible to stop. She sobbed and Catherine held her, she cried until her eyes burned with the salt and her body had nothing left inside to cry. Catherine rubbed her back in easy circles, until she could draw in a horrible, ragged breath and reach for some kind of calm.

"You're tired, my girl. Up, up then, and let's get you back to bed."

Grace could almost imagine what it might have been like to have Catherine as a mother after that, finding herself guided back to the bed with sure and steady hands.

Catherine tucked Grace in beneath the counterpane, her pillows resettled behind her head and her foot up on its bolster again. She didn't even blink while Grace fought to contain her tears, handing over one handkerchief after another from a neatly folded stack she'd pulled out of a drawer.

The grief that boiled within her was a gaping maw, a black hollow that nothing in her life had ever been able to fill, not until *him*. But she couldn't focus, couldn't think. For once the intensity of the scraped-raw edges of her nerves was too much to ignore or push aside, a lifetime of loneliness and failure pouring out.

You've been strong for so long.

That's what Isaac had said, and now look at her, a weeping mess all streaked with tears and her hair a tangle. Grace pulled in a shuddering breath again, not daring to look over at the woman who sat beside her, calmly handing over another clean handkerchief.

"I'm sorry," Grace began, and got shushed for her trouble.

"Nonsense. You let it out. I have the feeling you haven't had a proper cry in a year of Sundays." Catherine's words were joking but her tone was soft, the circles she rubbed on Grace's back the best and worst sort of kindness. "That's it. Lance the boil and let the poison out. Then you can start to heal."

Grace hiccupped.

Catherine chuckled kindly, and dipped a kerchief in the washbasin, handing it to Grace to wipe her face. The cool water stung on her swollen-hot eyes, enough to start bringing her back from the brink. Grace held the cloth to her face as the odd and deep-down pain started to fade.

Where did that come from? What is wrong *with me?*

"That's better, isn't it?" Catherine's voice came from beside her, then there was the sound of the chair pushing back, and someone puttering about in the small room. "You can only keep a brew bottled up for so long, you know. Sooner or later, any cork will have to pop."

It was a metaphor, Grace's brain too muddled and thick from tears to pick it apart properly.

"I popped all over your shawl," she said mournfully, her tongue thick in her mouth as she tried to start apologizing, Catherine's nice green shawl now wrinkled and half-soaked from tears.

"It'll dry. Believe you me, after bringing up three children, my clothes have seen a great deal worse."

Catherine stepped outside the room for a minute, spoke quietly to someone, then came back in and settled in the chair beside Grace's bed. "Now, will you take tea with me? Nicolas is down with his father in the inn, and I long for conversation that doesn't revolve around seasonings, coffee shipments, or beer."

Grace was hardly in a state to take tea with anyone, the way her nose was running, and her face doubtless all blotches and red. But the offer was well-meant, and she had absolutely no desire to be alone in her misery again. "Yes, I will," she croaked out, blowing her nose and clearing her throat so that she could speak and sound like herself. "But forgive me—I thought you were a brewer yourself?"

"Oh, I am, that I am. But even talking recipes gets dull, on occasion." Catherine chuckled. There was a quiet knock at the door and she went to it, taking a tray from the solidly built older woman in an apron on the other side.

Wonderful smells wafted off the tray as Catherine brought it back over, laden with bowls of some thick, rich stew and a plate of buttered bread. The steam rose off the bowls and Grace's stomach rumbled in loud agreement. How long had it been since breakfast? And she'd been too nervous about the day to eat much then.

"We don't stand on ceremony around here, my girl. Eat up." Catherine fluffed the pillows behind Grace and helped her sit fully up, then set the tray before her with a flourish. "You'll need to build up your strength if you want that foot of yours to heal right. Mr. Caird—my husband, that is, not one of the boys—his mother swears by a good stew fortified with marrow to strengthen the blood. And she's still alive at the rare old age of eighty-and-three, so I put great stock by her remedies."

It was all too overwhelming, and for one horrible moment, Grace imagined she might start to cry again. She sniffled discreetly instead, dabbing the dampness from the corners of her eyes with a clean handkerchief. "Does she live in London?" Grace asked instead, turning the conversation to something normal, something easy.

"Mother Caird? No, you'd never catch her this far south. She's fond of the lowlands, even if they have been having more troubles the last few years, since abolition passed. Some people can't stand the thought of change, even when it's for the better."

"Some people can't stand the thought of anything that might inconvenience themselves, you mean." Grace's tone was sharper than was polite, but Catherine, her skin white as cream and hair like spun gold, didn't bat an eyelash.

"Times are changing, thank the good Lord," she said instead. "Not fast enough, but it's already better now than five years ago, when the slave trade was still protected by law. In a decade from now, a century—imagine what else we'll see."

Grace cocked her head and looked at Catherine, and a few more pieces of the puzzle fell into place. "You're an abolitionist," she guessed, and Catherine smiled.

"How could I not be, with my Andrew?" she replied, her voice filled with such fondness that it felt almost too personal. "You should have heard the noise people made when Andrew insisted on starting the sugar boycotts here. Oh, the complaints when we stopped shelving rum! We held our ground, though. I'd rather use honey for all my cooking or spend extra for the India sugar than send any coin to the plantations, may the slavers rot in Hell.

"We women almost got arrested for tucking some of Clarkson's anti-slavery pamphlets under townhouse doors in Mayfair, and that caused quite a to-do! Isaac might remember some of that—he was old enough. But I'd only just weaned Nicolas, and he was still in short pants."

The image popped to mind completely formed: Andrew, fierce and proud, and a younger Catherine, a babe on her hip, Isaac in tow—and her basket full of seditious broadsheets, determined to convert the idle wealthy to the cause of human freedom. "Isaac's never mentioned it," Grace murmured.

"No, I don't suppose he would have." Catherine tapped Grace's bowl with the edge of her spoon, reminding her to eat. Grace dipped her own spoon into the thick broth and tasted it cautiously, the savory warmth of it sinking down into her very bones. Her next few spoonfuls were much less careful.

"It's nice to have another woman in the house," Catherine said after they'd eaten in silence for a moment. She slid two thick slices of buttered bread onto Grace's tray. "Our Nan got married three years ago, bless her, and it's only me in a houseful of men. Mrs. Sedgewick's only here in the afternoons sometimes, when I could use the extra hands. It does get lonely."

Grace bit into the bread, discovering that it was fresh. The butter melted into the nutty brown slice, the crust crisping between her teeth. "Nicolas isn't married?"

"No." Catherine chuckled, but there was a tinge of something else there. Wistfulness, maybe? Not quite sadness, but something. "I don't know if I see that in his future."

"Not fortune telling, I hope." Grace had had more than enough of that.

"Some men are born to be bachelors." Catherine said it rather diplomatically, but Grace thought, perhaps, she caught the meaning.

Or Catherine might just be speaking of the fact that his older brother was a gad-about who didn't seem likely to settle down, either. "Isaac too, I suppose," she said, just a little bit out of spite.

Catherine's eyebrows went up. "Not him, no, my dear

girl. He's been looking for someone to stand beside him for a long time now."

That stirred up thoughts that Grace didn't want, and she stomped them down ruthlessly. "I'll wager he has."

"You'd be surprised, I think. He's not quite still waters, but there's a good piece of that boy that runs deep. There's nothing he wouldn't do for his brother or his sister, and that bodes well for anyone else he brings in under his wing." The look Catherine gave Grace was far too knowing for Grace's comfort, especially considering she was still trying desperately to stay furious with the man.

She finished her meal instead of pursuing the conversation, and Catherine seemed content enough to let it lie.

Catherine rose as the room darkened and vanished for a minute, only to come back with a taper and light a lamp that sat on the mantle. The warm golden glow spread out from the corner of the room, bathing the world in contentment and peace.

"Thank you," Grace said softly.

"For what now?" Catherine asked, puttering around tidying up the tray and the napkins.

"For all of this. I'm a stranger to you, and you're being so kind."

"Nonsense. You're a friend of my boys, and that makes you a friend of mine." Catherine set the tray down on the table, and she sat down on the bed by Grace's side. She looked down, and when Grace met her eyes, they held the same look of compassion and caring that Grace had once imagined seeing on Isaac.

"If you don't mind me saying so, poppet, it's written on your face. You look as though you haven't had anyone taking care of you in a long time. Everyone needs a little mother's love once in a while, even once you're all grown."

Grace pressed her lips together, ignoring the sting in her eyes. "I'm not sure I know what that's like. My mother...was not the affectionate sort."

The offended snort that came from Catherine was hardly dignified, but it was reassuring. "Then you'll just have to stop by more often until you learn how it feels, and then stay until you start taking it for granted. Now you get some rest."

She patted Grace's hand, and for some reason that simple gesture was enough to send a wave of something new and powerful racing through Grace's chest. It was as though, somewhere deep inside, an ancient, nameless wound had begun to heal.

"Damnation!" Isaac slammed the door of the loft behind him. The walls shook with the force of it, the rush so satisfying that he did it again for good measure. He stormed across the floor, kicking aside a bucket that was in his way, and it tumbled across the space to smash up against the table leg and stop there. It did a little to release the anger and the pressure building up inside, but not enough. Not nearly enough.

He yelled, a wordless cry of frustration that echoed off the loft's high ceiling. He needed to focus, be clear-headed and tackle the mystery like an intelligent man, but the fear-fueled rage clouded everything.

When he closed his eyes, all he could see was her, blue silk tumbling down through the darkness. When the room was silent, all he could hear was the sound of impact. It ripped through his brain, the echo of dreams dying, all of it compressed into that single moment when he had been so sure that she was dead.

And in that moment, too, he had learned one vital thing.

He was desperately in love with her.

Beyond her body, her beauty, her wit—he had pursued Grace for all of those things, but she was so much more. And that point when time had stopped in turn had shown him everything he had just lost: her kindness, the soft vulnerability in her eyes when she looked at him and thought he wasn't watching back. The soft unfolding as she had begun to trust him, the stirring in his soul that made him want to hold her close and be her shelter against the world.

A life without her wry smile and the softness of her lips was no life at all.

Grace Owens was the one woman he knew who could ever complete him, who saw his mind and shared it. And she lived! She lived, and now she surely hated him. He'd seen her fury first-hand.

How could he blame her?

He kicked the corner of the trunk for good measure, accomplishing nothing but to dent in the toe of his boot and send a shock through his leg. He could almost hear Grace's acid commentary in his mind the moment he'd done it.

Was that supposed to be helpful?

She would have snorted a laugh, the corner of her

mouth curled up just so, in that way that told him to get his head screwed on correctly.

You're pitching a childish fit. Go back to the nursery until you can behave like a man.

"You're right," Isaac told the air. If he were going mad, at least it was the woman he loved who would haunt his despair. "I need to get to work."

The lamp flared to life under his fingers, the flint and tinder catching easily. The shadows in the corners moved and he looked over sharply, but there was nothing there except the play of light across the boards.

I'm getting paranoid.

But was it truly unreasonable to be concerned when something had happened that very afternoon?

Isaac sat down at his workbench, bringing the lamp as close as he dared. He unwrapped the bundle of parts he'd collected from the stage and spread them out on the tabletop, in as close to proper configuration as he could manage in the flat.

Something in here would tell him what had happened.

And then, when he knew—what then?

He turned the broken pulley over in his hands, the smooth-sanded wood familiar and warm in his palms. At first glance it looked normal, nothing soft or rotten through.

Then why had it snapped?

He leaned back in his chair, tapping one finger against the pulley in his hands. The other half sat on the table and he picked it up, turning it over in the light before fitting it back against its mate.

And there, there in the light when Isaac held the wood up and turned it around—he saw it.

Tooling marks that had not been there before. Split by the place where the wood had broken, invisible except in the lamp's direct light, the wood bore the undeniable sign of a dragging file. The marks had been made recently, cutting through the smooth-sanded surface, carving fault lines into an otherwise sturdy piece.

Now that he knew what he was looking for, he ran his fingertips over the other side of the broken pulley and found the rough spots there, as well.

"This was done on purpose."

He spoke the words aloud and they fell, dead, into the silence of the room.

He'd considered it, of course, better than imagining that he had made such a horrific mistake. But now, seeing this, knowing with utter certainty that someone had set this up, perhaps intending Grace to die?

The rage washed over him again and this time he let it sweep him under. It passed a moment later, leaving his chest tight and his heart thumping painfully in his chest.

He had his answer, but it generated more questions than before. *Who did this?* Not anyone in the theatre, surely. The company squabbled and bickered amongst themselves, but *sabotage*? Never. Especially, he decided somewhat cynically, if there was any chance that the saboteur would be caught in the problem. That left out Colby and Tottenham completely. Outside the company, then—that gave him an obvious option. No-one but Thilby would want to see his work fail. But that he couldn't bring himself to believe.

Thilby was an ass, a shirker who hated hard work, and many other things besides, but he was also the boy who had swept stages with him, hung over balconies and dropped rye berries into fancy ladies' headdresses, and pooled money for sweets when they'd been working for pennies. There was a trust there that wouldn't be broken. Besides, how would he have gotten in? He'd never had a key to the Surrey.

If not Isaac, then the target had to have been Grace. But who would want to harm a dancer? And why in such a convoluted way, instead of sending a cutpurse after her, or an alley thug?

Until he had the whole story, Grace wouldn't be safe. And he couldn't go to her until he could promise her that, for once and for all. Then he would tell her everything, present her enemy's head—or at least news of his arrest— to her on a platter.

Colin and their parents would keep watch over her for now. Isaac had more work to do.

Chapter Sixteen

The sun had barely risen when Isaac woke, peeling his face off the worktable where he'd slumped at some point in the earlier hours of the morning. Isaac rolled up to sitting and stretched, the kink in his neck stabbing him with a painful reminder of why he should have pulled out a pallet and blanket while he'd had the chance. Groaning, he pushed himself up and stretched again, his shirt riding up and the bones of his spine cracking in a gratifying way.

He scratched at his chin, the stubble there bristling, but he hadn't the time to shave now, or really do anything except splash his face and hands with cold water from the washbasin and find the rest of his clothes. The broken pulley had given up all its secrets last night—he needed a new way to get his answers.

At least there was one thing about the theatre: *it* never slept. Someone was bound to have been about on Saturday night.

It had to have been done Saturday. Isaac had tested the rig that morning before heading home to get ready for tea with his mother and Grace. It had been working *fine.* Nothing had been out of order, or even the slightest bit loose. But then by Sunday afternoon, when they had all assembled, suddenly the pulleys that had held a fifteen-stone man in the air the day before had failed at the weight of a slender ballerina.

Isaac buttoned his waistcoat quickly and carelessly, pulling his coat on as he jogged down the attic stairs. Saturday night, he and Grace had been in bed together. He'd been indulging in pleasures of the flesh while someone else was fulfilling far darker designs.

It was his failure, then, even though his design had been sound. He could have kept better watch, set one of the boys to stay up and make sure nothing was tampered with.

The boys might be the answer. The backstage apprentices were like mice, scampering through the place at all hours. For all he knew, some of them slept in the dressing rooms overnight. He wouldn't put it past them, anyway.

The women's dressing room sat empty, stockings hung over a screen to dry and the tables covered with pots of creams and paints, lengths and curls of false hair, and a rather sad-looking half-eaten meat pasty.

The men's yielded up slightly better results. Someone lay along the battered old settee, head propped up on the arm with the split seam, stuffing coming out about the edges. A newssheet lay open over the person's face, shielding him from the light now filtering in through the streaky window panes.

"Oy," Isaac said aloud, and the figure stirred. He smiled grimly, crossed the floor and folded the paper in his hands.

John Bright, the bright young spark of the company, if you asked Elliston (the pain in the rear end barely out of school who was entirely too full of himself, if you asked anyone else), sat up with a start, blinking bleary-eyed into the morning. "Caird! What are you doing? Did I oversleep? Is it rehearsal?"

"Relax." Isaac couldn't help the grin. It wasn't exactly polite, but then, Bright had never been one for standing on ceremony, especially with the backstage hands. "You're not late. It's early enough you could even get yourself looking like a human being instead of one of the animals at the Exchange, if you cared to."

"Oh, har." Bright snorted and ran his hands through his shag of brown hair, then shook his head until it fell haphazardly into place. "What is it that you want?"

"Were you here Saturday night?"

Bright raised an expressive eyebrow and gave Isaac one of those disdainful looks he was notorious for. "Why? Has something gone missing? I don't have any interest in tool chests or hacksaws."

One look at his soft hands could have told Isaac *that*.

"Nothing like that," he said instead of falling into the temptation to bicker. "But it's important, or I wouldn't ask. Were you about on Saturday night? After the supper hour, I'd say."

Bright frowned, his arms folded, his breeches unbuttoned at the cuffs and his shirtsleeves rolled up in comfortable ease. Isaac could all but see the smoke rising from the boy's brainpan as he tried to think back. "Out. Down to Astley's for the show, then to Covent Garden for a girl." He grinned wide, proud of his own outrageousness as only a boy of sixteen with regular wages and no responsibilities could be. "A nice bit, too. I didn't leave until Sunday morning, when I walked her to church."

"And you went to service too, I suppose," Isaac drawled, amused despite himself.

"Not me, Mr. Caird. I'd spent all night in prayers already." Bright waggled his eyebrows, but eventually his mischievous smile dimmed. "It's a damned shame about Miss Owens, of course. I heard about that when I ran into Paddy Byrne at the pub last night. How's she faring?"

Of course he'd have to ask that question. "Well enough," Isaac hedged. The sour weight settled low in his stomach again, the guilt and grief nibbling around the corners of his forced calm. "She's being looked after now, and resting. She's had quite the fright."

Bright nodded, and there was only concern in his expression. *He didn't have anything to do with it.* "I don't doubt it. If there's anything that I can do to be of comfort to her, of course, just say the word."

"I don't think she's after your sort of comfort, my lad," Isaac replied dryly. "But you can be of help to me. Someone was in the building on Saturday night who should not have been, and I need to find out who."

Now that got a reaction. Bright came alert and sat upright. "You're after a saboteur," he guessed rightly, and something in the way he looked at Isaac had changed— approval, maybe, or more respect. "You daft bugger, you're going to try and chase him down yourself, aren't you?"

"That would be the plan." Isaac left out the part of the plan *he* liked the best, where he had the villain strung up by his toes and pelted with rotten fruit. Or perhaps just whipped around the town, like in the olden days. "But first I need to know who saw what."

Bright nodded, the easy street drawl coming back in to his voice as his enthusiasm grew. "I'll ask about, see if any of the fellows know anything. I'll tell you right off, the Byrnes were here late. Paddy said as much down t'pub. They've been working as long as their candle ends hold out to get the new costumes ready on such short notice."

Of course they would be—and there were any number of people coming in and out of the wardrobe who might be able to give him a clue. "You're a prince and a gentleman," Isaac said, clapping Bright on the shoulder in his sudden burst of enthusiasm. "That might just do it. But keep your eyes and ears open. Something is afoot here, and until we know who's at fault—"

"Let me guess. No one is safe, and none can be trusted?" Bright chuckled, but his eyes were alight.

"Off-book already, like the professional you are." Isaac left the boy behind and strode down the long hallway, his boots echoing on the uneven wooden floor. Maybe he'd been foolish to say anything, but then, Bright had guessed his motives right away. The saboteur would surely know that someone would figure it out, and sooner rather than later. He'd be covering his tracks, not catching naps in the dressing room.

It would probably be all right.

Isaac had to have faith in *something*.

He all but tripped over Red Peter, the propmaster's boy, who sat at the foot of the stairs dutifully sanding down a bucket full of wooden doorknobs. A small pile of finished ones sat to the side, and Isaac jumped a step rather than put his foot down in the precariously-placed bucket.

Peter looked up, the vivid pink birthmark on his face giving him a lopsided, roguish look, and smiled when he recognized Isaac. "Early morning for you, Mr. Caird?"

"Too early," Isaac agreed. He dropped down to sit on the bottom step, taking up a doorknob and a scrap of glasspaper to go with it. "You're about the place all the time, aren't you?"

"Here, there, and everywhere," Peter agreed easily, his fingers never stilling as he turned and smoothed the wood. No more than thirteen, fourteen maybe, he already had most of his grown height alongside a voice that still squeaked at inopportune moments. "Wherever Da needs an extra set of hands."

Moving the paper with its sparkling shards of glass made it twinkle in the dim light. It dragged slow against the wood when Isaac set them together, the rhythm of the movement somehow deeply satisfying. "How about Saturday?"

"Day or night? Daytime we was working here, building up the table for Act One. Banquo's got to run mad across the thing now, so's it had to get another beam nailed in under to hold Neddy up." Peter snorted, shaking his head. "You'd think they'd all have figured that one out before this week, but that's the way she goes. Nighttime, we went home. After the sun was down, mind, but not that much later. Ma had to go call on a neighbor who's lying-in, so we were needed."

Isaac nodded, the sawdust sparkling in the air around him. "Was anyone else still hanging about when you left?"

Peter frowned for a moment, thinking. "Wardrobe was open, but they've always got folks coming in and out. Other than them? Only Miss Sullivan, but she had her bonnet on and all, about to go not long after us."

Now that was a thought. If Lucy had been around, if she had seen anything—but no. She was a close friend of Grace's. If she knew anything at all, she'd have been the first to speak out.

"Keep your ears and eyes open, will you? Ask around the lads." Isaac dug out a coin and flipped it to the boy. "Someone was poking about Saturday night where they shouldn't have been. I mean to find out who."

"For another one of these when I get your answers," Peter retorted, his lopsided grin mercenary.

Isaac smiled. "You drive a hard bargain."

"But I deliver, every time."

They shook on it, the coin vanishing into Peter's pocket and the doorknob into the bucket, and the boy turned back to his work.

What now? He could go to Miss Sullivan. Maybe she'd noticed something that hadn't seemed important at the time. But he had no idea where she was. The Byrnes, on the other hand, were almost always easy to find.

Grace woke to the sounds of a house already in motion. The rise and fall of cheerful voices thrummed through the floorboards, words indistinct. Pots and pans clanked, a door opened and closed, carts rolled by on the cobblestone streets outside. A deep bass voice was singing somewhere in the house, the words indistinct and the gentle melody rising and falling. Someone had already been in the room while she lay asleep, the curtains drawn back to let in the light. Butter-yellow sunbeams touched the bedspread and pillow, warming Grace's slow drift back to consciousness.

All it needed was birdsong, or perhaps a bubbling brook, to be perfectly pastoral. Neither were terribly likely to be found in Chelsea. Grace smoothed her hands out across the wide bed. A tabby cat jumped down from the windowsill and landed on the bedspread with a thump. He bumped his head against her hand until she scratched behind his ears, and he settled in with a low rumbling purr.

She should be grateful. She should be luxuriating in the comfort, in the simple beauty of the morning.

All she could feel was the emptiness on both sides.

Only yesterday she had woken in her own bed, the sunlight blocked by the closeness of the buildings on either side of hers, voices outside shouting and grumbling at each other as Charing Cross began its day.

But she had been at peace, then. She had rolled over and pressed herself up against Isaac's broad, naked back, traced the lines of shadow on his muscled arms and the hollows of his hips. She had been able to bury her nose in the nape of his neck and drink in his scent, the edges flavored still with the musk of sex.

For all its finery, this soft feather bed piled high with pillows and pastel-colored bedclothes was a poor second to the few minutes when she had believed she was loved.

Had he come home last night? Maybe he was out there now, having let her sleep, waiting until she was awake again before he came in. Yes, that could be it. He would be pacing the hall, wondering what to say, perhaps planning and discarding myriad ways to apologize.

It was a lovely fantasy, the image in her mind's eye solid and punctuated by words she had heard Isaac murmur in his passions. *I adore you, you are everything.*

But the moment she needed him, truly needed him, he left. Unwilling to face the reality of his actions, he had run away.

How like a man. The moment things became difficult, he had fled. To a club, no doubt, or the tavern downstairs, to drown his failures in ale and doxies, a girl pulled across his lap to make him forget.

Some small part of her knew she was being unreasonable. The loneliness swallowed that voice whole.

She had always been able to work through these things before, drown the nagging voices and sour feelings in scripts and memorizing lines, and before that, in the purity of movement. Dancing around the room was out of question right now, but she could sink into her skin again without that. Grace pointed the toes on her injured foot, the drag and ache in the back of her ankle a faint warning not to push too far.

She ignored it until the faint alarm became a sudden scream. Grace released her muscles, flexed her foot this time until the strain pulled the other way, a rope pulled tight along the back of her ankle. It hurt, but that was familiar. This was the one thing she had always been able to rely on, even as the rest of the world collapsed down around her.

It would be better if Isaac were here, even though it

was his fault in the first place. But he would put his arms around her, his voice murmuring sweet words of encouragement, his shoulders solid enough to hold up the world, of which she was just one small and insignificant part.

The door handle turned.

Grace pushed herself up to sitting and dragged one hand through her curls, the wild black corkscrews refusing to be tamed. So be it—she had been wrong! He was here, and he was coming to her, to hold her in his arms and beg her forgiveness, to pledge himself for—

The door opened and Mrs. Sedgewick appeared, a bustling apron-clad form surmounted by a tightly coiled walnut-brown braid and a neat white cap.

Not him.

Bastard.

Grace bit the inside of her cheek to force her disappointment away from her face, and she smiled gently instead. "Good morning."

"And a good morning to you, my dear." Mrs. Sedgewick took a quick turn about the room, redoing the curtain ties and checking the fire before stopping by the bed. "Gyb, you nuisance of a thing. Go earn your keep." She nudged the cat until he glared at her and jumped to the floor, landing with an indignant thump. Mrs. Sedgewick drew back the covers without asking permission, exposing Grace's injured leg to her knee. "Let's see that ankle now."

"It feels much better," Grace reported dutifully. It did, honestly; a couple of mild pangs twinged at the injury site when Mrs. Sedgewick pressed her fingers against the tendon, but nothing like the sharp pain that had crippled her yesterday. "I'm sure I can walk on it now."

"You'll do nothing of the sort," Mrs. Sedgewick snorted. She turned Grace's foot, gently stretching out her ankle until the pain set in and Grace winced. "Mrs. Caird said you'd be impatient, and now I see what she means. I'll get another poultice put together, and you keep yourself right here."

"Yes, ma'am." Against her own better judgment, a smile tugged up at one corner of her mouth. Mrs. Sedgewick tucked the bolster back beneath Grace's ankle and propped her foot up in the air, where the sunbeam danced on her bare toes.

"Mrs. Sedgewick," Grace began, then fell silent. She didn't need to know. But Lord have mercy, she wanted to. "Did Mr. Caird—Isaac—did he come home last night?"

Mrs. Sedgewick pursed her lips. "I go home a'nights once the older Mr. Caird's got the kitchen ready for the evening guests, so I couldn't tell you rightly, but I daresay not. His door's open and his bed's made, and there were only the three Cairds about to sit to breakfast a minute ago." She looked almost apologetic. "Perhaps he spent the night at his sister's."

Was that the answer she wanted? Maybe. If he had come home and not come to see her, that would have been awful and all the proof she needed of his capriciousness.

But if he didn't come home at all—did that mean he couldn't even bear to be under the same roof as she was? Perhaps he was angry with Colin and his mother for taking her in, where she would be a constant reminder. Or perhaps he didn't care at all. Worse than the thought of his anger was the idea of his indifference.

And why should he care? She wasn't important, after all, just another dancer, and an old and broken one at that. He'd been curious about her, maybe even thrilled by the breeches she wore, the exotic questions of her desires. And now that he'd had her, now that he'd sated his curiosity, even though she'd not let him have everything—

She'd been useful and now she wasn't, so he had moved on.

The jagged pain through her chest was new and uncalled for, stealing her breath and her hope all in one.

Discarded and forgotten, again.

"Of course," Grace murmured. Mrs. Sedgewick gave her a deep and inscrutable look before gathering up the linens and bustling herself out the door.

No, this way was better. Then she could get well and go back to her regular life without having to face him directly. She would go back to the Olympic next season. Meg would be glad to act with her again, and Sarah could be prevailed upon to write a role for Grace into her next play. And then she would never have to look at Isaac Caird ever again.

So there.

The door opened a second time, and damn her, she sat right up again, because this time it might be him.

Catherine bustled in, a laden tray in her hands. Grace sagged back against her pillows, disappointment flooding through her just as that false bravado had done just a moment ago. Isaac's mother didn't seem to notice her reaction. She set the tray down across Grace's lap and laid a napkin across with as much pomp and circumstance as if she were serving a queen.

The rich smells of meat and eggs drifted up from the tray, and Catherine took the linen cover away to display a feast with enough food for at least three of Grace—sausage and eggs, yes, but also a rasher of bacon and a bowl of porridge swimming with berries and milk. "There's hot water coming for washing, and here's a little something to break your fast."

"This is 'a little something'?" Grace blurted out in her surprise.

Catherine didn't seem to take offense, snorting kindly. "You're all skin and bones, my dear. I know you dancers work long days—let me get some meat on you. I warn you, mind, it'll be an insult to my cooking if you don't try a bit of everything." She said that last in solemn tones, but she winked as well, and Grace stifled the unexpected chuckle that threatened.

"You're being very kind," she offered instead. "I'll never be able to repay your generosity."

"Pish tosh. Thank Isaac if you must carry on like that, for he's the one who began our acquaintance. I'm doing no more for you than I would for any of their friends who needed help, if that makes you feel any better." Catherine smiled a roguish smile so much like Isaac's for a moment that Grace's heart fluttered and ached at the same time.

"I would, if he were here," she said, and this time let the pain sink over her, anchors on her arms and legs that would drag her down into sorrow and loss.

Catherine looked at her with amusement, though, and

some sympathy. "My son," she sighed. "He's a contradiction in many ways, you know. Of course you do, for you'll have seen it. He's a man of science, of deep thought, but if he's not moving, not *doing*, he feels useless. And so he sets off explosions in my kitchen on the regular instead of writing papers for the college."

And that...did not surprise Grace as much as it probably should have. All she could think to say in return was the truth. "He let me down."

Catherine made a soft noise that hovered half between agreement and not.

What was I thinking? She's his mother, and a good one. Of course she would always think the best of him.

Grace changed the subject. "Mrs. Sedgewick was in earlier. My ankle really is much better now. I think I'll be able to take my leave of you today."

"I think you need to have Isaac sit down with you and go over sums again," Catherine retorted quickly, seemingly relieved to leave the other topic of conversation behind. "Unless I'm mistaken, one day of rest is not equivalent to three."

"Ah, but I'm healthy and young, so I heal faster than a doddering old physician."

"Young and foolish, you mean, and like all young folks, prone to ignoring the advice that would do you the most good!"

Grace tried to smile. Catherine smiled back, determination, amusement, and maybe even something like affection in the way she argued back. Maybe she meant what she said, and Grace was no burden on her.

It was a strange thought, but the more Grace poked at it, the more she discovered that it was a notion she liked.

She would just have to make sure she was long gone before Isaac came home and broke her heart again.

A wide set of stairs led down into the bowels of the theatre. The hallways had begun to fill again with the bits and pieces for the new show—a witches' cauldron piled high with wooden goblets for the feast, a boxful of daggers already splashed with red, a pile of armor pieces of varying shapes and sizes, a bloody severed head resting cheerfully on the top.

Isaac patted the top of the Thane of Cawdor's paint-matted scalp as he headed by, for luck. "Better days, Mac."

Byrne and his wife were in the wardrobe when Isaac opened the door and poked his head in, a fire banked in the hearth and the ubiquitous tin kettle sitting on the stones. Only one of Byrne's apprentices was about this time, the lanky youth with olive skin sitting cross-legged on one of the long tables. He glanced up when Isaac entered, then turned back to stitching on an oddly shaped piece of canvas molded into a curve over his hand.

"Caird!" Byrne set an extravagant crown down on the trestle table in the center of the room and flapped a harried hand at Isaac. "What is it you need? And don't be saying that something's been cut or added again, because I told Elliston yesterday, he gets what he gets at this point, and if he doesn't like it well enough, he can go—"

"Mr. Byrne!" Mrs. Byrne's scolding reprimand from

the fireside cut him off before he could finish. The stout, balding Irishman in the shockingly salmon banyan cocked an eyebrow at Isaac as though to say *"women"*.

Isaac shook his head. "Nothing like that. It's about yesterday, and Saturday night."

"You mean poor Miss Owens." Byrne nodded sagely. "Damn shame that, damn shame. Nice girl, that one, if a bit standoffish. More girls should wear breeches about. It don't half brighten the place up."

"Mr. Byrne!"

"Sorry, mum." He grinned, not looking sorry in the slightest.

"You're a terror, you are."

Normally Isaac would have gleefully joined in with the teasing, but this morning he had a much more serious purpose in mind. "Were you here Saturday night? Red Peter said he thought you might have been."

"Saturday?" Byrne looked over at his wife, his brow furrowed, and she nodded briskly.

"Ay, there was the green cloak missing the clasp, and the boots that had to go to the cobbler, and the—"

"—the witch skirt that needed bringing up, but I still can't understand how a girl can shrink in height in the span of a week."

"As if the span of a year would make it more likely?" Mrs. Byrne snorted, half-buried in the pile of cotton petticoats she was stitching on.

"Saturday?" Isaac interrupted again, his fingers tapping restlessly on his thigh.

"Oh, aye." Byrne nodded thoughtfully. "An honest day's work is never done."

"Who else was here?" Isaac pressed. "Someone did some damage Saturday night, and there are only so many ways they could get into the building. Someone had to have seen them."

"There was a noise upstairs," Mrs. Byrne said.

"There are always noises upstairs, mum."

"If your ears are that good, why can't you hear me when I'm talking to you half the time?"

"I saw someone."

The bickering Byrnes fell silent and Isaac turned at the soft voice. The teenage boy sitting on the table regarded him solemnly, his hands stilled and the needle still clasped between his fingers. He nodded to Isaac, a jerky, awkward sort of movement, like he was still becoming accustomed to the length of his limbs.

Byrne made a vaguely surprised noise in his throat. "Caird, Simon. Simon, Caird."

"Go on, Simon," Isaac urged, crossing the space between them with three long strides. "Tell me. Any detail you can recall."

Simon cleared his throat with a low-lung cough before he spoke. "We were here late, myself, the Byrnes, Richards who does the goldwork stitching, and Mrs. Winkler the milliner who has the shop off Sloane Square. I thought I heard something—the door, or maybe Devenish come back to help with the pressing, so I went up. I saw someone mucking about in the wings, but I assumed it was one of the hands."

He fell silent, his eyes darting anywhere but at Isaac.

"What else?" Isaac demanded, slamming his open hand down on the edge of the table. The slap echoed and his palm stung, fueling his impatience. "If you're protecting someone or holding anything back, then out with it!"

Simon flinched, his eyes flashing with panic, and guilt settled low in Isaac's gut. "Believe me, sir—at the time, the ghost light was the only thing lit, so I couldn't see faces. I thought it were just Colby, or Tottenham. Or you."

"How d'you know it wasn't?" Byrne asked, the voice of reason that Isaac didn't want to hear. He wanted—no, he *needed*—to make some kind of headway, to know that he was coming closer, however short the steps. "It could've been anyone in those circumstances, lad."

Simon shook his head, his shoulders settling back down from up around his ears. "Thinking back on't, I don't think so. Colby left at sundown, Tottenham wasn't about at all, and if Mr. Caird wasn't around—I should have gone closer, taken another look."

Two figures in the dark—it was something, but not enough. Nowhere near enough. And if that was all he would have to go on, then Grace's attackers would be left free to roam the city unpunished. That thought soured his stomach and sent spears of pain through his heart.

Someone walked by in the hall outside, conversation echoing, indistinct but undeniably there.

Isaac leaned in, seizing on to that faint spark of hope. "Maybe you couldn't see, but I'll wager you could hear. If your ears are good enough to pick up an opening door from down here."

"I don't know, honest I don't," Simon said, his uncertainty writ large across his face. "I suppose...I might have, but it's not at all clear."

It was worth the attempt. "Put down your work for a moment," Isaac urged. "We'll try to jog your memory."

"If this involves a punch to the brainpan, I'll ask you to cease and desist," Byrne broke in from the fireside, where he'd settled in to the overstuffed wing chair with a box of buttons and a pair of britches. "He's the only one of my apprentices with any sense at all."

"Nothing so dire." Isaac stood tall and looked into Simon's eyes, tried to impress upon him the absolute importance of his answers. How had the mesmerizer done it in his miracle show last winter?

"Look at me and ignore the rest of the room. Think back two nights, remember the feeling of walking up the stairs."

He felt like a ruddy great idiot like this, half-remembering phrases and intentions he'd watched from the wings. Simon seemed to be following, though, a frown of concentration settling in on his face.

"You came in to the theatre," Isaac prompted. "It was mostly dark, so you couldn't see much. What did you hear?"

"Nothing. I didn't see or hear anything!"

"Didn't you? Think, man!"

"The door closing," Simon said finally. "Footsteps, there were three of them. Not three feet, three men. One stayed by the door. The others went up, past the ghost light, into the wings. I think—feet on the ladder. I heard feet on the ladder, scuffling."

"And their voices. What of their voices?"

Simon shook his head. "I don't know! They were mumbling, I didn't stay long." He looked away, closing his eyes.

After a moment he breathed deep, the frown line back between his brows. "Voices. One sounded older. Deep voice, grumbling. He didn't want to be there. The other…"

Simon paused, and Isaac had to hold himself back from growling at him again. Then Simon's eyes opened, and he smiled a grim smile. "The other—it was an odd sound. Like he had an accent, perhaps. Or a lisp."

Chapter Seventeen

Like an accent. The description haunted Isaac the rest of the morning, even as all his other avenues gave him nothing. Nothing that was of any use, anyway. Old Tom thought he remembered a drunkard pissing in the alley behind the theatre that night, but that was nothing out of the ordinary. Nor were the girls hanging about the stage door waiting for the young men to come in search of entertainment. No matter who he spoke to, how many hints he followed or coins he slipped into eagerly open palms, he couldn't seem to find anything more than what Simon had been able to tell him. And that was almost worse than useless.

Isaac stopped on the street corner and looked around, considering his options. A carriage sped by, almost bowling over a handful of children running pell-mell after a rolling ball. Housekeepers and maids out to market bustled up and down, while a pair of schoolgirls walked arm in arm, peering in windows and giggling to each other. It was a beautiful summer's day, and that was maddening. By all rights the sky should be low and storming, the rumbling of thunder a grim counterpoint to Isaac's dark and angry mood.

Chelsea's busy thoroughfare steadfastly refused to play the role of a setting in a ghastly sort of novel, and Isaac was left to deal with the low-banked rage and damned *impotence* all on his own.

He could find Red Peter and find out if the boy had discovered anything, but how likely was that, if Isaac had come up empty? His stomach growled at him, and settled the question. Home first, to eat and change clothes, and then take stock of his situation. Colin had said that Grace was in the pink bedroom, and that he could easily avoid. Because how could he face her without answers?

All she would have to do was take one look at him, and she would know that he had failed. He had sworn to find the men responsible, and he was barely any closer now than he had been yesterday. Grace deserved better. All her life she had been disappointed by men, put her faith in them only to find it abused. He had to be the exception.

The fire of his renewed determination carried him as far as the kitchen door. There were voices beyond, hardly unusual for the lunch hour. But he could have sworn, just for a moment, that he'd heard Grace laughing.

The tight squeeze around his heart and the rush of air out of his lungs were just surprise. It had nothing to do with the longing that bubbled up in his chest. Besides, Grace was bedridden, doctor's orders. She would hardly be up stirring soup or filling pies.

Encouraged by the reminder, Isaac pushed open the green-painted door and went inside. He ducked his head to avoid crashing it into the low beam, and the cheerful buzz of conversation died. Isaac's heart, only just started to lift, sank down to his toes once again.

Grace sat ensconced in one of the cushioned chairs from the parlor, of all things, incongruous in its floral cheer in the otherwise utilitarian kitchen. Her foot was wrapped in a bandage and carefully propped up on a bolster positioned on a stool. She had a simple day dress on, a ribbon wrapped around her head to hold back her cloud of curls, and a bowl of peas, half-shucked, on the wooden table before her. Colin sat across from her, of all people, slicing a ham into fine portions. Colin set his knife aside and nodded, but Grace stared at him coldly, ice in her eyes.

"Don't let me interrupt," Isaac said, for lack of any better ideas. "I've just come home for a few minutes. To wash. And eat."

"Of course," Grace spoke, and there was no affection in her voice, every word a fine-honed dagger sticking in his chest. She hated him, of course she did. He was a fool to have thought otherwise, even for a moment. "I'm sure you've had very important business to attend to."

What could he say, that he had come back with nothing, after promising her everything? No, the only way to get out of this and save face was to say as little as possible, and try to make it to the door before anyone asked him how his search had gone. "Important enough. Mother is making sure you're comfortable, I hope?"

He could see the answer for himself. Grace might be injured, but there had been a life in her eyes and in her smile moments ago that he'd only seen a few times before. She seemed so at ease in her throne, a queen reigning over her domain, so at home that he could picture her as somehow always having been part of this space, and his life.

"She has, thank you. I have been made very welcome."

A thread of something other than anger wove through her clipped reply, but she didn't say enough for him to be sure that he had heard it. She was an actress, after all, and had her face so tightly composed and controlled that a mentalist would be hard-pressed to guess at any of her thoughts.

"Good," Isaac said, and from the corner of his eye he saw Colin wince. He glared at his brother, then tried to find words. "Good," he said again, for lack of any other inspiration.

It wasn't at all what he wanted to say. He would much rather take her by the waist and lift her into his arms, press kisses along every inch of her throat and pledge his fealty, soothe the furrows in her brow with his fingertips and swear to be her knight errant for the rest of her days.

Instead, what came out was anything but. "I'll, ah. Be going. And let you get back to your work."

She didn't argue. She turned away instead and reached for the bowl, giving him a good view of the back of her head, and the back of her shoulder.

He had been dismissed, and even as he made his way out into the hallway, he felt the ache of it deep inside his bones.

The sunlight in the hallway seemed dimmer, the rays too cold to warm him through as he headed up the creaking stairs. His room was dark, the curtains drawn, all the light in the world left downstairs at the kitchen table beside his little brother.

I'm thinking nonsense. I can't let myself be distracted now.

There was a proper order of events, just like with his

experiments. First do the research, then prove or disprove the theory, and only after that worry about the clean-up.

Isaac stripped, shaved and washed in the cool water left in the jug, splashing his face briskly so the shock would finish clearing his head. He dragged a clean shirt on over his head, the door opening while he was blinded by the billowing linen.

Grace!

No—how could it be? She couldn't walk.

He tugged his shirt down and almost got his head stuck in the armhole for his troubles. Colin stood in the doorway, his mouth twisted like he'd been about to laugh. He stepped inside and closed the door behind him, though, instead of poking fun.

"Did you learn anything?" Colin asked, dropping down on the end of Isaac's bed and sitting there, cross-legged. Thank God for Colin. He cut right to the important question, leaving Isaac free not to think about what had been making him and Grace laugh so freely.

He's not courting her; I can be sure of at least that much. If Colin had been anyone else, mind you!

But leave that behind. He'd been asked a question and needed to answer. Isaac shook his head, then paused, nodded, then waggled his hand in the air in a vague sort of way. "Perhaps." He changed his breeches and tucked in his shirt-tails as he carried on.

"One of Byrne's apprentices saw three men skulking about backstage after hours, but he couldn't give me anything about what they looked like. Only that one of them had an accent. I thought perhaps it might have been Cortez, the new Spanish hand who still works at the docks, but what cause would he have to want to hurt Grace? As far as I know, they've never even met."

Colin frowned, worrying his thumbnail between his teeth. "Is that what you suppose happened? That someone is after Miss Owens specifically?"

"Of course. What else could it be?" Isaac slid his braces up on his shoulders, the rote actions oddly soothing. "A rival, perhaps, or something to do with her parents." The thought had occurred to him before, but there was no way to know for certain without going through weeks, if not months, of passenger lists.

It was a far cry to imagine that somehow Grace's father had heard of her dancing again, from wherever he might be resting overseas, and then either sending someone to harm her or even come himself. How would he even have heard about the play changes, never mind found his way into the theatre? The Surrey had appreciative audiences, certainly, but none that obsessive. "No, not her parents. The last she knew they were in Austria, and the war lies in between us and them."

He sat on the edge of the bed beside his brother, his confidante. Colin laid a hand on Isaac's shoulder, the contact a comfort in a world gone cold. "And yet she has no rivals that I can find, either," Isaac confessed. "Miss Mayes at the school says that the corps think well of her, esteeming her work ethic and skills. The actors have no reasons—she's not in competition with any one of them for roles."

A flash of red hair in the wings. *Miss Sullivan was just leaving*— Impossible.

But then again, a quiet voice murmured inside his mind, Miss Sullivan had known where he'd be on Saturday afternoon.

"You're pondering something," Colin prompted, sprawling back on his elbows and nudging Isaac's thigh with his knee. "Out with it."

"It's nothing."

"Out with it!"

"Miss Sullivan," Isaac admitted, and even in the stillness and privacy of his room, the whole thing sounded absurd. "She's been acting oddly the last little while, even dangling after me at one point, when she knew—or must have known—that I've been courting Grace."

Courting her—was that what he was doing? Of course it was, whether he'd realized it at first or not.

"You're right," Colin cracked. "That is extremely odd. What would any girl, never mind two, see in that ugly mug of yours?"

Isaac shoved him in the hip and Colin rolled off the edge of the bed. He landed on the floor with an echoing thump, and burst into chuckles from below. "Your charm, now, perhaps that might attract them."

"She's got a way about her," Isaac continued, turning the puzzle over and again in his mind. "I can't put my finger on it."

Colin stood, tugging his waistcoat back into place. "That's hardly enough to go accusing someone."

"No accusations. Only a sensation that there's more to her than meets the eye."

"She's a woman," Colin observed sagely. "That's always the way."

"As though you would know."

"Are you going out again?" Colin changed the subject as Isaac pulled on his boots.

"I am. I've got some things to look after at work." Isaac finished dressing, buttoning his jacket and brushing it down. There. Now he didn't look like he'd been sleeping in a cathouse, he could hunt on more respectable grounds. "Take care of her for me. She's angry now, you saw what she was like downstairs. But once I solve this, it will be different."

Colin picked a tiny thread off Isaac's jacket, and brushed down his shoulders. "I'll keep an eye on her," he promised. "But only until this mess is over. I'm not the one she needs, you know."

Isaac nodded at the reminder, slow and not entirely sure of it himself. He wasn't sure of anything. "When this is over, once I have her answers, she'll see that she can rely on me. I'll make it all up to her, every last minute."

His brother's scowl wasn't terribly reassuring. "Want my advice? Don't wait too long."

Grace had managed to hold her composure until the kitchen door closed behind Colin. The moment it clicked home, though, leaving her alone in the warm, sunny room, the wave of anger and grief rose up to sink her.

How dare he?

How dare he come in and pretend that they were barely acquainted? As though they hadn't been lying, sweaty and replete, in each other's arms only two, no, three days before?

To humiliate her like that, and in front of his brother, who doubtless knew far more about Grace and Isaac than he had let on!

Grace shoved the bowl away roughly and wrapped her arms tightly around her chest, hugging her tears back in. She'd been a fool to come down to the kitchen in the first place. Colin had been convincing, even sweet, cajoling her with promises of company and busy work, to keep her mind off things.

Had he been part of a plan? Had Colin known that Isaac would come in through that door and made some arrangement to put her in his path, or he in hers? For what purpose? Some kind of...perverse satisfaction at seeing her upset?

It seemed impossible. He'd been so kind. But kindness didn't mean anything coming from men—Isaac had been kind as well, and now look at how he acted once she was no longer of use! She couldn't be his "angel" if she couldn't dance, and unable to move as she was, she was probably of little use to him as a carnal outlet.

And there it was. She had outlived his need for her, and so he had moved on.

So much for his pledges and his promises. He was no different than any of the men she had ever known. Unreliable, untrustworthy, and selfish.

The tears threatened again, stinging hot at the corners of her eyes. Something heavy and sour sat in her throat, blocking her breath.

Was it worse this time because she had started to trust? Served her right for listening to him in the first place. She had been right before; she was better off alone.

A noise from the hallway made her snap her head up and listen. Nothing followed, but that wouldn't last. Isaac or Colin would be back soon enough, or if not them, Catherine with her keen eyes and friendly curiosity. Grace couldn't face any of them right now, not with a tear trickling down her cheek.

On impulse, Grace slowly, carefully, rolled her injured foot, first this way, then that. The soft cushion gave way beneath her, still gently supportive, and the snugly wrapped bandage held her ankle in a solid embrace. It ached a little, to be sure, but the pain was dulled now rather than sharp. She'd lived with worse. God's blood, she'd *danced* on worse, once upon a time.

Three days of rest, the doctor had said. Stuff that. She had always been a fast healer.

Carefully, Grace bent her knee, slid her foot free from the pillow on its stool, and pushed herself up in the deeply cushioned chair that Colin had cheerfully dragged in for her from somewhere else in the house.

Mrs. Sedgewick had teased him and Colin had flushed, then gently helped her to sit, made sure she was comfortable. He was exactly the sort of boy she would have liked to have had as a brother, except that if he'd been her brother in truth, he'd no doubt pester her mercilessly, rather than come to her aid…

No, don't think on that. Focus on what must be done.

Her good foot touched the floor and that was no problem. She pushed herself up to standing, hands firm on the table, then slowly, slowly, touched her other toe to the floor.

She braced for another bright shock of pain and something like that jolted up the back of her leg. Tears sprang to her eyes, but she tried again, resting on the ball of her foot now, and the shock dulled into a bone-deep ache. Her whole foot, then, and the pain dulled more. Right, then. She put her weight on both feet, the shoe on the one and the bandage on the other. The tabletop rough under her tight grip, her fingertips digging into the wood, Grace took a step.

Her ankle held.

It hurt, to be sure, but in the nature of a deep bruise rather than the hot knives that had seemed to pierce her the day before. She could do this.

One step, then another, her ankle unsteady as she let go of the support of the table, but by the time she reached the garden door she was walking well enough to make good time. There would be no running, nor walking much farther than the road, perhaps, but it was something that she had done, she herself. What did she need men for?

The bright sun outside and the sweet summer breeze passing over the tiny back garden were a balm to her soul. Grace stood in the doorway and breathed in for a moment, imagining that she could smell the flowers blooming in St James Park, not too far away.

She could go. Pick up her hem and walk away, find herself a little grassy nook in the park and watch the geese swimming on the pond. Forget men, forget Elliston and his show, forget dancing again—and just for a moment find peace like the kind she had imagined she had known in Isaac's arms.

Him again. Drat the man!

He haunted her even when he wasn't speaking to her. The less she saw of him, the faster that wound would also heal.

She made it down the steps with care, but without a shoe on her foot—either above or below the bandage, it hardly mattered when it was a hypothetical shoe—she wasn't going to be travelling much farther than this. Still, she was invisible here from the kitchen window, especially if she sat against the wall.

Voices echoed from inside, and Grace tucked her skirts up and took a seat, the sunbeams playing gently over her legs. Her ankle twinged, but it was the good sort of feeling that came from pushing oneself just to the next point beyond one's usual limits.

"Mrs. Sedgewick should go into business selling her poultices," Grace remarked aloud, her voice like a stranger's in her own ears. "The woman's near on to being a genius."

No one answered, not that she had expected anyone to.

Grace leaned back against the side of the house, the stone steps cool beneath her and the sun beating down upon the world.

She would wait here, just until she knew that Isaac had left the house. Then she could go back in, pack up her own belongings, and make a new, better plan. One that didn't involve relying on anyone but herself.

The sound of the front door opening and closing again must have been lost in the noise of the world around her. The creak of the window opening beside and above her head was the thing that startled her out of her thoughts. That and Colin's head appearing in the space, followed by arms that he folded casually on the windowsill.

"He's gone," Colin said, and raised an eyebrow at her. "Are you going to come back inside or are you planning to run? Because I feel it's only fair to mention that I promised to keep an eye on you, and I really don't feel like chasing an injured woman through the streets of Chelsea. People might get the wrong idea."

Grace snorted, rolling her head back to look up at him. "I hope you're not suggesting I'm a prisoner here."

"Perish the thought. But if we don't get the preparations finished before Mother and Father get back from the market, you and I will both be condemned to a full evening of dishwashing, injury or no." He grinned, and it was so much like Isaac's smile that Grace's heart ached anew. "You're under Mother's wing now, which makes you practically family. Which means if I face my maker, you do too."

His cheer was infectious, the warmth of his welcome so innocent and so complete that Grace felt her mood lifting despite herself. Was this what it would have been like, to grow up in a family where love and care were the currency, instead of ambition and pride? It was what had made Isaac the way he was—or the way she thought he had been!

No. I'm determined to stay angry at him, but that's going too far. One mistake doesn't mean the end of everything, does it?

That depended entirely on him.

"Far be it from me to court certain doom." Grace

levered herself up, carefully, gently, and grabbed hold of the stair rail to finish pulling herself on to her feet. Yes, her ankle was definitely feeling better. Perhaps one more day would be enough, one or two more of Mrs. Sedgewick's magical poultices, and then she could leave.

Isaac had left again, and without even saying goodbye. Whatever else it meant, that gave her another afternoon, perhaps another evening, to pretend that she had found somewhere where she truly belonged.

For the first time in years, perhaps ever, the theatre didn't feel like home when Isaac walked in the door. There was a moment in the artists' entrance when the familiar walls were close about him and he could point out every scuff and nick on the skirting board, but then he stepped into the theatre proper, saw the stage, and it all came rushing back.

She screamed, she fell, and I couldn't stop it.

Isaac turned on his heel and left down the backstage stairs, taking the long flight down into the bowels of the building. He still needed to prepare his torches, check the fire buckets. A thousand and one little chores that even the chaos of the last two days could not excuse him from.

Colby was already in the paint shop, putting final touches on a drop cloth that had been nailed to the ceiling beams and the walls to keep it stretched. A Scottish moor unfurled across the backdrop, the vibrant greens and blues of the paint vivid and unnatural in this light. Once it was installed upon the stage, though, the yellow glow of the argand lamps would shade them into the proper muddy sort of northern landscape the audience would see.

"Afternoon," Colby grunted, running his hand over the top of his paint-speckled head. He stepped back and regarded the drop with a critical eye. "Stay back there," he ordered in his usual taciturn way. "Squint some. What do y'see here?" and he gestured vaguely at the upper right corner.

Isaac did as he was told, squinting and peering at the section under debate. "Thunderclouds," he guessed, "and a flock of birds. Magpies?"

"Ravens." Colby snorted. "Half the old biddies in the boxes need spectacles to see past their own noses anyway; I suppose it'll do."

That meant he'd be carefully adjusting it for another hour at least.

"Anything new come down from above?" Isaac asked, stepping around a half-roll of canvas taller than his head, a horned skull mounted on a tall spear, and a large sheet of polished plate glass that had been carefully set against the wall, cushioned with rolled fabric about the edges.

"Opening's pushed back a week," Colby grunted. "On account of Miss Owens being hurt and the actors all being superstitious ninnyhammers. They're calling it the Scottish Curse, the great bloody lot of them. Elliston threw a fit, but there's nothing for it. They won't go on until St. John's Day's been and gone, being as it's a witch's Sabbath and all."

"There's no such thing as curses," Isaac pointed out, rummaging in the bins along the wall until he found the carefully stoppered bottle he'd been looking for. "Miss

Owens was hurt by the cruelty of man, not witchcraft—and certainly not Mac's curse."

And even though he didn't believe in black magic, or witches, or the supposed bad luck of the Scottish Play—he still couldn't bring himself to say the full name while he stood within the Surrey's walls.

Why tempt fate?

"Try telling them that. I'll wish you luck."

Isaac snorted at the notion. "Have you seen Peter at all?"

"Last I saw he were up putting out rat-traps, round the back way."

A quick thank-you and Isaac was off again, purpose driving back the nerves that had settled thick in his chest. He skirted the main hall on his way up, crossing the backstage without looking up at the flies or the ladder in the wings. If Peter's luck had been better than his, maybe the day would not be a wash after all.

The figure he came across in the stairwell wasn't Peter. Lucy Sullivan lingered at the bottom of the stairs, staring out into the darkness of the wings, a script in her hands and an odd, distant expression on her face. She snapped out of her pensive reverie when he came into view, flashing him a smile as bright as it was obviously false. The back rows might see it from the stage, but the warmth didn't touch her glittering green eyes.

"Mr. Caird!" Lucy laid her hand on his arm by way of greeting, something eager and a little hungry in the tilt of her head and wideness of her eyes. "Have you news for us? How is Grace doing?"

"She's—" *Further away from me than even before we introduced ourselves; she hates me and everything I do seems to hurt her even more; I love the woman and she cannot stand the sight of me.* "Mending well," he said aloud. "I saw her not an hour ago, sitting up and laughing as though she hadn't a care in the world."

A strange shadow crossed Lucy's expression, but the relief that followed seemed real enough. "I'm so pleased, you have no idea, Mr. Caird. I cannot seem to shake that terrible moment from my mind." She shuddered, drawing closer to him as though by instinct, but when he stepped back she stayed where she was.

"I think most of us feel the same way, except, of course, for those who caused the accident in the first place." he said, but while he watched her carefully, she didn't blink or flinch.

"Caused it?" Lucy frowned, her brow furrowing. Her look of horror certainly seemed real enough. "You know what's being said, of course." She leaned in closer. "That it was witches, Mr. Caird. The curse."

"Not you too, Miss Sullivan!" Isaac bit back a groan. But then, hadn't she been the one who had taken Grace to some kind of fortune-teller, and kept a book of star charts on her dressing table? He should have known better than to expect any sense coming from her.

"'There are more things in heaven and earth, Horatio,'" she quipped.

"Wrong play."

"So it is." She shrugged expressively and sighed. That felt false, like choreography she had memorized long ago.

"You've heard that we've delayed opening, of course. Do tell darling Grace? I know she'll be ever so thrilled to know that she'll have time to get back on her feet. I suppose you'll be pleased as well. It will give you more time to decide on a course of action."

"I'm sorry?" He blinked.

"With your effects, silly." Lucy frowned affectedly. "Unless you mean to concede your bet now. Don't you have to have something in place for opening? I'd so hate to see Mr. Thilby gloating all over London."

Oh, that.

That was a much safer topic of conversation. "Hardly," Isaac snorted. "I have some other things to take care of first, but you can rest assured, the Surrey's honor will be quite safe with me." Sooner or later he would have to consider his next step, whether Grace could still dance, whether she would at all, or whether he could convince someone like Miss Mayes to take her place instead if Grace would not.

But he had another week to figure that all out. He had more important problems right now.

"I knew we could count on you," Lucy replied, with another one of those smiles that didn't reach her eyes. "May the best man win."

She patted his arm again, a little too familiarly, and nodded her farewells. She moved off into the wings and Isaac continued on his way, pushing open the back door and stepping out into the vaguely fetid stench of the back alleyway.

It wasn't until after he'd chased down Red Peter and started to interrogate the boy about his findings that the thought occurred to him, bright and sharp.

Lucy Sullivan was an actress, not a hand. As far as he knew, he, the Byrnes, and one or two of the dressers were the only crew she spoke to.

So how in hell did she *know about the bet?*

Chapter Eighteen

"Ow!"

Dr. Marshall, white of hair and bent of back, would never know just how close he had come to being kicked in the face. "Hold yourself still, girl," he groused instead, palpating the back of Grace's bare ankle as though it held the combination to unlock some secret treasure.

Grace bit the inside of her cheek and resisted the overwhelming urge to pull away. Meg, perched on the windowsill in a bright blue gown like the ornamental flower she was, met Grace's eye and stifled a giggle. Lucy, prim in sprigged calico and sitting cross-legged in one of the soft parlor chairs, shot Meg a look of irritation but held her tongue.

Grace was the odd one out in her breeches and boy's shirt, but the notion of putting on stays and a gown today had felt immeasurably *wrong*. Something had shifted again, and the face that looked back at her in the mirror from under her ribbons and curls had been sad. Lucy had wrinkled her nose, Meg smiled, and Dr. Marshall was carefully trying not to show that he had noticed her transgression.

"There's still no sign of a tear, and the swelling's all

but gone," Dr. Marshall pronounced, rising to his feet with the help of his young assistant. He ruffled himself back into order, an old gray goose checking his feathers. "You may get up and walk, but only for short distances, and rest frequently. If the pain increases, soak the foot and ankle in a cold-water bath, infused with lavender. Further trauma may cause deeper injury, so take care not to place undue stress on the joint."

"We'll make sure she takes her ease," Meg chirped, idly winding one of her long black curls about her finger. "And don't give me that sour look, sweetheart. If we have to tie you to that chair, we shall." Her eyes gleamed, the doctor's boy turned red in the face, and Marshall harrumphed his goodbyes before hustling them both out the door.

Voices in the hallway suggested that Catherine was paying the man's fee, and Grace stared at her hands. She could get up, she could leave…and she found herself both eager and reluctant at the same time. What could she ever do in order to repay Catherine and the Cairds for their kindnesses? And yet. Isaac hadn't come home last night either.

Where was he sleeping?

And what would she say to him when he did return? It would be better for everyone if she left now.

"What are you thinking about, darling?" Meg settled delicately on the arm of Grace's chair. Grace had been so tied up inside her own mind that she hadn't seen the girl move. "Your mind is churning like a millstone, round and round in circles. I swear I can smell the flour from here."

"Charming, Miss Ceniza," Lucy replied dryly. "As

always." She crossed the room as well, tugging a chair up to Grace's other side.

"What to do next," Grace admitted, glancing from one friend to the other. "I should pack and take my leave. The last thing the Cairds need is an extra unpaying mouth to feed."

"That's true," Lucy said, at the same moment Meg snorted, "Says who?"

Grace's lip twitched.

"They're innkeepers, for heaven's sake." Meg waved airily. "If they don't have the capacity to feed an extra person, then who could? And has Mrs. Caird said that you're intruding?"

"No," Grace admitted quietly. "Quite the opposite."

"Well then!" Meg leaned back against the chair and Grace's arm as though everything were settled. "You do need to repair things with that strapping man of yours, and how better than by living in his very house? I'll tell you what—tonight, while he's sleeping, you creep into his room and—"

"Margaret!" Lucy gasped, as though scandalized. As if she hadn't had liaisons of her own. "That's absurd, especially considering what's already transpired. What Grace needs is her own home, her own space, and time away from Isaac Caird. He's dangerous."

The set of Lucy's jaw made her look fierce, fiercer than anything Grace had seen her show off stage. She had been unusually solicitous this visit as well, come to think of it, pouring Grace's tea and bringing her a plate of sweets, ensuring her pillows were set just so. *What is that girl feeling guilty for now?*

"Dangerous?" Meg scoffed before Grace had the chance to speak. "That pussycat?"

"Don't you remember Madame Raiza's foretelling? Change and pain, a man keeping you in chains, and falling in the dark? You've had the pain, Grace, and Mr. Caird tied you up in the flying wire, didn't he? It's not chains, but close enough. And then you fell from the darkness! Exactly like Madame prophesied."

There had been other bondage too, but Grace wasn't about to tell either of the pair of nattering gossips about any of *that*. "That's ridiculous," she objected as a matter of rote, but was it? Was it really?

"It's hogwash," Meg snorted. But then, Meg was hardly the expert on things that were sensible.

"Just consider it, Grace," Lucy pleaded, leaning forward and grasping Grace's hands. "What's next? Fire. Oh, I couldn't bear it if you were hurt again."

"Fire could mean anything." Meg glared at Lucy from her perch beside Grace's shoulder. "From a warm and cozy hearth, to candles on a pretty moonlit night. Maybe she'll meet the love of her life wandering the paths at Vauxhall, for all that."

"Or torches," Grace murmured, the image of Isaac's sketches impressing themselves upon her memory.

"Exactly," Lucy said, triumphantly. "Isaac Caird is bad news, Grace. Stay away from him and his inventions."

"And why are you so agog to have her set him aside, Lucy Sullivan?" Meg asked, leaning in. Lucy recoiled a little, but not far enough to leave Grace out of the middle. "You don't have eyes for him yourself, do you? What price is sisterhood?"

"For that one? Unlikely." Lucy tossed her hair, red curls bouncing. Her eyes glittered, sharp and cunning. "I think Grace deserves better, as any good friend would. Why, I'll wager he wasn't even going to share that five pounds with you, despite the role he's had you play in his schemes."

"The which?" Grace asked, suddenly not entirely sure that she had heard correctly.

"The five pounds," Lucy said again, and she watched Grace intently.

Meg pulled in air in a kind of reverse-gasp of surprise. "She didn't know, Lucy, look at her face."

"That cad!" Lucy cried out, pressing her hand to her chest. "I told you he was a bad lot."

"Would someone please tell me what on God's green earth the two of you are babbling on about!" The volume of Grace's voice surprised even herself, but it had the effect she needed of startling the girls into silence.

"I'm sorry, Grace, I assumed he'd have told you." Lucy settled her hands primly back into her lap. "Mr. Caird and Mr. Thilby over at the Theatre Royal laid a bet on the new shows. Whichever one can come up with the greatest, most spectacular technical effect for opening night wins five pounds off the other. It's ridiculous, of course, but then men usually are."

"My James heard it from Mr. Byrne when he was delivering stays to the Surrey," Meg sighed. "And they say *women* are gossips."

"Five pounds," Grace repeated, the sum of money beyond belief even as she said it. "On an *effect*?"

"On a spectacular effect," Lucy clarified.

"No wonder he's been so obsessed," Grace mused aloud.

Meg gripped her arm with a fierce hand. "You don't think he did something on purpose, Grace. Why would he hurt you if he was trying to create something wonderful?"

"He wouldn't," Grace said, the pieces of the puzzle beginning to fall very firmly into place. "But what he would do is rush ahead in pursuit of his own glory, with no thought given to anyone else who might get hurt along the way."

And when she said it like that, the patterns became terribly clear.

"If you would be so kind as to help me pack my bag, ladies, I have some things I need to take care of immediately."

Henrietta Crosby from the ballet corps disliked Grace because she found her arrogant. But Miss Crosby was seen at the Bell and Whistle at the same time Simon saw the three men sneaking into the Surrey...

Isaac frowned at the scrap of paper with the names on them, but he tucked a tacky piece of gum arabic behind the note anyway and stuck it firmly to the wall. The section beside his workbench was covered with notes already—some longer, some as short as a single name. And none of them getting him close enough to the answer he needed.

He had a particular suspicion, sinking and terrible, but as of yet no proof. Peter had been sent out with a pocketful of coins on another hunt, but even so, there was no telling how long it might take him.

The door to the loft swung open and for a moment Isaac imagined his own thoughts had summoned the lad, but no. It was not Peter who came through. *Grace* stood on the other side leaning heavily on a walking stick, dressed in her boy's clothes and knee-high leather boots, and with a look of murder burning in her dark brown eyes.

It was a tribute to the perversity of man that his first reaction was instant and hot right through his blood. He wanted—no, he *needed*—to pull her against him, to kiss the fury from her lips, to bear her down to the floor and turn that energy into something incandescent. *God have mercy, she's stunning.*

"Five pounds!" she shouted, and he froze. "That is what my life was worth to you? Five pounds?"

"What are you talking about?" When and how had she found out? He crossed the space between them with long strides and reached out for her elbow. Contact, support— *her ankle must be damned sore*—"That wager had nothing to do with your *life.*"

She wrenched her arm away before he could get a hold, her whole body rigid and anger coloring her cheeks dark red. "You risked my life with an unproven, unreliable *machine* for a paltry five pounds? All you've ever cared about was making your own fortune, and to hell with the rest of us. You're the same as my father."

Five pounds was hardly paltry, but that was another argument that would be extremely unwise to make. The accusation stabbed through him, his pride taking the punch.

"Unfair! I am *nothing* like your father." How could she, how dare she, when he'd spent every moment since looking for answers?

"True," she spat back. "At least *he* sold me out for more!"

"Dammit, Grace—listen to me for once instead of hiding behind your anger! I made a wager on my skills, yes, but the rig was reliable!" He reached out again to seize her elbow, and this time he took hold. He spun her before she could pull away. "There—do you see?" The repaired harness hung from the new pulley system, rigged to one of the loft's beams. A full sack of cannonballs was suspended from it, four-pounders he'd "borrowed" from the thunder run in order to make his tests.

Isaac made the three paces toward it, gave a fierce shove to the harness and its contents. The rig swung menacingly, the ticking of an infernal pendulum, but nevertheless, it held firm. "See for yourself—it holds! I didn't do this, Grace—the accident was not my fault. Nor was it an accident at all. The first one was *sabotaged*, a pulley sawn almost clean through." He stabbed his finger at the offending mechanism, the new, solid block holding firm.

"Please believe me," he added, when she said nothing—nothing! Only stood and stared at the harness, her chest rising and falling rapidly with her breath. Would she? Could she see through the red haze of her anger and give him the benefit of the doubt? He came back to her side, the place he should never have left.

"I would give anything in the world for this to have been my fault," he said, and she stared at him incredulously. He grabbed her hand and held it to his chest, pressing her palm open over his heart. "Because then I could spend the rest of my life making amends, knowing that if I worked hard enough, I could turn myself into a better man—a smarter man, a more careful one—and still give you a life free from further harm."

Grace drew in a long, shuddering breath. She blinked quickly, a few times over, clearing the tell-tale sparkle of tears from her eyes. Her cheeks still flushed red, her shoulders heaved with the storm of emotion that had to be surging through her.

So close—if he could just say the right thing that would tip her over into understanding! "I've been working to find out who did this," he promised her, setting his hands on her shoulders. He willed her to look at him, to see the truth of his oath in his face. "I swear to you, I won't rest until I find him and make him pay for hurting you."

She slapped his hands away, shaking her head. "Don't touch me!"

"Grace!"

"You *left*," she spat out, her shoulders hunching up toward her ears.

He what? Isaac faltered, because what the hell was she talking about now? "I what?"

She pushed him in the shoulders, knocking him a half-step back out of sheer surprise.

"You walked away! I was lying there on the stage, thanks to your horrible contraption, and you left me in the hands of *strangers.*"

Oh, hell. He didn't like the direction this was heading. He had the sinking suspicion that it was not going to fall out in his favor at all.

"My brother and Mrs. Elliston aren't *strangers*," he began, but that wasn't going to work—he could see the recoil in her eyes, the walls slamming back up between them. "You told me to go!"

"You weren't supposed to listen!"

The agony that ripped out of her was unfeigned, each word invested with the kind of razor-sharp pain that spoke of a lifetime spent bleeding, unseen.

Wait, what is happening here?

Is *this my fault?*

He hadn't caused the accident, had not made any careless mistakes on his plans or the build, but—oh God— he *had* been careless with something more important.

But how? That was what he couldn't fathom. He had bollixed things up terribly, but *how*? There were no manuals or methods to talk him through this particular disaster, no soda ash on hand to put out this kind of fire.

"You told me to leave," he began, spreading out his hands in confusion. "And I did. I don't quite see how I was in the wrong here."

"You walked right by me in your own home and didn't check on me once!" Grace didn't leave him time to work out the problem, shoving him in the chest once more. He held firm, a still, solid point in a world gone utterly mad, her frustration not enough to bowl him over.

"I checked in with Mother, Father and Colin every day, to find out how you were, if you needed anything. Grace, I thought you hated me. You did everything but say so directly. I was giving you time, and space." She was so close that he could reach out and wrap his arms around her, if he could be assured she wouldn't break his nose in return.

"I do hate you—for leaving me alone when I needed

you!" Grace's voice caught then, the last half of her sentence turning plaintive and small. She dashed tears away from her eyes with the back of her hand, a swift, impatient gesture that sent another stab of pain right through his heart.

"I didn't leave you. I've never left you." He grabbed for her hands and caught them this time, so cold and small between his own. He held them there between his palms to warm and soothe them. She was trembling, shivers racing across her skin, and he needed to fix that too, with a cloak, or stoking up the fire.

"I've been here working, and out there in Town, looking for the bastard who did this. Every moment of the last three days has been devoted to protecting you. I thought—I thought my family's company would be enough. At least until I could prove to you that I'd made your world safe again."

His brother's words echoed in his memory. *I'm not the one she needs, you know.*

"Grace," Isaac said quietly, and her name caught on his tongue. "I am so very sorry."

That was when the dam broke, Grace's shoulders crumpling and a harsh and angry sob ripping from her throat. She pulled away from him, shifting her weight to one foot, a wince tightening her face.

She's still injured, you unbelievable numbskull! How thick can you possibly be?

He'd let her think that he'd abandoned her once, and the guilt of that sank in to his own bones, cold and unforgiving. He wouldn't make that mistake twice. Isaac gathered Grace into his arms, pulling her close against his chest. She pulled away at first, but not with any force, and he tugged her back into his embrace.

Grace resisted, but only for another moment, then she pressed her face against his chest and grabbed fistfuls of his shirt. He set his arm around her waist so she could lean her weight on him, feather-light as she was. He buried his face in her hair, the airy black curls bright with the scent of apple blossoms, or lavender.

How do I fix this? What are the right steps?

"You disdain words," he started, picking his way through the bramble hedge of language. It was a field of poisonous snakes, and one misstep would lose him the most precious thing in his world. "I wanted to earn your approval back through action. To prove that I could protect you."

Isaac trailed off at that last, drawing her in close. He needed to feel her breath, to pull her inside and make her a part of him, so she could feel the waves of need, and of love, that poured from him now. "I am here now. And I will never give you cause to doubt me again."

Grace's weeping slowed, her breath shuddering and her shoulders shaking as she struggled. He waited, held her, splayed his hands out across the small of her back to try, in some small way, to cover her with his support and his contrition. She shivered despite the warmth of the room.

"I needed you and you weren't there," she said, and his own heart cracked down the center at the utter desolation in her voice.

"I will be from now on," he promised recklessly, meaning every word. "Every need you have in the future, I will fill it. Every time you reach for me, I'll be there. I swear on everything holy, you will never feel unloved again."

She sniffled, her shoulders hiking with a strangled sob. He held firm, his arms around her, soaking in her warmth. If only he could project his feelings through their skin, make her *feel* how sorry he was, how determined to make this right.

"Forgive me, give me the chance to prove it to you." He pressed his lips against the top of her head, his anger and surprise and sorrow shot through with the memory of her falling, blue and white in the darkness. But she was here, now, safe and in his arms, and he would never let her go.

Grace took a deep breath, and then another. She pressed her forehead against his chest then slowly raised her head, her eyes swollen and her cheeks streaked with tears. And she was still the most beautiful, precious thing he had ever seen. He wiped away one of those tears with the pad of his thumb, and she leaned into his touch.

"I'm still angry with you," she said, but the heat was gone from her voice.

Relief was the most glorious sensation in the world. It flooded his body from his toes up, and Isaac nodded. "That's all right, I deserve it. I'm happy as long as we're talking."

Her blood still boiled but it was calmer now, a simmer raging low in her veins. She had come up the stairs prepared to fight, to show him exactly what damage he had done, and just like that, he had disarmed her.

No, now she was in *his* arms. They were strong and

safe, his chest broad, his shoulders wide enough to rest the world upon. His heart thundered under her ear, a rapid drumbeat that echoed in her own chest.

Warring impulses tore her apart. She should pull away, tell him all the ways in which he was a terrible person, demand that he...what? He had already apologized, promised everything she could have asked and more.

She could stay right here instead, accept the warmth of his body, the firm muscle under her palms, the faint scent mix of leather and oil, paint and charcoal that seemed to follow Isaac wherever he went.

Standing still wasn't enough, letting him hold her wasn't enough, the rush and burn of the fight-that-wasn't still surging like the tide inside her. She wore breeches today—strength in her armor—no frail or wilting flower waiting for the eventual attention of the bee.

Grace rose on her toes. Her ankle shrieked pain at her and she lifted her foot to touch just her toe to the floor, gripping Isaac's shoulders to keep her balance. Her lips found his, not in the sweet and delicate reclamation that might be expected, but a fierce and potent kiss that sent her head swirling. She drew his lower lip between her teeth, tugged at it, and demanded more.

His hesitation and surprise only lasted for a moment before he was kissing her back, arms tight around her. His thigh rode high against her, thick and taut with hard muscle that she could lean on, ride against, send shockwaves rippling through her body.

Here she was wanted, she was safe, she was—being picked up, Isaac's hands sliding beneath her arse and lifting her off her feet. She yelped and he laughed, then deposited her down on the end of his workbench, her weight off her feet.

"There," Isaac murmured against her lips. "Much better." He stroked his broad hands down her thighs, stepping close between them. She wrapped her arms about his shoulders. His swelling cock pressed against her stomach, the hard evidence of his need for her. Desire washed over her, the restless energy of battle converted to a raging heat deep inside.

She bit his lower lip, just to show him that he wasn't going to get away with being so...*him.* He only laughed, though, returned the fierceness with a soul-melting kiss of his own that reverberated down to her toes.

"How will you have me?" His voice rumbled low against her ear, his lips following in nipping kisses down the side of her throat. His hand pressed up between her thighs, cupped her groin and palmed the rise of her sex through her breeches. "Like this?"

He took his hand away and pressed her back until she arched, then put his mouth to the tip of her breast, the linen of her shirt soft against her skin, until it dampened from the wet heat of his mouth. She ground her hips against him, her groin against the thick pressure of his cock, and the relief that the contact promised. "Or like this?"

"Your mouth," Grace ordered him, or at least she tried to, for the sound came out as more of a breathy plea instead. "I need your mouth on me, show me how much you would care for me."

"Your wish is my command."

He tugged her legs swiftly, until her hips rested on the

edge of the table, the firm heat of him between them, but not touching, the wretch! At his nudge Grace let her knees fall a little ways apart, and he slid smoothly between.

Despite watching, feeling the trembling in his arms as he held himself still and slowly leaned into her, the first hot press of his mouth to Grace's inner thigh made her gasp.

Grace arched and cried out before remembering they were not alone in the building, not this time. Biting her lip helped keep the noise inside until he turned his head, pressed tiny kisses and nibbles along the seam of her breeches on her other thigh, the sensation light and tickling before he was gone.

She barely had time to make a noise, low in her throat, and then he was on her again, kissing down the collar of her shirt, tugging it lightly aside to graze the edge of his teeth along her collarbone. Grace lifted her hips so he could tug her shirt up, and he groaned against her skin. His mouth moved down her chest, and he fastened his lips tight around her nipple. He cupped the side of her breast in his hand, solid and sure, his tongue tracing circles around the hard bud, across her skin.

One of his hands slipped down between her legs again and his fingers teased, rubbing circles across the cotton of her breeches, further down between to where she ached for him, rocked up against his hand.

Grace's fingers gripped hard at the wood of the table beneath her, a solid support as the world gave way.

Isaac sucked and bit at her other breast then sat back, his face flushed and dark brown eyes heavy-lidded. He grasped the hem of his own shirt in both hands and stripped it off over his head.

His chest was a sculpture that could have been the prize of any museum, a column of sleek, defined muscle. His nipples stood out in the faint light, darker brown circles against his golden skin, and a fine trail of tight black curls traced line from the middle of his chest down across his flat stomach, vanishing beneath his waistband. "Suddenly I find myself too warm." His eyes roved down her half-naked body, her thighs spread wide for him. "God above, Grace," he groaned. His skin was spotted with sweat, his muscles tight, his face flushed hot. "I need to be inside you."

His trousers tented obscenely now, his desire obvious. She wanted—there was nothing stopping her from popping the buttons on his fall-front, sliding her hand down inside, touching him and stroking him and bringing him up and inside the slick heat of her body.

Except the sudden burst of laughter from somewhere on the floor below, the knowledge that at any moment they might be interrupted.

"Not here." She shook her head, a rush of panic firming up her decision. "I want your mouth on me, love, your hands—later," she promised. But something had changed. His eyes had gone fierce and possessive, and when he bent down to kiss her, his hips hard against her cunt, it felt like he was staking a lifelong claim.

Love—I said it, and he heard me.

Grace's mouth went dry. She trailed her fingers down along his shoulder, the thick muscle of his upper arm, the long line of his collarbone. He grazed her nipples with his teeth and she dug her nails into his shoulders. "Hey!" he objected, but not loudly.

He took her thighs instead, one in each broad hand, and

spread them wider, only to the point where she resisted. With two fingers he smoothed the fabric down across her cunt, the renewed contact a shock of lightning up through her body. Grace gasped again, her hips rising up of their own accord.

"Easy," he murmured low, and bent down to slide his mouth over the wet cotton between her thighs.

Heat, slick pressure and fire—his mouth was everywhere all at once, one of his hands holding her thigh down, the other rubbing circles against the damp cotton. The pressure was muted by the layers of clothing but his rhythm was insistent, his mouth closing over that spot, sucking hard, seizing the fabric with his teeth and letting go again. The rhythm pulsed inside her, drove her up, away from the worry about being overheard or discovered.

Isaac groaned against her body and the sound set up an answering tremor in her belly. It built up beyond rational thought, raced through her body, exploded out along her arms, legs, spine, like bolts of lightning from a cloudless sky.

Grace's body arched, her hips pushing up against his greedy mouth, his fingers rubbing hard against her entrance, nothing but flimsy cloth preventing him from finding his way inside. She shook apart, he *took* her apart, and she collapsed, spent and sweat-damp, on top of his workbench.

His hands stayed on her, stroking long passes along her thighs, low across her belly, gentle touches down between her legs where his touch set off another little series of tremors. She lay there for a moment, lost in the pleasure-fog that settled over her, made her limbs languid and heavy.

Eventually he drew his hands back and she sat up. He

captured her mouth with his and she could taste a faint musk on his lips that had not been there before. His chest was flushed right down, his nipples tight, and he shivered with agony when she brushed her hands across his skin.

"I'm not as skilled as you at working around obstacles," she teased, shifting forward and taking the front of his trousers down. His prick rose proudly, thick and hard for her, and she wrapped her hand around him. He slid up into her fist, his eyes snapping closed and his hands grabbing on to the bench on either side of her knees for balance.

"You're doing remarkably well as it stands," he managed to reply, and she squeezed him tighter, just to feel the tremors through his body.

"If you're capable of making puns, you're obviously not enjoying yourself enough yet," Grace told him archly.

"Oh, no, believe me," Isaac gasped, hips rocking up in rhythm with her hand, his trousers sitting precariously on his narrow hips. "I'm enjoying myself immensely." He leaned in and kissed her, devoured her, as she worked her hand between them.

He was hers, all hers, and she had him vulnerable in her hands, had been laid open and bare before him and beneath him. All her fury was a distant memory now, swept away by the tidal force of their pleasure.

"Now!" he cried against her lips, as his body began to shake. "Grace, love, my love." He came over her hand, sticky and white. He trembled against her, buried his head in her shoulder as he pulsed, stilled, then let out a long, slow and shuddering breath.

His arms came around her and she settled inside them, their chests pressed together and the rapid beat of his heart thundering beneath her ear. There it was, that sensation she thought had been ripped away from her forever. Here, in the curve of his arms, she was safe.

Safe and sticky, as her body reminded her a minute or so later, and she nudged him gently until he unraveled from around her. A few moments with the washing jug and their shirts back on and they were slightly more presentable again, if not actually *tidy*. She could bathe properly and change once she was home, and she briefly regretted that she wouldn't have the chance to try Meg's audacious suggestion of sneaking out of her room at night.

"Are you all right?" Isaac traced his finger down the curve of her cheek, his eyes soft and warm, his touch a blessing. "How is your ankle feeling now?"

"I forgot about it entirely, at least for a little while in there." She tipped her chin up, and he brushed a kiss against her lips.

"I'll have to do better than that—I want to make you forget everything except the pleasure your body is capable—"

The door opened.

Grace pulled back and whipped her head around. Their position was compromising, to say the least, but there was no time to move. At least they had their clothes back on— God forbid someone had come in just ten minutes earlier!

Isaac made a noise of distress deep in his throat and stepped back, his hands still resting on Grace's hips.

The door swung all the way open and one of the

backstage boys poked his head around. He made a started sort of squawk when he saw them and vanished again. "Sorry, Mr. Caird!"

Isaac gave her a rueful smile, skimming his fingertips across her jaw. "It's all right, Peter," he called out. "Come back."

"What's this about?" Grace asked, tilting her head and frowning at him.

"I have an idea," he admitted, then stopped when the boy reentered the room.

"Miss." Peter knuckled his cap and flashed Grace a cheeky grin, but he lost his smile when he turned his attention to Isaac. Grace stayed where she was on the table's edge, rolling her ankle gently to feel the sore tendon stretch and pull.

Peter put his hands behind his back and drew himself up to height before he started to make his report. "I did what you suggested and talked to some of the lads up at the other theatres. Marcus Green over at th'Royal knew what I was talking about, and he took me into the workshop there. That's where I saw it, plain as day—or as the red on my face," he joked, and his easy manner startled a soft laugh out of Grace. "'e's got a copy of your machine in there." Peter nodded at the rig hanging from the ceiling beams, stuffed full of cannonballs to weigh it down.

Isaac's face seemed to change, shock and betrayal twisting his expression into something pained. "That low-down cheating son of a bilge whore!" Isaac glanced at Grace and shut his mouth tight on the finale of his string of insults.

"I've heard worse," she reminded him with a wry smile. "Don't stop on my account."

Peter drew some folded papers from his pocket and was pointing things out on what looked like a fast and basic sketch of whatever it was he had seen. So Isaac's rival had stolen his idea. It was hardly the end of the world, was it? She wasn't annoyed with him any longer, but the thought of his wager still rankled.

Grace's gaze fell on a series of papers pasted on the wall next to the workbench, all of them notes in Isaac's tidy hand. *Miss Mayes says no one odd has been at the school* and *pulley sawn through—tech knowledge needed* and others along the same theme.

What was all that?

I've been here working, and out there in Town, looking for the bastard who did this. Every moment of the last three days has been devoted to protecting you.

How many hours had he been here mapping out these connections, searching the city for clues and scraps of knowledge that might point toward his answer?

For me. He has been doing this all for me.

And to prevent losing his five pounds, but nevertheless.

The knowledge hit her squarely in the gut, bringing a wave of guilt at the words she'd thrown like weapons.

"And I'll wager anything that Mr. Thilby didn't come across those plans on accident," Peter said firmly, and Isaac nodded.

"He's involved in this up to his neck, and there's no doubt about it." He paused, looked up as though only just remembering something or making a connection.

"An accent," Isaac said, apropos of nothing. "An accent or a *lisp*—that goddamned *whistle*. The misbegotten troll was *here*." His eyes blazed with anger and Grace's breath caught in her throat. From ardent lover to focused thief-catcher to a hero riding to her rescue like a cavalier of old, Isaac all but glowed with the power of his righteous fury.

No one in Grace's entire life had ever been that passionate about her—not toward her, nor because of her, nor in her defense. The power of it was overwhelming.

"I'm going to murder him where he stands."

"Not the best idea, Mr. Caird," Peter said quickly. "Given that it's not your usual trade and all, and I'm pretty sure that's against one of the commandments."

"Only 'pretty sure'?" Grace asked, and it was only then that both of them seemed to remember she was in the loft at all. "I think you need more Bible."

"What I need is to call him up and make him pay—for cheating, yes, but mostly for putting you in the way of danger."

A vein throbbed along the edge of Isaac's jaw, the muscle clenched tight. "Him, and whomever he was working with."

"Do you know who they are yet?" Grace asked the question more as a distraction than anything else, but her curiosity was beginning to burn. "How many? And was it just about this bet of yours, or something more?"

"I've no idea," Isaac admitted. "We've been at odds before, but never anything serious. Thilby's a colleague, occasionally a friend—or so I thought."

"It looks as though you thought wrong."

"It's not the first thing I've been wrong about, and likely won't be the last. But this I will make right."

Ankle almost forgotten, Grace turned the scenario over in her mind. "Assume for a moment that it is only about the bet, and not about me at all. What could make it so important that he'd be willing to resort to such measures?"

"The Regent's tour. You remember, Mr. Elliston said it that day when we switched plays," Peter suggested, looking back and forth from one to the other. Both Isaac and Grace fell silent. "I overheard Da talking about it t'other night. The Prince said he was going to go to all the opening nights this year, whether his father be ill or no."

"Elliston did say as much," Isaac confirmed. "And Thilby will want to keep the Prince Regent's favor for the Royal, even if it means stealing my plans and sabotaging my work."

"Would he go that far to impress the Regent?" Grace asked, but she had the feeling she already knew the answer.

Isaac nodded grimly. "He's always wanted the most glory for the least work, and royal patronage can make a man for life. He wouldn't risk the chance that I might succeed, even if he opened the day before. There would always be the chance that the Surrey's audience would like our version better."

"Except with your version of the rig unusable, you would have had no time to build and test anything new." She finished the thought for him, and Isaac nodded. "The ballet would have to be changed, or scrapped. And if we couldn't do the ballet, then the Surrey wouldn't be allowed to perform the Scottish play at all. Thilby would win by default."

"If you hadn't been hurt, if the cast hadn't refused to open on the original day, if we hadn't tested the rig when we did—if I'd been as sloppy as he usually is, and left everything to the last minute—it might have worked."

"So what happens next?" Grace asked. Isaac's mind was already working through a hundred combinations; she could see the flickering thoughts passing behind his eyes.

"For you, nothing," he said firmly, and Grace's indignation flared. Isaac turned back to her before she could say anything, and stroked his hands down her arms, solid, strong and firm. "I won't permit you to place yourself in any possibility of danger. Not again."

"You won't, won't you?" she retorted, though the small, lonely child deep inside thrilled at the care in his voice.

Isaac shook his head and didn't pull his deep, dark, and intense gaze away from hers. He seemed to be staring right into her soul, as though his eyes were commanding her to understand. "No. Peter and I will go. You're going to allow me to do this, to look out for you the way I should have been doing all along."

She wanted to object, should object—she was as capable as he was, maybe even more so. But the way he held her now, as though she were something precious to be protected, to be *fought for*—it was everything that her soul needed to finally begin to heal.

"Fine," she said, nodding slowly.

"Fine?" Isaac blurted out, as though he hadn't expected her to agree.

"That's what I said. But I won't sit idle, either. Give me something to do here that will help." She lifted her chin and met his eyes, challenge accepted. "We have an opening to plan for, after all. One that will bring all of London to its feet."

Chapter Nineteen

Isaac couldn't say that he was ecstatic about leaving Grace behind at the Surrey, even though the idea had been his. In a perfect world, he would have been able to convince her to return to his house and the watchful eyes of Colin and their father, knowing that she was utterly out of harm's way.

Not that he really imagined anything would happen to her at the theatre, but then, he hadn't predicted the last time either.

The sun was slowly setting as he and Peter rode the back of Quentin's mail coach up over Blackfriar's Bridge, the Thames rippling with the red and gold reflection of the light. The wheels of the coach bumped and rattled, his teeth rattling with them. Peter held on beside him, flashing a bright grin under his wide-brimmed hat when he caught Isaac's glance. The port-wine staining on his face wasn't nearly so startling in this light, and the young man was looking almost handsome. As far as a boy could, at his age.

"Green said he'd leave the door unlatched 'round the back." Peter jumped down first as they rattled past the Savoy, Quentin waving Isaac off as he followed. It was easy enough to lose themselves in the alleys of Covent Garden, wending their way toward the rear entrance of the Royal.

Thilby would know that Isaac knew the moment he saw Isaac and Peter arrive. If he saw them, then their expedition for proof—something real and solid that he could wave under Thilby's thieving nose—would be all for naught.

No, Isaac needed to be in there before Thilby saw him coming, before he could destroy anything that would link him to the break-in at the Surrey.

And then what? Turn him in to the magistrates on suspicion that he'd come into a semi-public building, where no one had seen him clearly?

There would be no help coming from that direction.

"Their opening night is tomorrow." Isaac strode down the alleyway, ignoring the doxy in the low-cut gown who blew kisses to him from her stoop. "They'll be in dress with properties and sets tonight, at least part-way. If they keep the same schedule as usual, then everyone will have been released for a supper hour at six o'clock. That gives us…" He glanced up at the clock tower that loomed in the distance, squinting to make out the numbers. "Three quarters of an hour before they're back. It should be ample time."

Peter scurried to keep up with Isaac's long strides. "The scene-painting room's right up at the stage. The backstage crossover opens right onto it. If anything's in there, we'll never get to it without being seen."

"We'll cross that bridge when we come to it."

Green had left the door unlatched, as he had promised, and Isaac pushed gently against the heavy wood. It swung in to the dark hallway beyond on silent hinges, lending an ominous air to an endeavor that was already making the hair on the back of Isaac's neck stand on end.

Voices echoed from somewhere deeper into the building, but the way before them stayed clear. Titles of old shows and woodcut faces of former performers stared down at them from the playbills plastered on the walls, some scrawled with autographs and others simply stark reminders of performances that had been and gone.

A set of stairs ran from the hallway up toward the offices and galleries. Footsteps echoed on the stairs and Isaac grabbed Peter's collar, hauling him back behind a crate and into the shadows, tucked beneath the staircase. The boy squawked in surprise then clapped his hand over his mouth, his breathing heavy in Isaac's ear.

Conversation floated down to them along with the heavy tread of work boots, rough voices echoing off the walls. "…when I find out who keeps emptying the wine bottle on the properties table, I'm going to shove it straight up their ape-drunk arse."

"Fill it with absinthe tonight. That'll give 'em one hell of a shock."

"You have that kind of blunt lying about? Keep the absinthe for yourself and use a purging draught instead. Serve the bugger right."

Not one of them was Thilby; none had his telltale whistle in his voice. Laughter followed and then the sound of the door at the end of the hall opening and closing once more.

Isaac sagged back against the wall for a moment, his heart beating rather faster than it should. Peter nodded, tugged his shirt and jacket back into place, and rubbed at his neck.

"Sorry for that," Isaac apologized, and Peter only shrugged.

"Worked, din' it?"

And then it was their turn to step back out into the dim half-light, a faint flicker from a lantern coming from a partly open door. "This way." Peter nodded to the right, a vast dark room beyond there offering glimmers of shapes and nothing more. A ladder, a roll of canvas, a pile of rags in the doorway. The image of a job almost complete.

Isaac followed Peter into the wings. He ducked under the lines running off a winch for the scene drops, keeping close to the black curtains that blocked the house's view of the backstage and all of its unromantic mechanisms. And there, right where he would have placed it himself, the proof he was looking for.

His rig, or a poor copy of it, hanging from pulleys in the flies of the Royal Theatre's stage.

"Son of a syphilitic whore," Isaac cursed under his breath, damning Thilby with all of his might.

Peter shook the ladder that attached to the wall, and the base at least held firm. "What'd'you plan to do now?"

"Put an end to this, right here and now."

Isaac grabbed the rungs of the ladder and swung himself upward with all the ease of experience. Up into the black he climbed, hands and feet finding their marks as sure as if he'd been here before. Nine, ten feet—the Royal's flies were higher than the Surrey's, the backstage larger. He reached the platform and sat on the edge, feet dangling over the empty space below.

Once he had the rig in his hands, however, his

pocketknife unfolded, he hesitated.

Cutting through the ropes, or half-slicing them as he'd originally planned—that would make him no better than Thilby. Someone would be hurt, and an innocent at that.

Not to mention ropes are easy to replace at a moment's notice.

Peter hovered around the bottom of the ladder, keeping his eye on the hallway and the stage alike. He raised no alarm.

Isaac still had time.

Unwinding the rigging took longer than he wanted, the knots tangling even as he untied them.

Finally one end sprang free and Isaac could reach the pulleys that ran the rigging along the beam. The wood was rough in his hands, unfinished and half-heartedly sanded, a job done with too much haste and not enough care. That bilge-rat didn't deserve to take the credit for Isaac's design, even on a simple craft level. It stung the pride, that's what it did.

"Hsssst!" Peter shook the ladder and caught Isaac's attention. "Door's opening."

Isaac re-strung the ropes as quickly as he could manage. They went back faster than he'd been able to take them apart, but not fast enough. A door slammed and voices echoed back up his way again. He grabbed the rails of the ladder and slid down to the stage below, his feet barely skimming the rungs as he descended.

They only had moments to get out of there. Isaac took one of those precious seconds to look up at his handiwork. Nothing would seem out of place to the casual observer from below.

Good enough.

Isaac made for the door to the hallway, but a figure appeared in the gap and Isaac drew up short.

"What ho, Caird," Thilby greeted him, his smile not quite so gregarious and cheerful this time. His shirt was stained with sweat beneath the arms, his thinning brown hair pushed back from his forehead. He folded his meaty arms and filled the doorway with his bulk. "To what do we owe this unexpected honor? Come to wish us luck for opening, or to make your first payment on my five pounds?"

"Call me the thief-taker, instead." Isaac strode toward him, ignoring Peter's coughed warning behind. "What kind of a man cheats and lies his way through life, Thilby? You're no better than a blackleg swindler."

"You mean I outsmarted you, Caird, and you're bitter because you've lost. You used to think you were so much smarter than the rest of us, eh? Don't it hurt some to get a taste of your own medicine right back."

The mockery in his voice raised Isaac's hackles, but what had he expected? That Thilby would roll over and show his belly, admit his crimes and his guilt in one?

"You mean you couldn't beat me on your own goddamn terms!" Face to face with Thilby now, Isaac stared his old colleague dead in the eye, saw the bully and the coward in the eyes of the apprentice boy he'd once been. Had they ever been friends, or had he been fooling himself all this time? "You've been riding my coattails since we were young, and now that I'm not carrying you along, you come back to steal my work."

Thilby sneered, his breath stinking of stale tobacco and

beer. "I've already beaten you. Ned may have liked you better, taught you more, but I've got the better contract, and now I'm going to have the Prince Regent's commission to boot. I haven't just won this bet, *boy*. I've finally won it all."

"*Boy*? Is that what you called me?" Isaac's hand balled up into a fist. "You'll be crawling on your knees to ask my forgiveness when—"

A sharp *"hssst"* came from behind him and the boiling in his blood abated just long enough to remember. *Don't give up the game. He'll go look at his so-called work, he might still have time to fix things.*

"You're a bastard goat-fucker," Isaac finished instead. Thilby puffed up his chest and stepped forward, crowding Isaac into taking a couple of steps back. *Yeah, come on, get into an open space, you sweat-greased walking turd.*

"Better than your mother." Thilby made the "joke" about Isaac's women just as he had a dozen times before, but now there was no fun in it. Frustrated ambition had been driving him, turned his heart sour and his intentions worse. Isaac was so beyond feeling sorry for him.

"Heard about your dancer—rough luck, that. Easier to get her on her back now that she can't run, mind you." Thilby's grin broadened to a smug and fleshy leer.

Red fury filled Isaac's vision, heat and rage thundering in his blood, and above it all, the vision of blue silk, falling through the air.

Peter didn't stop him this time.

The satisfying crunch of Thilby's nose going sideways more than drowned out the memory of Grace's scream.

The Surrey buzzed with activity downstairs, but up in Isaac's workshop, Grace had the space to herself.

Look through the chest, those had been Isaac's parting instructions, among others. And now she flipped the crumble-edged pages of a folio that should have been dust a half-century ago, a lamp glowing gently on the table, and one ear and eye on the door. There was nothing to this collection but sketches of dancers costumed as nymphs and dryads in varying stages of undress—so she was not at all surprised that it had remained in the folio. It wasn't going to be of any help at all, mind you. Not for a spectacle.

She closed the card cover and set it aside, but something in the way the pages sat caught her eye. Some smaller papers had been tucked inside the back pages, scribed in a different hand and with numbers jotted down the side, as though the unseen writer had been taking notes from a larger book.

Nouvelles récréations physiques et mathématiques, the French words read. "New physical and mathematical amusements." *Et la déception du fantôme de Guyot.* There was one thing to thank her parents for, if nothing else; her French was still adequate, even after these years of living back in England. Now—who, or what, was Guyot?

The door creaked open and Grace slammed the folio closed, trapping the pages with their cramped handwriting tightly within. She set it aside, and waited for Lucy to realize she was there.

It took a beat or two longer than Grace would have thought, Lucy's attention caught for a moment too long on the repaired flying rig, still hanging in the middle of the space.

The last question Grace had found its answer in Lucy's eyes. *How could you?*

Grace moved in her seat, propping her foot up on the edge of the worktable, her leather boots gleaming in the lamplight. Lucy whipped around and let out a little squeak of shock, a mask of flustered concern slipping down over her expressive features.

"I didn't see you there, you dreadful thing," Lucy scolded, moving into the circle of the lamplight. The sun was slowly setting outside, the clouds on fire with pink and orange. "How is your ankle? Are you sure you should be up and about?"

"Well enough, thank you." An actress Grace might be, but she was finding it hard to bite her tongue and keep her voice sweet. "Were you looking for Mr. Caird? He's not here at the moment."

"I can see that. And no—that is, yes." Lucy cocked her head and frowned at Grace, her lips pressed together in the gesture of deep thought. "I have time to spare before I'm called to rehearsal. I thought, given the circumstances, he might need an extra set of hands to help out with whatever it is he might be working on to replace…that thing." She gestured toward the flying rigging with obvious distaste.

"I'm not sure when he'll be back." How had she not seen the quirks in Lucy's expressions before? The way her eyes darted to the things she felt guilty about? Or was Grace only imagining things based on Isaac's half-formed suspicions?

"Oh, but Grace," Lucy blurted out. She knelt at Grace's side, hands on the arm of the chair Grace was sitting in. "Why are you hanging about that man? His own troubles have already cost you so much. Leave him to his wagers and his rivalries, and remember who your real friends are."

"Why do you care so much, Lucy?" Grace asked. "It's more than simple envy, of that I'm sure. I know you made eyes at Isaac, and I also know he turned you down. My leaving his side won't change that."

"No, but it might save your life!" Lucy's eyes went wide after that, and she clamped her mouth shut again.

Now they were on to something.

"How am I in danger?" Grace asked, swinging her boots down to the floor and leaning forward. "And how do you know so much about it?"

Lucy stood up and paced halfway back to the door in a flurry of skirts and fluster. "Madame Raiza," she said after a moment, any surprise or roughness in her voice gone. She had her composure back, and when she turned to face Grace, Lucy looked the same as she ever had. "I know you don't believe in fortune-telling, Grace, but it's all too clear to me. The life you know will end in fire, remember? And who do we know who is always meddling with flame, flint, and tinder, and other such nonsense?"

"We're past the point where I believe that, even from you." Grace stood, her hand resting on the table to give her support.

Where was the sad and tired Grace who would have nodded and moved on, swept the conversation beneath the rug in the hopes of keeping the peace? That girl's weakness was gone, replaced by the reminder of Isaac's strong arms, Meg's laughter, Colin's gentle encouragement, Andrew's courtesy, Catherine's warm embrace. Grace's breeches hugged her thighs and waist, her boots strong and solid, grounding her feet.

"You told Thilby about Isaac's designs, didn't you?"

Grace let the accusation hang there in the air, and refused to take it back.

Lucy didn't answer.

"No," Grace thought aloud. "More than that. It had to be, or you wouldn't be so tangled up over my foot. You've never been this solicitous before, Lucy Sullivan, and I almost believed it of you this time. You gave him the plans?"

Lucy rolled her eyes and sighed dramatically. She shrugged, her green eyes cold and glittering in the lamplight. "And let him in to the building. You must know." The expression slipped for a minute, something very much like guilt coming through. "You were never meant to be injured, Grace. That was never part of the deal. And I do think you should stay away from Caird, for your own safety. Unless you can convince him to concede now, of course. I have no idea what else they might do."

Grace's reply would have sounded better coming from one of the longshoremen down at the docks, but Lucy didn't flinch at the curse. It went a little way toward repairing the feeling of betrayal that stabbed home, now that Lucy had confirmed what Grace had never wanted to believe.

"Why?" Grace finished with the question that mattered most.

"It's business, Grace, that's all. Nothing personal. There's been nothing but bit parts for me here at the Surrey, and I've been promised a lead at the Royal for the winter season. It's a patent theatre, with royal patronage and full houses every night! Madame Raiza predicted it all, you know. I will be famous throughout the land." Lucy at least had the good grace to look guilty. "You were never meant to be involved. But it looks as though you're healing well enough, so…" She waved her hand airily, as though the miracle of Grace's minor injury suddenly made everything better. "No hard feelings, I hope."

"Famous throughout the land," Grace repeated, then she smiled, grim amusement slowly taking over from her anger. "As long as you trust the right people, wasn't it? Exactly how much pull do you think Thilby has over casting, Lucy? Especially since Isaac is over there right this moment, making sure that little toad of a man answers for his crimes. You're a status-hungry sneak, and this time you've thrown your lot in with the wrong side."

The color drained from Lucy's face, as slowly and surely as the fire burned back up into Grace's.

"You should have trusted your true friends, Lucy Sullivan. And now we know *exactly* what kind of person you are beneath."

"You, I," Lucy spluttered. "Oooooh!" There was little pleasure to be found in watching months of supposed friendship crumble to the ground, but Lucy's tantrum more than made up for it. She stomped her foot in rage and stormed out of the loft, slamming the door behind her. It didn't slam, not well, the bottom of the door catching on some scuff marks on the uneven floor. The hinges creaked as it started to swing home, but much more gently than it otherwise might.

Lucy reappeared, her cheeks red. She grabbed the door

handle and dragged it past the rough spot on the floor. She yanked on the door and only then it slammed properly, the noise loud in the wide-open space of the loft.

The sound of running footsteps down the stairs echoed through the closed door. Grace sat back down in Isaac's chair and laughed until she cried.

"Yer hand's a bit of a mess," Peter informed Isaac needlessly, wrapping the strip of clean linen around Isaac's bruised knuckles. "Yer lucky you didn't break anything of yours."

"Oh, but it was worth it," Isaac said, though in his heart of hearts he was wondering.

He sat in the back parlor of the Surrey, a washbasin at his elbow and his shirt ripped across the neck from where Thilby had gotten one good grab in. Most of the blood that stained the water red wasn't Isaac's. Thilby was a worse fighter than he was a machinist, and two good hits had been all that Isaac needed.

It wasn't the beating that was gnawing at him. Thilby deserved it, and worse, for what he'd done, and for the terrible ends they'd only avoided by chance or the grace of God. It was the remembering. They'd never been the greatest of friends, but they'd been apprentices together, and surely that had to count for something.

Apparently not, at least once professional pride and the Prince Regent's approval were on the line.

"Is that going to be enough, though?" Peter's brow furrowed and he sat, his back against the wall. "You didn't take down the rigging, so now what's to stop them from using it tomorrow?"

Isaac reached into his coat pocket with his unbandaged hand, his fingers closing around the circles of rough-hewn wood. The thrill raced through him, the certain knowledge that this time, he had won.

He drew his hand out again and displayed the two custom-designed pulleys to Peter, whose delighted cheer was enough to turn Isaac's mood entirely. "He'll have a great deal of trouble getting it to work tomorrow without these."

A few minutes later Isaac was mounting the stairs to the loft two at a time. He half expected to see Grace in a similar sort of condition, her knuckles bruised, or Lucy Sullivan laid out after a proper thrashing, if she'd played the part in things that he'd suspected.

And yet he was equally unsurprised to find nothing of the sort. Grace was in his chair, one leg up and the other curled beneath her, poring over a sheaf of papers in the light of his work lamp. She looked up when he entered, her gaze immediately dropping to the white bandage that glared brightly against his dark skin. "You fought him?" she guessed immediately, her eyes widening.

"If you can call it a fight." Isaac grinned, striding across the floor to seize her and plant a kiss on her upturned lips. "The man has a glass jaw to go with his decayed ethics. Did Miss Sullivan make an appearance?"

Grace nodded, and didn't seem nearly as upset as he'd expected. "Like you predicted. I think she'd come up to see what your replacement project was going to be. We had words. I don't think she'll be a problem from here on in. At the very least, everyone will know she's not to be trusted." She reached up for him, sliding her hand along the back of his neck and sending shivers running down his spine.

"Mm. Do that again."

"I might still be mad at you."

"I thought we fixed that?" Isaac sank down to a crouch to put himself a little below her eye level. He was going to say more, to apologize again, but there was a twinkle in her eyes that was so unlike her, and so welcome, that he closed his lips tightly on the thought. "Or I could always apologize again," he offered instead, a purr of anticipation in his grin and his voice.

Grace's smile echoed his own, and she tipped forward, brushing her lips against his. "That might help."

"Have I mentioned before how delicious you look in these?" Isaac murmured, running his hands up over the fullness of her thighs, the breeches stretched tight across them.

"Hmm, can't say as I remember."

"Obviously remiss on my part. I'll have to make sure you hear it every day from now on." He rose up and sought her kiss, that haven where everything in the world made sense. She opened to him, her lips parting, and her mouth warm and sweet. He kissed her as though the past few days had been nothing but a bad dream.

Grace melted against him, her hands playing out across his arms. This, this was where he belonged, where his soul had found its match. The words were on his lips, all he had to do was say them. Honor. Love. Cherish.

"Phantasmagoria."

"I'm sorry, what?" The orchestra playing arias in Isaac's mind screeched to a stop and the universe came back into focus around him. He sat back on his heels and Grace reached for the pages she'd been reading when he'd come in the room.

"I've found the answer we've been looking for. Both for the ballet and for Duncan's ghost."

He recognized the pages, the thin paper covered in numbered notes in a small, cramped hand, and in French. He could recognize the language for what it was, but that was where his knowledge ended. He'd dismissed them as unimportant the first time, and tucked them away. Now he looked up at Grace with new interest, standing to rest his hips against the table at her side. "I cannot read French," he confessed. "What do they say?"

"They're notes from someone who had a chance to look at a copy of a manuscript regarding visual illusions and conjuration tricks. Here." She shuffled the pages, turning one over to show him yet more text that he couldn't comprehend. "This talks about a book by the inventor of the camera obscura. It seems simple enough: a mirror, a light, a plate of glass."

Disappointment chased elation in short order. Isaac shook his head. "The camera obscura works only in a small, dark room. It cannot be changed to an effect for the stage."

"Cannot, or has not?" Grace insisted. "I saw a phantasmagoria show in France where the projections were made on a hanging sheet, and the assistant moved the sheet to make it seem as though the scene was moving."

"Yes, but that requires a projection directly in front of the screen, or the light could never reach so far." An idea was niggling at the back of his mind, though, and he grabbed for paper and a pencil stub. He licked the pencil and traced a couple of lines on the page, not knowing yet what the image would be. "But the camera obscura is a mirror trick, and we already use mirrors to change the colors of the stage lights, make a flame redder or a forest greener."

"A combination of the two, then." Grace tucked her head beneath his elbow to get a look at the raw idea as he roughly sketched the layout of the Surrey's stage.

"With a mirror, and a plate of glass," he echoed her words. "And a magic lantern ghost that will bring down the house. It's never been done before."

"Do you think you can manage it?"

Isaac smiled and ran his hand down her back, the thrill of discovery doubled—no, tripled!—now that she was with him too. "With your help. We'll put on a show the likes of which London has never seen."

Chapter Twenty

The five days until dress rehearsal passed by in a blur of late nights and early mornings, of waking up in the guest bedroom at the Cairds' home and falling asleep on the old chesterfield in the dressing room at the ballet school.

She should have gone home, should have resumed her old life now that she was back on her feet, and yet.

Her bag had been packed. It sat in her dressing room at the Surrey, left there when she had stormed out of the Cairds' home intent upon ripping Isaac's skin from his bones. That night, though, she had sat and stared at the large satchel, reluctant to rise, take it up, and begin the lonely walk home.

Isaac had made the decision for her, stepping into the dressing room only long enough to sweep the straps onto his shoulder and hold out his arm for her to take. The Cairds had barely blinked upon her return, Andrew setting supper for them both upon the tavern's bar without hesitation.

Of course Andrew had then handed Isaac an apron and ordered him to work despite the lateness of the hour. And for Grace, he drew up a chair instead. Waving off her attempt to pay for her meal, he'd placed an overflowing tankard of good beer in front of Grace instead. Then he'd followed it with small glasses of fine spirits that, he claimed, required tasting to ensure that they were of quality sufficient to serve his customers.

They were very good.

Grace had slept soundly that night for the first time in ages.

The notes about Grace's friends and enemies vanished from the wall of Isaac's workshop, replaced with diagrams and sketches, pages of obscure geometries and equations that Isaac claimed were measures of light and how it reflected. She couldn't quite figure out how that would be helpful, exactly, but he seemed convinced.

Grace's ankle improved daily, with a little assistance from Mrs. Sedgewick's poultices, and while she wouldn't be rising to any number of *fouetté* turns on her left side any time soon, by the third day back she crossed the center of the rehearsal hall at speed, the corps applauding her final held arabesque with honest joy.

"You were lovely." Miss Mayes tucked her arm through Grace's after practice, and pressed a happy kiss on Grace's cheek. "Do you feel ready for tomorrow?"

"I think so, perhaps." Grace frowned, taking back her arm and rising up on her toes. Her ankle held, only a twinge up the back to remind her that she had been injured. "Assuming nothing else dreadful happens," she said flippantly and Miss Mayes swatted her on the shoulder.

"Don't say that! You'll call down trouble."

"We've had enough of that already to last a lifetime."

"Exactly what I mean!"

"Are you going to turn three times, spit, and curse?" Grace teased her, moving for her bag and towel with more ease than she'd felt in weeks. On top of that were nerves and excitement, of course, and a faint yet growing sense of panic that all would not be ready in time.

Miss Mayes knelt to unlace her dance slippers and laughed, but uneasily. "Perhaps I should, if you think it will help. Are you going to the Surrey tonight?"

Grace nodded, patting the sweat from her face and neck with the clean linen. "Directly. They may need more hands to finish setting up, and I promised Mr. Caird I would be by to witness the first tests."

"Be careful," Miss Mayes warned her, her eyes round and wide. "No more flying, you hear?"

"None of that," Grace promised. "You'll see, tomorrow."

When, precisely, had she regained her faith in him? Had it been the moment he kissed her, or when he'd come racing back with Thilby's blood on his hands? No...after that, when their minds had met, the pages spread out upon the worktable, trading ideas and inspiration back and forth.

There, that was it. It had been the moment she realized that *he* had faith in *her.*

It was an uncommon feeling, one she wasn't entirely sure that she would ever be used to.

Grace washed, laced her stays, and slipped into a clean gown. The face that stared back at her from the mirror today was a soft one, something warm creeping back into her eyes.

She could *be* soft today and feel safe in it, and she held on to that sensation as tightly as she could.

Grace stopped at a newsagent on the way, one more errand to be done. The Surrey stage was in an uproar by the time she arrived, untying the ribbons on her bonnet and drawing off her gloves.

"Put it there."

"No, you great blunderer—the marks are to your left, your left—your *other* left!"

"Shift it back this way—back—back—back—*forward*!"

"If you break it, I'll cut your balls off and feed them to you one at a time."

Four or five of the hands shuffled about the stage, Isaac and Mr. Colby shouting instructions over top of one another as they maneuvered a vast sheet-covered set piece into position. Two of the backstage boys scrambled about with lines and wires, while some of the other apprentices lounged about in the seats in the pit, catcalling to their friends.

She lingered there in the darkness of the opposite wing, watching Isaac. He moved with confident ease, entirely in his element. He'd rolled his shirtsleeves up to his elbows again, exposing the muscles in his powerful arms. His waistcoat was half-unbuttoned, a cravat loose about his neck and so much like a sailor's kerchief that she had the momentary vision of him decked out in proud uniform, a captain's hat beneath his arm.

"Sorry, miss!" Grace jumped aside at the sound of the voice behind her in the door to the wings.

"Pardon, miss!"

Two boys rushed past her with rolls of soft wool in their hands, pinched from wardrobe, no doubt. Isaac pointed at the floor, Colby barked an order, and the boys tucked the wool rolls against the bottom of the tall, flat whatever-it-was while the adult hands fitted wooden beams along each side.

She turned aside to let them work, setting her bonnet and shawl on one of the empty properties tables to free up her hands. By the time she'd turned around Isaac was striding toward her in the semi-darkness, with a smile on his lips and a gleam of purpose in his eyes.

"You're here!" He set his arms around her waist and gave her a little spin. The laugh burst from her, surprising both of them, and he set her down again gently.

"I said I would be, didn't I?"

His face was so close to hers, his breath sweet on her cheek. He trailed his lips across her jaw, the barest brush of contact, but it was as electric as the first time they had touched. It had been a week since they'd last lain in each other's arms, since they'd had the time, coinciding schedules, energy, and privacy all at the same moment. Now even this gentle contact—his hands on her waist, the heat of his body in front of hers, the whisper of his kiss—made her mouth go dry.

"You did," he murmured, his voice low music, and he took that half-step closer that let their bodies touch, her breasts to his chest, his arms beneath her hands, his hips against hers. "Will you stay?"

Always, she was about to answer, and *forever*, until she realized that his mind had not gone where hers had fled. "Tonight?" she hazarded a guess. She moistened her suddenly dry lips with the tip of her tongue, his hungry gaze following the movement.

"That too…" Isaac took her hand, tracing his thumb across the cup of her palm. She flushed, her cheeks hot, until a shout came from the stage and Isaac coughed once, stepping back half a step and breaking the spell.

"Keep that notion close to your heart," he teased, his eyes merry. "But I meant now. We're all but ready to make the first test. The team of Caird and Owens presents the first-ever stage showing of the miraculous 'Guyot's Ghost.'"

He spread his hands in the air as though demonstrating the high headlines on a playbill or broadsheet, and she laughed at him. "Hardly 'Owens.' You're the one who's done the work."

"But you're the reason for it all in the first place, and I'll brook no arguments on that score."

"Then I won't argue." But before he could say more, Grace tapped his chest with the rolled-up newssheet, glee making her smile. "Have you seen the news from the Royal?"

"No! Is there news?" Isaac reached for the paper but she pulled it away, snapping the paper open and holding it to the light so that she could read off the cramped text with the proper dramatic flourish.

"'*Skirts of the Camp* opened to audiences at the Royal two nights ago'—oh, but we know that part."

"Wench!" Isaac laughed. "Give it here!" He reached for it but she dodged, moving into clearer light.

Grace cleared her throat. "'To audiences such as the London season normally sees…' and on he prattles for a bit about who among the beautiful people were there to see it.

Oh, did you know that the 'divine' Lady K.—mustn't name names, after all—was seen in the company of a man not her husband? Scandal!"

Isaac groaned. "Would you get on with it? What does it say about the *play*?"

She skimmed down a bit, looking for the lines that had caught her eye before. "Here it is. 'It is a shame that such a noble and well-respected theatre should give itself over to performing such lowbrow tripe as this, and to be so unprepared on opening night is a travesty of the noble arts. A long pause in the middle of the second act, where one would naturally expect something far more exciting, looked as though everyone on stage had forgotten what few lines they had to learn. The production never seemed to recover from the disruption, and distraction seemed to be the byword for the night. All credit to the actors, who seemed to be trying to rally, but shame on the crew who so badly disappointed their calling. I expected better from a stage which has seen the performances of such luminaries who have trod the boards in previous years… and so on."

Grace closed the paper and handed it to Isaac with a brilliant smile. "It looks as though Thilby's grand plans came to nothing after all."

"There's a part of me that wishes he had succeeded," Isaac remarked frankly, and she stared at him, confused. "Because then your injuries would not have been for nothing."

"I think I can accustom myself to the notion, considering that it ended with his failure and what is sure to be your rousing success."

"Our success," Isaac corrected her again. "Come see."

He led her by the hand out onto the stage so she could see the installation for herself. Isaac and Tottenham drew back the sheets to display what lay beneath.

The vast glass plate she'd first seen in the scene painting shop was mounted now in a wooden frame that sat on little wooden wheels. She could see right through it, no silver turning it into a mirror like she'd thought at first glance.

"It's magnificent," she marveled, stepping lightly around the piece as Elliston joined them on the stage to look over the creation.

"It's big and expensive, certainly," the manager grunted around his cigar. "But will it work?"

Isaac bowed and gestured, ever the showman. "Take your seats in the house, if you please."

"Even me?" Grace asked, glancing behind him at the table and chair set up in the nook just offstage.

"Even you, at least for now. I want you to be in the first group to see it—either our rousing success, or our equally rousing failure." From the sparkle in his eye, she didn't think he believed the latter.

She didn't say "good luck"—that was a thing you never said, especially not now with the Scottish moors painted on the drop behind them and so much riding on this moment. "*Merde*," Grace wished him instead, like she would any of the dancers, and he grinned wide to show he understood.

Grace trotted lightly down the stairs and into the house, taking a seat with the other cast and crew who had come to watch. The hands and machinists fussed and puttered on the stage, guiding the glass sheet this way and that, Isaac moving the lights and their colored shades to ease them into place.

A tweak, and the stage brightened, light flashing off the reflectors. Another, and the glass divider seemed to vanish entirely, the wood frame blending in to the wood rails and banisters of the castle set, and the light not reflecting off it at all.

Two of the boys on the side of the stage turned the lampshades with their colored reflectors, and the stage fell into red-hued dimness.

A light struck at that same moment and two torches flared into life. A gentle mist rose, smoke trickling from the wings and fanning toward the center of the stage.

"What are we supposed to be looking for?" Mrs. Elliston asked from the row in front of Grace, and Grace held her breath.

There—as the torches burned higher and the light dimmed, a pale white figure appeared in the center of the stage, as though created from the swirling fog. Mrs. Elliston gave a little gasp, Frederick Poole yelped in surprise, and Grace felt the smile spreading helplessly across her face. The white creature, long and shimmering, swayed in the empty space, nothing above it but air.

"How on God's green and fertile earth?" Elliston said aloud, and Grace's heart leapt with pride.

He had done it. It should have been impossible, even as Isaac called out some orders and the stage lights flared bright again, the torches dimmed. The ragged sheet-marionette ghost danced on its strings as whomever was handling it on the catwalk ran along the top beam from one side of the stage to the other, making haunting banshee sort of noises.

"Now we have Miss Owens in her dancing dress behind the partition," Isaac began explaining halfway through his answer, gesturing at something off the other side of the stage. "When we light the torches *here* and dim them *there*, she appears as a reflection in the glass, as ephemeral as our poor makeshift ghost. We can project other things as well—in effect, a magic lantern show that needs no screen."

Grace followed the manager up to the stage, the lights up now and the effect faded, but she still needed to see it, touch it, for herself.

"It's to do with the angle of the glass—," Isaac was trying to explain the principles behind the thing to Elliston, who only grunted as he examined the construction.

"Can you repeat it?" Elliston asked briskly.

"As many times as needed," Isaac replied, looking a wee bit deflated. He watched Elliston's back as the man stalked off across the stage.

Grace let her hand rest on his arm, firm beneath her touch. "I find it interesting," she offered, and he flashed a grin back at her.

"Too kind, I'm sure."

"Mm. Because I often tell such trifling fibs." She was teasing, but couldn't help it, angling to draw out his easy smile again and again.

He gave her what she wanted, the corners of his eyes crinkling gently with his grin. "Oh yes. You're terrible for deceit."

"Caird!" came the shout from the other side of the stage, and Isaac sighed, his fingertips twitching against the closest fold of her skirt.

"I need to work," he apologized. "Will you be here when we're done?"

She could say yes, could stay and even take a chance at testing the effect for herself—but the night was still young, though her muscles were tired, and the sweet hidden caress of his thumb inside the palm of her hand again made up her mind.

"No." She shook her head, continuing before the flash of hurt in his eyes could settle in. "I'm going to go home— to my home—and I'll wait for you there. Assuming, of course, that such an offer appeals to you…"

While his body seemed to yearn toward hers, there were still so many things yet to be resolved, so much still left unsaid.

"Oh, it appeals." The words seemed to tangle on his tongue, and Isaac cupped her elbow in his hand. "I will finish here as quickly as possible, and then I'll come. You'll be safe to get home in the evening light? Let one of the boys walk you home."

"I'll be fine," she insisted, though the protectiveness in his eyes thrilled her down to the core of her bones.

"Peter!" Isaac was already moving across the stage, flagging down the propmaster's eldest son. A quick conversation later and Peter was heading in her direction, knuckling his cap with a grin and a nod.

"I can take care of myself well enough," Grace informed him.

The young man—what was he, fourteen at the eldest?—shook his head. "That may as well be, Miss Owens, but Mr. Caird's given me strict instructions not to let you out of my sight until you're safe inside your lodgings."

Grace sighed, setting her chin in her hand. "I suppose there's no misplacing or outpacing you."

"I'm afraid not, miss. Shall we?" He offered her his arm with an excess of dignity and poise, though he'd not yet had his full height and was perhaps an inch shorter than she was. Still, Grace retrieved her shawl, gloves and bonnet, tucked her hand in Peter's offered arm, and let him escort her home.

It wasn't until she was lighting the final candle end and setting it in its sconce that Grace paused to consider. It had been a little more than an hour since she had left the Surrey, a little less than that since she'd arrived at home. She'd had time to tidy the room, stoke the fire up a little to counteract the evening's chill, even to bathe and slip into a dressing gown.

The fine amber silk smoothed over her damp skin as sensual as a caress, the finest and most laughably frivolous thing she owned. It had been a gift from Meg, frippery given *her* by a former patron, and she'd pressed it upon Grace, insisting that only her complexion would do the color justice.

Privately, Grace rather agreed.

Only now, with all of her minor time-filling chores

completed, her riotous curls tied back with a ribbon and Meg's foolish silk robe wrapped around her, Grace felt the weight of time pressing in.

What if he didn't come? What if he had changed his mind, or worse yet, forgot? It would be just like him to get caught up in his work and forget all about a spur-of-the-moment promise he had made while his mind had no doubt been elsewhere.

The smart thing to do would be to pinch out the candles that she had set around the room, change into a sensible nightdress, and take herself to bed.

He said he would come. I have to learn to trust at some point; it may as well be now.

The knock on her door sounded only a moment after the fleeting thought had crossed her mind. The dark mood vanished as quickly as it had settled down upon her, and Grace caught herself all but running to lift the latch.

She opened the door and he was standing there, tall and solid, far more real than any dream she could conjure up. His dark green coat hugged his shoulders, the fine wool snug around the muscles of his arms. He'd buttoned his waistcoat again, his cravat neatly tied, and when he moved, her eyes were immediately drawn to the buff wool and the way it cupped and highlighted the sleek firmness of his rear, his fine legs. He had a small basket in his hands, and his hat perched jauntily on his head.

Isaac looked every inch the proper gentleman, and there she was in a brown dressing gown.

Still, a slow, warm appreciative smile spread across Isaac's face as he took her in. "Might I come inside?" He held up the basket as though to draw her attention toward it. "I come bearing gifts—my excuse for the delay."

The distinct smell of spices carried on the air when he moved, and Grace stepped aside to let him in. "What have you got in there? It can't possibly be what I think it is."

His only reply was to twitch aside the corner of the linen kerchief covering the contents. The smile broke through, washing away all her previous irritation as though it had never been. Four Chelsea buns nestled inside, warm enough that the scent still carried, the glaze on top of the rolled currant-filled pastries still looking as though it had only just been brushed on.

"The Bun House keeps early hours, there's no chance these were just baked—it's the middle of the night!"

"Not quite so late. And I bought them this afternoon." Isaac set the basket down on the small table and turned to clasp Grace's hands, interrupting her quiet reach for one of the sweet treats. "I had no idea how or when I would have the chance to bring them to you, but Mrs. Byrne kept them warm by her fireside just in case."

His hands were warm, the palms broad enough to encompass hers altogether. Grace didn't fight the touch, letting the simple knowledge of his nearness sink into her bones. "You know my weaknesses."

"Science is about repeating experiments to get consistent results." His roguish grin made her laugh, her fingertips falling just short of the handle.

"People aren't that predictable," she objected.

"You certainly aren't," Isaac agreed with an affectionate snort. He kept hold of her hand with one of his and nudged the basket closer to her with the other. "Perhaps that's what I need most—someone who will always keep me learning."

Grace let her hand fall away, bringing Isaac's fingers close enough to brush against her lips just once before she let go of him, as well. The disappointment came from everywhere and nowhere at once, a fog that dimmed the candles' glow. "That's not what I need. I need someone who will never make me doubt, or guess at his intent." She hadn't known what she would say until the words came out, the truth in them exposing so much of her soul that she felt the wound opening already.

Except that Isaac retook her hands and kept his gaze focused on her so defiantly that she had to return the look. Their eyes locked, and then he spoke. "I don't know if I can ever promise perfection, Grace. No one can. But I can promise that I will never break my word to you. When I say that I will be by your side, I will be, come hellfire, storm, or flood. You will never have to guess at my intent, because it will only ever be this—to be happy with you."

She should search for the lies and the half-truths, pick out the things he wanted to believe from the things he really meant, so she could prepare for them. She was safer that way, always on the watch, half an ear trained for the waver in the voice that meant something hurtful was on its way.

And yet. She raised her hand to his and their palms almost met, held no more than a hairs-breadth apart. He stayed there, steady and rock-sure, an ever-fixed mark on which she could finally rest.

Grace nodded slowly. "I believe you."

He didn't blink at the way she said it, only relaxed, and

the smile blossomed, erasing his furrowed brow. Isaac pressed his palm against Grace's, then closed his fingers about her hand. He drew her into the center of the room where the light shone the brightest and scudded the pad of his thumb across the fullness of her lower lip.

No words passed between them—none were needed. He bent his head and kissed her, as soft and gentle as a virgin's tentative courting. She kept still, let him set the pace, dropping little kisses at the corners of her mouth, nibbling and tasting the curve of her lip as though for the first time.

Grace slipped her hands up beneath his waistcoat, the warm linen of his shirt all that remained between her and the smooth heat of Isaac's skin. He deepened the kiss and she opened to him, parting her lips and letting the tip of his tongue inside.

It could have been moment or hours that they stood there, arms close about each other, chests pressed tight, all lips and tongue and teeth. Grace's breath caught in her chest, the wave of need to be closer—closer—under his skin breaking over her from whatever dam she'd constructed against her deepest desires.

Isaac seemed to know, despite his jokes about not being able to read her. He scooped her up in his arms and, crossing the small room in two long strides he laid her down upon her own bed.

Grace sat up partway, her arms bracing her and the amber silk sliding halfway down one of her shoulders to leave the skin dark and bare. Now it was Isaac's turn for his breath to stutter, the hunger burning in his half-lidded dark brown eyes.

The steps of this dance were becoming familiar, and they moved together as though he heard every one of her cues. By the time their clothes were abandoned on the floor and he nestled between her thighs, his mouth hot against her skin, she was beyond any hope of redemption. His hand slid up her hip, reaching for her, and she seized it. Their fingers intertwined and she held on, her rock, her anchor in the storm. Lightning burst from the base of her spine and sent shockwaves through her limbs, every inch tingling, arching, pleasure searing its way across her skin.

Somewhere in the distance, she thought she heard Isaac cheerfully murmur, "One."

And then—then he didn't stop. Even as her hips resettled on the bed, her back and brow slick with sweat and fireworks still bursting behind her eyes, he put his mouth on her again, more gently this time, a soft and gentle caress with the flat of his tongue, his lips, that coaxed her back up from blissful repose.

He knew what she needed, somehow, and while her fingers clenched fistfuls of her bedclothes and she could hear her own voice crying out from a distance, he slipped a finger inside of her, then another, coaxing and curling to beckon her onward. Onward she went, his thumb joining his tongue to drive her utterly and completely mad.

She clenched tight around him and came again, this time from somewhere deep inside, a rocking, body-shaking climax that stripped her muscles of their power. She sobbed out his name and he laughed, the vibrations of his pleasure sending tingling waves through her stomach and her groin.

"Two."

"What?" Grace lifted her head to see what he was

talking about, but he planted a kiss on the mound above her sex and moved toward her on all fours.

"Doesn't matter." Isaac crooked a finger beneath her chin and angled her face toward him for a kiss. She tasted herself on him and felt a flicker of desire still lingering somewhere deep inside. He planted his hands on either side of her, his cock pressing hard against her hip.

She'd once thought, when the time came, she'd have to consider her decision carefully. It turned out there was no decision to be made at all. Grace set her hands on Isaac's hips, digging her fingertips into the firm muscle. A gentle tug and he followed, moving to kneel between her thighs.

He groaned, his muscles trembling from the exertion of holding himself back. "Please," he groaned against her mouth. "Grace, love, queen of all."

Grace nodded, murmured, "Yes" against his lips.

Isaac moved and pressed the tip of his prick against her, the catch in his voice somewhere between a plea and a sob. One swift roll of his hips and he was inside, pressing home as though they had done this, moved together, since the dawn of time.

Grace cried out at the intrusion. It had been so long, too long, but his fingers before had eased the way, her cunt still slick with her arousal and the wet of his mouth. And he waited, though his arms trembled and his forehead beaded with sweat. He waited until her tension ebbed, pressing kisses down her jaw, her throat, her shoulder. Once she could relax around him, he began to move. She had forgotten how good this could feel, pressed open and exposed, his cock filling every empty, aching space inside.

He tipped up her hips, one hand beneath her, and thrust in again, striking a place inside that burned and sparked so intensely that her head swam.

Every inch of her still smoldered from her orgasms, every movement three times as intense as it would have been before. Grace's body responded with renewed desire, and she met him thrust for thrust, her hips rocking with his.

Isaac kissed her, their mouths locking together as their bodies were locked, his chest and arms slick.

Grace dug her nails into Isaac's back and he laughed in triumph, grabbing her hips and pulling her in tighter.

He took her up, up again and over, this set of shocks softer now, warmer, curling outward through her stomach from the place where their bodies joined, a soothing wave of sunshine.

The moment her convulsions slowed he pulled out, the red flush creeping down his chest and his breath coming in short, sharp gasps. Isaac stripped his cock once, twice, then threw his head back and cried out, coming over his own hand. Shuddering, shaking, he stroked himself through his aftershocks, nestled tight between Grace's thighs. Some of his emissions landed hot on her belly, white against the dark of her skin. She found she didn't care.

He curled in against her shoulder and she wrapped her arms around him, settling in with her head on the strength of his chest. They lay like that as the candles burned low, his heartbeat gently slowing beneath her ear and the sounds of the evening world outside seeming like they were a thousand miles away.

Isaac traced idle circles on Grace's shoulder, nuzzling

his face down into her hair. She should swat him, tell him to leave off or he would be the one who would have to bind it into tidy braids later, but she couldn't bring herself to care too much about that, either.

"Three," he murmured softly, sounding very pleased with himself.

"Three?"

"I like to set myself challenges," he teased lightly, running his palm down over the curve of her stomach to rest above her pubic bone.

Ohhh.

"That's what that was?" Grace asked archly. "A challenge?"

He chuckled warmly. "I'll try for four next time, unless you want me to stop."

She didn't need to consider her answer at all. "Perish the thought. Carry on."

As thought and memory filtered back in, she pressed a gentle kiss to Isaac's collarbone and asked the question that had been drifting idle in her mind. "Will your family be there for the opening tomorrow night?"

Isaac's voice was sleepy and pleased when he answered, "I imagine so. They haven't missed one yet."

"I wish I'd known what that was like," Grace replied wistfully. Father had been there, but always to judge, never to celebrate, greeting her with his endless lists of things she could have improved upon. "I wouldn't have minded a family like that."

Isaac propped himself up on one elbow and looked down at her, his eyes alight and impulsive. "What if they could be yours as well?"

Grace didn't catch on immediately, and furrowed her brow up at him. "I'm sorry?"

"I mean, you'd have to take me along with them, but I thought that might be a sacrifice you'd be willing to make."

That was when the understanding hit her full-force, a question so gargantuan that it left her breathless and spinning, unable to remember how to form words.

And still Isaac waited, even as she struggled to breathe. If she said no, or even "leave me time to think," what was the likelihood of having the time she needed to understand what had just happened, what she wanted, or...or anything at all? If she said yes, she would never know if she would have made the same answer if she had been prepared.

Grace moistened her lips and fought back the instinctive terror. "Will you ask me again, after the show?" His eyes suggested he didn't understand, so she tried to smile. "I need to be sure you're not going to drop me again, after all."

That did make him laugh, and then she could relax. "I'll ask again," Isaac promised. "And if you tell me to wait again, I'll still be here. That offer will always be open to you, so take as long as you need. When you're ready to give me an answer, I'll be here."

Tears pricked the corners of Grace's eyes, though she couldn't explain exactly what part of anything was turning her into an infant again. "I don't deserve you," she whispered.

"Balderdash," Isaac replied cheerfully, and he got out of bed to search out the washbasin and cloths, bringing the buns back to bed with him as well.

Falling asleep in his arms after that was easy, once they'd washed and slipped beneath the covers. Grace curled in close, the tastes of spices, currants, and Isaac lingering on her lips as she fell away into dreams.

Chapter Twenty-One

"Will you to Scone?"

Frederick's voice echoed across the packed theatre, the final conversation of the second act drawing to a close. Isaac mouthed the words along with the actors, the script embedded in his mind. After rehearsals and trials and endless hours working this damned show, he could probably do the entire thing himself, in his sleep.

"No, cousin; I'll to Fife."

He checked the torches one last time, the cloths impregnated with sulfur wrapped close about the torches, ready to be set alight. The ballet corps waited to enter as the ghosts, the girls in their gauzy robes.

Those with fair faces had whitened them further, painted their eyes in purples and grays, sunk and gaunt. Those who were dark had hollowed their cheeks and eyes further yet with the shadows of death.

Byrne and his missus had outdone themselves on that one. Isaac had come around the corner earlier and all but run into Miss Mayes, looking like she'd just risen from her grave.

Isaac hadn't yelped, precisely.

He paused now at the side of the stage, watched Grace

step in and out of the rosin box then rise up on her toes, her arms arched just so. She seemed to feel his eyes on her for she dropped out of her posture and offered him a worried smile, the soft blue layers of her gauzy gown turning her into the ghostly epitome of innocence, lost.

"Farewell, Father." The line came from the stage, and Isaac stepped in at Grace's side.

"Are you ready?" he murmured low in her ear. Her hand found his and gripped it tightly.

"Colby told me that the Prince Regent really is in the house tonight," Grace breathed out, her uncertainty showing. "He said he would, I know, but he actually came. The *Prince Regent.* Would it matter if I said no?"

"Not at this point." He couldn't let himself think about the stakes, not now when they were so close to the moment of truth. He brushed his lips lightly against hers, the red stain of her lip rouge forbidding anything more. "You'll be brilliant."

"God's benison go with you!" Charleston proclaimed on stage, his voice creaking with pretended age.

"That's the cue," Grace reminded him, and Isaac nodded. He brought her hand to his lips and kissed it fervently before letting it go.

"Then let us proceed," he said, and Grace nodded, smiled, and moved to take her place upon the blacked-out riser in the dark and hidden space behind the glass.

The dancers formed their lines, crossing their fingers and whispering to each other. Isaac lit his candle, a cover shielding the glow from outside eyes, and took up his position behind the curtain.

Success or failure all rode upon this moment.

"And friends of foes!" Charleston spoke his last line, the last of the act, and the actors strode off the stage in regal, measured paces. They broke character the moment they had cleared the wings, collapsing once again from princes and lords to ordinary men jostling about in bearskins and plaids.

Time moved like molasses in winter, seeming to slow until Isaac could see every instant with perfect clarity.

A whistle came from above, quiet enough that the audience would not hear it over the orchestra's swell.

Isaac set the candle flame to the torches and they flared to life. Red Peter set the smoke bucket alight and the boys dimmed the stage lights, turning the shields to block some of the glare. Grace rose up on her toes, the music swelling in a minor key and gauze veils floating from her outstretched arms.

She reflected in the glass that was invisible to the audience, a ghost that stood on nothing and seemed to dance on air. A gasp went up from the house itself, and a woman shrieked. Grace spun and bent, bowed and rose up like a thing possessed. The roiling tendrils of fog picked up the uncanny green and yellow of the torches, and the glass sent Grace's image out into the world as a dervish manifesting from the depths of Hades itself.

Grace slowed, stopped, raised her arms in benediction—or in supplication—and the music rose in the eerie wail of condemned souls.

On the signal from Mrs. Elliston the corps took the stage, a dozen spirits taking up the banshee's cry of doom, though more corporeal than Grace's image in the glass.

Isaac whistled the cue, low and long. Peter materialized at his elbow and together they dimmed the torches, the green eldritch fire going dim and shadow blacking out the backstage room. The lights rose on stage and finished the illusion, Grace stepping down from the platform once her reflection was gone.

She barely had time to cast him a smile, beaming and exhilarated, before she paused in the wings, smoothed her veils down once more, set her feet just so, and all but took flight across the stage.

Isaac had seen her dance before, but not like this, with the air as wings beneath her. She transcended beauty, and his heart lodged tight in his throat. A bird on the wing, no, more exquisite than that—the angel she was pretending to be, the smoke roiling around her ankles, the lights reflecting off the silver threads Byrne had woven into Grace's costume.

He had to struggle for breath, his chest tight.

He barely registered the presences gathering at his elbows and at his back, one quick glance telling him all he needed to know. The crew had gathered behind him, for this moment alone forgetting cues and places, petty irritations and busy-work. They stood and they watched as though none of them had ever seen dancing before.

The roar of the audience as they surged to their feet only showed that they were seeing what he already knew.

Grace Owens was magnificent.

Then the moment passed, as they always did, ephemeral and elusive.

She sank low in her curtsey, the corps following, and

cries of *"brava"* echoed from the house.

Tottenham grunted and groaned at the ropes, hauling down with the weight of his body to send the curtains flying closed.

Grace ran lightly off the stage and right into his arms in the wings, her satin slippers not making a trace of sound. Isaac swept her up into his arms, her body molding against his, loose and limber.

Their lips met, and it could only be for a moment—the whistle sounded again, the crew racing back to their assigned duties. The interval was only a quarter of an hour, long enough for the lords and sots upstairs to have their tipple, but not long enough to get anything done beyond setting the stage for the next act, and the next.

"Brilliance," Isaac murmured, and the gleam in Grace's eyes was thanks enough.

She pressed her fingertips against his lips and shook her head in warning. "I've one more to go yet; don't you dare curse me now."

"You'll be just as brilliant again," he vowed.

Grace made a disgusted noise in her throat, but her smile never wavered. She darted off, barely favoring her ankle, and joined the cluster of ballet girls moving for the stairs and their dressing room above.

And then there was no more time to watch her go. Isaac dusted his hands and set his back to the winch, cranking the ropes until the Scottish moors flew up and away into the blackness of the flies, revealing the painted backdrops of the court at Cawdor.

The show would indeed go on.

Ghost ballet, murder Banquo, Banquo's ghost—end Act Three. Witches, apparitions, more murders. Out damn spot, more blood to clear off the stage, second ballet. Fake-as-arse trees on wheels because *that* was original, Mac's bloody head held aloft, and finally, *finally*, the curtain closing upon the bows, the stage a shambles of discarded weapons and bits of distressed costume.

Isaac leaned upon the winch and could not strike the broad smile from his face. There was only a moment allowed for rest there as well, because the moment the actors fled the stage it was the crew's turn to replace them, clearing away the debris of the performance and resetting for the following day.

The glamour of the stage, indeed.

Isaac was halfway through refilling his smoke buckets when Colby called his name from the stage left wing. "Oy, Caird! Ye've people at the stage door."

"They never learn," Isaac groaned. It would be his parents, of course—who else? "Every time, I say 'we have to reset first,' and every time they come early."

"Don't think you're getting out of work that easy." Colby shook his fist in Isaac's general direction, then moved off to supervise his boys with their labors.

Isaac wiped his hands off on his kerchief and shoved it back into his rear pocket. He ducked around the moving pieces of set and at least four wheeled wooden trees to get himself to the stage door. Grace was only just coming down the stairs, her face washed clean of the dramatic cosmetics, and breeches hugging her delicious thighs and hips.

"Caird. A moment." Isaac wheeled around at the sound of the familiar voice, with the very unfamiliar sound of humility layered within. Thilby stood at the closed door, the purple and green bruising Isaac's fists had given him swelling large about both eyes.

In all the years he'd known the man, from their apprenticeships on through, had he ever seen him like this? Thilby was usually jocular, often rude, recently hateful, but never contrite. He bragged and bullied his way through life, never came to anyone with his hat quite literally in his hand.

Until now.

Good.

"What do you think you're doing, coming here?" Isaac replied sharply, placing himself solidly between Thilby and the stairs, Grace behind him.

One of the dressers scurried by, a pile of cloaks higher than her head stacked up on one shoulder.

"I believe I owe you something," Thilby admitted, air whistling between his teeth on that damned "s". He held out a small coin purse, jingled it in the air so Isaac could hear the coins clinking together inside. The next words seemed to pain him, coming out as slowly as they did. "For the better man."

Grace made a surprised sound behind Isaac, and Thilby's attention pulled toward her. "And to you, Miss Owens. I owe you an apology." He ducked his head, and when he raised it back up, his face twisted with regret, or shame. "Things should not have gone as far as they did."

It wasn't exactly taking responsibility, but it was more than Isaac had expected. He was about to open his mouth and reply with something to that effect when Grace came down the rest of the stairs to stand by his side. She cocked her head and regarded Thilby for a moment, as though memorizing his face and form. He couldn't meet her eyes, the slope of his shoulders more convincing than his words had been.

"Apology accepted," Grace said finally, much to Isaac's surprise. "Though I hope you'll understand, Mr. Thilby, when I say that I pray we are never in a position to meet again."

Thilby nodded, winced at the movement, and handed Isaac the coin purse. Then, after a beat of time, he fished in his coat pocket and drew out a familiar green ledger, stained and crinkled at the corners. He handed that back to Isaac as well, not meeting his eyes. "The *Prince Regent,* Caird." He spread his hands, as though that explained everything.

Isaac nodded. "I know." After tonight, in some ways, he could afford to be magnanimous. He shook the coin purse and Thilby groaned. "Better luck next time."

"The hell with you, Caird." And things were, if not back to normal, at least back to *usual*. Thilby pushed his way out of the backstage, almost tripping over a couple of the ballet girls in their pretty evening dresses.

"So much for that," Isaac grumbled, and tucked the purse into his belt without looking at it again. Thirty pieces of silver, indeed.

Grace seemed thoughtful, and he laid his hand gently against the small of her back to lend her his strength, his support. She leaned back into him and he took her weight with gladness. Lucy Sullivan scuttled past them both, still dressed in her witch's costume, and didn't meet either of their eyes.

"I know she was your friend, and didn't do anything out of malice, but it still seems wrong that Miss Sullivan should get away with it all scot-free."

"Oh, she won't," Grace said, with a honeyed sweetness that immediately sent all his senses on high alert.

"No?"

The predatory gleam in Grace's eyes did nothing to ease his sudden concern. "You remember my friend Meg."

"Who could forget?" he said, with feeling. The ingénue was notorious, both for her winsome personality and her overflowing bodices.

Grace snorted at him. "Behave yourself. Her patron is James Glover, the staymaker. He does work on costumes as well. For the Olympic, generally, and sometimes for the Royal."

"I still don't see what that has to do with Miss Sullivan."

"I've had it directly from Meg that James has agreed to partake in a little revenge on our behalf. He owes me a debt for services rendered," she added, with an odd expression on her face that he wasn't quite sure he wished to understand. "Lucy goes to the Royal Theatre for the winter season. And every few nights while she's there, her stays and skirts will be taken in again, less than a finger's-breadth at any one time. Just enough over the course of months to drive her slowly mad."

The image of a panicking and oblivious Miss Sullivan in her slowly shrinking costume was the picture of perfection. "You're devious," he said, a certain amount of fear laced with appreciation.

"That I am."

"Remind me never to get on your bad side again."

Grace brushed a kiss across his cheek. "You're doing well so far."

"Isaac my boy!" His father's voice echoed through the space as the great ruddy pack of them (if three could be considered a pack—no, six, because here came Mrs. Sedgewick as well as a very heavily pregnant Nan on her husband's arm) burst through the stage door and headed for him. "Amazing, simply amazing!"

"He told everyone within four rows of us that the magician was our son," his mother added, following in his father's jovial wake.

"She's not joking," Colin added, bringing up the rear. "And that the prima ballerina was your lady. Father was shushed by a *countess.* I think that's our closest brush with the aristocracy yet."

"You were a dream come to life, dear girl." Andrew reached out and took Grace's hands in his wide ones, affection warm in his eyes. "Truly magnificent. We're all so very proud of you."

"Thank you," Grace said, but her voice caught oddly, and she drew in a shaky breath. "I'm very pleased that you enjoyed the show, especially after all the work Isaac put into it... Excuse me, won't you?"

"Grace?" Isaac turned, but she was already gone, a faint shape in white breeches moving silently up the stairs and away.

She'd been able to face Thilby without qualms, even

379

talk about Lucy without feeling the stab of betrayal, but at the moment, dealing with all those Cairds—because there were an awful lot of them, even when there were only six—was utterly beyond her capacity. So Grace fled, up the stairs and to the dressing room, then out the creaking window to sit herself down on the gable roof overlooking Covent Garden.

The city bustled beneath her, carriages picking up the theatre-goers, glamorous ladies in their gowns and jewels, feathers in their hair. And there, the gentlemen in their suits and cloaks, sweeping dark figures forming a guard around the dazzling fledglings of the *ton.*

That was a world with its own rules, customs and patterns so different from the one she knew. They might as well be from different countries and Grace a student of the language, forever from the outside.

The Cairds straddled that line, respectable and solid, beloved by their community, even though their world centered on Chelsea and not Mayfair. It was a good life, mind you, at least from what she had seen. Stable, warm, with love enough to spare for a family-less girl plucked up from nowhere in particular.

We're all so very proud of you.

Seven words, and each one had struck a wound deeper than a sword ever could.

On the one hand, one simply couldn't marry a man for his family. Parents and brothers were not what one was left to bed down with at the end of the day, or stare at across the breakfast table.

On the other, a man's family showed who he could become.

Isaac was brilliant, passionate, giving, trusting—he'd been willing, even eager, to submit to her. At the same time he was just as capable of taking control, overpowering her better judgment, and taking her breath away.

He was loyal. She had imagined that he wasn't, but she'd been so very wrong.

Fine, so he was an example of how a good man could come from a family based on love.

It worked the other way just as easily, though. If she accepted that, then mustn't she also accept the more painful truth? That her own circumstances meant that she'd be a dreadful partner to whatever poor man was unlucky enough to fall for her?

At twenty-seven she was long past her marriageable prime, she was quick to anger and slow to trust, and she had no experience at all in managing a home. Half the time she wasn't a girl inside at all, and that certainly wasn't what your average fellow was searching for.

Will you have me?

I don't know.

The nighttime breeze toyed with her hair and the sleeves of her shirt, a gently tugging reminder of the world outside her head. Grace wrapped her arms about her knees and sat there, watching it all go by, no closer to an answer now than yesterday.

It took Isaac a little time first to extract himself from his family and then to figure out where Grace had gone. The flash of white outside on the roof granted him his final clue, though boosting himself through the window of the men's dressing room and picking his way across the tiled gable had probably not been the best method of getting to her side.

Still, he was there now.

Isaac cleared his throat and Grace looked up at him, as though she had been waiting for him all along.

"I'm too much like my father, and I dislike the idea of having children," Grace blurted out.

"All right," Isaac replied slowly, trying to keep his face still and calm while he frantically backpedaled in his memory to understand what conversational thread she was picking up now.

He sat down beside her as a way to buy himself time, drawing his knees up to his chest in a mirror of her posture.

My proposal. Marriage. That must be it. Too much Mr. Owens, no babies?

He shrugged. "I'm sure you inherited the best of his qualities, and I don't mind spending myself elsewhere to keep us from unhappy accidents. But what has any of that to do with the price of salt?"

Grace frowned at him. "Why me?"

That one was easy. "Because you complete me."

She recoiled, as though his answer offended her. "No, never say that! I'm not a rib, to be put back into place in someone else's chest."

Oops.

"A fair point," he conceded. "You are certainly no one's spare parts." Isaac sat for a minute, rethought the words he had been going to say.

"You inspire me, let me say instead. Your ideas fuel mine, your joy makes mine brighter, and frankly, I think you're better at using your prick than I am." He waggled his eyebrows and was rewarded with the surprised peal of her laugh.

She sighed, then, and looked as though she wanted to lean in, but didn't end up moving. "I'll never be a sweet and docile wife, making tea cozies and stitching table runners."

"God forbid! If I wanted that sort of thing, I'd marry Mrs. Sedgewick." He took a calculated risk, reaching out and clasping her hand in his. Her skin was cool and he tucked her hands between his, warming them against the night. "But she's not the glorious hoyden I've fallen in love with."

"Hoyden?" Grace snorted.

"You have a better word?"

"How about plain and simple Grace?"

It was Isaac's turn to laugh now, but with delight. "There's nothing either plain or simple about you, darling." He brought her hands to his lips, and pressed a kiss to her knuckles. "I will never tire of watching you unfold to me, of coaxing these little trusting treasures from your lips. I love you in gowns or in breeches, or better yet, in nothing at all. And whether you marry me or not, I'll still be by your side."

She moved in toward him then, leaned against his side. The breeze picked at them, and he slipped his arm around her shoulders to draw her close, and keep her warm.

He took Grace into his arms and let himself fall back, bringing her with him to lie beside him on the roof, beneath the stars.

Something hard lodged under the small of his back and he grunted at the impact. Reaching behind him, he fished out the coin purse from Thilby, the contents clinking gently.

"Well now," Grace said softly, and she cocked her head up at him. "Your five pounds, I presume."

It only took a moment to untie the purse and glance inside. More money than Isaac normally made in a month glinted back at him in the light pooling from the dressing room window. "You would presume rightly." A thought occurred to him even as he did so, and Isaac held the purse out to Grace. "It's rightfully yours, you know. You took the injury, discovered the text that led to our success, and performed the role. I was only the facilitator."

Grace closed his hand around the purse and shook her head. "And where would I have been without your glass and torchlight, your smoke and science? I may be the figure, but you are the alchemist. We won this together. Put it aside," she suggested, a smile on her lips. "The beginning of a nest egg for a house of our own."

"A house?" His heart leapt, caroused, ran about in circles inside his chest, and his breath caught.

"Naturally," Grace said easily, as though everything was already perfectly settled. "As lovely as your parents are, you can't imagine that we'll live with them forever."

"Naturally," he echoed, and then he did pull her into his arms, met her lips with his.

A popping noise echoed over the city, and he opened his eyes. Fireworks burst in the sky above Vauxhall, the flashes of brilliant yellow and orange reflecting in the glass of the windows, the reflective pools of water in the park.

Isaac held Grace close and she turned her head to watch the spectacle.

"Evening's fire," she said, laughing as she reached out toward the showers of falling stars half a city away.

"I'm sorry?" he asked, not catching the reference.

She tipped her chin and kissed him again, her lips soft and lush and carrying that promise of forever. His Grace, until death did them part.

"Nothing," she murmured, warm and safe in his arms. "Only that I may owe Madame Raiza an apology after all."

Author's Note

If you enjoyed this book, please leave a brief review at your online bookseller of choice. Thank you!

Going to the theatre was an extremely popular pastime in the Regency era, but while we know a great deal about the stars on stage, a theatre needs a vast number of backstage crew in order to function. Their stories tend to get lost in the sparkling world of fame and fortune-hunting, and information about their lives is not always as easy to find. I've pulled upon a wide variety of sources in my research for Grace and Isaac's story, and I'd like to call attention to a few that are referenced in the text, or that I found exceptionally useful.

First and foremost, some modern sources that I found myself consulting time and again throughout writing *Treading the Boards* in general, and *That Potent Alchemy* specifically: Edmund Fairfax's book *The Styles of Eighteenth Century Ballet* (2003), Peter Stoneley's *A Queer History of the Ballet* (2007), Gretchen Gerzina's magnificent book *Black London: Life Before Emancipation* (1995) and *The Oxford Handbook of the Georgian Theatre, 1737-1832*, written by Julia Swindells and David Francis Taylor (2014).

Some of the effects that Isaac researches were invented by real-life set and stage designers from the sixteenth through the eighteenth centuries. The "rock that opens to release horse and rider" and the "chariot designed as a cloud that descends from the flies with a winged cherub riding" were originally created in the early 1600s by Inigo Jones. He designed sets and costumes for Ben Jonson's masques, elaborate spectacles written for King James I. "Guyot's Ghost" is a more contemporary effect, created in the late eighteenth century as an extension of the technology behind the *camera obscura*, a very early form of motion-picture making. The description Grace translates is from a real book of magic tricks and illusions, *Nouvelles récréations physiques et mathématiques*, written by Edme-Gilles Guyot in 1769. The original text can be found digitized on The Internet Archive.

Isaac and Madame Raiza's flame tricks are commonly done in chemistry classrooms around the world these days as burn tests. Green could be made by burning borax and turmeric, orange with sea salt, and "witch meal" is a name for vegetal sulfur, a common ingredient in Georgian stage tricks. Isaac's pistachio experiment was one I ended up trying myself, since the sources were mysteriously quiet on the potential results. (Don't do any of these at home, kids.)

Lucy's tarot card readings are from an eighteenth century form of the deck, the tarot of Antoine Court de Gebelin (1781). As with anything, the meanings and emphases have changed considerably over the years.

The Ellistons were real people, though in all likelihood not as represented here. Robert Elliston was praised as an actor for his comedy skills and his versatility, though he ended his career first with a bankruptcy in 1826, and then death (likely) from alcoholism in 1831. Some of his choicer moments in this book are dedicated to directors I've worked for in the past. Cheers.

St. John's Day is June 23rd, and was believed—and is still considered, by some—to be one of the witches' Sabbaths, days where the power of the occult would be at its strongest. Not necessarily a date on which anyone would want to be performing one of the most notoriously "cursed" plays in the English canon!

About the Author

Tess has been a fan of historical fiction since learning the Greek and Roman myths at her mother's knee. Now let loose on a computer, she's spinning her own tales of romance and passion in a slightly more modern setting. Years of obsession with history have provided the basis for her current novels, most especially with the performing arts communities of Georgian London. She is a PhD candidate in early modern history, which has proven very useful for things that would utterly dismay her professors.

Tess lives in the Canadian Maritimes with her partner of eighteen years and two cats who should have been named Writer's Block and Get Off the Keyboard, Dammit.

Learn more about Tess and her projects at her website, http://tessbowery.com, or on social media at @tessbowery on Twitter, and http://tessbowery.tumblr.com.

ALSO BY TESS BOWERY

Rite of Summer

Treading the Boards Book #1

ISBN: 978-1-7753003-0-4 (digital)

ISBN: 978-0-9866184-9-9 (print)

Love is a terror worse than stage fright.

Violinist Stephen Ashbrook is passionate about three things—his music, the excitement of life in London, and his lover, Evander Cade. It's too bad that Evander only loves himself. A house party at their patron's beautiful country estate seems like a chance for Stephen to remember who he is, when he's not trying to live up to someone else's harsh expectations.

Joshua Beaufort, a painter whose works are very much in demand among the right sort of people, has no expectations about this party at all. Until, that is, he finds out who else is on the guest list. Joshua swore off love long ago, but has been infatuated with Stephen since seeing his brilliant performance at Vauxhall. Now he has the chance to meet the object of his lust face to face—and more.

But changing an open relationship to a triad is a lot more complicated than it seems, and while Evander's trying to climb the social ladder, Stephen's trying to climb Joshua. When the dust settles, only two will remain standing...

Warning: Contents under pressure. Contains three men, two beds, one erotic piercing, and the hottest six weeks of summer the nineteenth century has ever seen.

She Whom I Love

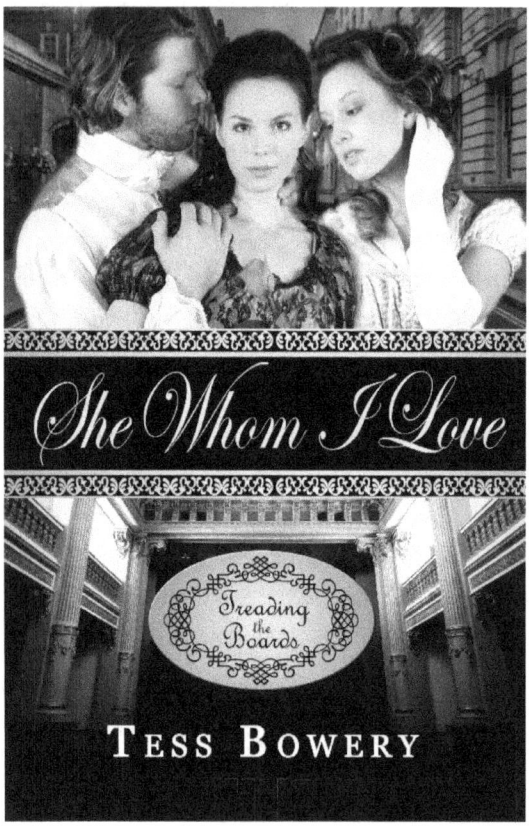

Treading the Boards Book #2

ISBN: 978-1-7753003-1-1 (print)

ISBN: 978-1-7753003-2-8 (digital)

Love would be simpler if it came with a script.

Marguerite Ceniza dies on the London stage each night, but her own life has barely begun. The ingénue is on the prowl for a lover, but while she burns with desire for Sophie, a confession could ruin their decade-long friendship. In the meantime there are always men vying to be her patron, and square-jawed, broad-shouldered James Glover can't help but catch her eye.

Sophie Armand has been a lady's maid for too long, and she's sick of keeping secrets. Her hidden scripts and the story of her birth are only the beginning. Her nights are haunted by desperate thoughts of the beguiling Marguerite, and of James, the handsome tradesman who whispers promises of forever into her ear.

James has the kind of problem a lot of men would kill for—two women, both beautiful, both sensual, and both willing. Sophie wants marriage, while Marguerite's only in it for fun, and choosing between them isn't easy.

What's the worst that could happen if he secretly courts them both?

Warning: Contains a lady's maid with secret desires, a corset-maker who knows his way around a woman's body, and an actress who never has to fake it. Rated for adult audiences only.